Foe-Farrell

by

Arthur Thomas Quiller-Couch

Foe-Farrell
by Arthur Thomas Quiller-Couch

ISBN: 978-93-61424-05-2

Published by

DOUBLE 9 BOOKS

2/13-B, Ansari Road
Daryaganj, New Delhi – 110002
info@double9books.com
www.double9books.com
Tel. 011-40042856

ABOUT THE AUTHOR

Sir Arthur Thomas Quiller Couch was a British author who wrote under the name Q. He was born on November 21, 1863, and died on May 12, 1944. Even though he wrote a lot of novels, he is best known for his literary criticism and the massive book The Oxford Book of English Verse 1250–1900 (later expanded to 1918). Many people, including the American author Helene Hanff, who wrote 84, Charing Cross Road and its follow-up, Q's Legacy, were inspired by him even though they never met him. His Oxford Book of English Verse was a favorite of Horace Rumpole, a figure in John Mortimer's stories. Arthur Quiller-Couch was born in England in the town of Bodmin in the county of Cornwall. He was born to Dr. Thomas Quiller Couch (d. 1884), a famous doctor, folklorist, and scholar who married Mary Ford and lived at 63 Fore Street, Bodmin, until he died there in 1884. Thomas was born from the marriage of two very old families in the area: The Couch family and the Quiller family. Arthur was the third smart person in the Couch family to come from that line. Jonathan Couch, his grandpa, was a naturalist, a doctor, a historian, a classicist, an apothecary, and an artist (mostly of fish). He had two younger sisters named Florence Mabel and Lilian M. who were also artists and folklorists.

CONTENTS

BOOK I
INGREDIENTS

If the red slayer thinks he slays,
Or if the slain think he is slain,
They know not well the subtle ways
I keep, and pass, and turn again.
EMERSON: *Brahma*.

The best kind of revenge is not to become like him.
MARCUS AURELIUS ANTONINUS.

PROLOGUE

Otway told this story in a dug-out which served for officers' mess of a field-battery somewhere near the Aisne: but it has nothing to do with the War. He told it in snatches, night by night, after the manner of Scheherazade in the *Arabian Nights Entertainments*, and as a rule to an auditory of two. Here is a full list of:

PERSONS OF THE DIALOGUE

NARRATOR.

Major Sir Roderick Otway, Bart., M.C., R.F.A.

AUDIENCE AND INTERLOCUTORS.

Lieut. John Polkinghorne. R.F.A., of the Battery.
Sec. Lieut. Samuel Barham, M.C. R.F.A., of the Battery.
Sec. Lieut. Percy Yarrell-Smith. R.F.A., of the Battery
Sec Lieut. Noel Williams, R.F.A., attached for instruction.

But military duties usually restricted the audience to two at a time, though there were three on the night when Barham (Sammy) set his C.O. going with a paragraph from an old newspaper. The captain—one McInnes, promoted from the ranks—attended one stance only. He dwelt down at the wagon-lines along with the Veterinary Officer, and brought up the ammunition most nights, vanishing back in the small hours like a ghost before cock-crow.

The battery lay somewhat wide to the right of its fellows in the brigade; in a saucer-shaped hollow on the hill-side, well screened with scrub. Roughly it curved back from the straight lip overlooking the slope, in a three-fifths segment of a circle; and the officers' mess made a short arc in it, some way in rear of the guns. You descended, by steps, cut in the soil and well pounded, into a dwelling rather commodious than large: for Otway— who knew about yachts—had taken a fancy to construct it nautical-wise, with lockers that served for seats at a narrow saloon table, sleeping bunks excavated along the sides, and air-holes like cabin top-lights, cunningly curtained by night, under the shell-proof cover.

"It cost us a week," he wrote home to his sister, "to get the place to my mind. Since then we have been adding fancy touches almost daily, and now the other batteries froth with envy. You see, it had to be contrived, like the poet's chest of drawers."

> A double debt to pay:
> Doss-house by night and bag-of-tricks by day.

And here we have lived now, shooting and sleeping (very little sleeping) for five solid weeks. All leave being off, I have fallen into this way of life, almost without a thought that there ever had been, or could be, another, and feel as if my destiny were to go on at it for ever and ever. And this at thirty-five, Sally!

"It must be ever so much worse for the youngsters, one would say. Anyway I have had ten good years that they are missing... Cambridge, Henley, Lord's; Ascot, and home-to-tidy, and afterwards the little Mercedes, and you and I rolling in to Prince's and the theatre, whilst good old Bob is for the House, to take *his* exercises walking the lobbies; clean linen after the bath, and my own sister beside me—she that always knew how to dress—and the summer evening over Hyde Park Corner and the Green Park.... No, I mustn't go on. It is *verboten* even to think of a white shirt until the Bosch hangs out the tail of *his*.

"My youngsters are missing all this, I tell myself. Yet they are a cheerful crowd, and keep smiling on their Papa. The worst is, a kind of paralysis seems to have smitten our home mails and general transport for close upon a fortnight. No letters, no parcels—but one case of wine, six weeks overdue, with half the bottles in shards: no newspapers. This last specially afflicts young Sammy Barham, who is a glutton for the halfpenny press: which again is odd, because his comments on it are vitriolic.

"No books—that's the very worst. Our mess library went astray in the last move: no great loss perhaps except for the *Irish R.M.*, which I was reading for the nth time. The only relic that survives, and follows us everywhere like an intelligent hound, is a novel of Scottish sentiment, entitled *But and Ben*. The heroine wears (p. 2) a dress of 'some soft white clinging material'— which may account for it. Young Y.-Smith, who professes to have read the work from cover to cover, asserts that this material clings to her throughout: but I doubt the thoroughness of his perusal since he explained to us that 'Ben' and 'But' were the play-names of the lad and his lassie.... For our personal libraries we possess:

"R.O.—A hulking big copy of the *International Code of Signals*: a putrid bad book, of which I am preparing, in odd moments, a recension, to submit to the Board of Trade. Y.-Smith borrows this off me now and then, to learn up the flags at the beginning. He gloats on crude colours.

"*Polkinghorne*—A Bible, which I borrow, sometimes for private study, sometimes (you understand?) for professional purposes. It contains a Book of Common Prayer as well as the Apocrypha. P. (a Cornishman, something of a mystic, two years my senior and full of mining experiences in Nevada and S. America) always finds a difficulty in parting with this, his one book. He is deep in it, this moment, at the far end of the table.

"*Sammy Barham*, so far as anyone can discover, has never read a book in his life nor wanted to. He was educated at Harrow. Lacking the *Daily Mail*, he is miserable just now, poor boy! I almost forgave the Code upon discovering that his initials, S.B., spell, for a distress signal, 'Can you lend (or give) me a newspaper?'

"*Yarrell-Smith* reads Penny Dreadfuls. He owns four, and was kind enough, the other day, to lend me one: but it's a trifle too artless even for my artless mind.

"Young *Williams*—a promising puppy sent up to me to be walked—reads nothing at all. He brought two packs of Patience cards and a Todhunter's *Euclid*; the one to rest, the other to stimulate, his mind; and I've commandeered the *Euclid*. A great writer, Sally! He's not juicy, and he don't palpitate, but he's an angel for style. 'Therefore the triangle DBC is equal to the triangle ABC—pause and count three—'the less to the greater'—pause—'which is absurd.' Neat and demure: and you're constantly coming on little things like that. 'Two straight lines cannot enclose a space'—so broad and convincing, when once pointed out!—and why is it not in *The Soldiers' Pocket-Book* under 'Staff Axioms'?

"When you make up the next parcel, stick in a few of the unlikeliest books. I don't want Paley's *Evidences of Christianity*: I have tackled that for my Little-Go, and, besides, we have plenty of 'em out here: but books about Ireland, and the Near East, and local government, and farm-labourers' wages, and the future life, and all that sort of thing. "Two nights ago,

Polkinghorne got going on our chances in another world. Polkinghorne is a thoughtful man in his way, rising forty—don't know his religion. I had an idea somehow that he was interested in such things. But to my astonishment the boys took him up and were off in full cry. It appeared that each one had been nursing his own thoughts on the subject. The trouble was, none of us knew very much about it—"

Otway, writing beneath the hurricane-lamp, had reached this point in his letter when young Barham exclaimed to the world at large:

"Hallo! here's a tall story!"

The C.O. looked up. So did Polkinghorne, from his Bible. Sammy held a torn sheet of newspaper.

"Don't keep it to yourself, my son," said Otway, laying down his pen and leaning back, so that his face passed out of the inner circle of the lamplight.

Sammy bent forward, pushed the paper nearer to this pool of light, smoothed it and read:

"'THAMES-SIDE MYSTERY'"

"'A Coroner's jury at C—, a 'village' on the south bank of the Thames, not a hundred miles below Gravesend—'"

"Seems a lot of mystery about it already," observed Polkinghorne. "Don't they give the name of the village?"

"No; they just call it 'C—,' and, what's more, they put 'village' into inverted commas. Don't know why: but there's a hint at the end."

"Proceed."

Sammy proceeded.

"'—Was engaged yesterday in holding an inquest on the body of an unknown man, found lying at highwater mark in a creek some way below the village. A local constable had discovered the body: but neither the officer who attended nor the river police could afford any clue to the deceased's identity. Medical evidence proved that death was due to drowning, although the corpse had not been long immersed: but a sensation was caused when the evidence further disclosed that it bore an incised wound over the left breast, in itself sufficient to cause death had not suffocation quickly supervened.

"'The body was further described, in the police evidence, as that of a middle-aged man, presumably a gentleman. It was clad in a black 'evening-dress' suit, and two pearl studs of some value remained in the limp shirt-front; from which, however, a third and fellow stud was missing. The Police Inspector—who asked for an open verdict, pending further inquiry—added that the linen, and the clothing generally, bore no mark leading to identification. Further, if a crime had been committed, the motive had not been robbery. The trousers-pockets contained a sovereign, and eighteen shillings in silver. In the waistcoat was a gold watch (which had stopped at 10.55), with a chain and a sovereign-purse containing two sovereigns and a half-sovereign: in the left-hand breast pocket of the dinner-jacket a handkerchief, unmarked: in the right-hand pocket a bundle of notes and a worn bean-shaped case for a pair of eyeglasses. The glasses were missing. The Police had carefully dried the notes and separated them. They were nine one pound notes; all numbered, of course. Beyond this and the number on the watch there was nothing to afford a clue.'—"

Here Barham paused for a glance up at the roof of the dug-out, as two explosions sounded pretty near at hand. "Huns saying good-night," he interpolated. "Can't have spotted us. Nothing doing aloft these three days."

Polkinghorne looked across the light at the C.O., who sat unaccountably silent, his face inscrutable in the penumbra. Taking silence for "yes," Polkinghorne arose and put his head outside for a look around.

"Queer story, you'll admit, sir?" put in Sammy Barham during this pause. "Shall I go on, or wait for the rollicking Polly to hear it out?—for the queerest part is to come."

"I know," said Otway, after some two or three seconds' silence.

"Eh?... But it's just here, sir, the thing of a sudden gets mysteriouser and mysteriouser—"

Polkinghorne came back. "Nerves," he reported. "They're potting all over the place.... Here, Sammy, pass over that scrap of paper if you've finished reading. I want to hear the end."

"It hasn't any," said Otway from the shadow.

"But, sir, when I was just warning you—"

"Dashed good beginning, anyway," said Polkinghorne; "something like *Our Mutual Friend*."

"Who's he?" asked Sammy.

"Ingenuous youth, continue," Otway commanded. "Polky wants to hear the rest of the paragraph, and so do I."

"It goes on just like a detective story," promised Sammy. "Just you listen to this:—

> "'An incident which may eventually throw some light on the mystery interrupted the Coroner's summing up and caused something of a sensation. This was the appearance of an individual, evidently labouring under strong excitement, who, having thrust his way past the police, advanced to the Coroner's table and demanded to have sight of the body. The man's gestures were wild, and on being asked his name he answered incoherently. His manner seriously affected one of the jury, who swooned and had to be removed from Court.

> "'While restoratives were being applied at the 'Plume and Feathers' Inn (adjacent to the building in which the inquest was held), the Coroner held consultation with Police and Foreman of the Jury, and eventually adjourned for a second inspection of the body, the stranger accompanying them. From this inspection, as from the first, representatives of the Press were excluded.

> "'Returning to Court at the expiration of forty minutes—by which time the absent juror had recovered sufficiently to take his seat—the Coroner directed an open verdict to be entered and the inquiry closed.

> "'The intrusive visitor did not reappear. We understand that he was found to be suffering from acute mental derangement and is at present under medical treatment as well as under supervision of the police, who are closely watching the case. They preserve great reticence on the whole subject and very rightly so in these days, considering the number of enemy

plotters in our midst, and that the neighbourhood of 'C—' in particular is known to be infested with their activities.'"

"Is that all?" asked Polkinghorne.

"That's all; and about enough, I should say, for this Penny Reading."

"When did it happen?"

"Can't tell. The top of the sheet's torn off." Barham pushed the paper across. "By the look, it's a bit of an old *Daily Chronicle*. I found it wrapping one of my old riding boots, that I haven't worn since I took to a sedentary life. Higgs must have picked it up at our last move—"

"Do you want the date?" put in Otway. "If so, it was in January last—January the 18th, to be exact."

"But—"

"I mean the date of the inquest. The paper would be next morning's—Wednesday the 19th," Otway went on in a curious level voice, as though spelling the information for them out of the lamplight on the table.

Barham stared. "But—" he began again—"but *how*, sir?"

Polkinghorne, who also had stared for a moment, broke in with a laugh. "The C.O. is pulling your leg, Sammy. He tore off the top of your paper—it was lying around all this morning—noted the date and thought he might safely make a pipe-spill."

"That won't do," retorted Barham, still searching Otway's face on which there seemed to rest a double shadow. "For when I turned it out of my valise this morning I carefully looked for the date—I'll swear I did—and it was missing."

"Then you tore the thing in unpacking, and the C.O. picked up the scrap you overlooked. Isn't that the explanation, sir?"

"No," said Otway after a pause, still as if he spoke under control of a muted pedal. He checked himself, apparently on the point of telling more; but the pause grew into a long silence.

Barham tried back. "January, you said, sir?… and now we're close upon the end of October—"

He could get nothing out of the C.O.'s eyes, which were bent on the table; and little enough could he read in his face, save that it was sombre with thought and at the same time abstracted to a degree that gave the boy a sudden uncanny feeling. It was like watching a man in the travail of second sight, and all the queerer because he had never seen an expression even remotely resembling it on the face of this hero of his, with whose praise he filled his home-letters—"One of the best: never flurried: and, what's more, you never catch him off his game by any chance."

Otway's jaw twitched once, very slightly. He put out a hand to pick up his pen and resume writing; but in the act fell back into the brown study, the trance, the rapt gaze at a knot in the woodwork of the table. His hand rested for a moment by the ink-pot around which his fingers felt, like a blind man's softly making sure of its outline and shape. He withdrew it to his tunic-pocket, pulled out pipe and tobacco-pouch and began to fill....

At this point in came young Yarrell-Smith. Young Yarrell-Smith wore a useful cloak—French cavalry pattern—of black mackintosh, with a hood. It dripped and shone in the lamplight.

"Beastly night," he announced to the company in general and turned to report to Otway, who had sat up alert on the instant.

"Yes," quoted Otway,

"'Thou comest from thy voyage—
Yes, the spray is on thy cloak and hair.'"

That's Matthew Arnold, if the information conveys anything to you. Everything quiet?"

"Quite quiet, sir, for the last twenty minutes; and the Captain just come in and unloading. No accidents, though they very nearly met their match, five hundred yards down the road."

"We heard," said Polkinghorne.

"I tucked the Infant into his little O.P., and left him comfy. He won't see anything there to-night."

"He'll *think* he does," said Sammy Barham with conviction.

"The Infant is quite a good Infant," Otway observed; and then, sinking his voice a tone, "Lord, if at his age I'd had his sense of responsibility..."

Barham noted the change of tone, though he could not catch the words. Again he threw a quick look towards his senior. Something was wrong with him, something unaccountable....

Yarrell-Smith noted nothing. "Well, he won't see anything to-night, sir; and if Sammy will pull himself together and pity the sorrows of a poor young man whose trembling knees—"

"Sorry," said Sammy, turning to the locker and fishing forth a bottle.

"—I'll tell you why," Yarrell-Smith went on as the tot was filled. "First place, the Bosch has finished hating us for to-night and gone to bye-bye. Secondly, it's starting to sleet—and that vicious, a man can't see five yards in front of him."

"I love my love with a B because he's Boschy," said Sammy lightly: "I'll take him to Berlin—or say, Bapaume to begin with—and feed him on Substitutes.... Do you know that parlour-game, Yarrell dear? Are you a performer at Musical Chairs? Were you by any chance brought up on a book called *What Shall We do Now?* The fact is—" Sammy, who could be irreverent, but so as never to offend, stole a look at Otway—"we're a trifle hipped in the old log cabin. I started a guessing-competition just now, and our Commanding Officer won't play. Turn up the reference, Polky— Ecclesiastes something-or-other. It runs: 'We are become as a skittle-alley in a garden of cucumbers, forasmuch as our centurion will not come out to play with us.'"

Otway laughed. "And it goes on that the grasshopper is a burden.... But Y.-S. has given you the name, just now."

"*I*, sir?" Yarrell-Smith gazed, in the more astonishment to find that Otway, after his laugh, reaching up to trim the lamp, looked strangely serious. "I'm blest if I understand a word of all this.... What name, sir?"

"*Hate*," said Otway, dropping back into his chair and drawing at his pipe. "But you're warm; as they say in the nursery-game. Try '*Foe*,' if you prefer it."

"Oh, I see," protested Yarrell-Smith, after a bewildered look around. "You've all agreed to be funny with a poor orphan that has just come in from the cold."

Barham paid no heed to this. "'Foe' might be the name of a man. It's unusual.... But what was the Johnny called who wrote *Robinson Crusoe?*"

"It *was* the name of a man," answered Otway.

"*This* man?" Barham tapped his finger on the newspaper.

Otway nodded.

"The man the inquest was held on?"

"That—or the other." Otway looked around at them queerly. "I think the other. But upon my soul I won't swear."

"The other? You mean the stranger—the man who interrupted—"

At this point Yarrell-Smith sank upon a locker. "I beg your pardon, all of you," he moaned helplessly; "but if there's such a thing about as First Aid—"

"Sammy had better read you this thing he's unearthed," said Polkinghorne kindly.

Barham picked up the newspaper.

"No, you don't," Otway commanded. "Put it down.... If you fellows don't mind listening, I'll tell you the story. It's about Hate; real Hate, too; not the Bosch variety."

NIGHT THE FIRST
JOHN FOE

John Foe and I entered Rugby together at fourteen, and shared a study for a year and a term. Pretty soon he climbed out of my reach and finally attained to the Sixth. I never got beyond the Lower Fifth, having no brains to mention. Cricket happened to be my strong point; and when you're in the Eleven you can keep on fairly level terms with a push man in the Sixth. So he and I were friends—"Jack" and "Roddy" to one another—all the way up. We went through the school together and went up to Cambridge together.

He was a whale at Chemistry (otherwise Stinks), and took a Tancred Scholarship at Caius. I had beaten the examiner in Little-go at second shot, and went up in the same term, to Trinity; where I played what is called the flannelled fool at cricket—an old-fashioned game which I will describe to you one of these days—

"Cricket? But I thought you rowed, sir?" put in Yarrell Smith. "Yes, surely—"

"Hush! tread softly," Barham interrupted. "Our Major won't mind your not knowing he was a double Blue—don't stare at him like that; it's rude. But he will not like it forgotten that he once knocked up a century for England v Australia.... You'll forgive our young friend, sir; he left school early, when the war broke out."

Otway looked across at Yarrell-Smith with a twinkle. "I took up rowing in my second year," he explained modestly, "to enlarge my mind. And this story, my good Sammy, is not about me—though I come into it incidentally because by a pure fluke I happened to set it going. All the autobiography that's wanted for our present purpose is that I went up to Trinity College, Cambridge, in the footsteps (among others) of Francis Bacon and Isaac Newton, and—well, you see the result. May I go on?"

But although they were listening, Otway did not at once go on. Sammy had spoken in his usual light way and yet with something of a pang in his voice, and something of a transient cloud still rested on the boy's face. Otway noted it, and understood. When the war broke out, Sammy had been on the point of going up to Oxford....

Before the cloudlet passed, Otway had a vision behind it, though the vision came from his own brain, out of his own memory—a vision of green turf and of boys in white on it, a small regiment set orderly against a background of English elms, and moving orderly, intent on the game of games.

O thou, that dear and happy Isle,
The garden of the world erstwhile....
Unhappy! shall we nevermore
That sweet militia restore?

Snatches of an old parody floated in his brain with the vision — a parody of Walt Whitman —

Far off a grey-brown thrush warbling in hedge or in marsh; Down there in the blossoming bushes, my brother, what is that you are saying?...

The perfect feel of a "fourer "!...

The jubilant cry from the flowering thorn to the flowerless willow, "smite, smite, smite."

(Flowerless willow no more but every run a late-shed perfect bloom.)

The fierce chant of my demon brother issuing forth against the demon bowler, "hit him, hit him, hit him."

The thousand melodious cracks, delicious cracks, the responsive echoes of my comrades and the hundred thence-resulting runs, passionately yearned for, never, never again to be forgotten.

Overhead meanwhile the splendid silent sun, blending all, fusing all, bathing all in floods of soft ecstatic perspiration.

Otway lifted his stare from the rough table.

They have skinned the turf off Trinity cricket-ground... Such turf, too! I wonder who bought it, and what he paid for it. ... They have turned the field into a big Base Hospital — all tin sheds, like a great kraal of scientific Kaffirs. Which reminds me...

Foe read medicine. Caius, you must know, is a great college for training doctors, and in the way of scholarships and prizes he annexed most of the mugs on the board. All the same I want you to understand that he wasn't a pot-hunter. I don't quite know how to explain.... His father had died while he was at Rugby, leaving him a competence; but he certainly was not over-burdened with money. Of that I am sure.... Can't say why. He never talked of his private affairs, even with me, though we were friends, "Jack" and "Roddy" to each other still, and inhabited lodgings together in Jesus Lane. He owed money to no one. Unsociable habit, I used to call it; destructive of confidence between man and man.

But he was no pot-hunter. I think — I am sure — that so long as he kept upsides with money he rather despised it. He had a handsome face — rather curiously like the pictures you see of Dante — and his mind answered to it, up to a point. Fastidious is the word,... gave you the impression he had attached himself to Natural Science much as an old Florentine attached himself to theology or anatomy or classics, with a kind of cold passion.

The queerest thing about him was that anything like "intellectual society," as they call it, bored him stiff. Now you may believe it or not, but I've always had a kind of crawling reverence for things of the mind, and for men who go in for 'em. You can't think the amount of poetry, for instance, I've read in my time, just wondering how the devil it was done. But it's no use; it never was any use, even in those days. No man of the kind I wanted to worship could ever take me seriously. I remember once being introduced to a poet whose stuff I knew by heart, almost every line of it, and when I blurted out some silly enthusiasm—sort of thing a well-meaning Philistine does say, don't you know?—he put the lid down on me with "Now, that's most interesting. I've often wondered if what I write appealed to one of your—er—interests, and if so, how."

Well that's where I always felt Foe could help. And yet he didn't help very much. He read a heap of poetry—on the sly, as it were; and one night I coaxed him off to a talk about Browning. His language on the way home was three-parts blasphemy.

Am I making him at all clear to you? He kept his intellect in a cage all to itself, so to speak.... What's more—and you'll see the point of this by and by—he liked to keep his few friends in separate cages. I won't say he was jealous: but if he liked A and B, it was odds he'd be uneasy at A's liking B, or at any rate getting to like him intimately.

This secretiveness had its value, to be sure. It gave you a sense of being *privileged* by his friendship.... Or, no; that's too priggish for my meaning. Foe wasn't a bit of a prig. It was only because he had, on his record already, so much brains that the ordinary man who met him in my rooms was disposed to wonder how he could be so good a fellow. Get into your minds, please, that he *was* a good fellow, and that no one doubted it; of the sort that listens and doesn't speak out of his turn.

He had a great capacity for silence; and it's queer to me—since I've thought over it—what a large share of our friendship consisted in just sitting up into the small hours and smoking, and saying next to nothing. *I* talked, no doubt: Foe didn't.

I shall go on calling him Foe. He was Jack to me, always; but Foe suits better with the story; and besides... well, I suppose there's always something in friendship that one chooses to keep in a cage.... The only cage-mate that Jack—I mean Foe—ever allowed me was Jimmy Caldecott, and that happened after we had both moved to London.

He—Foe—had taken a first-class in the Tripos, of course; and a fellowship on top of that. But he did not stay up at Cambridge. He put in the next few years at different London hospitals, published some papers on the nervous system of animals, got appointed Professor of Animal Morphology, in the South London University College (the Silversmiths' College), and might wake up any morning to find himself a Fellow of the Royal Society. He was already—I am talking of 1907, when the tale starts—a Corresponding Member of three or four learned Societies in Europe and the U.S.A., and had put a couple of honorary doctorates to his account besides his Cambridge DSc.

As for me, I had rooms at first in Jermyn Street, then chambers in the Inner Temple—my father, who had been Chairman of Quarter Sessions, holding the opinion that I ought to read for the Bar, that I might be better qualified in due time to deal out local justice down in Warwickshire. I read a little, played cricket a good deal, stuck out three or four London Seasons, travelled a bit, shot a bit in East Africa (Oh, I forgot to say I'd put in a year in the South African War); climbed a bit, in Switzerland, and afterwards in the Himalayas; come home to write a paper for the Geographical Society; got bitten with Socialism and certain Fabian notions, and put in some time with an East-End Settlement besides attending many crowded and unsavoury public meetings to urge what was vaguely known as Betterment. When I took courage and made a clean breast of my new opinions to my father, the old man answered very composedly that he too had been a Radical in his time, and had come out of it all right. ... By all means let me go on with my spouting: capital practice for public life: hoped I should take my place one of these days in the County Council at home: wouldn't even mind seeing me in Parliament, etc.—all with the wise calm of one who has passed his three-score years and ten, found the world good, made it a little better, hunted his own harriers and learnt, long since, every way in which hares run. So I returned and somehow found myself pledged to compete as a Progressive for the next London County Council—for a constituency down Bethnal Green way. In all this, you see, my orbit and Foe's wouldn't often intersect. But we dined together on birthdays and other occasions. One year I took him down to the Derby, on the ground that it was part of a liberal education. In the paddock he nodded at a horse in blinkers and said, "What's the matter with that fellow?" "St. Amant," said I, and began to explain why Hayhoe had put blinkers on him. "Where does he stand in the betting?" asked Foe. "Why, man," said I, "at 5 to 1. You can't risk good money on a horse of that temper. I've put mine on the French horse over there—Gouvernant—easy favourite—7 to 4 on." "Oh," said he, in a silly sort of way, "I thought St. Amant might be your French horse—it's a French name isn't it?... As for your Gouvernant, I advise you to run for your life and hedge: the animal is working up for a stage fright. A touch more and he's dished before the flag drops. Now, whether the blinkers have done it or not, that St. Amant is firm as a rock." "How the devil—" I began. "That's a fine horse, too, over yonder," he said, pointing one out with his umbrella. "John o' Gaunt," said I: "ran second to St. Amant for the Guineas, and second to Henry the First in the Newmarket, with St. Amant third. The running has been all in-and-out this season. But how the devil you spotted him, when I didn't know you could tell a horse's head from his stern—" "I don't profess to much more," said Foe; "but it's my job to read an animal's eye, and what he's fit for by the quiver under his skin. Now, I'd only a glimpse of St. Amant's eye, across his blinkers, and your John o' Gaunt is a stout one—inclined, you tell me, to run in second place. But if your money's on Gouvernant, hurry while there's time and set it right. If you've thirty seconds to spare when you've done that," he added, "you may put up a tenner for me on St. Amant—but don't bother. Your book may want some arranging."

The way he said it impressed me, and I fairly shinned back to the Ring. I hadn't made my book on any reasoned conviction, you understand; for the horses had been playing at cat's-cradle all along, and as I went it broke on me that, after all, my faith in Gouvernant mainly rested on my knowing less of him than of the others—that I was really going with the crowd. But really I was running to back a superstition—my belief in Foe, who knew nothing about horse-racing and cared less.

Well, the race was run that year in a thunderstorm—a drencher; and if Foe was right, I guess that finished Gouvernant, who never looked like a winner. St. Amant romped home, with John o' Gaunt second, in the place he could be trusted for. Thanks to Foe I had saved myself more than a pony in three strenuous minutes, and he pocketed his few sovereigns and smiled.

That was also the day—June 1st, 1904—"Glorious First of June" as Jimmy Collingwood called it—that Foe first made Jimmy's acquaintance. Young Collingwood was a neighbour of mine, down in the country; an artless, irresponsible, engaging youth, of powerful build and as pretty an oarsman and as neat a waterman as you could watch. Eton and B.N.C. Oxford were his nursing mothers. His friends (including the dons) at this latter house of learning knew him as the Malefactor; it being a tradition that he poisoned an aunt or a grandparent annually, towards the close of May. He was attending the obsequies of one that afternoon on the edge of the hill, in a hansom, with a plate of *foie gras* on his knees and a bottle of champagne between his ankles. His cabby reclined on the turf with a bottle of Bass and the remains of a pigeon pie. His horse had its head in a nose-bag.

"Hallo, Jimmy!" I hailed, pausing before the pastoral scene. "Funeral bake-meats?"

"Hallo!" Jimmy answered, and shook his head very solemnly. "Sister-in-law this time. It had to be."

"Sister-in-law! Why you haven't one!"

"Course not," said Jimmy. "That's the whole trouble. Ain't I breaking it to you gently?... Case of *angina pectoris*, if you know what that means. It sounds like a pick-me-up—'try Angostura bitters to keep up your Pecker.' But it isn't. Angina—short 'i'; I know because I tried it on the Dean with a long one and he corrected me. He said that angina might be forgiven, for once, in a young man bereaved and labouring under strong emotion, but that if I apprehended its running in the family I had better get the quantity right. He also remarked rather pointedly that he hoped his memory was at fault and that my poor brother hadn't really lost his deceased wife's sister."

"Do you know where bad boys go?" I asked him.

"Silly question," said Jimmy, with his mouth full of *foie gras*. "Why, to the Derby, of course. Have something to eat."

I told him that we had lunched, introduced him to Foe as the Malefactor, and invited him to come back and dine with us at Prince's before catching the late train for Oxford. He answered that fate always smiled on him at these funerals, paid off his cabby, and joined us.

Our dinner that evening was a brilliant success; and we left it to drive to Paddington to see the boy off. He had dropped a few pounds over the Derby but made the most of it up by a plunge on the last race: "and what with your standing me a dinner, I'm all up on the day's working and that cheerful I could kiss the guard." He wasn't in the least drunk, either; but explained to me very lucidly, on my taxing him with his real offence—cutting Oxford for a day when, the Eights being a short week off, he should have been in strict training—that all the strength of the B.N.C. boat that year lying on stroke side (he rowed at "six"), one might look on a *Peche Melba* and a Corona almost in the light of a prescription. "Friend of my youth," he added—addressing me, "and"—addressing Foe—"prop, sole prop, of my declining years—as you love me, be cruel to be kind and restrain me when I show a disposition to kiss yon bearded guard."

As the tail of the train swung out of the station Foe said meditatively, "I like that boy,"... And so it was. That autumn, when Jimmy Collingwood, having achieved a pass degree—"by means," as he put it, "only known to myself"—came up to share my chambers and read for the Bar, he and Foe struck up a warm affection. For once, moreover, Foe broke his habit of keeping his friends in separate cages. He was too busy a man to join us often; but when we met we were the Three Musketeers.

My father died in the Autumn of 1906; and this kept me down in the country until the New Year; although he had left his affairs as straight as a balance-sheet. Death duties and other things.... His account-books, note-books, filed references and dockets; his diaries kept, for years back, with records of rents and tithe-charges, of farms duly visited and crops examined field by field; appraisements of growing timber, memoranda for new plantings, queer charitable jottings about his tenants, their families, prospects, and ways to help them; all this tally, kept under God's eye by one who had never suffered man to interfere with him, gave my Radicalism a pretty severe jerk.

You see, here, worked out admirably in practice, was the rural side of that very landlordism which I had been denouncing up and down the East-End. The difference was plain enough, of course; but when you worked down to principle, it became for me a pretty delicate difference to explain. I was pledged, however, to return to London after Christmas and run (as Jimmy Collingwood put it) for those Bethnal Green Stakes: and in due time—that's to say, about the middle of January—up I came.

I won't bore you with my political campaign. One day in the middle of it Jimmy said, "To-night's a night off and we're dining with Jack Foe down in Chelsea. Eight o'clock: no theatre afterwards: 'no band, no promenade, no nozzing.' We've arranged between us to give your poor tired brain a rest."

"When you do happen to be thoughtful," said I "you might give me a little longer warning. As it is, I made a half-promise yesterday, to speak for that man of ours, Farrell, across the water."

"No, you don't," said Jimmy. "Who's Farrell? Friend of yours?"

"Tottenham Court Road," I said. "Only met him yesterday."

"What? Peter Farrell's Hire System?... And you met him there, in the Tottenham Court Road—by appointment, I suppose, with a coy carnation in your buttonhole. A bad young baronet, unmarried, intellectual, with a craving for human sympathy, on the Hire System'—"

"Don't be an ass, Jimmy," said I. "He's a Progressive, and they tell me his seat's dicky."

"They mostly are in the Tottenham Court Road," said Jimmy. "But if you've made half a promise, I was a week ahead of you with a whole one. We dine with Jack Foe."

The night was a beast. Foe's flat, high up on a block overlooking the Chelsea embankment, fairly rocked under squalls of a cross-river wind. He had moved into these new quarters while I was down in Warwickshire, and the man who put in the windows had scamped his job. The sashes rattled diabolically. Now that's just the sort of thing he'd have asked me to see to before he installed himself, if I had been up at the time: or, rather, I should have seen to it without being asked. That kind of noise never affected *him*: he could just withdraw himself into his work and forget it. But different noises get on different men's nerves, and, next to the scratching of a slate-pencil, a window on the rattle or the distant slam-slam of a door left ajar makes me craziest. You'd think a man out here would get accustomed to anything in the way of racket. Not a bit of it! Home on leave those particular sounds rasp me as badly as ever.... Moreover I have rather an eye for scamped carpentry: learned it off my father, going about the property with him. His own eye was a hawk's for loose fences, loose slates, badly-hung gates, even a broken sash-cord.

Foe's notions of furnishing, too, had always been bleak. He had hung his few pictures in the wrong places, and askew at that. He understood dining, though, and no doubt the dinner was good, though I gave very little attention to it.

"Otty's hipped to-night," said Collingwood, over the coffee. "Politics are all he can talk in these days. Wake up, Otty, and don't sit thinking out a speech."

I woke up. "I don't need to think out a speech," said I. "After a fortnight's campaigning a fellow can make speeches in his sleep."

"That's just what you're doing; and my fear is, you'll stand up presently and make one in ours."

"I'm sorry, Jack," I apologised. "Fact is, I'm worried by a half-promise I made to your man Farrell, over the river—"

"*My* man Farrell?" says Foe. "Farrell?... Farrell?... Never heard of him. Who's Farrell?"

"Never heard of him?... Why, Farrell's our candidate over there! ... *Your* candidate; because, if elected, he'll represent you; because your College and—if you choose to narrow it down—your own laboratories and lecture-rooms—will belong to his constituency. The rates on your buildings, the trams that bring your poorer students, the public money that pays their scholarships—"

"My dear Roddy," he broke in. "You know that I never could get up an interest in politics. As for local politics—"

That fired me up at once. "Pretty silly sneer, that! Doesn't there lurk, somewhere down in your consciousness, *some* sense of belonging to the first city in the world?... Oh, yes, you use it, fast enough, whenever you go back to Cambridge and play the condescending metropolitan in Combination Room. *There*, seventy minutes from Liverpool Street, you pose—yes, *pose*, Jack—as the urbane man, Horatius Flaccus life-size; whereas your job as a citizen is confined to cursing the rates, swearing if a pit in the wood pavement jolts you on the way home from the theatre, supposing it's somebody's business, supposing there's graft in it, and talking superciliously of Glasgow and Birmingham, provincial towns, while you can't help to cheapen the price of a cabbage in Covent Garden!"

"Dear Roddy," Foe answered—very tolerantly, I'll admit—"you'll get elected, to a dead certainty."

"Oh, I'm all right," said I, cooling down. "Wish I could be so sure of your man Farrell, across the bridge."

"Farrell?"

"That's his name.... Think you'll be able to remember it?"

Here Jimmy dropped the ash of his cigar into his coffee-cup and chipped in judiciously.

"Otty has the right of it, Professor—though we shall have to cure him of his platform style. *Somebody* has to look after this country and look after London; and if you despise the fellows who run the show, then it's up to you, my intellectuals, to come in and do the business better. But you won't. It bores you. 'Oh, go away—can't you see I'm busy? I've got a malignant growth here, potted in a glass bottle with a diet of sterilised fat and an occasional whisky and soda, and we're sitting around until the joker develops D.T. He's an empyema, from South America, fully-grown male—'"

"Heavens alive!"

"I dare say I haven't the exact name," confessed Jimmy. "Fact is, I happened on it in the dictionary when I was turning up 'Empiricist' in a bit of a hurry. Some Moderate fellow down at Bethnal Green had called Otty in one of his speeches 'an ignorant empiricist'; so naturally I had to look up the word. I'd a hope it meant something connected with Empire-building, and then Otty could have scored off him. But apparently it doesn't."

"Are you sure?" asks Foe.

"Well, I used the dictionary they keep at Boodle's, not having one of my own. If you tell me it's not up to date, I'll write something sarcastic in the Complaint-Book."

Foe dropped the end of his cigar into the ash-tray and pushed back his chair. "Well", said he, "it's about time we got into our coats, eh?"

"My dear fellow—" I began. "You don't tell us—" I began again.

He understood, of course. What he said was, "The late Mr. Gladstone, they tell me, used to address Queen Victoria as if she were a public meeting. She complained that she didn't like it... and anyway, if you two can't help it, I can't help the acoustic defects of this flat.... Some more brandy? You'd better. It's a beast of a night; but your faithful dog shall bear you company."

NIGHT THE SECOND
THE MEETING AT THE BATHS

Foe's man, after whistling ten minutes or so for a taxi, returned upstairs, powdered with sleet. There wasn't, he said, so much as a four-wheeler crawling in the street. We went down and waited in the hall while he whistled again.

"Where is this show of yours being held?" Foe asked, after a bit.

"In the Baths," I told him, "just across the bridge. Yes, actually *in* the great Swimming Bath…. You needn't be afraid, though. They drain it."

"I don't care if they omitted that precaution," said he. "This is an adventure, and I'm for taking it in the proper spirit. Let's walk."

He pushed back the catch of the lock. The door burst open, hurling him back against the wall, as his man came flying through, fairly projected into our arms by the pressure of wind in the porch.

"Make up the fire, put out the whisky, and go to bed," Foe bawled at him. "Eh?… Yes, that's all right; I have my latch-key."

I couldn't have expostulated if I'd wanted to. The wind filled my mouth. We butted out after him into the gale, Jimmy turning in the doorway to let out a skirling war-whoop—"just to brace up the flat-dwellers," he explained afterwards. "I wanted to tell 'em that St. George was for Merry England, but there wasn't time."

We didn't say much on the way. The wind took care of that. On the bridge we had to claw the parapet to pull ourselves along; and just as we won to the portico of the Baths there came a squall that knocked us all sideways. Foe and Jimmy cast their arms about one pillar, I clung to another; and the policeman, who at that moment shot his lantern upon us from his shelter in the doorway, pardonably mistook our condition. He advised us—as a friend, if he might say so—to go home quietly.

"But there's a public meeting inside," said I.

"There might be, or there might not be," he allowed. "It's a thin one anyway. You'll get no fun out of it."

"And I am due to make a speech there," I went on. "That's to say, they want me to propose or second a vote of thanks or something of the sort."

"If I was you, sir," advised the constable, kindness itself, "I wouldn't, however much they wanted it."

I gave him my card. He held it close under the ray of his bull's-eye and altered his manner with a jerk. "Begging your pardon, Sir Roderick—"

"Not at all," I assured him. "Most natural mistake in the world. If there's a side entrance, now, near the platform—"

He led us up a gusty by-street and tapped for us on the side door. It was opened at once, though cautiously, by a little frock-coated man ornamented with a large blue-and-white favour. After an instant's parley he received us obsequiously, and the constable pocketed our blessing.

"Of course," he said by way of Good night, "I knew from the first I was dealing with gentlemen. I made no mistake about that."

The little steward admitted us to a sort of lobby or improvised cloak-room stowed somewhere beneath the platform. While helping us off with our coats he told us that the audience was satisfactory "considering the weather." "A night like this isn't calculated to fetch out doubtfuls."

"It has fetched out one, anyhow," said I. "This is Professor Foe, of your University College."

"Greatly honoured, sir, I am sure!" The little man bowed to Foe, and turned again to me: "Your friends, Sir Roderick, will accompany you on the platform, of course. Shall we go in at once? Or—at this moment Mr. Jenkinson is up. He has been speaking for twenty minutes."

"—And has just started his peroration," said I; for though it came muffled through the boarding, I had recognised Mr. Jenkinson's voice, and the oration to which in other parts of London I had already listened twice. I could time it. "There's no hurry," I said. "Jenkinson—good man, Jenkinson—has finished with the tram-service statistics, and will now for a brief two minutes lift the whole question on to a higher plane. Then he'll sit down, and that's where we'll slip in, covered by the thunder of applause."

He divided a grin between us and a couple of assistants who had been hanging up our coats and now came forward.

"To tell you the truth, Sir Roderick, our candidate wants strengthening a bit, for platform purposes; though they tell me he's improving steadily. The kinder of you to come, sir, and help us. As for Jenkinson, he's the popular pet over here, as a speaker or when he comes across to play at the Oval. As a cricketer yourself, Sir Roderick, you'll know what Jenkinson does with his summer?"

"Certainly," said I. "Being on the Committee of the M.C.C.—"

"You don't mean to say that it's Jenko?" Jimmy chipped in. "You don't tell me it's our long left and left-handed Jenko, that has bowled me at the nets a hundred times?—alas, poor Jenko!"

"Why, of course, it is," said I. "Didn't you know?... How the deuce else do you suppose that a cricket pro. supports himself during the winter?"

"I'd never thought of that," said Jimmy. "One half of the world never knows how the other half lives."

"Well," said I, "that's Jenkinson's winter occupation—public oratory— advocacy of social and municipal reform—mostly on Fabian lines. The man's honest, mind you.... But he's finishing.... Come along! Are you for the platform, Jack?"

"Not if I can sit somewhere at your feet and look up at you," said Foe. "I'm not at all certain that I approve of your candidate, either, or his political platform—"

"Our Mr. Farrell, Professor? Oh, surely!—" the little steward expostulated. "But maybe you've never made Mr. Farrell's acquaintance, sir?"

"Never set eyes on him, to my knowledge," Foe assured him.

"Then, Professor—if I may make bold to say so—it's impossible to disapprove of Mr. Farrell. He's a bit what-you-might-call *opportunist* in his views; but, for the gentleman himself, he wouldn't hurt a fly—not a headache in a hogshead of him, as the saying goes.... Certainly, Sir Roderick, if you're ready.... Mr. Byles, here, will conduct the Professor to a chair close under the platform. We usually keep a few front seats vacant, for friends and—er—eventualities."

"I'm an eventuality," said Foe.

"You'll be one of *us*, sir, before you've finished, never fear!" the little steward promised genially.

We entered amid salvos of applause, again and again renewed. It was none of our earning nor intended for us. Jenkinson (I was afterwards told) had varied his peroration with a local allusion very cleverly introduced. "They probably knew him" (he said)—"those, at any rate, who happened to live near Kennington probably knew him—for one who earned his living by a form of sport, by a mere game, if they preferred so to call it." (Cheers.)

"He was not there to defend himself, still less to defend cricket." (Hear, hear.) "He would only say that cricket was a game which demanded some skill and— especially when one bowled at the Oval" (loud cheers) "against Surrey" (cheers loud and prolonged)—"often some endurance." (Laughter.) "He would add that cricket was a thoroughly English game." (Renewed cheers.) "Why do I mention cricket to-night, sir?"—Jenkinson swung round and demanded it of the Chairman, who hadn't a notion. "I mention it, sir, because players have sometimes said to me, 'Jenkinson, I wonder you always seem to enjoy yourself at the Oval.' 'Why not?' says I; 'the crowd's friendly and the pitch perfect.' 'That's just it,' they say; 'perfect to break a bowler's heart.' 'Never you mind.' I answers: 'Tom Jenkinson, when he gets into Surrey, isn't out for averages.'" (Can't you hear the cheers at that?) "'He's out for fine art and a long day at it in pleasant surroundings: and,' I winds up, 'if you reckon I sometimes take a while, down there, to bowl a man *out*, just you wait till I come down and help to bowl a man *in*!' Your servant, Mr. Farrell!"

Neat, eh? Well, we made our entrance right on top of it: and though the great Bath was no more than three-parts full, you couldn't see a vacant seat, the audience rocked so.

Now I must tell you a queer thing.... You know what it feels like when you're talking away easily, maybe laughing, and all of a sudden the Bosch puts in one that you feel means business? Something in the sound of the devil makes you scatter.... Well, I can't explain it, but through the noise of the stamping, hand-clapping, cheering, all of a sudden and without rhyme or reason, I seemed to hear the shriek of something distant, sinister, menacing.... Oh, I'm not an imaginative fellow. Very likely it was a note set up by the wind outside. I can't even swear that I *heard* it; sort of took it down my spine. Shrill it was for a moment—something between a child's wail and the hiss of a snake—and, the next moment, not shrill at all, but dull and heavy, like the flap of a great wing beating the air, heavy with evil.... Yes, that was the sense of it—heavy with evil. I pulled up with a shiver. The Chairman was on his feet, waiting for the applause to cease, ready to announce the next speaker. The little steward touched him by the arm; he wheeled about and shook my hand effusively as I was introduced. "Delighted! Flattered!" he said, and shook me by the hand again. The shiver went out of me: but it took something out of me at the same time. I had a most curious feeling of depression as I found my place.... I looked about for Foe, and spotted him. They had given him a chair close under the platform, a little to my right. He had taken his seat and was scanning the platform attentively. The arc-light shone down on his face, and showed it white, bewildered, a trifle strained.... But this may have been no more than my fancy.

The Chairman asked for silence. He was a bald-headed small man of no particular points and (as Jimmy whispered) seemed to feel his position acutely. He said that, whatever their personal differences, they would all agree that Mr. Jenkinson's speech had uplifted them above ordinary politics. He had felt himself speaking not as their Chairman but as a private individual—or, in other words, as a man— uplifted into a higher plane, and he would now call upon their respected candidate, Mr. Farrell, to address the meeting.

Mr. Farrell stepped forward. I must try to tell you what Mr. Farrell looked like, because it belongs to the story.... You'll find that it becomes pretty important.

He was of medium height and carried a belly. Later on, when I came to know him, I heard him refer to it as his "figure" and say that exercise was good for it. I don't know about that: but he certainly was given exercise to reduce it, later on.... He could not have been ashamed of it either, just yet: for it was clothed in front with sealskin and festooned with two loops of gold chain.

Two or three locks of hair, cultivated to a great length and plastered by means of pomade across his cranium, concealed a certain poverty of undergrowth thereabouts; while a pair of whiskers, sandy in colour and stiff in texture, and a clean-shaven upper lip and chin, threw out a challenge that Mr. Peter Farrell could grow hair if and where he chose. His eyes bulged like gooseberries. They were colourless, and lustreless in comparison with the diamond pin in his neckcloth. His frock-coat and pepper-and-salt trousers were of superfine material and flashy cut. They fitted him like a skin in all the wrong places. Get it into your heads—Here was a prosperous reach-me-down person of the sort you will find on any political platform, standing for Parliament or seconding a vote of thanks.

He was not in the least bumptious. He began very nervously with a carefully prepared Shakespearean quotation—"'I am no orator as Brutus is,'" in compliment to Jenkinson. Then he gave *me* a lift. He said that my presence there was a proof, if proof were needed, of the solidarity—he would repeat the word—of the solidarity existing in the Progressive ranks. He was sure—he might even say, confident—that this graceful act on the part of the right honourable baronet (as he chose to call me) would give the lie to certain reports—hints, rather—emanating from certain quarters which called themselves newspapers. He would not soil his mouth by giving them their true name, which was Rags. "We are all solid here," announced Mr. Farrell, and was answered with applause.

After this spirited opening he consulted a sheaf of notes, and was straightway mired in a ploughland of tramway finance and sticky statistics. After ten minutes of this he turned a furrow, so to speak, and zigzagged off into Education "Provided" and "Non-Provided," lunging and floundering with the Church Catechism and the Rate-Book until I dare say his audience mistook the two for one single composition.

"Poor old Jack!" I thought. "This will be boring him stiff.".... And with that I sat up of a sudden, listening. Sure as fate I heard the damned thing coming... coming...

"This brings me," said Mr. Farrell, "to the subject of Grants—Grants from the Imperial Exchequer and Special Grants from the London County Council to certain University Colleges, of which you have one in your midst—" It was at this point that I sat up.

"I may claim," went on Mr. Farrell, "to be no foe of Higher Education. I am all for the Advancement of Science. In my own way of business I have frequently had occasion to consult scientific experts, and have derived benefit—practical benefit—from their advice. I freely own it. What's more, ladies and gentlemen, I am all for Research, provided you keep it within limits.

"What do I mean by limits?... I have here, in my hand, ladies and gentlemen, a document. It is signed by a number of influential persons, including several ladies of title. This document alleges— er—certain practices going on in a certain University College not five hundred yards from where I stand at this moment; and it asks me what I think of them, and if public money—your money and mine— should be voted to encourage that and similar forms of Research—"

"Great Scott!" groaned Jimmy, and touched my arm. "Otty, look at the Professor's face! To think we—"

"I have also," pursued Mr. Farrell, "a supplementary paper, extensively signed in the constituency, supporting the document mentioned and asking for a Public Inquiry; asking me if I am willing to press for a Royal Commission. It was put into my hands as I entered the hall; but I have no hesitation whatever in answering that question.

"A certain Professor is mentioned—I have not the pleasure of his acquaintance—and a certain—er—" Mr. Farrell consulted his papers— "Laboratory of Physiological Research. I made my own way in the world. But I am an Englishman, I hope; and when such a document as this, influentially signed, is put into my hands and an answer demanded of me, what sort of answer do I give? The answer I give, ladies and gentlemen, is that I keep a spaniel at home, though not for sporting purposes, and still less for purposes of Physiological Research"—Every time the ass came to these two words he made elaborate pretence of consulting his papers.

"Nine times out of ten this dumb friend and dependent of mine greets me in the hall as I reach home after a hard day's business, wagging his tail in a way almost more than human. And when I think of me going home to-night, with this document—signed, as I say, by persons of title and supported by this influential body of rate-payers—and look into his dumb eyes and think it might happen to my Dash to be laid on a board in the interests of this so-called Research, and there vivisected alive, then I say—"

"It's a lie!"

Foe was on his legs, and he fairly shouted it. Shell-shock? *Phut!*—It exploded right at our feet below the platform. Farrell came staggering back, right on top of us; but the reason may have been partly that Jimmy had reached forward, too late, and gripped his coat-tails. Of course the man's offence was unpardonable; but I could hardly recognise Jack's face, so drawn it was and twisted in white-hot hate.

There was silence while you might count five, perhaps. The audience, taken right aback for that space, had begun to rise and crane forward. "Who is it?"—you could almost hear the question starting to run.

Then again, for a few seconds, things happened just as they do in rowdy public meetings. While the Chairman thumped the table, Farrell wrenched his coat-tails from Jimmy's grip and stepped to the edge of the platform.

"Who are you?" he demanded. There was a queer throaty sound in his voice; yet he held himself (I thought) in fair control.

"My name is Foe," came the answer. Jack was still on his feet, his face ashen, his eyes blazing behind his glasses. I had known him all these years and never guessed him capable of such a white rage. But the words came very slowly and deliberately. "My name is Foe. I am the Professor with whom, just now, you said you hadn't the pleasure to be acquainted—"

"Throw him out!" called a voice from one of the back rows.

I had expected that; had, as you might say, been waiting for it. What caught me unprepared was its instant effect on Mr. Farrell.

He raised a fist and shook it. He fairly capered. "Yes, throw him out! Throw him out!" He choked, spluttered and let it out almost in a scream. I leaned forward for a sideways sight of his face.

"Gad! he's going to have a fit and tumble off the platform. Stand by, Otty." Jimmy, reaching out a hand again for Mr. Farrell's coat-tails, spoke the warning close in my ear, for by this time twenty or thirty voices had taken up the cry, "Throw him out!" the Chairman was hammering like mad for Order, and there was an ugly shuffle of feet at the far end of the hall.

"Throw him out! Throw him out!" Farrell kept screaming above the hubbub. "How would *he* treat a dog?—"

"The man's demented," said I—and with that I heard a bench or a chair go crack like a revolver-shot. It might have been a shot starting a sprint; for close on top of it about a dozen fellows leapt out into the gangway, while three or four charged forward through the audience, where the women had already started to scream.

There was nothing for it but prompt action. Jimmy and I swung ourselves down over the front of the platform. This gave us a fair start of the crowd, but it didn't give us any time to argue with Foe, who still stood glaring up at Farrell, ready to put in another retort as soon as he could get a hearing. Of the danger rushing down on him either he wasn't aware or he cared nothing for it. Jimmy caught him by the waist, and grinned intelligently as I pointed to the emergency exit around the corner of the platform.

"Right-O! Hold the curtain aside for me.… Along you come, Professor! Be a good child and don't kick nursy…"

"Take him home," said I. "Policeman will help if there's a row outside."

Then I dropped the curtain on them and faced about. The audience by this time were standing on benches and chairs, but of course my first job was with the hustlers who had reached the end of the gangway and were coming on under the lee of the platform. They looked ugly at first, but the job turned out to be a soft one.

"You wanted him turned out," said I, "and we've obliged you. Rather neatly, eh?—You can't say no to that."

I wanted someone to laugh, and by the mercy of Heaven someone did—someone back in the third or fourth row. In five seconds or so quite a lot of people were laughing and applauding.

"Now stand where you are," said I, catching hold of this advantage; "and one of you give me a leg up to the platform. I'm going to propose a vote of thanks.… Won't keep you standing long. But please don't go back to your seats; because some of the women are frightened."

Well, they gave me a leg up, and somebody above gave me a hand, and there I was, none the worse, on the platform.

Farrell had collapsed in his seat by the Chairman's table and sat with his face in his hands. The Chairman was paralytic. So I did the only thing that seemed possible: started to propose a vote of thanks. Pretty fair rubbish I must have started with, too: but by and by I slipped into my own election speech and after that it was pretty plain sailing. You see, when a man runs for candidate, he begins by preparing half a dozen speeches; but by the time he's half through he has them pretty well boiled down into one, and he can speak that one in his sleep. After ten minutes or so I forgot that I was moving a vote of thanks to somebody and moved a vote of confidence instead—confidence in Mr. Farrell.

Nobody minded. Two or three speakers followed me and moved and seconded all sorts of things at random. We were all in a hopeless muddle, and all quite good-humoured about it; and we wound up by singing "God Save the King!"

NIGHT THE THIRD
THE GRAND RESEARCH

The little Chairman followed me into the lobby and thanked me effusively, while a couple of stewards helped me into my great-coat. He threw a meaning glance over his shoulder at Farrell, who stood in a corner nervously winding and unwinding a long silk comforter about his neck and throat. He seemed to be muttering, saying something over to himself. His face twitched—it was still red and congested— and he kept his eyes on the floor. He had not spoken to either of us since the meeting dissolved. Very likely he did not see us.

"A bit rattled," I suggested quietly.

"You may bet on that, Sir Roderick." The steward, who was turning up my coat collar, said this almost in my ear. "You don't think, now—"

He did not finish the sentence, and I faced about on him for the rest of it. He tapped his forehead gently.

"Oh, nonsense!" said I. "He's not broken to public life and he doesn't ruffle well, that's all; and, after all, it isn't every man who enjoys being called a liar to his face and before some hundreds of people."

"His face, sir," the steward persisted. "That's it; you've given me the word. Did you see his face? No, of course you didn't, for you were sitting sideways to him—and so was you, Mr. Chairman, sir. But I was standing by the main door when it happened, and had him in full view, and—Well!" he wound up.

"Well?" said I.

He dropped his voice to a whisper almost. "It frightened me, sir.... I think it must have frightened a good few of the audience, and that's what held the rush back and gave you and the other gentleman time. You wouldn't think, to look at his face now"— with a glance across at Farrell, who was sending out to inquire if his car had arrived, and looking at his watch (for, you'll understand, the meeting had broken up early in spite of my oratorical effort)—"you wouldn't believe, Sir Roderick, that there was anything deep in the man. Nor perhaps there isn't. It didn't seem to me, just half a minute, that it was Mr. Farrell inside Mr. Farrell's clothes and looking out of his eyes."

"Then *who*, in the world?" I asked.

The steward gave himself a shake. "Speak low, sir, and don't turn round.... I was a fool to mention his name—folks always hear their own names quicker than anything else. He's looking our way, suspicious-like.... Now if I was to say 'Satan,' or if I was to say that he was a party possessed— Well, any way, Sir Roderick, I wish we had someone else for a candidate, and I don't see myself happy, these next few days, working on Committee for him."

"Well, you have the advantage of me," said I. "You saw him full-face, whereas I had to study him from the rear. From the rear he looked funny enough.... But look here," I went on; "if there were any slate loose on the man's roof, as you're hinting, you may bet that a great Furnishing Company in Tottenham Court Road wouldn't be taking any risks with him as Chairman of Directors."

"All I can say, sir," he muttered, shaking his head, "is that I don't like it. And, anyway, he isn't a gentleman."

The Chairman had left us to say good night to Mr. Farrell, whose car was just then announced. I went across, too, to shake hands and wish him good luck on polling-day. As our eyes met he started, came out of the torpor in which he had been gazing about him, and bowed to me in best shop-walker fashion.

"Ah, Sir Roderick!" he said, not very coherently. "You must excuse me—remiss, very. Owe you many thanks, sir—not only for coming— great honour—But saved very awkward situation. Overwrought, sir— that's what I'm suffering from—overstrain: not used to this sort of thing.... My God, I am tired... all of a sudden, too; so tired you can't think.... Can I have the pleasure of driving you a part of the way, Sir Roderick?"

"Thank you, Mr. Farrell," said I. "But you're for Wimbledon, I believe, and I'm for Chelsea. Fact is"—I ventured it on an impulse—"I'm going to call on that friend of mine, Professor Foe, who so unhappily interrupted you to-night, and tell him that he made a fool of himself." I watched his eyes. They were merely dull— heavy. "You did provoke him, you know, Mr. Farrell," I went on: "I'm morally certain he is guiltless of the practices alleged in that document of yours; and, if I can persuade him to receive you in his laboratory and show you his work and his methods—"

By George, I *had* called back that look into Mr. Farrell's gooseberry eyes! This time it lasted for about two seconds.

"Meet him?—*him?* Your pardon, Sir Roderick." He brushed his hand over his eyes, but they were dull again.... "No, thank you"—he turned to the Chairman—"It's only two steps to the car; I don't want anyone's arm.... Well, yes, I'm obliged to you. Queer, how tired I feel.... Good night, gentlemen!"

The car purred and glided away. "I feel a bit uneasy about our Candidate," said the Chairman as we watched the rear-light turn the corner. "He's had a shock.... Well, we live in stirring times, and one more evening's over!"

"But it isn't!" I cried out on a sudden thought. "Man, we've forgotten the reporters! If they've left the building the whole town will be red before we're well out of our beauty-sleep."

We made a plunge back for the hall and, as luck would have it, found three of the four reporters at the table. The early close had left them ahead of time, and two were copying out their shorthand while the third was engaged on a pithy paragraph or two under the headline of "Stormy Proceedings—A Professor Ejected. What happens to Dogs in the Silversmiths' College?"

I won't say how we prevailed with the Fourth Estate, except that it wasn't by bribery. The man writing the Pithy Pars did some cricket reporting at Lord's during the summer—some of the best, too. I was taking bread out of his mouth, and knew it. But it had to be done, and it was done, as a favour between gentlemen. He saw to the others.... God help those people who run down Cricket!

I knocked in at Foe's flat well on the virtuous side of midnight. Jimmy was in charge of the patient. Foe had got into an old Caius blazer and sat very far back in a wicker chair—lolled, in fact, on his shoulder-pins, sucking at a pipe and brooding.

"Give me a whisky-and-soda," said I. "If ever a man has earned it!"

"I somehow knew you'd turn up," said Jimmy, mixing. "Not a scratch? Tell us."

So I told. I didn't tell all, of course. I left out all the business in the lobby, what the steward had said, what Farrell had said, and my traffic with the reporters. I humped myself on my display of oratory.

I must have thrown this—necessarily thrown it—somewhat out of proportion.

Jimmy said, "Rats! I know all about Caesar's funeral, and you couldn't do it. You can't come it over us with your spellbound audience. What you've done is you've kept the bridge ever since the proud Professor and I started back, and, when they cut it behind you, you swam the river."

"Have it which way you like," said I, dropping into a chair. "Now tell me how you two have been getting along."

"Our motto," said Jimmy, "has been Plain Living and High Thinking. We have fleeted the time in earnest discourse. It began on the way home with the Professor asking me some innocent question concerning what he called the 'Science' of Ju-Jitsu. I told him that it was of Japanese origin, as its name implied, and further that he did wrong to call it a Science; it was really an Art. I engaged that I could prove this to him in thirty seconds, but said I would wait until we reached home, lest he might be trying his discovery on the Police. This led to a discussion on the Art of Self-Defence, in the course of which he let fall the incredible remark that he had never been inside the National Sporting Club."

"Give him time," said I. "Jack's a methodical worker, as every man of science should be. He'll come to it; but, so far, his researches have been confined to the lower animals."

Jimmy looked puzzled. "Eh?... Oh, you mean politicians. Well, it occurred to me that if he meant to attend any more political meetings, there was no time to be lost. So—"

"But I don't," Jack growled.

Jimmy corrected himself. "Perhaps we'd better say, then, that I thought it well he should know the difference between some public gatherings and others. So we've been talking about the N.S.C. and the Professor is under promise to visit it with me, one night, and see how an argument ought to be conducted."

I lit a pipe and looked at Foe over the match. "Jack," said I, "a holiday for you is indicated. With Jimmy's leave I'm going to speak seriously for a moment.... Down in the country, among other jobs, I have to sit on an Asylum Committee: and from the start I've been struck by the number of officials in charge of lunatics who seem, after some while at it, to go a bit dotty themselves. Doctors, male attendants—it doesn't seem to affect the women so much—even chaplains—after a time I wouldn't give more than short odds on the complete sanity of any of 'em. Why, even our Chairman... I must tell you about our Chairman.... He's old, and you may put it down to senile decay. Before we discharge a patient, or let him out as harmless, it's our custom to have him up before the Committee with a relative who undertakes to be answerable for him. Well, our Chairman, of late, can't be trusted to tell t'other from which: and it's pretty painful when he starts on the vacant-looking patient and says, pointing a finger at the astonished relative, 'You see, Mr. So-and-so, the apparent condition of this poor creature. It is with some hesitation that we have given this case the benefit of the doubt; and we cannot hand him over unless satisfied that you feel your responsibility to be a grave one.'"

Foe got up, smiling dourly, knocked out his pipe, and chose a fresh one from the mantelpiece. "You'll make quite a good story of that, Roddy," he said, "with a little practice. But, as I don't work among lunatics, what's the bearing of it?"

"You're working," said I, "—for years now you've been working and overworking—on these wretched animals, and neglecting the society of your fellow-men. You pore over animals, you probe into animals, you're always thinking about animals; which amounts to consorting with animals—at their worst, too.... I tell you, Jack, it won't do. I've had my doubts for some time, but to-night I'm sure of it. If you go on as you're going, there'll be a smash, my boy."

I was half afraid he would fly out on me. But he lit his pipe thoughtfully, dropped the match into the fire, and watched it burn out before he answered.

"And I'm to consort with my fellow-men, eh?—with the sort you led me among to-night?" He laughed harshly, with a not ill-humoured snort. "Is that your prescription? Thank you, I prefer my bad beasts."

"No," I said. "After to-night it's not my prescription. I'll give you another. I know your work, and that your heart's in it. But ease down this term as far as the lecture-list allows, and then at Easter come with Jimmy and me to Wastdale and let me teach your infant footsteps how to mountaineer. There's nothing like a stiff climb and a summit for purging a man's mind.... I've come to like mountains ever so much better than big game. They are the authentic gods, high and clean; they're above desecration; the more you assail them the more you are theirs.... Now there's always a kind of lust, a kind of taint, about big-game hunting. No harm to a man if he's in full health—but beastliness, and menagerie smell, if he's not."

"Mountains!" scoffs he.

"You needn't despise them," said I. "They're apt to be heavenly, just before Easter, with the snow on 'em; and Mickledore or Gable or the Pillar from Ennerdale will easily afford you forty-four ways of breaking your neck.... If you're good and can do a little trick I have in mind on Scawfell I'll reward you by bringing you home past a farm where they keep a couple of savage sheep-dogs. For a good conduct prize, I have a friend up there—a farming clergyman—who will teach you words of cheer by introducing you to a bull that can't pass the Board of Trade test because he's like Lady Macbeth's hand— however you babble to him in a green field he makes the green one red. But these shall be special treats, you understand, held in reserve. Most days you'll just climb till you're tired, and your dinner shall be mutton for three weeks on end…. Now, don't interrupt. I may seem to be on the oratorical lay to-night, but God knows I'm in earnest. If I wasn't, I shouldn't have spoken out like this before Jimmy, who's your friend and will back me up."

"I might," said Jimmy judiciously, "if I understood what you meant by all this chat about savage animals. What is it, at all? Does the Professor keep a menagerie? And, if so, why haven't I been invited?"

"Why, don't you know?" I asked.

"Know what?" asked Jimmy, leaning back and sucking at his pipe. "Whatever it is, I probably don't: that's what a Public School and University education did for me. As I seem to remember one Farrell's remarking in the dim and distant past, for my part I never indulged in Physiological Research—I made my own way in the world…" He murmured it dreamily, and then sat up with a start. "Lord's sake!" he cried out. "You don't tell me that Farrell… that the Professor actually—"

"Don't be a fool," I interrupted. "Of course, Jack doesn't. Jack, tell him about the Grand Research. Enlighten his ignorance, that's a good fellow."

"Enlighten him yourself, if you want to. You'll tell it all wrong: but I'm tired," declared Foe.

"Well, then," said I, "it's this way, dear James…. You behold seated opposite to you on the right of the fireplace, and smoking the beast of a brier pipe with the modesty of true genius, a Scientific Man—a Savant, shall I say?—of European reputation. It isn't quite European just yet: but it's going to be, which is better."

"I always prophesied it," said Jimmy. "What's it going to be *for*?"

"Listen," said I. "Having received (as you assure us) a liberal education, either at Eton or B.N.C., you probably made acquaintance with that beautiful poem by Dr. Isaac Watts beginning—"

'Let dogs delight to bark and bite—'

"Continue the quotation, with brief notes on any obscurities."

"Certainly," said Jimmy.

'Let dogs delight to bark and bite,
'Tis manners so to do—'

"No, that sounds a bit off."

> 'Let dogs delight to bark and bite,
> For God hath made them so;
> Let bears and lions growl and fight, For 'tis their nature
> toe.'

"Good boy!" said I. "Now that's where Dr. Watts—"

"Don't interrupt," said Jimmy. "It isn't manners so to do, when I'm just getting into my stride—"

> 'But, children, you should never let
> Such angry passions rise:
> Your little hands were never made
> To tear each other's eyes...'

"Please, I don't know any more."

"Nor need you," I assured him, "for, according to Jack, it's completely out of date."

"'M'yes!" Jimmy agreed. "But he won't get a European reputation by discovering *that*. They don't tear each other's eyes at the N.S.C., even—it's against the rules. Come and see for yourself, Professor."

"Angry passions," I went on patiently; "envy, hatred, and malice—especially hatred—are Jack's special lay; the Grand Research we call it. Take simple anger, for instance. What is it makes a man angry?"

"Lots of things.... Being called a liar, for one."

Foe took the mischief in the boy's eye, and let out a laugh. "I can't be angry with *you*, anyway. Go on, Roddy. You're doing it quite well so far, though I'm almost too sleepy to listen."

"It isn't as simple as you think," I pursued seriously (but glad enough in my heart to have heard Jack laugh—he wasn't given to laughter at any time). "All sorts of things happen inside you; all sorts of mechanisms start working: nerves and muscles, of course, but even in the blood-vessels there's a change of the corpuscles as per order—you put an insult into the slot and they do the rest. The levers of the machine—the brakes, clutches and the rest are in the forebrain: that's where you change gear when you want to struggle with suppressed emotion, run her slow or let her all out: and that's what Jack means to do with us before he has finished. Does he want us to love or to hate?—He'll press a button, and we shall do the rest, automatically. He will call on a Foreign Minister or an ambassador and make or avert a European War. He will dictate—"

"He's telling you the most atrocious rubbish," cut in Foe, addressing Jimmy.

"I am suiting this explanation to the infant mind," said I, "and I'll trouble you not to interrupt.... You may or may not have heard, my dear child, either at Eton or Oxford, that the brain has two hemispheres—"

"Just like the globe," said Jimmy brightly.

"Aptly observed," I congratulated him: "though that is perhaps no more than a coincidence. Taking the illustration, however, if we can only eliminate the Monroe Doctrine and work the clutch between these two—Jack, you are reaching for the poker. Don't fire, Colonel: I'll come down.... Reverting, then, to the forebrain, you have doubtless observed that in man it is enormously larger than in the lower animals, as in our arrogance we call them—"

"I hadn't," said Jimmy.

"It's a fact, nevertheless," said I. "I assure you.... Well, Jack, so far, has dealt only with the lower animals. I don't say the lowest. I doubt if he can do much with an oyster who has been crossed in love. But by George! you should watch him whispering to a horse! or, if you want something showier, see him walk into a lion's cage with the tamer."

"I say, Professor! Have you *really?*—" I knew Jimmy would sit up at this point.

"Of course he has," said I. "It began on a trip we took together in Uganda, just after leaving Cambridge. I was after lions: Jack's game was the mosquito and other bugs. One day—oh, well, Jack, we'll keep that story for another occasion.... The long and short was, he found he had a gift—uncanny to me—of dealing with animals in a rage, and raising or lowering their angry passions at will. He switched off bugs, their cause and cure, and on to this new track. He started experimenting, made observations, took records. He's been at it now—how many years, Jack? He'll play on a dog-fight better than you can on a penny-whistle: as soon as he chooses they're sitting one on each side of the gramophone, listening to Their Master's Voice. Vivisection?—Farrell's an ass. The only inhuman thing I've ever known Jack do was to domesticate a wild-cat and restore her to the woods unprotected by her natural amenities. These people hear a shindy going on in the laboratory in `—` Street, and conclude that he's holding the wrong sort of tea-party. Now, if he'd had an ounce of practical wisdom to-night, he'd have arisen quietly, invited Farrell to drop in at 4.30 to-morrow, arranged a moderate dog-fight, and given that upholsterer ten minutes of glorious life. Farrell—"

"I'm going to turn you both out," said Foe, getting up suddenly. "Help yourself to another whisky-and-soda, Roddy.... I'm so beaten with sleep it's odds against getting off my boots." As a fact, too, his face was weary-white. He turned to Jimmy, however, with a ghost of a smile. "Roddy has been talking a deal of nonsense. But if you really care to inspect my little show, come around some morning .... Let me see—to-day's Wednesday. Saturday is my slack morning—What d'you say to breakfasting here on Saturday, nine o'clock? and we'll walk over at half-past ten or thereabouts. I keep a yellow dog there that will go through some tricks for you.... Right? Then so long!... You can come along, too, Roddy, if you'll behave yourself."

NIGHT THE FOURTH
ADVENTURE OF THE POLICE STATION

I opened my newspaper next morning in no little anxiety. I ought rather to say "my newspapers": for the L.C.C. campaign was raging at its height, and a candidate cannot afford to neglect in the morning any nasty thing that any nasty fellow has written overnight.

Jephson—yes, he's the same good Jephson who wouldn't exchange my button-stick for a Field-Marshal's baton—Jephson brought in my morning tea and laid across the foot of my bed a bundle of newspapers as thick as a bolster.

I sat up, reached for them and began to read almost as soon as he switched on the light. I was honestly nervous.

I took the hostile papers first, of course. Pretty soon it began to dawn on my grateful soul that all was right with the world. The reporters had stood shoulder to shoulder. Two or three headlines gave me a shake. "BRISK SCENES ACROSS THE WATER," "MR. FARRELL SPEAKS OUT," "AN INTERRUPTER EJECTED." One headline in particular gave me qualms—"WHAT'S WRONG WITH SILVERSMITH'S COLLEGE? PUBLIC ENDOWMENT WITHOUT PUBLIC CONTROL: MR. FARRELL PUTS SOME SEARCHING QUESTIONS." But it had all been toned down in the letterpress and came to very little. The reporters, using their own discretion, had used such phrases as "An interrupter, apparently labouring under some excitement," "At this point a gentleman in the front row caused a diversion by challenging... The audience were in no mood, however,..." "Here an auditor protested warmly. It was understood that he had some official connection with the institution referred to by the candidate," and so on.

I hugged myself over my success. To be sure, the vague impression derivable was that the "scene" had its origin in strong drink. But the name of Professor John Foe nowhere appeared. Greatest blessing of all, there was no leading article, no pithy paragraph, even. I arose and shaved blithely. Across the stairhead I could hear Jimmy shouting music-hall ditties—his custom in his bath. Yes, all was right with the world.

Nothing happened that day, except that I interviewed my agent after breakfast, worked like a nigger until nightfall, canvassing slums; got back to the Bath Club, had a swim, dined, and returned to my constituency for the night's public meeting. Arduous work: but what you might call supererogatory. I could have shot my opponent sitting, and he knew it. My rascal of an agent knew it too, but he was an honest man in his way—and that's politics.

Next morning, same procedure on Jephson's part: similar bolster of papers, neatly folded and laid across the foot of my bed. This time I poured myself a cup of tea and reached for them lazily. The *Times* was topmost. Jephson always laid the *Times* topmost.

Five minutes later... But listen to this—

(*To-night before resuming his story Otway had laid on the table beside him a small but bulging letter-case, from the contents of which he now selected a newspaper cutting.*)

PUBLIC ENDOWMENT OF RESEARCH

To the Editor of *The Times*:—

Sir,

A Memorial, influentially signed by a number of ladies and gentlemen variously eminent in Society, Politics, Literature and Art but united in their friendship for the dumb creation, was recently addressed to the Principal of the South London ("Silversmiths'") University College, situated in the constituency for which I am offering myself as representative in the next London County Council. In this Memorial the Principal was invited to ease the public mind with respect to rumours (widely prevalent) concerning certain practices in the laboratories under his charge, either by denying them or inviting a public inquiry. I was not aware of this document— to which I should have been happy to add my signature— until last night, when a copy of it was put into my hands, with an additional list of signatures by more than a hundred local residents. This morning I have had an opportunity to peruse the answer sent by the Principal (Sir Elkin Travers) to the Hon. Secretary of the Memorialists.

I cannot consider this answer satisfactory. Sir Elkin is content to meet the allegation with a flat denial, and rejects the reasonable request for a public inquiry in language none too courteous. Unfortunately a body of testimony by residents in the close vicinity of the College, as to the noises and outcries heard proceeding from the laboratories from time to time, if not in direct conflict with the denial, at least suggests that, with the growing numbers of his professors and students, Sir Elkin cannot know what is going on, at all times, in every department of the Institution: while his peremptory rejection of an investigation which he might have welcomed as an opportunity for allaying public suspicion will be far from having that effect. If all is well inside his laboratories, why should Sir Elkin fear the light?

May I point out that considerable sums of public money are spent on these University Colleges, and even, indirectly, in promoting the very researches incriminated by the Memorialists. We should insist on knowing what we are paying for and whether it is consistent with the consciences of those among us who look upon dumb animals as the friends and servants of man.

I am, Sir, Your obedient servant,

P. FARRELL.

The Acacias, Wimbledon,
Thursday, March 7, 1907.

I dressed and breakfasted in some haste. I heard Jimmy splashing and carolling in his tub, and for one moment had a mind to knock in and read him the letter, which worried me. But I didn't.... It really wasn't Jimmy's business.... Good Lord! if I'd only acted on that one little impulse, which seemed at the time not to matter two straws!—

I took a taxi to Chelsea, carting the newspapers with me and rooting Farrell's truffles out of a dozen or so on the way. It was just as bad as I feared. The man had used a type-copier and snowed his screed all over Fleet Street. There were one or two small leaders, too, and editorial notes: nasty ones.

I caught Foe on his very doorstep. "Hallo!" said he. "What's wrong? ... Looks as if you were suddenly reduced to selling newspapers. I'm not buying any, my good man."

"You'll come upstairs and read a few, anyway," said I; and took him upstairs and showed him the *Times*. He frowned as he read Farrell's letter. I expected him to break out into strong language at least. But he finished his reading and tossed the paper on to the table with no more than a short laugh—a rather grim short laugh.

"Silly little bounder," was his comment.

"You didn't treat him quite so apathetically, the night before last," said I. "It might be better for you if you had. Look, here's the *Morning Post, Standard, Daily News, Mail, Chronicle, Express....* He has plastered it into them all."

"I don't read newspapers," was his answer.

"Other people do," was mine; for I was nettled a bit. "Here are some of the editors asking questions already, and I'll bet the evening papers will be like dogs about a bone. This man may be a damned fool, but he's dangerous: that's to say he has started mischief."

"Oh, surely—not dangerous?" Foe queried, with an odd lift of his eyebrows.

"If I were you, at all events, I'd go straight and consult your man— what's his name? Travers?—at once. My taxi is waiting, and I'll run across in time to interview him before you start your morning's work. Did he show you his answer to these precious Memorialists before he posted it?"

For the moment Foe ignored my question. "Dangerous?" he repeated in a musing, questioning way. "Do you really think... I beg your pardon, Roddy... Eh? You were asking about Travers. Yes, he showed me his answer. Very good answer, I thought. It just told them to mind their own business."

"Did he say that, in so many words?" I asked.

"Let me think.... So far as I remember he put it rather neatly. ... Yes, he wrote that he was not prepared to worry his staff with vague charges, or to invite an inquiry on the strength of representations which—so far as he could attach a meaning to them— meant what was false. But he added that if the Memorialists would kindly put these charges into writing, defining the practices complained of, and naming the persons accused, they should be dealt with in the proper way which (he understood) the law provided."

"Capital," said I. "Your Principal is no fool. Go off straight and consult him. Take these papers—the whole bundle—"

Foe took them up and pushed them into the pockets of his great-coat.

"*You* think he's dangerous?" he asked again, in an absent-minded way.

"Eh?… Oh, you're talking of Farrell?" said I. "Farrell's a fool, and fools are always dangerous."

Thereupon Jack Foe did and said that which I had afterwards some cause to remember. He passed his hand over his forehead, much as a man might brush away a cobweb flung across his evening walk between hedges. "That man makes me tired," he said; "extraordinarily tired. For two nights I've been trying not to dream about him. It was very good of you to come, Roddy. You shall run me over in your taxi and I'll speak to Travers. If the man is a fool—"

"A dangerous fool," I corrected.

"Coward, too, I should judge. Yes, certainly, I'll speak to Travers."

I put down Foe at the gates of his College and speeded home. Jimmy had breakfasted and gone forth to take the air. I sat down to open my letters and answer them. In the middle of this my agent arrived. We lunched together and spent the afternoon canvassing. This lasted until dinner, for which I returned to my Club. Thence a taxi took me East again to Bethnal Green for a meeting. The importance of these details is that they kept me from having word with Jimmy, or seeing fur or feather of him, for more than twenty-four hours.

Nor did I find him in my chambers when I got home, soon after eleven. He was a youth of many engagements. So I mixed myself a drink and whiled away three-quarters of an hour with a solitary pipe and the bundle of evening papers set out for me by Jephson, who lived out with his wife and family and retired to domestic joys at 9.30.

The evening papers had let down the Silversmiths' College pretty easily on the whole. But one of them—an opposition rag which specialised in the politics, especially gutter politics, of South London and was owned by a ring of contractors—had come out with a virulent attack, headed "Vivisection in Our Midst." The article set me hoping that Travers was a strong man and would use the law of libel: it deserved the horsewhip. It left a taste in the mouth that required a second whisky-and-apollinaris before I sought my bed, sleepily promising myself that I would call on Farrell in the morning, however inconvenient it might be, and help to put an end to this nonsense…. I would, if the worst came to the worst, even drag the fool to Jack's laboratory and convince him of his folly.

And this promise, as will be seen, I carried out to the very last letter.

A rapping on my bedroom door fetched me out of my beauty sleep. I started up in bed and switched on the electric light.

"That you, Jimmy?" I called. "Come in, you ass, and say what you want. If it's the corkscrew—"

"If you please, Sir Roderick—sorry to disturb you—" said a voice outside which I recognised as the night-porter's.

"Smithers?" I called. "What's wrong?... Open the door, man.... Is the place on fire?"

The door opened and showed me Smithers with a tall policeman looming behind him.

"Hallo!" said I, sitting up straighter and rubbing my eyes.

"Constable, sir," explained Smithers, "with a message for you. Says he must see you personally."

The constable spoke while I stared at him, my eyes blinking under the bed-light. "It's a dream," I was telling myself. "Silly kind of dream—"

"Gentleman in the Ensor Street Police Court, sir. Requires bail till to-morrow—till ten-thirty this morning, I should have said. Gave your name for surety." The constable announced this in a firm bass voice, respectful but business-like. "Said he was a friend of yours."

"What's his name?" I demanded.

"Gave the name of James Collingwood, sir—and this same address."

I gasped. "Jimmy?—Oh, I beg your pardon, Constable!—What has Mr. Collingwood been doing?"

"He's *charged*, sir," the constable answered carefully, "with resisting the police in the execution of their duty."

"What duty?"

"There was another gent took up, sir: and I may say, between ourselves, as your friend, sir, put up a bit of a fight for him. Very nimble with his fists he was, sir, or so I heard it mentioned. I wasn't myself mixed up in the affair. But from the faces on them as brought him in I should say, strikly between ourselves, he's lucky the word isn't assault—even aggeravated. But the Inspector took the report... and the Inspector, if I may say so, knows a gentleman when he sees one."

"Was he—" I began, and corrected myself. "Was Mr. Collingwood drunk?—strictly between ourselves, as you put it."

"No, sir." The honest man gave his verdict slowly. "I shan't be called for evidence: but I seen him and talked with him. Sober and bright, sir; and, when I left, in the best of sperrits. But I wouldn't say as how he hadn't been more than happy earlier in the evening."

"Thank you, Constable," said I. "You'll find a decanter, a syphon, and a glass set out for the prodigal's return, all on the table in the next room. Possibly you'll discover what to do with them while I dress. Smithers, turn on the light out there, and get me a taxi if you can. For I suppose," said I to the constable, "this means that I've to turn out and go with you?"

"I am afraid so, sir, and thanking you kindly. But as for the taxi, I came in one and took the liberty to keep it waiting—at this hour."

"Very thoughtful of you," said I, with a look at my watch. The time was 12.50.

"Not at all, sir. Mr. Collingwood turned out the loose change in his pocket and told me not to spare expense. Here it is, sir—one pound, seventeen—and I'd be glad if you took it and paid the whole fare at the end of the run."

"Good," said I, amused. "Jimmy is obviously sober. I never knew him drunk—really drunk—for that matter." I had my legs out of bed by this time, and the constable was bashfully withdrawing, Smithers having turned on the lights in the outer room. "Stop a moment," I commanded. "You may not believe it, but I'm a child at this game. How much money shall I have to take?... I don't know that I have more than a tenner loose about me—unless I can raise something off Smithers."

The constable relaxed his face into a smile, or something approaching one. "There is no money needed—not at this hour of the night. Your recognisances, Sir Roderick—for a fiver or so, if you ask me. But—" and here he hesitated.

"Well?"

"There's the other gentleman, sir. Mr. Collingwood *did* mention—"

"Oh, did he?" I cut in. "It was silly, maybe, to have forgotten him all this time—I'm a sound sleeper; and even when awake my mind moves slowly. But who the Hades is this other gentleman?"

"When arrested, sir, he gave his name as Martin Frobisher," said the constable with just a tremor of the eyelids, "and his address as North-West Passage; he wouldn't say more definitely. At the station he asked leave to correct this, and said that his real name was Martin Luther, a foreigner, but naturalised for years, and we should find his papers at the Reform Club, S.W."

"I don't seem to have met either of these Martins—or not in life," I said thoughtfully.

"Well, sir, if you ask *me*," he agreed, "I should be surprised if you had; for between ourselves, as it were, I don't believe he's either of his alleged Martins. And the Station don't think much of his names and addresses."

"Does *he* want to be bailed out, too?" I asked.

"He didn't ask it. He weren't in no condition, sir—as you might put it—when I left. But Mr. Collingwood, he says to me (I took a note, sir, of the very words he used)"—the man pulled out a note-book from his breast-pocket, and held it forward under the light—"'You go to Sir Roderick,' he says, 'and tell him from me that the prodigal is returned bearing his calf with him.'" The constable read it out carefully, word by word. "I don't know what it means, sir; but that was his message, and he said it twice over."

"There seems to be more in this than meets the eye," said I, pondering the riddle.

"You wouldn't say so, sir, if you'd seen Hagan's," said he, retiring with the last word and, on top of it, a genially open grin.

I was dressed in ten minutes or so, and we sped to Ensor Street. There I found my young reprobate sober and cheerful and unabashed.

"Sorry to give you this trouble, old man," was his greeting. "Sort of thing that happens when a fellow gets mixed up in politics."

"You shall tell me all about it," said I, "when we've gone through the little formalities of release.... What have I to sign?" I asked the sergeant who played escort.

"Oh, but wait a moment," put in Jimmy. "There's another bird. The animals came in two by two—eh, Sergeant Noah? I say, Otty, you'll be in a fearful way when you see him. But I couldn't help it—upon my soul I couldn't: and you'll have to be kind to him."

"Who is it?" I demanded.

"It's—Well, he gave the name of Martin Luther. But you judge for yourself. Sergeant Bostock—or are you Wombwell?—take Sir Haroun Alraschid to the next cage and show him the Great Reformer."

To the next cell I was led in a state of expectancy that indeed justified his allusion to the *Arabian Nights*. And the door opened and the light shone—upon Mr. Peter Farrell!

It was a swollen eye that Mr. Farrell upturned to us from his low bed, and a swollen and bloodied lip that babbled contrition along with appeals to be "got out of this" and lamentations for the day he was born; and as on that day so on this a mother had found it hard to recognise him. He wore a goodly but disorganised raiment; a fur-lined great-coat, evening dress beneath it; but the tie was missing, the shirt-collar had burst from its stud, the shirt-front showed blood-stains, dirty finger-marks, smears of mud. Mud caked his coat, its fur: apparently he had been rolling in mud. But the worst was that he wept.

He wept copiously. Was it the late Mr. Gladstone who invented the phrase "Reformation in a Flood"? Anyhow, it kept crossing and re-crossing my mind absurdly as I surveyed this wreck that had called itself Martin Luther. All the wine in him had turned to tears of repentance, and he was pretty nauseous. I told him to stand up.

"This—er—gentleman," said I to the police-sergeant, "is called Farrell—Mr. Peter Farrell. He lives," I said, as the address at the foot of the *Times* letter came to my memory, "at The Acacias, Wimbledon."

The sergeant nodded slowly. "That's right, sir. I knew him well enough. Attended a meeting of his only last Saturday—on duty, that's to say."

We smiled. "He's not precisely a friend of mine," said I. "But we have met in public life, and I'll be answerable for him. We must get him out of this."

"There's no difficulty, sir, since we have the address. There was no card or letter in his pocket, and he said he came from Wittenberg through the Gates of Hell. I looked him up in the Directory and the address is as you state…. But to tell you the truth, sir, I didn't ring up his telephone number, thinking as a nap might bring him round a bit…. We keep a taxi or two on call for these little jobs, and I'll get a driver that can be trusted. I'll call up Sam Hicks. There was a latch-key in the gentleman's pocket, and Sam Hicks is capable of steering a case like this to bed and leaving the summons pinned on his dressing-gown for a reminder…. But perhaps you'll call around for him to-morrow morning, sir, and bring him?"

"I'll be damned if I do," said I. "He must take his risks and I'll risk the bail…. Look here!"—I took Mr. Farrell by the collar and my fingers touched mud. "Pah!" said I. "Can't we clean him up a bit before consigning him?… Look here, Farrell! I'm sending you home. Do you understand? And you're to return here on peril of your life at ten o'clock. Do you understand?"

"I understand, Sir Roderick," sobbed Farrell. "Angels must have sent you, Sir Roderick…. I have unfortunately mislaid my glasses and something seems to be obscuring the sight of my left eye. But I recognised your kindly voice, Sir Roderick. The events of the past few hours are something of a blank to me at present: but may I take the liberty of wringing my deliverer by the hand?"

"Certainly not," said I. "Sit up and attend. Have you a wife? Sit up, I say. Will Mrs. Farrell by any chance be sitting up?"

"I thank God," answered Mr. Farrell fervently, "I am a widower. It is the one bright spot. Could my poor Maria look down from where she is, and see me at this moment—"

"It *is* a slice of luck," I agreed. "Well, you're in the devil of a mess, and you've goosed yourself besides losing a promising seat for the party. What on earth—but we'll talk of that to-morrow. You must turn up, please, and see it out. I don't know what defence, if any, you can put up: but by to-morrow you'll have a damnatory eye that will spoil the most ingenious. My advice is, don't make any. Cut losses, and face the music. This is a queer country; but the Press, which has been ragging you for weeks, will deal tenderly with you as a drunk and incapable."

"But the scandal, Sir Roderick!" he moaned.

"There won't be any," said I. "You've lost the seat: that's all. ... Now stay quiet while I sign a paper or two."

Jimmy (redeemed) and I together packed Mr. Farrell into his taxi. Mr. Samuel Hicks, driver and expert, threw an eye over him as we helped him in and wrapped him in rugs. "There's going to be no trouble with this fare," said Mr. Hicks, as he pocketed his payment-in-advance. "Nigh upon two o'clock in the morning and no more trouble than a lamb in cold storage."

NIGHT THE FIFTH
ADVENTURE OF THE "CATALAFINA": MR. JAMES COLLINGWOOD'S NARRATIVE

"Well now," I asked, as my taxi bore us homeward, "what have you to say about all this?"

"I say," answered Jimmy with sententiousness, after a pause, "that you should never take three glasses of champagne on an empty stomach."

"I don't," said I.

"Nor do I," said Jimmy. "I took five, on Farrell's three… eight glasses to the bottle. It was a Christian act, because I saw that was he exceeding. But he insisted on ordering two bottles: so it was all thrown away."

"What was thrown away?"

"The Christian act…. I say, Otty," he reproached me, "wake up! You're not attending."

"On the contrary," I assured him, "I am waiting with some patience for the explanation you owe me. After dragging me out of bed at one o'clock in the morning, it's natural, perhaps, you should assume me to be half-asleep—"

Jimmy broke in with a chuckle. "Poor old Otty! You've been most awfully decent over this."

"Cut that short," I admonished him. "I am waiting for the story: and you provide the requisite lightness of touch; but the trouble is, you don't seem able to provide anything else."

"Don't be stern, Otty," he entreated. "It is past pardon. I know, and to-morrow—later in the morning, I should say—you'll find that the defendant feels his position acutely. Honour bright, I'll do you credit in the dock…. Wish I was as sure of Farrell. But, as for the story, as I am a sober man, I don't know where to begin. There's a wicked uncle mixed up in it, and a wicked nephew and a taxi, and a lady with a reticule, and a picture palace, and a water-pipe, and heaps upon heaps of policemen—they're the worst mixed up of the lot—"

"Begin at the beginning," I commanded. "That is, unless you'd rather defer the whole story for the magistrate's ear."

"The whole story?" He chuckled. "I'd like to see the Beak's face. … No, I couldn't possibly. My good Otty, how many people d'you reckon it would compromise?"

"You've compromised Farrell pretty thoroughly, anyhow," said I grimly: "and you've compromised the cause in which I happen to be interested. Has it occurred to you, my considerate young friend, that Farrell has receded to 1000 to 1 in the betting?—that, in short, you've lost us the seat?"

"*I* compromise Farrell?"—Jimmy sat up and exclaimed it indignantly. "*I* lose you his silly seat?… Rats! The little bounder compromised himself! He's been doing it freely—doing it since ten o'clock—two crowded hours of glorious life… 'stonishing, Otty, what a variegated ass a man can make of himself nowadays in two short hours, with the help of a taxi and if he wastes no time. When I think of our simple grandfathers playing at Bloods, wrenching off door-knockers…. Oh, yes—but you're waiting for the story. Well, it happened like this,—

"Farrell called on you this morning, soon after breakfast-time, and found me breakfasting. He was in something of a perspiration. It appeared that he'd fired off a letter to the *Times* directed against our dear Professor; and, having fired it, had learnt from somebody that the Professor was a close friend of ours. He had come around to make the peace with you, if he could—he's a funny little snob. But you had flown."

"I had gone off," said I, "to catch Jack Foe and warn him that the letter was dangerous."

"Think so? Well, you'd left the *Times* lying on the floor, and he picked it up and read his composition to me while I dallied with the bacon. It seemed to me pretty fair tosh, and I told him so. I promised that if his second thoughts about it coincided with my first ones, I would pass them on together to you when I saw you next, and added that I had trouble to adapt my hours to political candidates, they were such early risers. That, you might say, verged on a hint: but he didn't take it. He hung about, standing on one leg and then on the other, protesting that he would put things right. I hate people who stand on one leg when you're breakfasting, don't you?… So I gave him a cigar, and he smoked it whilst I went on eating. He said it was a first-class cigar and asked me where I dealt. I said truthfully that it was one of yours, and falsely that you bought them in Leadenhall Market off a man called Huggins. I gave him the address, which he took down with a gold pencil in his pocket-book…. I said they were probably smuggled, and (as I expected) he winked at me and said he rather gathered so from the address.

He also said that he knew a good thing wherever he saw it, that you were his *bo ideal* of a British baronet, and that we had very cosy quarters. This led him on to discourse of his wife, and how lonely he felt since losing her—she had been a martyr to sciatica. But there was much to be said for a bachelor existence, after all. It was so free. His wife had never, in the early days, whole-heartedly taken to his men friends: for which he couldn't altogether blame her—they weren't many of 'em drawing-room company. A good few of them, too, had gone down in the world while he had been going up. He instanced some of these, but I didn't recollect having met any of 'em. There were others he'd lost sight of. He named these too—good old Bill This and Charley That and a Frank Somebody who sang a wonderful tenor in his day and would bring tears to your eyes the way he gave you *Annie Laurie* when half drunk: but again I couldn't recall that any of them had been passed down to me. 'You see, Mr. Collingwood,' he said, 'when one keeps a little house down at Wimbledon, these things have a way of dropping out as time goes on.' 'Just like the teeth,' said I. He thought over this for a while, and then laughed—oh, he laughed quite a lot—and declared I was a humorist. He hadn't heard anything so quick, not for a long while. 'Mr. Collingwood,' he said, 'I'm a lonely man with it all. I don't mind owning to you that I've taken up these here politics partly for distraction. It used to be different when me and Maria could stick it out over a game of bezique. She used to make me dress for dinner, always. We had a billiard-room, too: but that didn't work so well. I could never bring her up to my standard of play, not within forty in a hundred, by reason that she'd use the rest for almost every stroke. She had a sense of humour, had Maria: you'd have got along with her, Mr. Collingwood, and she'd have got along with you. You'd have struck sparks. One evening I asked her, 'Maria, why are you so fond of the jigger?' 'Because of my figger,' says she, pat as you please. Now, wasn't that humorous, eh? She *meant*, of course, that being of the buxom sort in later life—and it carried her off in the end—' Why, hallo!" Jimmy exclaimed. "Are we home already?"

"We have arrived at the Temple, E.C.," said I gently, "but scarcely yet at the beginning of the story."

He resumed it in our chambers, while I operated on the hearth with a firelighter.

"Well," said Jimmy, smoking, "to cut a long story short"—and I grunted my thanks—"he told me he was a lonely man, but that he knew a thing or two yet. Had I by any chance made acquaintance with the 'Catalafina,' in Soho? 'Oh, come!' said I bashfully, 'who is she?' 'It's a restarong,' said he: 'Italian: where the cook does things you can't guess what they're made of. Just as well, perhaps.' But the results, he undertook to say, were excellent."

"Do I see one?" I asked.

"No, you don't," answered Jimmy, sipping his whisky-and-soda. "That's just *it*, if you'll let me proceed.... He said that they kept some marvellous Lagrima Christi—if I liked Lagrima Christi. For his part, it always soured on his stomach. But we could send out for a bottle of fizz—I'm using his expression, Otty—"

"I trust so," said I.

"He called it that. He said he would take it as an honour if I'd join him in a little supper this very evening at the 'Catalafina.' He had a meeting at 7.30, at which he would do his best to soften down this letter of his in the *Times*; he would get it over by 9.30. Could we meet (say) on the steps of the 'Empire' at ten o'clock? He would hurry thither straight from the Baths, report progress—for me to set your mind at rest—and afterwards take me off to this damned eating-house. I should never find it by myself, he assured me. He was right there; but I'm not anxious to try. My hope is that it, or the management, won't find *me*.... Well, weakly-and partly for your sake, Otty—I consented. He said, by the way, he would be greatly honoured if I'd persuade you to come along too. 'It's Bohemian,' he said; 'if Sir Roderick will overlook it.' 'You told me it was Italian,' said I: 'but never mind. Sir Roderick, as it happens, is a bit of a Bohemian himself and is dining to-night with a club of them—the Lost Dogs, if you've ever heard of that Society.' I saved you, anyway. You may put it that I flung myself into the breach. They found you, but it was literally over my prostrate body... and here we are."

"Is that the story?" said I.

Jimmy leaned back on his shoulder-blades in the armchair. "It is the preliminary canter," he announced. "Now we're off, and you watch me getting into my stride,—

"Farrell turned up, on time. He was somewhat agitated, and I suspect— yes, in the light of later events I strongly suspect—he had picked up a drink somewhere on the way. I got into his taxi, and we swung up Rupert Street, and out of Rupert Street into what the novelists, when they haven't a handy map or the energy to use it, describe as a labyrinth leading to questionable purlieus. I am content to leave it at purlieus. The driver, as it seemed to me, had as foggy a notion as I of what, without infringing Messrs. Swan and Edgar's *lingerie* copyright, we'll call the 'Catalafina's' whereabouts. Farrell spent two-thirds of the passage with his head out of window. I don't mean to convey that he was seasick: and he certainly wasn't drunk, or approaching it. He kept his head out to shout directions. He was pardonably excited— maybe a bit nervous in a channel that seemed to be buoyed all the way with pawnbrokers' signs. But he brought us through. We alighted at the entrance of the 'Catalafina'; Farrell paid the driver, and I advised him to find his way back before daylight overtook him.

"I will not attempt to describe the interior of the 'Catalafina.' Farrell saved me that trouble on the threshold. 'Twenty years or so,' he said, pausing and inhaling garlic, 'often makes a difference in these places. One mustn't expect this to be quite what it used to be.".... Well, I hadn't, of course, and I dare say it wasn't. It had sand on the floor, and spittoons. It was crowded, between the spittoons, with little cast-iron tables, covered with dirty table-cloths spread upon American cloth and garnished with artificial flowers and napkins of Japanese paper. Farrell called them 'serviettes.' He also said he felt 'peckish.' I—well, I had taken the precaution of dining at Boodle's, and responded that I was rather for the bucket than the manger. He considered this for some time and then laughed so loudly that all the anarchists in the room looked up as if one of their bombs had gone off by mistake.... Oh, I omitted to mention that all the space left unoccupied by cigarette-smoke and the smell of garlic was crowded with anarchists, all dressed for the part. They wore black ties with loose ends, fed with their hats on, and read Italian newspapers—like a musical comedy. The waiters looked like stage-anarchists, too; but you could easily tell them from the others because they went about in their shirt-sleeves.

"Farrell caught the eye of one of these bandits, who came along with a great neuter cat rubbing against his legs. Farrell began with two jocose remarks which didn't quite hit the mark he intended them for. 'Hallo, Jovanny!' he said pretty loudly, 'I don't seem to remember your face, and yet it's familiar somehow.'—Whereat Giovanni, or whatever his name was, flung a look over his shoulder that was equal to an alarm, and all the anarchists looked up uneasily too—for Farrell's voice carries, as you may have observed. He followed this up by smiling at me over the *carte du jour* and observing in a jovial stentorian voice that he felt like a man returned from exile. Fifteen years—and it must be fifteen years—is a long stretch.... 'Oh, damn your Italian,' said Farrell suddenly, dropping the card. 'In the old days we used to make orders on our fingers, in the dumb alphabet, and risk what came.'

"By this time he had Giovanni, and several anarchists at the nearer tables, properly scared. But he picked up the card and went on, innocent as a judge,' We used to have a code in those days. For instance, you crooked one finger over your nose and that meant 'sea-urchins.'' 'Why?' I asked. 'That was the code,' Farrell explained. 'They used to have a speciality in sea-urchins, straight from the Mediterranean. You rubbed a soupsong of garlic into them with three drops of paprika.... Now what do you say to sea-urchins?'

"'Nothing, as a rule,' said I. 'Safer with oysters, isn't it? They don't explode.' I dropped this out just to try its effect on the waiter, and he blanched. One or two of our *convives* began to clear.

"Farrell ordered two dozen of oysters, to start with, and sent a runner out for—no, Otty, I won't say it again—for two bottles of Perrier-Jouet; *two* bottles and '96, mark you. On hearing this command about a dozen *habitues* of the 'Catalafina' arose hastily, drained their glasses and vanished.

"Farrell perceived it not. He had picked up the card again and was ordering some infernal broth made of mussels and I-don't-know-what. 'What do you say to follow?' he asked me.

"'Something light,' I suggested. 'Liver of blaspheming Jew, for choice: it sounds like another speciality of this kitchen.'

"In the interval before the wine was brought Farrell gave me a short account of the meeting he had just left: and he didn't lighten the atmosphere of suspicion around us by suddenly sinking his voice to a kind of conspirator's whisper. The meeting (it appeared) had been lively, and more than lively. Our small incursion—or the Professor's, rather—had been a fool to it. For the Professor's loyal pupils, stung by that letter in the *Times*, had organised a counter-demonstration. 'Their behaviour,' Farrell reported, 'was unbridled.' They would hardly allow me a hearing. I give you my word—and I wish Sir Roderick to know it—I was prepared to tell them that information had come to me which put a different complexion on the whole case. I was even prepared to tell them that, while I should ever insist on the South London University College and all similar institutions being subject to a more public control with an increased representation of local rate-payers on their governing bodies, I was confident that in this particular case the charge had been too hasty.... I have the notes of my speech in my great-coat pocket; I'll give them to you later and beg you as a favour to show them to Sir Roderick. But what was the use, when they started booing me because I wore evening dress?'

"'Why did you?' I asked.

"'Because, as I tried to explain, I had another engagement to keep immediately after the Meeting—a Conversatsiony, as I put it to them.'

"'Then perhaps,' said I, 'they took exception to some details of the costume—for instance, your wearing a silk handkerchief, and crimson at that, tucked in between your shirt-front and your white waistcoat.'

"'Is that wrong?' Farrell asked anxiously. 'Maria used to insist on it. She said it looked neglijay.... But I suppose fashions alter in these little details.' He stood up, removed the handkerchief, and stowed it in a tail-pocket.

"'That's better,' said I.

"'I'm not above taking a hint,' said he, 'from one as knows. It'll be harder to get at…. But I don't believe, if you'll excuse me, that any one of these students, as they call themselves, ever wore an evening suit in his life—unless 'twas a hired one. No, sir; they came prepared for mischief. They meant to wreck the Meeting, and had brought along bags of cayenne pepper, and pots of chemicals to stink us out. They opened one—phew! And I have another, captured from them, in the pocket of my greatcoat on the rack, there. I'll show it to you by and by. Luckily our stewards had wind, early in the afternoon, that some such game was afoot, and had posted a body of bruisers conveniently, here and there, about the hall. So in the end they were thrown out, one by one—yes, sir, ignominiously. It don't add to one's respect for public life, though.'

"At this point the wine made its appearance, and—if you'll believe me—it was genuine: Perrier-Jouet, '96. A little while on the ice might have improved it, but we gave it no time. The oysters arrived too; but they were tired, I think. Something was wrong with them, anyhow…. Then—as I seem to remember having told you—Farrell put down three glasses of champagne on an empty stomach."

"You did mention it," said I; "somewhere in the dim and distant past."

"For my part," went on Jimmy seriously, "my potations were moderate. After trying the first oyster, I was sober enough to let the others alone. Then came on the alleged mussel-soup. I tried it and laid down my spoon…. Do you happen to know, Otty, which develops the quicker typhoid or ptomaine? and if they are, by any chance, mutually exclusive? Farrell will like to know.

"He swallowed it all. But when he had done he looked full in the eyes and said in a loud, unfaltering voice, 'This restarong is no longer what it was.'

"'The champagne is, and better,' I consoled him.

"'Well, what do you say now,' he asked,' to a pig's trotter farced with pimento? *That* sounds appetising, at any rate.'

"I think it was at this point, accurately, that I began to suspect him of having exceeded or of being on the verge of excess. But the suspicion no sooner crossed my mind than he set it at rest by getting up and walking across the room to his great-coat, on the rack by the door. His gait was perfectly steady. He drew certain articles from the pockets, returned with them, and laid them on the table: a cigar-case, a mysterious round box of white metal—sort of box you buy 'Blanco' in—and another round object concealed in a crushed paper-bag. He opened the first.

"'Have a cigar,' he invited me. 'They smoke between the courses in this place—proper thing to do.'

"'Sanitary precaution,' I suggested. 'I'll be content with a cigarette for the present. What are your other disinfectants?'

"He laughed, very suddenly and violently. 'Disinfectants?' he chortled; 'that's a good 'un! They're exhibits, my dear sir—pardon-liberty-calling-you-Dear-sir. Stewards collected a dozen, these infernal machines—'

"'There's no need to shout,' said I. No, Otty I was sober. … But I looked around and it struck me that the faces at the near tables were bright, and white, and curiously distinct in the cigarette-smoke.

"'I am not shouting,' Farrell protested: but he was, and at that moment. 'Disinfectants? That box, there—there's a bottle inside— sulphuretted hydrogen. T'other joker's a firework of sorts. I brought 'em along for evidence.… Wha's that?' He jerked himself bolt upright, staring at a dish the waiter held under his nose.

"'It's the *tete de veau en spaghetti* you ordered, sir,' said Giovanni.

"'Did I? I don't remember it. Do *you* remember my ordering tait-de-whatever it calls itself?' he asked me earnestly.

"Well, I couldn't, and I said so.

"'If I did,' commanded Farrell, 'take it away and let me forget it. This place is not what it was.… Take it away, you Corsican Brother, and bring me the bill! Look here,' said he as Giovanni departed. 'We'll get out of this and try something better. What do you say to looking in at the Ritz?' He lit his cigar and poured out more champagne.

"'As you like,' said I. 'Let's get out of this anyway. For my part, I've had enough.'

"'Well, *I* haven't,' said he, and fixed a stare on me. 'Oh, I see what you mean. I'm drunk.… It's no use your pretending,' he caught me up argumentatively. 'I've taken too much t'drink. Tiring day. Hope you're not a prude?'

"'Well then,' I confessed, 'it did strike me you were punishing the other fellow a bit too fast in the opening rounds. But you walked over to your corner, just now, steady as a soldier—'

"'Peculiarity of mine,' he explained. 'Ought t'have warned you. Takes me in head, long before legs. Do you a sprint down the street—even money—when we're outside.... Wha's this? Oh, the bill.... Thought it was more spaghetti.... Yes, I know.... Custom of house... pay the signora in the brass cage. My dear sir, if you'll 'scuse fam'liarity—'

"'Right,' said I, as he dived a hand into his pocket and fetched out a fistful of coin. 'Here's half-a-crown for Giovanni—he will now run along and poison somebody else. This being your show, I further abstract two sovereigns for the bill. I shall, I perceive, have to hand you ninepence in cash with the receipt.... But since you are intoxicated and I am what in any less sepulchral caravanserai might be described as merry, let us order our retreat with military precision. First, then, I fetch you yonder magnificent garment which has been drawing revolutionary hatred upon us ever since we entered...'

"'It was a present from Maria,' he said, as I helped him into it. 'Her last. She said it was a real sable.'

"'She spoke truthfully,' I assured him. 'Now gather up these light articles and steer for the door as accurately as you can, while I gather up my inexpensive paletot and pay at the desk.'

"'If I had my way with this blasted restarong,' he observed with sudden venom,' I'd raze it to the ground!'

"I walked over to the desk. I was right in supposing that ninepence was the sum I should receive from the Esmeralda behind the brass barrier. But her eyes were bright and interrogated me: the brass trellis between us shone also with an unnatural lustre: I was dealing with another man's money, and it seemed incumbent on me to count the change twice, with care.

"While I was thus engaged, Farrell went past me for the door with the shuffle and hard breathing of an elephant pursued by a forest fire.

"'Hurry!' he gasped.

"'What is it?' I demanded, catching him up on the fifth stair.

"He panted. 'I couldn't help it.... Sodom and Gomorrah ... basaltic, I've heard... we'd better run!'

"'What the devil have you done?' I asked, close to his ear.

"'Opened that stink-pot,' Farrell answered, taking two steps at a time. He gained the pavement and paused, turning on me.

"'Lucky they can't afford to keep a commissionaire.—How long do these things take, as a rule, before going off?'

"'What things?' I asked.

"'Maroons, don't you call 'em?' said he, feeling in a foolish sort of way at his breast-pocket, as if for his pince-nez. 'I got the slow-match going with the end of my cigar, careless-like. How long do they take as a rule?'

"Well, a handsome detonation below-stairs answered him upon that instant.

"Farrell clutched my arm, and we ran."

NIGHT THE SIXTH
THE ADVENTURE OF THE PICTUREDROME

"Farrell could sprint," continued Jimmy. "You may have noticed that a lot of these round-bellied men have quite a good turn of speed for a short course. In spite of his fur coat he led by a yard or two: but this was partly because I hung back a little, on the chance of having to fight a rear-guard action.

"I could hear no shouts or footsteps in our wake, and this struck me as strange at the time. On second thoughts, however, I dare say the management and frequenters of the 'Catalafina' have more than a bowing acquaintance with infernal machines. A daisy by the river's brim... to them a simple maroon would be nothing to write home about, nor the sort of incident to justify telephoning for an inquisitive police. By the mercy of Heaven, too, we encountered no member of the Force in our flight. I suppose that constables are rare in Soho.

"Farrell led for a couple of blocks as an American writer would put it; dived down a side street to the right; sped like an arrow for a couple of hundred yards; then darted around another turning, again to the right. I put on a spurt and caught him by his fur collar. 'Look here,' I said, 'I don't hear anyone in chase. We are the wicked fleeing, whom no man pursueth. I don't quite understand why. Maybe sulphuretted hydrogen's their favourite perfume. They don't use it in their bath, because... well, never mind. What I have to talk at this moment is mathematics. I don't know how you reason it out; but to me it's demonstrable that if we keep turning to the right like this we shall find ourselves back at the door of your infernal 'Catalafina.' Inevitably,' I said, nodding at him in a way calculated to convince.

"'Allow me,' he answered, and promptly wrung my hand. 'I ought t'have warned you—I always run in circles, this condish'n. Bad habit: never could break myself. 'Scuse me; haven't been drunk for years.' He pulled himself up and eyed me earnestly. 'Wha's your suggest'n under shirkumstanches? Retrace steps?'

"'As I figure it out,' said I, sweet and reasonable, 'that also would lead us back to the 'Catalafina.''

"'Quite so,' he agreed, nodding back as I nodded. 'Case hopelesh, then. No posh'ble way out.'

"'Well, I don't know,' said I. 'If we go straight on until we find a turning to the left.... And look here,' I put in, grabbing him again, for he was starting to run. 'Since there's no one in chase apparently, I suggest that we walk. It looks better, if we meet a constable: though there seems to be none about ... so far.'

"'Scand'lous!' said Farrell.

"'What's scandalous?' I asked.

"'Lax'ty Metr'pl't'n P'lice.' He took me by a buttonhole, finger and thumb. 'Dish—district notorious. One-worst-Lond'n. Dish—damn the word—distr'ck like this, anything might happen any moment. Mus' speak about it.... You just wait till I'm on County Counshle.'

"I took him by the arm and steered him. I did it beautifully, though it's undeniable that I had taken wine to excess. I did it so beautifully that we met not a living soul—or if we did, Otty, I failed to remark it.... I don't suppose it was really happening as I felt it was happening. I just tell how it felt.... Farrell and I were ranging arm-in-arm through a quarter that had mysteriously hushed and hidden itself at our approach. There were pianos tinkling from upper storeys: there were muffled choruses with banjo or guitar accompaniments humming up from the bowels of the earth: there were chinks of light between blinds, under doorways, down areas. There was even a flare of light, now and again, blaring to gramophone accompaniment across the street from a gin-palace or a corner public. But the glass of these places of entertainment was all opaque, and there were no loungers on the kerb in front of any.... I held Farrell tightly beneath the elbow, and steered through this enchanted purlieu.

"'S'pose you know where you're heading?' said Farrell after a while.

"'On these occasions,' said I, 'one steers by the pole-star.'

"'Where is it?' he demanded.

"'At this moment, so far as I can judge,' I assured him, 'it is shining accurately on the back of your neck.'

"Of a sudden we found ourselves at the head of a pavement lined with the red stern-lights of a rank of cabs and taxis. I had not the vaguest notion of its name: but the street was obviously one of those curious ones, unsuspected, and probably non-existent by day, in which lurk the vehicles that can't be discovered when it's raining and you want to get home from a theatre. 'Glow-worms!' announced Farrell.

"I tightened my grip under his funny-bone, and hailed the first vehicle. It was a hansom. 'Engaged?' I asked.

"'All depends where you're going, sir,' said the cabby.

"'Wimbledon,' shouted Farrell, and broke away from me. 'Wimbledon for pleasure and the simple life!… You'll excuse me—' he dodged towards the back of the cab: 'on these occasions— always make a point take number.'

"'It's all right,' I spoke up to the cabman. 'My friend means the Ritz. I'm taking him there.'

"'I shouldn't, if I was you,' said the man sourly; 'not unless he's an American.'

"'He is,' said I, 'and from Texas. I am charged to deliver him at the Ritz, where all will be explained': and I dashed around to the rear of the cab, collared Farrell, and hoicked him inboard.…

"The cab was no sooner under way and steering west-by-south than Farrell clutched hold of me and burst into tears on my shoulder. It appeared, as I coaxed it from him, that his mind had cast back, and he was lamenting the dearth of policemen in Soho.

"The hole above us opened, and the cabman spoke down.

"'Are you sure you meant the Ritz, sir—really?'

"'I don't want to compromise you,' said I. 'Drop us at the head of St. James's Street.'

"He did so; took his fee, and hesitated for a moment before turning his horse. 'Sure you can manage the gentleman, sir?' he asked.

"'Sure, thank you,' said I, and he drove away slowly. I steered Farrell into the shelter of the Ritz's portico, facing Piccadilly."

"They draw the blinds now (put in Otway) under the Lighting Order: but in those days the Ritz was given—I won't say to advertising its opulence—but to allowing a glimpse of real comfort to the itinerant millionaire. Jimmy resumes:—

"'Now, look here,' said I, indicating the show inside: 'I wasn't hungry to start with: and I suggest we've both inhaled enough garlic to put us off the manger for a fortnight. As for the bucket, you've exceeded already, and I have taken more than is going to be good for me—a subtle difference which I won't pause here and now to explain. It's a kindly suggestion of yours," said I; 'but I put it to you that it's time for good little Progressives to be in their beds, and you'll just take a taxi from the rank on the slope, trundle home to Wimbledon and go bye-bye.'

"Farrell wasn't listening. He had his shoulders planted against a pillar of the portico, and had fallen into a brown study, staring in upon the giddy throng.

"'When we look,' said he slowly, like an orator in a dream—'when we are privileged to contemplate, as we are at this moment, such a spectacle of the idle Ritz—excuse me, the idle Rich—and their goings on, and countless poor folk in the East End with nothing but a herring—if that—between them and to-morrow's sunrise— well, I don't know how it strikes you, but to me it is an Object Lesson. You'll excuse me, Mr.—I haven't the pleasure to remember your name at this moment. I connect it with my Maria's two pianners—something between the Broadwood and the Collard and Collard—you'll excuse me, but putting myself in the place of the angel Gabriel, merely for the sake of argument, this is the sort of way it would take *me*!'

"Before I could jump for him, Otty, he lifted his hand and flung something—I don't know what it was, for a certainty, but I believe it was the 'Blanco' tin of sulphuretted hydrogen, that he had been nursing all the way from the 'Catalafina.'… At any rate the missile hit. There was an agreeable crash of plate glass, and we ran for our lives.

"You know the long rank of taxis on the slope of Piccadilly. We pelted for it. Before an alarm whistle sounded I had gained the fifth in the row. The drivers were all gathered in their shelter, probably discussing politics. I made for a car, cried to Farrell to jump in, hoicked up the works like mad, and made a spring for the seat and the steering-gear. Amid the alarm-whistles sounding from the Ritz I seemed to catch a shrill scream close behind me, and looked around to make sure that my man was inside. The door slammed-to, and I steered out for a fair roadway.

"There was a certain amount of outcry in the rear. But I opened-out down the slope and soon had it well astern. We sailed past Hyde Park Corner, down Knightsbridge, and cut along Brompton Road into Fulham Road, and rounded into King's Road, cutting the kerb a trifle too fine. Speed rather than direction being my object for the moment, Otty, I rejoiced in a clear thoroughfare and let her rip for Putney Bridge. There was a communication tube in the taxi, and for some while it had been whistling in my ear, with calls and outcries in high falsetto interjected between the blasts. 'Funny dog's ventriloquising,' thought I, and paid no further attention to the noises. Our pace was such, I couldn't be distracted from the steering.… I was quite sober by this time: sober, but considerably exhilarated.

"My spirit soared as we took the bridge with a rush, cleared the High Street and breasted Putney Hill for the Heath. The night was clear, with a southerly breeze. The stars shone, and I seemed to inhale all the scents of a limitless prairie, wafted past the wind-screen from the heath and the stretch of Wimbledon Common beyond.... Why should I miss anything of this glorious chance? Why should I tamely deliver Farrell at a house the name of which I had forgotten, the situation of which was unknown to me, the domestics of which, when I found it by painful inquiry, would probably receive me with cold suspicion, as a misleader of middle-age? In fine, why should I not strike the Common and roam there, letting the good car have her head while Farrell slept himself sober. A line or two of the late Robert Browning's waltzed in my head:"

> 'What if we still ride on, we two?'
> —Ride, ride together, for ever ride.'

"I brought the car gently to a halt on the edge of the heath, under the stars, climbed out, and opened the door briskly.

"'Look here, Farrell,' I announced. 'I've a notion—'

"'Then it's more than *I* have, of the way you're treating a lady!' answered a voice; and out stepped a figure in skirts! By George, Otty, you might have knocked me down with a—with a feather boa: which was just what this apparition seemed preparing to do. I had brought the taxi to rest close under a gas-lamp, and in the light of it she confronted me, slightly swaying the hand which grasped the boa.

"'Good Lord! ma'am,' I gasped,' how in the world... ?'

"'That's what I want to know,' said she, with more show of menace. 'What is your game, young man? Abduction?'

"'I swear to you, ma'am,' I stammered, 'that my intentions would be strictly honourable if I happened to have any.... I may be more intoxicated than I felt up to a moment ago.... But let us, at all events, keep our heads. It seems the only way out of this predicament, that we keep strictly in touch with reality. Very well, then.... You entered this vehicle, a middle-aged gentleman something more than three sheets in the wind. You emerge from it apparently sober and of the opposite sex. If any explanation be necessary,' I wound up hardily, 'I imagine it to be due to *me*, who have driven you thus far under a false impression—and, I may add, at no little risk to the transpontine traffic.'

"'Look here!' said this astonishing female. 'I don't know how it's happened, but I believe I am addressing a gentleman—'

"'I hope so,' said I, as she paused.

"'Well, then,' she demanded, smoothing her skirt, and seating herself on the edge of the grass, under the lamplight. 'The question is, what do you propose to do? I place myself in your hands, unreservedly.'

"I managed to murmur that she did me honour. 'But with your leave, ma'am,' said I, 'we'll defer that point for a moment while you tell me how on earth you have managed to change places with my friend, whom with my own eyes I saw enter this vehicle. It must have been a lightning change anyhow: for all the way from Piccadilly I have been priding myself on our speed.'

"'Change places?' she exclaimed. 'Change places? I'm a respectable married woman, young sir: and as such I'd ask you what else was due to myself when he sat down on my lap without even being interjuiced?'

"I made a step to the door of the taxi, but turned and came back. 'He's inside, then?' I asked.

"'Of course he's inside,' she retorted. 'What d'you take me for? A body-snatcher? Inside he is, and snoring like a pig. Wake him up and ask him if I've be'aved short of a lady from the first.'

"'He's incapable of it, ma'am,' said I. 'Or, rather, I should say, *you* are incapable of it. By which I mean that my friend is incapable of—er—involving you otherwise than innocently in a situation of which—er—you are both incapable, respectively. Appearances may be against us—'

"'Look here,' she chipped in. 'Have you been drinking too?'

"'A little,' I admitted. 'But you may trust me to be discreet. How this responsibility comes to be mine, I can't guess: but it is urgent that I restore you to your home, or at any rate find you a decent lodging for the night. Where is your home?' I asked.

"'Walsall,' said she. 'And I wish I had never left it!'

"'Well, ma'am,' said I, 'I won't be so ungallant as to echo that regret. But, speaking for the moment as a taxi-driver, I put it that Walsall is a tidy distance. Were you, by some process that passes my guessing, on your way to Walsall when we, as it seems, intercepted you in Piccadilly?'

"'Not at all,' she answered. 'On the contrary, I was wanting to get to Shorncliffe Camp.'

"I mused. 'From Walsall?... They must have opened a new route lately.'

"'It's this way,' she told me. 'My husband's a sergeant in the Royal Artillery. He's stationed at Shorncliffe: and I was to meet him there to-night, travelling through London. When I got to London, what with the shops and staring at Buckingham Palace, and one thing and another, I missed the last train down. So, happening to find myself by a line of taxis, I had a mind to ask what the fare might be down to Shorncliffe and tell the man that my husband was expecting me and would pay at the other end. I was that tired, I got into the handiest taxi—that looked smart and comfortable, with a little lamp inside and a nice bunch of artificial flowers made up to look like my Christian name—And what do you think that is? Guess.'

"'I'm hopeless with plants, ma'am," said I, looking hard at the taxi. 'Might it be Daisy?'

"'No, it ain't,' said she. 'There now, you'll take a long time guessing, at that rate. It's Petunia.… Well, then as I was saying, I got in and sat back in the cushions, waiting for the Shofer, if that's how you pronounce it; and I reckon I must have closed my eyes, for the next thing I remember was this friend of yours sitting plump in my lap without so much as asking leave. Before I could recover myself we were off. And now, I put it to you as a gentleman, What's to become of me? For, as perhaps I ought to warn you, my husband's a terror when he's roused.'

"'He's at Shorncliffe. We won't rouse him to-night,' I assured her. 'It's funny,' I went on, 'how often the simplest explanation will—' But I left that sentence unfinished. 'Have you any relatives in London?' I asked brightly.

"She hesitated, but at length confessed she had a sister resident in Pimlico.

"'Ah!' said I. 'She married beneath her, perhaps?'

"Mrs. Petunia looked at me suspiciously in the lamplight. 'How did you guess that?' she asked.

"'Simplicity itself, ma'am,' I answered. 'She could hardly have done less. And from Eaton Square to Pimlico, what is it but a step?… Or, you may put it down to a brain-wave. Yes, ma'am. And I'm going to have another."

"I stepped to the door of the taxi, threw it open, and shouted to Farrell to tumble out.

"'Wha's matter?' he asked sleepily. 'Where are we?'

"'We're on the edge of Putney Heath,' said I.

"'Ri'!' said he in a murmur. 'You're true friend. First turning to the left and keep straight on. Second gate on Common pasht pillar-box.'

"I haled him forth. 'Look here,' said I. 'Pull yourself together. I find that we've, in our innocence, abducted this lady, who happened to be resting in the taxi when you jumped in.'

"Farrell, making a mental effort, blinked hard. 'That accounts for it,' said he. 'Thought I felt something wrong when I sat down.'

"'That being so,' I went on, 'you will agree that our first duty, as we are chivalrous men, is to restore her to her relatives.'

"'B'all means,' he agreed heartily. 'R'shtore her. Why not?'

"'As it happens, she has a sister living in Pimlico.'

"'They all—' he began: but I was on the watch and fielded the ball smartly.

"'And you, unless I'm mistaken,' said I, 'are a member of the National Liberal Club?'

"'We all—' he began again, and checked himself to gaze on me with admiration. 'Shay that again,' he demanded. "'You are a member of the National Liberal Club?' I repeated.

"'I am,' he owned; 'but I couldn' pr'nounce it just at this moment, not for a tenner. An' you've said it twice! Tha's what I call carryin' liquor like a gentleman: or else you've studied voice-producsh'n. Wish I'd studied voice-producsh'n, your age. Usheful, County Council.'

"'County Council!' put in the lady sharply. 'Don't tell me!'

"'He's but a candidate at present, ma'am,' I explained.

"She eyed us both suspiciously. 'No kid, is it?' she asked. 'You ain't a dress-clothes detective? What?... Then, as between a lady and a gentleman, why haven't you introduced him? It's usual.'

"'So it is, ma'am. Forgive me, this is Mr. Peter Farrell. Mr. Farrell, the—the—Lady Petunia.'

"'And very delicately you done it, young man.' The Lady Petunia bowed amiably. 'This ain't no—this isn't—no time nor place for taking advantages and compromising.' She pitched her voice higher and addressed Farrell. 'I'm pleased to make your acquaintance, if I caught your name correctly. Mr. Farrell?—and of the National Liberal Club? The address is sufficient, sir. It carries its own recommendation—though I had hoped for the Constitutional.'

"'It's still harder to pronounce, ma'am,' I assured her. 'That is my friend's only reason.'

"'It was you that started my-ladying me,' she claimed. 'Why don't you keep it up? I like it.'

"'My dear Lady Petunia,' said I, 'as you so well put it, the National Liberal Club carries its own recommendation. What's more, it's going to be the saving of us.'

"'I don't see connecshun,' objected Farrell. 'They don't admit—'

"'They'll admit you,' I said; 'and that's where you'll sleep to-night. The night porter will hunt out a pair of pyjamas and escort you up the lift. Oh, he's used to it. He gets politicians from Bradford and such places dropping in at all hours. Don't try the marble staircase—it's winding and slippery at the edge.... And don't stand gaping at me in that helpless fashion, but get a move on your intelligence.... We're dealing with a lady in distress, and that's our first consideration. Now I can't take you on to Wimbledon, however willing to be shut of you: first, because it would take time, and next because I'm not sure how much petrol's left in the machine. So back we turn for be lights of merry London. We deposit the Lady Petunia at—what's the address, ma'am?"

"'Never you mind,' said she helpfully. 'Put me down somewhere near the end of Vauxhall Bridge, and I'll find my way.'

"'Spoken like an angel,' said I. 'And then, Farrell, you're for the National Liberal Club. The servants there are not known to me, but I'll bet on their asking fewer questions than I should have to answer your housekeeper.'

"I think Farrell was about to demand time for consideration. But the Lady Petunia gripped him by the arm. 'Loveadove!' she exclaimed. 'There's a copper coming down the road!' We bundled him back into the taxi. 'It's a real copper, too,' she warned me as she sprang in at his heels. 'Spark her up, and hurry!—I can tell the sound of their boots at fifty yards.'

"Well, Otty, I sprang to the stirrup, and Joris and she.—She was right. The policeman came up and drew to a halt as, without an indecent show of haste, I dropped into the driver's seat, started up and slewed the wheel round.

"'Anything wrong?' he asked.

"'There was,' said I. 'Over-succulence in the bivalves: but she'll work home, I think.'

"I pipped him Good night, and we sailed down the hill in some style. Sharp to the right, and by and by I opened a common on my right— Wandsworth? Clapham?—Don't ask *me*. I named it Clapham. 'To your tents, O Clapham!' I shouted as I went: but the warning was superfluous. As the poet—wasn't it Wordsworth?—remarked on a famous occasion, Dear God! the very houses seemed asleep....'

"It must have been five or six minutes later that our petrol gave out and my trusted taxi came gently to a halt in the middle of the roadway. I climbed out, opened the door and explained. 'Step out, quick,' said I, 'and make down this street to the left. We must tangle the track a bit, with this piece of evidence behind us.'

"The Lady Petunia considerately took Farrell's arm. 'Why, he can walk!' she announced. 'I'm all ri'!' Farrell assured her. 'You may be yet,' she answered, 'if you keep your head shut.' Farrell asked me if I considered that a ladylike expression. To this she retorted that she couldn't bear for anyone to speak crossly to her: it broke her heart.

"'Capital!' said I. 'Voices a tone lower, please—but keep it up, and you're husband and wife, returning from an evening at the theatre. Taxi broken down—wife peevish at having to walk remaining distance. Keep it up, and I'll undertake to steer you past half the police in London.'

"Well, I steered them past two, and without a question. Not one of us knew our bearings, but we were making excellent weather of it, and at length came out by the by-streets upon a fine broad thoroughfare with an arc-lamp at the corner.

"I stared up at the building on my left, against which he lamp shone. There was no street-sign at the angle, and an inscription in large gilt letters on the facade was not very hopeful—ROYAL SOUTH LONDON PICTUREDROME—yet to some extent reassuring. We were at any rate lost in London; and not in Byzantium, as we might have deduced from other architectural details.

"'And yet I am not wholly sure,' said I. 'We will ask the next policeman. *Picturedrome* now—barbaric union of West and East.— Surely the word must be somewhere in Gibbon. Ever met it in Gibbon, Farrell?'

"'No, I haven't,' he answered testily. 'Never was in Gibbon, to my knowledge. Where is it?... But I'll tell you what!' he wound up, fierce and sudden; 'I've met with too many policemen to-night; avenuesh, we've been passin'. Seems to me neighb'rhood infested. Not like Soho. 'Nequal dishtribush'n bobbies. 'Nequal distribush'n everything. Cursh—curse— modern shivilzash'n—damn!'

"'Our taxi,' I mused, 'may have been a magic one. We are in a dream, and the Lady Petunia is part of it. She may vanish at any moment—'

"But Petunia had turned about for a glance along the street behind us. Instead of vanishing, she clawed my arm sharply, suppressed a squeal, and pointed.... Fifty yards away stood a taxi, and two policemen beside it, flashing their lanterns over it and into its interior.

"Between two flashes I recognised it…. It was *mine*, my Arab taxi, my beautiful, my own…. Farrell's fatal propensity for steering to the right had fetched us around, almost full circle.

"There she stood, with her mute appealing headlights. 'Wha's matter?' asked Farrell. 'Oh, I say—Oh, come! *More* of 'em?'

"'I dragged him and Petunia back into the shadow under the side-wall of the Picturedrome, and leaned back against the edifice while I mopped my brow. My shoulder-blade encountered the sharp edge of a rainwater pipe. A bright and glorious inspiration took hold of me. Farrell had made all the running, so far: it was time for me to assert my manhood.

"'Wait here,' I whispered, 'and all will be well. In three minutes—'

"'Here, I say!' interposed the Lady Petunia. 'You're not going to do a bilk?'

"'Dear lady,' I answered, 'for at least twenty minutes you have been complaining, and pardonably, that my friend and I have enjoyed the pleasure of your company yet repaid it with no form of entertainment. I fear we cannot offer you Grand Opera. But if your taste inclines to the Movies—'

"'Get along, you silly,' she rebuked me. 'Ain't you sober enough to see the place is closed?'

"'If I were sure it wouldn't be used as evidence against me,' I answered gallantly, 'I should say that Love laughs at Locksmiths. Here, take my overcoat; my watch also—as evidence of good faith and because it gets in one's way, climbing…. Wait by this door, which (you can see) is an Emergency Exit, and within five minutes you shall be reposing in a plush seat and admitting that the finish crowns the work.'"

"Well, at this hour, Otty, I won't dwell on my contribution to the evening's pleasure. Besides, it was nothing to boast of. I was a member of the Oxford Alpine Club, you know: and the water-pipe offered no difficulties. The stucco was in poor condition—I should say that it hardens more easily in Byzantium—but for difficulty there was nothing comparable with New College Chapel, or the friable masonry and the dome of the Radcliffe.

"I let myself down through a skylight into the bowels of the place: found, with the help of matches, the operating box and the gallery, switched on the lights, and shinned down a pillar to the stalls. After that, to open the Emergency Exit and admit my audience was what the detective stories call the work of a moment. I re-closed the door carefully, and climbed back to manipulate the lantern.

"I had helped to work one of these shows once, at a Sunday School treat—or a Primrose Fete—forget which—down in the country. It's quite simple when you have the hang of it.... I made a mull with the first reel: got it upside down; and Petunia, from somewhere deep under the gallery, called up 'Gar'n!' It was a Panorama of Pekin, anyway, and dull enough whichever way you took it.

"After that we fairly spun through 'The Cowpuncher's Stunt'—a train robbery—'The Missing Million,' and a man tumbling out of the top storey of Flat-Iron Building, New York. He went down, storey after storey, to the motto of 'Keep on Moving,' and just before he hit the ground he began to tumble up again. On his way up he smacked all the faces looking out at the windows—I often wonder, Otty, how they get people to do these things: but I suppose the risk's taken into account in the pay.

"Farrell took a great fancy to 'Keep on Moving.' Up to this we had been snug as fleas in a blanket; but now he started to make such a noise, encoring, that I had to step down to the gallery and lean over it and request Petunia to take the cover off the piano and play something, if she could, to deaden the outcries. 'Something domestic on the loud pedal,' I suggested. 'Create an impression that we're holding a rehearsal after hours.'

"She came forward, looked up, and said that I reminded her of Romeo and Juliet upside down.

"'Of course!' I explained. 'We're in Pekin. Get to the piano, quick.'

"'I've forgotten my scales,' she answered back, between Farrell's calls of ''Core! 'Core!'—'Will it do if I sit on the keys?'

"She went to the instrument. 'Often, and *con expressione*!' I shouted; 'and back-pedal for all you are worth!' Then I climbed down and collared Farrell, for the police had begun to hammer on the door. I grabbed for his head: but it must have been by the collar I caught him—that being where he wore most fur.... There was a stairway between the stalls and the gallery. I whirled him up it, and leaned over the gallery rail, calling to Petunia. She had dragged off the piano-cover and was rolling herself up in it.... Then, as the police crashed in, I switched off the lights.

"Somehow or another I hauled Farrell up and on to the flat roof. 'Now,' said I, after prospecting a bit in a hurry, 'the great point is to keep cool. You follow me over this parapet, lower yourself, and drop on to the next roof. It's a matter of sixteen feet at most, and then we'll find a water-pipe.'

"But he wouldn't. He said that he suffered from giddiness on a height and had done so from the age of sixteen, but that he was game for any number of policemen. He'd seen too many policemen, and wanted to reduce the number. I left him clawing at a chimney-pot, and—well, I told you the stucco was brittle, and you saw the state of his clothes. I think he must have got out a brick or two and put up a fight.

"For my part, I slid three-quarters of the way down a pipe, lost my grip somehow and tumbled sock upon the serried ranks of a brutal and licentious constabulary. They broke my fall, and afterwards I did my best. But, as Farrell had justly complained, there were too many of them. So now you know," Jimmy wound up with a yawn.

"What about the Lady Petunia?" I asked.

"Oh!" He woke up with a start and laughed: "I forgot—and it's the cream, too.... The police who grabbed me had been hastily summoned by whistle. They rushed me up two side streets and towards a convenient taxi. It was convenient: it was stationary.... It was my own, own taxi, still sitting. One constable shouted for its driver; another had almost pushed me in when he started to apologise to somebody inside. It was Petunia, wrapped in slumber. She must have slipped out by the Emergency Exit and taken action with great presence of mind. I don't know if they managed to wake her up, or what happened to her." Jimmy yawned again. "What's the time, Otty? It must be any hour of the morning.... *I* don't know. She forgot to return my watch."

NIGHT THE SEVENTH
THE OUTRAGE

Jephson awoke me at 7.30 as usual. But I dozed for another half an hour and should have dropped asleep again had it not been that some little thing—I could not put a name to the worry—kept teasing my brain; some piece of grit in the machine. An engagement forgotten? an engagement to be kept?—Nothing very important....

Then I remembered, jumped out of bed, and knocked in at Jimmy's room. I expected to find him stretched in heavy slumber. But no: he stood before his dressing-table, tubbed, shaven, half-clothed, and looking as fresh as paint.

"Hallo!" said he. "Anything wrong?"

"Just occurred to me," said I, "this is the morning you were due to breakfast with Jack. Thought I'd remind you, in case you might want to telephone and put him off."

"If I remember," said Jimmy thoughtfully, rummaging in a drawer, "this Jack's other name is Foe. If it were Ketch, I'd be obliged to you for ringing him up with that message.... It's all right. Plenty of time. Breakfast and conversation with the learned prepared for me right on my way to the Seat of Justice. Providence—and you can call it no less—couldn't have ordered it better. Here, help me to choose.—What's the neatest thing in ties when a man's going to feel his position acutely?"

Upon this I observed that his infamous way of life seemed to leave more impression upon his friends than on himself; and stalked back to my bedchamber.

"Ingrate!" he shouted after me. "When you've seen Farrell!"

So I breakfasted alone, read the papers (which reported that Mr. Farrell's meeting overnight had been "accompanied by scenes of considerable disorder "), dealt with some correspondence, and in due time was taxi'd to Ensor Street. There I found Jimmy on the penitents' bench, full of sparkling interest in the proceedings of the court and in the line—a long and variegated one—of his fellow-indictables. Farrell sat beside him, sprucely dressed but woebegone. He wore a sort of lamp-shade, of a green colour, over his eyes, and (as Jimmy put it) "looked the part—Prodigal Son among the Charlottes." By some connivance—on some faked pretence, I make no doubt, that I was his legal adviser—the police allowed Jimmy to cross over and consult me. He informed me that the Professor had put him up an excellent breakfast of grilled sole and devilled kidneys, and had afterwards shown him round the laboratory. "Wonderful man, the Professor! But you should see that dog of his he calls Billy— hairy little yellow beast that flies into rages like a mad thing, and then at a word crawls on its belly. Sort of beast that dies on his master's grave, in the children's books, like any human creature."

The charge was not called on the list until 12.30 or thereabouts. … They say that in England there's one law for the rich and another for the poor. I don't know about that: but there's one for the bright and young and another for the middle-aged and sulky. The police had already let Jimmy down lightly on the charge sheet: they showed further leniency at the hearing. Even the constable who faced the Bench with an eye like a damnatory potato contrived to suggest that he would have left it outside if he could— so benevolently, so appreciatively he made it twinkle as he gave evidence. Jimmy tried to take the blame; but the Magistrate, without relaxing his face, fined him two pounds and mulcted Farrell in five. He added some scathing remarks upon old men who led their juniors astray and called themselves Martin Luther when they were nothing of the sort. I wondered if he knew that he was admonishing a candidate for County Council honours. I had a notion that he did. His address lasted half a minute or less, and during it he kept his gaze implacably fixed on the culprit: but by the working of his under-jaw and of the muscles below it I seemed to surmise—shall we say—a certain process of deglutition.

Their fines paid, Jimmy—staunch to the last—brought Farrell forth to me, who waited outside by the doorstep.

"Look here, Otty; he's in trouble—"

"Of his own making, by all accounts," I put in sternly.

Farrell began to stutter. "A most untoward—er—incident, Sir Roderick—*most* untoward! Compromising, I fear?"

"You've lost us the seat, that's all," I told him.

"Oh, I trust not—I trust not!" he protested. "Might the reporters be—er—"

"Squared?" I suggested.

"Induced—yes, induced—to omit the—er—personal reference?"

"Like the Scarlet Mr. E's," suggested Jimmy, "or the Scarlet Pimpernel—rather a good name for you, Farrell. Better than Martin Luther, anyway. The Scarlet Pimpernel, or Two in a Taxi, Not to Mention the Lady. Or—wait a bit—Peter and Petunia, or Marooned in Soho. Reader, do you know the 'Catalafina'? If not, let me—"

"Jimmy," I commanded, "don't make an ass of yourself.... As for you, Mr. Farrell, let me remind you of a pretty wise saying of somebody's—that influence is jolly useful until you have used it. If I remember, I strained my little stock of it with these reporters two nights ago."

"I wouldn't jib at expense, Sir Roderick," he whimpered.

"Don't kick him, Otty," Jimmy implored. "He's down. And listen to me, Farrell," he went on, swinging about. "You can't help it: it's the Hire System working out through the pores. You don't perspire what you think you're perspiring, though you're doing it freely enough.... Now, Otty—for my sake—if you don't mind!"

"Well then, Mr. Farrell," said I, "I'm ready to do this much for you.—We'll find a taxi here and now for the Whips' Offices and take their advice. Having taken it, I am willing to drive straight back to your Committee Rooms with the Head Office's decision."

The man's nerves were anywhere. He clung to me for counsel—for mere company—as he would have clung to anybody.

So we found a taxi and climbed in, all three.

But I did not reach the Whips' Office that day.

There was a hold-up as we neared the bridge, and we to came a dead stop. I set it down to some ordinary block of traffic, and with a touch of annoyance: for Farrell by this time was arguing himself out as a victim of circumstances, and with a feebleness of sophistry that tried the patience. I remember saying "The long and short of it is, you've made a fool of yourself.... Why on earth can't this fellow get a move on?"—As though he had heard me, just then the driver slewed about and shot us back a queer half-humorous glance through the glass screen.

Jimmy, lolling crossways on one of the little let-down seats with his leg across the other, caught the glance, sprang up and thrust his head out at the window.

"Hallo!" said he. "Suffragettes? Dog-fight?... Pretty good riot, anyhow,"—and the next moment he was out on the roadway. I craned up for a look through the screen, and stepped out in his wake.

Some thirty yards ahead of us, close by the gates of the South London College, a dense crowd blocked the thoroughfare. It was a curiously quiet crowd, but it swayed violently under some pressure in the centre, and broke as we watched, letting through a small body of police with half a dozen men and youths in firm custody.

My wits gave a leap, and my heart sank on the instant. I stepped to the taxi door and commanded Farrell to tumble out.

"Here's more of your mess-work, unless I'm mistaken," said I.

"Mine?" He looked at me with a dazed face. "Mine?" he quavered. "Oh, but what has happened?… There would seem to be some conspiracy.…"

"Yes, you interfering ass. Out with you, quick! and we'll talk later." I turned my shoulder on him as I handed the driver his fare. "Now follow and keep close to me."

I stepped forward to meet the Sergeant in charge of the convoy. He would have put me aside. "Sorry, sir, but you must tell your man to take you round by the next bridge. Traffic closed here—half an hour, maybe." Then he caught sight of Farrell behind my shoulder, recognised him, and called his party to a halt. "Excuse me," he said, with a fine official manner committing him to no approval of us, "but is this the Candidate?… Well, you've come prompt, sir, but scarcely prompt enough. Situation's in hand, so to speak. Still you might be useful, getting the crowd to clear off peaceable." He pondered for a couple of seconds. "Yes, I'll step back with you to the gate, sirs, and pass you in. You, Wrightson," he spoke up to a second in command, "take over this little lot and deliver them: it's all clear ahead. Get back as fast as you can.… Now, sirs, if you'll follow me—there's no danger—the half of 'em no more than sightseers."

"Just a word, Sergeant," said I, catching up his stride. "I want to know how this started and how far it has gone."

He glanced at me sideways. "Not on oath, sir, nor official, eh? What isn't hearsay is opinion, if you understand. Far as I make it out—but we was caught on the hop, more by ill luck than ill management—it started with an open-air meetin' right yonder, at the corner of the Park. Your friend—that is to say Mr. Farrell, if I make no mistake-"

"Yes, he's Mr. Farrell all right. Go on."

"Well, he was billed to attend, sir; but he didn't turn up."

"He had another engagement," I put in.

"Well, and I did hear some word, too, to that effect," allowed the Sergeant, with another professional glance, subdolent but correct. "But, as reported to me, his absence was unfortunate. One or two of the wrong sort got hold of the mob, and there was a rush for the College gates.... Which the two or three constables did their best and 'phoned me up."

"Much damage?" I asked.

"Can't say, sir. I was given post at the gates, where for ten minutes my fellows was kept pretty busy bashing 'em and throwing 'em out. You see, it being Saturday, most of the students had gone home, and the porter was took of a heap and ran.... Or that's how it was reported. And whiles we was thus occupied, word came out that the game was over without need to call reinforcements, if we could hold the gate. We answered back sayin' if that was all we was doing it comfortably. Whereupon they began to hand us out the arrests, with word that some outbuildings had been wrecked and a considerable deal of glass broken. Lavatories, as I gathered."

"Laboratories," I suggested.

"Very like," the Sergeant agreed; "if you put it so. It struck me as sounding like the sort of place where you wash your hands.... We was pretty busy just then, or up to that moment; but from information that reached me, they was trying to wreck some part of the science buildings."

"One more question," said I—for by this time we had reached the edge of the crowd. "Do you happen to know if Professor Foe was in the building at the time?"

"He was not, sir. He had locked up for the day and gone home to his private house. They fetched him by 'phone.... I know, sir, having received instructions to pass him in: which I did, under escort. You needn't be anxious about him, if he's a friend of yours."

But I was.

The crowd, as the Sergeant had promised, was curious rather than vicious; much the sort of crowd that the King's coach will fetch out, or a big fire; and from this I augured hopefully (correctly, too, as it proved) that the actual rioters had been little more than a handful, excited by Saturday's beer and park-oratory.... The average Londoner takes very little truck in municipal politics, as I'd been deploring for a fortnight on public platforms. It costs you all your time to get one in ten of him to attend a public meeting: he's cynical and sits with his back to the ring where a few earnest men and women, and a number of cranks, are putting it up against the Vested Interests and the Press.

As we came up, some few recognised Farrell, and raised a cheer.... I dare say that helped: but anyhow the Sergeant worked us through with great skill, here and there addressing a man good-naturedly and advising him to go home and take his wages to the missus, because the fun was over and soon there might be pickpockets about. In thirty seconds or so we had reached the gate and were admitted.

The porter's lodge had escaped lightly. A trampled flower-bed, flowerless at this season, and a few broken window-panes, were all the evidence that the rioters had passed. A little farther on where the broad carriage-way, that ran straight to the College portico, threw out branches right and left to the Natural Science Buildings, a number of ornamental shrubs had been mutilated, a few of the smaller uprooted. Foe's laboratory lay to the left, and we were about to take this bend when a tall man came striding across to us from the right; a short way ahead of two others, one round and pursy and of clerical aspect, the other an official in the Silversmiths' uniform. The tall man I guessed at once to be the Principal, returning from a survey of the damage done: and I waited while he approached. He wore an angry frown, and his eyes interrogated us pretty sharply.

"Sir Elkin Travers?" I asked.

"At your service, sir, if you are sent to help in this business?" Sir Elkin's eyes passed on this question to the Police Sergeant and reverted to me. "From Whitehall?" he asked.

"No, sir," I answered. "My name is Otway—Sir Roderick Otway; and our only excuse for being here is that two of us are close friends of Professor Foe. Indeed, sir, for myself, let me say that I have for many years been his closest friend, and I am anxious about him."

"You have need to be, I fear," said Sir Elkin, speaking slowly. "I was going back to him at this moment. Will you come with me…. This, by the way, is Mr. Michelmore, our College Bursar."

"With your leave, gentleman," put in the Sergeant, "I'll be going back now. They've collared most of the ringleaders; but by the sound of it they're beating the shrubberies for the stray birds…"

"Certainly, Sergeant—certainly…. Your men have been most prompt." Sir Elkin dismissed him, and again bent his attention on us. "You are all friends of the Professor's?" he asked.

"Two of us," said I. "This third is Mr. Farrell, who has come to express his sincere regret."

The Principal's eyes, which had been softening, hardened again suddenly with anger and suspicion. What must that ass Farrell do but hold out his hand effusively? "Pleased to make your acquaintance, Sir Elkin," he began. "Assure you—innocent—slightest intention— quite without my approval—outrage—deplorable—last thing in the world—"

He stammered, wagging a hand at vacancy; for the hand it reached to grasp had swiftly withdrawn itself behind Sir Elkin's back, and remained there.

"We will discuss your innocence later on, sir. Be very sure you will be given occasion to establish it, if you can." Sir Elkin's glare, under his iron-grey eyebrows, promised No Quarter. "Since you have pushed your way in with these gentlemen, it may interest you to follow us and see the results of your ignorant incitement."

He shook Farrell off—as it were—with a hunching movement of the shoulder, and turned to me.

"Come, sir," he said, courteously enough. "I warn you it is a tragedy."

"But my friend is unhurt?" I asked anxiously. "The Sergeant told me—"

"Doctor Foe had left the building—whether fortunately or unfortunately you shall judge—half an hour before the mob arrived. Saturday is, for lecturing, a *dies non* with him, though he often spends the whole day here at his work." Sir Elkin paused. "By the way, did I catch your name aright, just now? You are Sir Roderick Otway?… Then I ought to have thanked you, before this. It was you who sent me a message yesterday. Foe himself made light of it—"

"I wish I had come with him," said I, with something like a groan.

"I wish to Heaven you had," he agreed very seriously. "For I have a confession to make…. I was a fool. I contented myself with warning a few of the teaching staff to be on their guard, and with setting an extra round of night-watchers. But I neglected to see to it that Foe removed his papers to the College strong-room. I did suggest it; but when he pointed out that it would involve an afternoon's work at least, and went on to grumble that it would probably cost him a month to re-sort them—that he hated all meddling with his records—"

"My God!" I cried. "You don't tell me his records—eight years' close work, as I know—"

"Eight years," repeated the Principal in grave echo as my words failed. "Eight years' work: that would have cost a few hours to secure—a week, perhaps, to rearrange; and in twenty minutes or so—" He broke off. "You see that smoke?" he asked. "Over there by the two tall Wellingtonias?… There, sir, goes up the last trace of those eight years of our friend's devotion. Patience amounting to genius, loyalty to truth for truth's sake so absolute that one careless moment is dishonour, records calculated to a hair, tested, retested, worked over, brooded over—there's what in twenty minutes your Hun and your Goth can make of it in this world!"

"But, sir," I broke in, "books and packed paper don't burn in that way! Foe's Regent-Park notes alone ran to thirty-two letter-cases when I saw them last. He brought home two bullock-trunks from Uganda, stuffed solid—"

Sir Elkin wheeled about sharply. "Mr. Farrell," said he, "you had a letter in yesterday's *Times*."

"If it had crossed my mind, Sir Elkin," pleaded Farrell with a wagging movement of his whole body, propitiatory, such as dogs make when they see the whip. "I do assure you—"

"I seem to recollect," interrupted Sir Elkin, "your saying that considerable sums of public money were spent on our laboratories. The grant allocated to this College for research was so munificent that, after building a physiological laboratory with a small lecture-theatre, we had to house the professor himself in a match-boarded room covered with corrugated iron. Between them"— he turned to me in swift explanation—"they made a furnace.... Yes, Mr. Farrell, and you asked why, if all is well inside my laboratories, I should fear the light. You would insist on knowing what you were paying for.... Well, here is the answer, sir—if it meet your demand."

In the clearing where Jack's laboratory stood surrounded by turf and a ring of conifers, a dozen firemen were busy coiling and packing lengths of hose. The fire had been beaten; its last gasp was out; and the main building stood, smoke-stained, water-stained, with gaping sockets for windows, but with its roof apparently intact. The trees were scorched to leeward, and the turf was a trampled morass. Charred benches and desks, broken bottles, retorts, and glass cases, bestrewed it. But of Jack's sanctum—of the room in which I had been allowed to sit while he worked, because, as he put it, "I made no noise with my pipe"—nothing remained save a mound of ashes and a few sheets of iron roofing, buckled and contorted. A thin wisp of smoke coiled up from the ruin.

"Jack!" I called.

"Let's try the theatre," Sir Elkin suggested. "I left him there."

We went in.

The rostrum Jack used for his lectures was low, flat-topped and semicircular, with a high raised desk in the middle. Being isolated, it had escaped the fire; as maybe it had proved too cumbrous for removal.

Anyhow, there it was; and Jack stood beside it busy with something he was laying out on the flat desk-top. It looked like some sort of jigsaw puzzle that he was piecing together very carefully, very— what's the word?— meticulously. He had a small heap of oddments on his left, and a silk handkerchief in his right hand. His game was, he picked out an oddment from the heap, polished it, fitted it more or less into the silly puzzle, and stepped back to eye it. He looked up, annoyed-like, as if we were breaking in on a delicate experiment.

"Drop that, Foe!" Sir Elkin commanded, sharp and harsh, but with a human tremble in his voice. His nails clawed into my arm. "It's his dog," he whispered me, "or what's left. The poor brute held the door, they say... sprang at their throats right and left... till someone brained him and they threw his carcass into the fire.... Drop it, Foe—that's a good fellow!"

Jack stayed himself, stared at us dully, and put down the handkerchief after dusting the bench with it.

"Is that you, you fellows?" he asked, with a smile playing about his mouth and twisting it. "Good of you, Roddy—though almost too late for the fun! Jimmy, too?... They've made a bit of a mess here, eh?... Ah, and there's Mr. Farrell! Will somebody introduce Mr. Farrell?... Good-morning, sir! We'll—we'll talk this little matter over—you and I—later."

BOOK II
THE CHASE

NIGHT THE EIGHTH
VENDETTA

"My dear Roddy,—Don't come around: and for God's sake don't send Jimmy. The word is 'No sympathy, by request.' You will understand.

"I shall call on you at 9 o'clock on Tuesday. Have breakfast ready, for I shall be hungry as a hunter.

"Don't fash yourself, either, with fears that I am 'unhinged' by this business. I am just off to Paddington—thence for the Thames—shan't say where: but it's a backwater, where I propose to think things out. I shall have thought them out, quite definitely, by Tuesday.

"I believe you keep a few bottles of the audit ale. Tell Jephson to open one for a stirrup-cup. You can invite Jimmy.—
Yours truly,
J.F.

"P.S.—I don't know, and can't guess, how you came to tumble in so promptly on the heels of that riot. But you have always been a cherub sitting up aloft and keeping watch over— Poor Jack.

"P.P.S.—This by Special Messenger…. Forgive my breaking away and leaving you all so impolitely. Nothing would do, just then, but to escape and be alone.— Until Tuesday."

A boy-messenger brought this missive at 5.30. I read it over in a hurry, and took cheer: read it over a second time, sentence by sentence, and liked it less. It left no doubt, anyhow, that to search for Jack on the reaches of the river would be idle, as to find him would be mean. So there was nothing to do but wait.

That week-end, as it happened, brought a false promise of spring, with a hard east wind and a clear sky.

Punctually at nine o'clock on Tuesday he arrived, clean and hale and positively bronzed. The old preoccupation of over-work rested no longer upon him. We had made ready with grilled sole, omelette, bacon and a cold game-pie. He ate like a cavalryman, talking all the while of his adventures. It appeared that he had chosen the "Leather Bottle" at Clifton Hampden for headquarters, and had spent a part of Sunday discussing Christian Science with an atheistical bagman. He said not a word of Saturday's happenings—talked away, in fact, as if he had returned to us, on perfect terms of understanding, out of a void. Jimmy played up and mulled some beer for us afterwards, on a recipe of which (he gave us to know) the College of Brasenose, Oxford, alone possessed the secret, to be imparted only to such of its sons as had deserved it by godliness and good learning.

Foe commended the brew, declined a cigar, and pulled out his old pipe.

"Infernal job," he began, "having to talk business, 'specially when you've tasted freedom."

He filled his pipe, lit it carefully, and went on. "I got back to London early yesterday morning. Spent the day clearing up my worldly affairs.... Don't look scared, Roddy. I've thrown up the Professorship—that's all."

"Why, in the world?" I wanted to know.

"You may put it," he answered easily, "that, as the clerics say, I've had a higher call."

"Don't understand," said I; "unless you're telling us that Travers—"
"Travers?" His eyebrows went up. "Oh, I see what you mean. No: Travers hasn't been running around and finding me a better-paid job as a solatium. He's a good fellow and quite capable of it. Even hinted at something of the sort when I broke it to him verbally, yesterday afternoon. I thanked him, but wasn't taking any. I get quite as much money as I want at the Silversmiths'; and I've saved a little, too. It's freedom, not money, I want; as a means to my little end. I want complete freedom for a couple of years, perhaps for three, or maybe even for longer. It may be I shall have to buy myself an annuity. I'd ask for absolute independence if it could be had—independence of all my fellow-creatures but one. But it can't be had: so I've come to you for help."

"Say on," I commanded.

"It's this way, Roddy. Like the late General Trochu, I have a Plan. Unlike his, it's a Great Plan.... Yes, I'll give you a glimpse of it by and by. It involves—or may involve—the cutting of all human ties—that is of all but one. Well, as you know, I haven't many, and those clients of Farrell's have lightened me of worldly furniture. What's become of Farrell, by the way?"

"He's retiring from the contest, and has been advised to travel for the good of his health. The Sunday papers settled it with their reports of the Police Court proceedings.... What! Haven't you heard?"

"Now I come to think of it, Travers tried to tell me some story... but I wasn't listening.... In trouble, is he? Good. Not going to hang him, are they? Good."

"The actual decision," said I, "was taken at the Whips' Office yesterday morning. Farrell goes. There's just time to put up a working-man candidate in his stead. But the seat's lost."

"Good," repeated Jack tranquilly. "Eh?... Oh, I beg your pardon, Roddy: I was looking at it from—well, from a different angle.... Let's get back to my plan. Wasn't it Huck Finn who wished it were possible to die temporarily? That's what I'm going to do, anyhow: and I want you to be my executor."

"I should need an inventory of your worldly goods, to start with," said I gravely.

"Drew it up, Sunday night.... Where's my coat?... here, catch!" He pulled out a long legal envelope, well stuffed, and threw it across to me. "Don't open it now. When you do, you'll find everything in order. I've a habit of neatness with my worldly affairs."

"All very well," said I. "But you'll have to tell a lot more before I commit myself. And, anyhow, things can't be done in this easy way. You'll have to see a solicitor and get me power of attorney or something of the sort—"

"Look here," he interrupted; "I thought it was understood that I'd come to you for *help*. Power of attorney? Bosh! Not going to commit yourself? Why, man, you're committed! The cheque's drawn and paid into your account at Hoare's.... I did it yesterday—caught 'em just before closing-time. You'll be hearing in a post or so. They have all the bonds too, and my written instructions.... I bank there, too, you know."

"Heaven alive!" said I, with a gasp. "Are you telling me you've chucked all you possess into my account?"

"Why not?" he demanded. "Oh, you can make me out an I O U some time, and get Jimmy to witness it, if you're so damned—what's the word?—

punctilious. If you can't do me this simple favour, why then you must sign the business over to Jimmy here."

"No, you don't," answered Jimmy, and in accents commendably clear considering that he uttered them with his nose deep in the tankard of mulled ale. "Up to now I have played the good boy who is seen but not heard. I break the self-imposed silence only to say: 'Woe betide the man who attempts to complicate my overdraft!'"

I addressed myself to Jack. "You'll be wanting money sent to you from time to time, and I'm to transmit.—Is that the idea?"

He nodded.

"Where am I to send it?"

"That's the uncertainty, of course. From time to time I shall keep you informed. It may be to a suburban villa, it may be to some *Poste Restante* in the Sahara. That's as the chase goes. Like Baal I shall be on a journey, or I shall be pursuing. Yes, anyway I shall be pursuing.... All I ask is that, on getting a call, you'll send out, as best you can, such-and-such a sum to the address indicated. You have between £6000 and £7000 to play with. Probably you will be surprised at my moderation in demanding: but anyway I shall keep well within the limit. My memory and the bank-book usually balance to a pound or two."

"Then it's travel you're after?" I asked.

He nodded. "On a journey—*and* pursuing."

"Big game?"

"You may call it the biggest. Or I'm out to make it the biggest. ... Jimmy, pass me the tobacco." He took the jar and, filling his pipe, lay back in the wicker chair with something like a groan. "Roddy, can't you *see*? These years, as you know, I've been working up my inquiry into rage in animals; beginning, that is, with animals, but always, as you know, intending to carry the inquiry up as soon as I had a solid working basis. Yes, it was all to proceed on induction—laborious tests, classifications—you know the system and that I didn't care if it took a lifetime. Well, all of a sudden, as I'm beginning to realise that, though the process is sound—must be sound—pursuit is probably hopeless because it must take twenty lifetimes—of a sudden, I say, this new way is revealed. Put it that I've come, all of a start, upon a little stream called Rubicon. Put it that I've burnt—no, put it that Farrell's myrmidons have burnt, at a stroke, every boat for me.

"—I might have gone on for years upon years, collecting statistics and ploughing out conclusions.... I begin to believe in the calculated interposition of Providence.... On the critical moment of transference the bridge breaks behind me. I have lost all my baggage. But, on the other shore, I have the jewel.

"—Listen, my boy.... The end of me may be empiricism.... They have destroyed eight years' work, and I have nothing left of it but memories of data which I can't produce for evidence—worthless, that is, for a man of my scientific conscience. *En revanche* and on the other side of the stream I find I have *it*; to carry on and test upon a fellow-man I have the diamond to cut all glass. With the brute beasts it was all observation, much of it uncertain. Henceforth it will be clean experiment. Farrell accused me of practising vivisection. As a matter of fact, I never did. Now I'm going to, and on Farrell."

Jimmy arose on pretence of seeking a match, and leaned his elbow on the mantelpiece while he stared into the fire.

"Oh, I say, Professor!" he blurted out. "Farrell, you know! He's no sort of class. He—he deserves punishing, but he don't mean any harm, if you understand." Here Jimmy faced about with an ingenuous smile. "I'm a bit of a fool myself, you see, and must speak up for my order."

"But you speak up too late, my boy," answered Foe. "What's the use of telling me that Farrell is no class? As if I didn't know *that*! ... Why, man, I didn't *choose* Farrell, to pay my attentions to him. If the gods had paid me the compliment of sending along the late Mr. Gladstone, or the present Archbishop of Canterbury (whoever he may be), or General Booth (if he's alive), to knock out eight years of my life like so many skittles in an alley, I'd have felt flattered, of course. But they didn't: they sent along Farrell, and I bow my head before a higher wisdom which, you'll allow, has been justified of its child. Could the late Mr. Gladstone—since we've instanced him—have done it more expeditiously, more thoroughly, with a neater turn of the wrist?... No. Very well, then! Better men than I have married their cooks and been content to recognise that it just happened so. You can start apologising for Farrell when I start complaining he's inadequate."

Jack's eyes, during this speech, were for Jimmy, of course, and I had used the opportunity to watch his face pretty narrowly. It was a little more than ordinarily pale, but composed, as his tone was light and his manner of speech almost flippant. I wondered....

"Jimmy meant," said I, "that *you're* too good to match yourself against Farrell. The harm he's done you is atrocious—I can hardly look you in the face, Jack, and speak about it.... All the same, Jimmy talks sense: an outsider like Farrell isn't worthy of your steel, as the writers say."

"We'll wait till he has felt it." Jack stood up, pushed his hands into his trouser-pockets, took one turn around the room, returned, and came to a halt on the hearth-rug. "There's another point," said he. "You fellows can never get it out of your heads that your thoroughbred is always, and necessarily, more sensitive than your mongrel. *It must be so*—you don't trouble about evidence: it's fixed in your minds *a priori*: which means that you're just as unscientific and at least as far from the truth as I should be if I posited the exact opposite… As a matter of fact, some miss in the breeding will usually carry with it an irritable protective nerve and keep the animal sensitive on points which the thoroughbred ignores. Your cripple thinks of his hip, your hunchback of his spine: your well-formed man takes his hip and spine for granted. Your bastard is sensitive on historical fact and predisposed to lying about it.… Stated thus, my counter-proposition is obvious. You won't be so ready to agree when I go on to assure you that sensitiveness in these mongrels and misfits often spreads from the centre over the whole nervous system.—But, anyway, you knew my poor hound, the pair of you. Not much breeding in Billy, eh?… Well, he bit four blackguards before they laid him out: bit 'em deep, too, and I won't answer for the virus. That dog died defending my papers. He fought on his honour, and he knew it, Roddy. He suffered, Jimmy—even if he was dead when they threw him into the fire. And—I'm going to give your Farrell the benefit of the doubt. … Where's the tobacco?"

I passed him the jar. "We'll allow for the moment that you are right, Jack," said I. "At all events, you've made out a case. But where do I come in? What's the part you propose for me in this show? Pull yourself together and admit that I'm asking a sweetly reasonable question."

"Didn't I explain?" Jack answered testily. "Surely I made it clear? All I ask of you is to post me out from time to time the money I ask for travelling expenses.… That doesn't compromise you, eh? … Damn it all, Roddy," he exploded, "I counted you were my friend to that extent!"

"That's all right, Jack," said I. "But a friend is one thing and an accomplice is another. What's your game with Farrell? You haven't told me yet, though you're asking what gives me the right to know."

He picked up his coat and hat and turned on me with a smile, very faint and weary and a trifle absent-minded.

"To tell you the truth," said he, as if searching for something at the back of his mind, "I haven't thought it out quite accurately. It's near enough to warrant what preparations I'm making: but it hasn't the shape of a clean proposition—which is the shape my conscience demands.… Don't hurry me, Roddy: let me come around again to-morrow.… I can't invite you to my flat, because I'm making arrangements to shut it up, and these details get in the way, all the time.... Tell you what.—Meet me, you two, at Prince's Grillroom to-morrow, one-fifteen, and you shall have the plan of campaign on a half-sheet of notepaper. I'm a brute, Roddy, to bother you with these private affairs in the middle of your politics. But one-fifteen to-morrow, if you can manage. Sure? Right, then.— So long!"

He wagged, at the door, a benediction on us with his walking-stick and went down the stairs, I strolled to the window and watched him cross the turfed square of the court. Jimmy had taken up the poker and started raking the lower bars of the grate.

"Queer how quietly the Professor takes it," began Jimmy. "I was half-afraid—Oh, drop it, Otty, old man—I'm sorry!"

We had both wheeled about together, and I held a window cushion, poised, ready to hurl.

"Of course I didn't mean that, really!" pleaded Jimmy, parrying with the poker-point. "Sit down and let's talk. Is he mad?... I don't like it."

NIGHT THE NINTH
THE HUNT IS UP

Well, I thought it over, and talked it over with Jimmy, and decided that, much as I loved Jack Foe, he'd have to be more explicit with me before I undertook this stewardship. You will say that, this being the only decent decision open, I might have done without the thinking and the talking.... And that's true enough. But, you see, I had lived with Jack pretty long and pretty close, and this was the first time I'd ever taken a miss with him. If anyone for the past ten or fifteen years had suggested to me, concerning Jack Foe, that a day might come when I shouldn't know where to find him, I—well, I should have lost my temper. It was inconceivable, even now. I told myself that, though he had expressly given me leave to invite Jimmy to the breakfast, he had taken a fit of reticence in Jimmy's presence and had shied off; that I should get more out of him when we were alone together.... Is that good English, by the way? Can two persons be alone?... Thank you, Polkinghorne—of course they can when they're real friends.

But that speculation wouldn't work, either: for again at Prince's, and again at Jack's invitation, we were to be a party of three.... I tell you of these doubts because through them, and (you may say) by way of them, it came to me—my first inkling that something was wrong with the man.

Anyway, as it turned out, Jimmy and I might have spared ourselves the discussion: for when we reached Prince's the head-waiter (an old friend) brought me a letter. It had been delivered by District Messenger almost two hours before. It ran—Here it is: I have all the documents but one, and I've sent home for that.

> "Dear Roddy,—Sorry to do a shirk: but circumstances oblige me to take the boat-train, 9.45, ex Victoria. I have locked up the flat. The porter has the keys, with instructions to lend to nobody but you or the landlord.

> "Address, for some little while, quite uncertain. I drew out a fair sum in circular notes and cash; enough to keep me solvent for some weeks. So you need not worry about the money.

"You needn't fash your consciences over the Plan, either. I'll tell you about it in my next, written from the first place when I find leisure. I'll unfold—no, the word insults its beautiful simplicity. Apologies to Jimmy. Tell him to buy a copy-book and write in it *Experiment is better than Observation*.

"So long! A great peace has fallen on me, Roddy. 'I am one with my kind,' like the convalescent gentleman in *Maud*. 'I embrace the purpose of—whatever Higher Power set Farrell going—'and the doom assigned.'

"Farrell is going strong. Yoicks!—Yours ever,"

"J.F."

I handed the letter across to Jimmy, and set myself to order, thoughtfully, something to eat.

"Well, what do you say to it?" I asked as Jimmy finished his perusal.

"I say," pronounced Jimmy in unfaltering voice, "that the crisis demands a gin-and-vermouth, at once, and that the vermouth should be of the Italian variety."

"Waiter!" I called.

"Nay," said Jimmy, "hear me out. I say further—did you mention a rump-steak underdone?"

"You did," said I.

"And with oysters on the top?"

"It's where they usually go," I pleaded. "I didn't specify. One takes a lot of these little things for granted."

"Then I say further that, this being one of those occasions on which no time should be lost, you will reach for that collection of *hors d'oeuvre* on the table behind you, and lift your voice for a bottle of Graves to follow the vermouth and quickly, but not so as to gall its kibe.... And I say last of all," he wound up reflectively, helping himself to two stuffed olives and a *hareng sauer*, "that the Professor is running a grave risk, and I wouldn't be in his shoes at this moment."

"You think—" I began nervously.

"Never did such a thing in my life," said Jimmy. "I *know*. He's in one of those beastly Restaurant Cars."

Silence descended on Foe for two months and more. Then I received this long letter:—

Grand Hotel, Paris,
May 27th.

"My dear Roddy,—The hunt is up. I took some time getting a move on it: but to-night Farrell has the real spirit of the chase upon him, and is in his room at this moment, packing surreptitiously with intent to give me the slip.

"You will have gathered from a glance at the above address that Farrell is with me; or rather, that I am with Farrell. I give him full scope with his tastes. It is part of the Plan. But to-night—knowing that he had gone to his room to pack surreptitiously, and that his berth in the *Wagon-lit* is booked for to-morrow night at the Gare d'Orleans—I gave myself what the housemaids call an evening-out. This is Paris, Roddy, in the time of the chestnut bloom. A full moon has been performing above the chestnuts. Beneath their boughs the municipality had hung a thousand reflections of it in the form of Chinese lanterns shaped and coloured like great oranges. The band at the *Ambassadeurs*—a band of artists and, as I should judge, conducted by somebody who couldn't forget that he had once been a gentleman—saw the moon rise and at once were stricken with Midsummer madness. It had been recklessly, defiantly, blatantly exploiting its collective shame on two-steps and coon song,—shouting its *de profundis*, each degenerate soul bucking up its lost fellow with a challenge to go one better and mock at its hell—when of a sudden, as I say, the moon rose, and the conductor caught up his stick, and the whole damned crew floated off on *The Magic Flute*.... It wasn't on the programme. It just happened, and no one paid them the smallest attention.... But there it was: ten minutes of ecstasy.

"They ceased upon the night: and the next news was that after five minutes' interval they were chained again and conscientiously throwing vim into *Boum-Poump* with the standardised five thumps of jollity on the kettledrum.

"So the champak odours failed—What is champak? Have the Germans synthetised it yet?—and I awoke from dreams of thee. I walked back by way of the Quais—by the river:"

Dissolute man!
Lave in it, drink of it
Then, if you can.

"But I have played for safety and am writing this with the aid of a whisky-and-Perrier to hope that it finds you well as it leaves me at present.

"I dare say it struck you as a poorish kind of trick—my inviting you to Prince's and leaving you to pay for the repast. The reason of my sudden bolt was a sudden report that Farrell intended to start at once for a holiday on the Continent of Europe—that he had been to Cook's and bought himself a circular ticket for the Riviera—Paris, Toulon, Cannes, Nice, etc.—on to Genoa, Paris by Mt. Cenis—that sort of thing. I should tell you that, being chin-deep in winding up my affairs, I had employed a man to watch his movements. Shadowing Farrell is a soft option, even now, when he's painfully learning the rudiments of flight: four months ago he had not even a nascent terror to make him suspicious. Oh, never fear but I'll educate him, dull as he is! Remember your *Ancient Mariner*, Roddy? Here are two passages purposely set wide apart by the author, that I'll put together for you to choose between 'em,—"

(1) As who, pursued with yell and blow,
Still treads the shadow of his—Foe,
And forward bends his head....

(2) Like one that on a lonesome road
Doth walk in fear and dread,
And having once turned round, walks on,
And turns no more his head;
Because he knows a frightful fiend
Doth close behind him tread.

"You may urge that Coleridge—a lazy man and a forgetful—is just repeating himself. But there's a shade of difference; and

I'll undertake to deliver back Farrell in whichever condition you
  prefer; or even to split the shade. But you must give me time.

"As it was, I risked nothing in paying an ordinary
professional. Farrell walked into the office, and my man
followed him. Farrell took some time discussing his route
with the clerk. My man borrowed the use of a telephone-
box, left the door open and rang me up. By the time he was
put through he had heard all he needed. So he closed the
door, and reported. I instructed him, of course, to buy me a
similar ticket. 'And,' said my man, 'he is inquiring which is
the best hotel at Monte Carlo, and it seems he hardly knows
any French." 'Right,' said I. 'Come along at once and collect
your fee, for I haven't any time to spare.'

"I thought it possible that Farrell might break his journey
to dally with the gaieties of Paris. But he didn't. I found out
easily enough at Cook's Office there that he had booked a
sleeper and gone straight through. So I went to the Opera,
listened to *Rigoletto*, idled most of the next day in the old
haunts, and took the usual Sud-Express, with a sleeper, from
the Gare de Lyons.

"No: I lie. You can't call it idling when you sit—say in the
Bois, on any chance bench anywhere—seeing nothing,
letting the carriages go by like an idle show of phenomena,
but with your whole soul thrilling to a new idea, drinking
it in, pushing out new fibres which grow as they suck in
more of it through small new ducts, with a ripple and again
a choke and yet again a gurgle, which you orchestrate into a
sound of deep waters combining as you draw them home....
Oh, yes—you may laugh: but I know now what conception
is: what Shakespeare felt like when he sat one night, in a
garden, and the great plot of *Othello* came teeming....

"Please bear one thing in mind, my dear Roddy, You are
never, now or hereafter, to pity me. *Qualis artifex*.... I used to
smile to myself in a cocksure youthful way when great men
hinted in great books that one had to make burnt-sacrifice of
the eye's delight, the heart's desire; the lust of the flesh, the
pride of the intellect; see them all consumed to a handful of
dust, and trample out even the last spark of that, before the
true phoenix sprang; that only when half-gods go the gods
arrive. But it's true, Roddy! It's true!

"I won't grow dithyrambic—not just yet. I was so sure of my man that it seemed quite worth while to tumble out at Avignon—a place I had never inspected—and fool away another spell among Roman remains, and Petrarch and the rival Popes, and the opening scenes of the Revolution, and just thinking—thinking.

"So I reached Monte Carlo next day, a little after noon; took a bath and a siesta; sauntered into the Casino there, a good forty-eight hours behind time; and caught my man, sitting.

"Are you superstitious, Roddy? Of course you are: and so are all of us who pretend that we are not.… Monte Carlo is the hell of a hole. I had never seen it before: but as I went into the Casino, all of a sudden I had a queer recollection—of a breakfast-party at Cambridge in young La Touche's rooms, in King's (he was killed in the South African War), and of his saying solemnly as we lit cigarettes that he'd had a dream overnight. He dreamed that he walked into the Casino at Monte Carlo, went straight to the first table on the left, put down a five-franc piece on Number 17, and came out a winner of prodigious sums.

"Well, we are all humbugs about superstition. I don't believe there's a man existent—that's to say, a tolerable man, a fellow who isn't a prig—who doesn't touch posts, or count his steps on the pavement, or choose what tie he'll wear on certain days, or give way to some such human weakness when he's alone. We so-called 'men of science' are, I truly believe, the worst of the lot. You can't get rid of one fetish but you have instantly the impulse to kneel to another…

"Anyhow, there was my man sitting, and the number 17 almost straight before him, a little in front of his right arm; and this recollection came to me; and I leaned over his shoulder and laid a five-franc piece on the number.

"It won. I piled my winnings on the original stake, *plus* all my loose cash; and Number 17 won again.

"That's all. You know my old theory that every scientific man should have a sense of mystery—it's more useful to him than to most of his fellows. Anyway I'd tried my luck on Bob La Touche's long bygone dream.

"Several pairs of eyes began to regard me with interest: and the croupier, as he pushed my spoil across, spared me a glance inscrutable but scrutinising. I make no doubt that had I helped to make up the next game, quite a number of the punters would have backed my infant fortune. But I didn't. Farrell had slewed about in his chair for to look up at the newcomer: and at sight of his dropped jaw, as he recognised me, I smiled, gathered up my wealth and walked out.

"I took a seat in the Casino garden, overlooking the sea. 'Sort of thing,' I found myself murmuring, 'might happen once in a blue moon,' and with that was aware that a sort of blue moonlight was indeed bathing the garden, though the moon's reflection lay yellow enough across the still Mediterranean. [Here, for description, turn up Matt. Arnold's *A Southern Night*: possibly still copyrighted.]

"Farrell came out. He spotted me at once; for to help the moon, as well as to dispel the heavy scent of the gaming-room, I was lighting a cigar. He took a couple of turns on the terrace and halted in front of me. His manner was nervous.

"'Excuse me, Professor—' he began.

"'Excuse me, Mr. Farrell,' I corrected him; 'I am a Professor no longer. You may call me Doctor Foe, if you like.... Did Number 17 win a third time?'

"'I—I fancy not," he stammered. 'To tell the truth, your sudden appearance here, when I supposed you to be in London—and at Monte Carlo, of all places—But perhaps you are a devotee of the fickle goddess? Men of learning,' he floundered on, 'find relaxation—complete change of interest. Darwin—the great Darwin—used to read novels: the worse the novel, the better he liked it—or so I've heard.'

"'As it happens,' said I, 'this is my first visit to Monte Carlo.'

"'Indeed?' He brightened and became yet more fatuous. 'Then we may call it a coincidence, eh?—a veritable coincidence. When I saw you—But first of all, let me congratulate you on your luck.'

"'Thank you,' I said. 'I will make a note that your first impulse on encountering me was to congratulate me on my luck.'

"This seemed to puzzle him for a moment. Then, 'Oh, I see what you mean,' he said. 'But we're coming to that.... You gave me a fair turn just now, you did, turning up so unexpected. But (says I) this makes an opportunity that I ought to have made for myself before leaving London. Yes, I ought.... But I want to say to you now, Dr. Foe—as between man and man—that I made a mistake. I was misled—that's the long and short of it. I never stirred up that crowd, Doctor, to make the mess they did of your—your premises. But so far as any unguarded words of mine may have set things going in my absence—well, I'm sorry. A man can't say fairer than that, can he?... And I've suffered for it, too,' he added; 'if that's any consolation to you.'

"'Suffered, have you?' I asked.

"'What, haven't you heard?' He was surprised.—Yes, Roddy, genuinely. 'Well, now I won't say it was all owing to that little affair at the Silversmiths' College.... There were other—er—circumstances. In fact there was what-you-might-call a combination of circumstances. The upshot of which was that I had a safe seat and took a bad toss out of it. No, I don't harbour no feelings against you, Doctor Foe. I'm a sociable, easy-going sort of fellow, and not above owning up to a mistake when I've made one.... I stung you up again just now, wishing you joy of your luck: meaning no more than your winnings at the tables. Not being touchy myself, I dessay it comes easy to advise a man not to be touchy. But what I say is, we're both down on our luck for the time, and we're both here to forget it. So why not be sociable?'

"'Suppose on the contrary, Mr. Farrell,' I suggested, 'that I am here to remember. What then?'

"'Then I'd say—No, you interrupted me somewhere when I was going to make myself clear. You won't mind what I'm going to say? ... Well, then, I gather those asses did some pretty considerable damage to your scientific 'plant'—is that so? ... Well, again, feeling a sort of responsibility in this business, I want to say that if it'll set things on their legs again, five or six thousand pounds won't break Peter Farrell.'

"I didn't strangle him, Roddy. It was the perilous moment: but I sat it out like a statue, and then I knew myself a match for this business. I didn't strangle him, even though he provoked me by adding, 'Yes, and now we're met, out here, you can be useful to me in a lot of little ways. Know French, don't you? Well, I don't, and we'll throw that in.... What I mean is, What d'ye say to our joining forces? I'm fed up with these Cook's men. They do their best, I don't deny. But this business of the lingo is a stiffer fence than I bargained for. Now, with a fellow-countryman to swap talk; *and* a gentleman, and one that can patter to the waiters and at the railway stations—What do you say to it, Doctor? Shall we let bygones be bygones?'

"I did not strangle him, Roddy, even for that. I sat pretty still for a while, pretending to consider.

"'It's odd, Mr. Farrell,' said I after a bit, 'that you should invite me to be your companion. You'll always remember that you invited me?'

"''Course I shall,' said he. 'Let's be sociable—that's my offer.'

"I threw away my cigar. 'Provided you make no suggestion beyond it, I accept,' said I. 'We will take this trip together. Do you mean to stay long at Monte Carlo?'

"'Pretty place,' said Farrell. 'Been up to La Turbie? No, of course; you've only just arrived. Well, I can recommend it— funny little railway takes you up, and the view from the top is a knock-out. But I'm your man, wherever you'll do the personally-conducting. I'm not wedded to this place. Only came here because I understood it was fast, and I wanted to see.'

"'Where's your hotel?' I asked.

"'Grand Hotel, next door,' he answered. 'What' yours?'

"'The same,' said I. 'We'll meet at *dejeuner*—same table. Twelve noon, if that suits.'

"'I don't know if you're wedded to this place—' said he.

"'Not one little bit,' I answered.

"'Inside there, for instance?'

"'You saw,' said I. 'I came out because I disliked the smell.'

"'And there's that pigeon-shooting. Goes on all day. I hate taking life—even if I could—'

"'You've once before,' said I, 'suspected me of being careless about the sufferings of animals; and you've, apologised. Shall we call it off? I don't shoot pigeons anyway.'

"'Me either,' Farrell agreed heartily. 'I'm here for fresh air and exercise. Don't mind confessing to you I've no great fancy for this place. Man told me at dayjooney this morning he'd just come in from sitting under the palms before the Casino entrance. ... All of a sudden a young fellow walked out and shot himself there, point-blank. Man who told me doesn't take any interest in play—over from Mentone for the day, just to see things.—Well, this young fellow, as I say, shot himself—put revolver to his forehead—there on the steps. And by George, sir, he was mopped up and into a sack within twenty seconds! One porter ready with sack, another to help, third with sponge to mop steps—stage clear almost before you could rub your eyes. ... I just tell it to you as it was told to me, and by a man pretty far gone in consumption, so that you'd say he'd be cautious about lying.'

"I lit another cigar. 'With so priceless a fool as this,' I said to myself, 'you must not be in a hurry, John Foe.' Aloud I said, 'I've no passion either, for this place. I wanted to see it, and I've seen it. I'll knock in at your room at eight o'clock, if that will suit you, and we'll discuss plans. For my part, I had a mind to go back to Cannes and start for a ramble among the Esterel.'"

"To be brief, we struck the bargain and—incredible as you may find it—have been running in double harness ever since…. I couldn't have believed it myself, in prediction: but here it is—*and until a few hours ago Farrell never guessed.*

"No: that is wrong. He never guessed at all. I told him.

"It came to me, after the first week, as habitually as daily bread. We put in a couple of days at Mentone, another couple at Nice; then for a fortnight we made Cannes our centre, with a trip up to Grasse and several long tramps among the mountains. After that came St. Tropez, Costebello, Toulon, Marseilles, Montpellier—with excursions to Aigues-Mortes, the Pont du Gard and the rest of it. From Montpellier we turned right about on our tracks; took Cannes again, Antibes; drove along the whole Corniche in a two-horse barouche. There was a sort of compact that we'd do the whole Riviera—French and Italian—as thoroughly as tourists can do it; and we did—from Montpellier to Bordighera, from Bordighera to Genoa. And he never guessed.

"I had two bad moments; by which I mean moments of unscientific impatience, sudden unworthy impulses to kill him and get rid of the job. Unscientific, unworthy—unsportsmanlike—to kill your priceless fish before he has even felt the hook!

"The second bad moment I overcame (I am proud to report) of my own strength of will. It happened at a bend of the Corniche, when our driver pulled up on the edge of a really nasty precipice and invited us to admire the view. It being the hour for *dejeuner,* we haled our basket out of the carriage, and spread our meal on the parapet. Farrell sat perched there with his back to the sea, and made unpleasant noises, gnawing at a chicken-bone. I wanted to see how he'd fall backwards and watch him strike the beach….

"Well, I was glad when the impulse was conquered and I had proved my self-control: because the previous temptation had been a close call, and I believe it would have bowled me out but for a special interposition of—Providence.

"We were following up a path in the Esterel: a little gorge of a path cut by some torrent long since dried. The track had steep sides—fifteen to twenty feet—right and left, and was so narrow that we took it single file. I was leading.

"Now, on our way westward out of Cannes, that morning, we had passed the golf-links, and Farrell had been talking golf ever since. I don't know why golf-talk should have such power to infuriate those who despise that game. But so it is, Roddy.

"I had the weapon in my pocket. I had my fingers on it as I trudged along, and was saying to myself, 'Why not here? In the name of common sense, why not here? Why not here and now?'— when a leveret, that had somehow bungled its footing on the high bank above, came tumbling down, not three yards ahead of us. The poor little brute picked itself up, half-stunned, caught sight of us, and made a bolt up the path ahead. From this side to that it darted, trying to climb and escape; but again and again the bank beat it, and from each spring it toppled back; and we followed relentlessly.

"At the end of two hundred yards it gave in. It just lay down in the path like a thing already dead and waited for what we should choose to do.

"I picked it up. I showed it to Farrell, keeping my fingers on the faint little heart.

"'They say,' said I, 'it's lucky when a hare pops out in your path. What do you think?'

"'Worth carrying home?' said Farrell. 'I'm partial to hare. But he's a bit undersized for Leadenhall Market'—and the fool laughed.

"'We'll let him go,' said I

"'I guess he's too far scared to crawl,' he suggested doubtfully.

"'Turn about and watch,' said I. 'It may have escaped your memory that you once accused me of being cruel to animals. Turn about, and watch. Don't move.'

"I undid the three upper buttons of my waistcoat, stowed the little fellow down inside, against my shirt, leaving his head free, so that I could stroke his ears and brainpan. I let Farrell see this, stepped past him, and walked slowly back down the path. At the end of twenty paces I lifted the little beast out, set him on the ground, and walked on. He shook his ears twice, then lopped after me like a dog, at a slow canter. At the point where he had tumbled I collected him again by the ears, lifted him, climbed the bank and restored him to his thicket, into which he vanished with a flick of his white scut.

"Then I went back very slowly to Farrell. 'Curious things, animals,' said I. 'If you don't mind, we won't talk any more golf to-day.'"

NIGHT THE TENTH
PILGRIMAGE OF HATE

"A map scored with the zigzags of our route would suggest the wanderings of a couple of lunatics. But that was the way of it. I would turn up at breakfast any morning and propound some plan for a new divagation. Farrell never failed to fall in with it. For a time, of course, I had him in places whence, with his ignorance of France, he might have found it hard to escape back to his own form of civilisation. But even when he had picked up enough of the language to ask for a railway ticket and something to eat, his reliance on me continued to be pathetic, dog-like.

"I know something of dogs. I have no experience of marriage. But from time to time I put this question to myself: 'Here is a widower—free, as he tells me, after twenty-seven years of married life almost entirely spent at Wimbledon. It is inconceivable that he did not, during that considerable period, look at least once or twice across the table at the late Mrs. Farrell and ask himself if the business was to go on for ever.' I supposed, Roddy, that the two had been in love, as such creatures feel the emotion. 'Well then,' thought I, 'here are we two, the one hating and hiding his hate, thrown together in constant companionship. How long will it take the other, who has never cut an inch of the ice encasing that hatred, before he finds my society intolerable?'

"That was the question; and I had the answer to-day.

"From Genoa we actually harked back to Cahors, for an aimless two weeks among the upper waters of the Lot and the Tarn. I led him over the roof of France, as they call it. I sweated him down valleys to Ambialet, to Roc-Amadour, I threaded him through limestone caverns wherein I could have cut his throat and left him, never to be missed. We struck up for the provincial gaieties of Toulouse. We attended the Opera there— *Il Trovatore*—and Farrell wept in his seat. I can see the tears now—oozing out between the finger-stalls of a pair of white-kid gloves he had been inspired to buy at the *Bon Marche*. We also went to the theatre, where the company performed *Les Vivacites du Capitaine Tic.*

"At the conclusion of this harmless comedy, Farrell said a really good thing. He said it was funny enough and even instructive if you looked at it from the right point of view; but for his part (and I might call him advanced if I chose) he liked the sort of musical comedy in which you spice a chicken to make 'em all fall in love when they've eaten it; or at least, if it's to be legitimate comedy, one in which they take off their clothes and go to bed by mistake.

"So we came on to Paris, and here we are at the Grand Hotel. Farrell's notion of Paris, was of course, the Moulin Rouge, and the kind of place on Montmartre where they sing some kind of blasphemy while a squint-eyed waiter serves you cocktails on a coffin.

"We were solemnly giving way to this libidinous humbug last night when he leaned back and said to me, 'This is all very well, Doctor; and I'm glad to have had the experience. But do you know what I want at this moment?'

"'Say on,' said I, looking up to return the nod of an acquaintance—a young American, Caffyn by name—who had risen from a table not far from ours and was making his way out. On a sudden impulse I called after him, 'Hi! Caffyn!'

"'Hallo!' Caffyn turned about and came strolling back. He is a long lantern-jawed lad with a sardonic drawl of speech. He has spent two years in the *ville lumiere*, having come to it moth-like from somewhere afar in Texas. His ambition—no, wait!—the ambition of his father, a 'cattle king,' is that he should acquire the difficult art of painting in oils. 'Want me?' asked Caffyn, as I pushed a chair for him. 'What for? If it's to admire the 'rainbow' you've been mixing, I'm a connoisseur and I don't pass it. Your hand's steady enough, one or two lines admirably defined, but you've gotten the pink noyau and the *parfait amour* into their wrong billets. If, on the other

hand, you want me to drink it, I'll see you to hell first."...
Then, as I introduced him, "Good evening, Mr. Farrell. I am
pleased to meet you in this meretricious haunt of gaiety. If I
may be allowed to say so, you set it off, sir.'

"'Sit down a moment,' said I. 'We didn't intrude upon your
solitary table, thinking—'

"'I know,' he caught me up. 'Natural delicacy of Britishers—
'Here's a fellow learning to take his pleasures sadly. We'll
give him time.' And I, gentlemen, allowed that it was 'way
down in Cupid's garden—Damon and Pythias discovered
hand in hand—no gooseberries, by request.... If you'd like
to be told how I was occupied, I was chewing—ay, marry
and go to— I was one with my distant father's most fatted
calf—fed up and chewing.'

"'And if you'd like to know how we were occupied,' said I,
'we were both wanting something—and the same thing. We
haven't told one another what it is, and you are called in to
guess.'

"'Oh, a thought-reading *seance*. Right.' He turned the chair
about, sat on it straddle-wise and crossed his arms over the
curved top bar. 'Let me see,' he mused, leaning forward,
pulling at his cigar and bringing his eyes, after they had
travelled over the crowd, back firmly to us. "Two souls with
but a single thought," he quoted, "two hearts that beat as
one.'... Well, now, if you were of my country and from my
parts I'd string you like two jays on one perch—How say'st,
prithee, and in sooth yes, sure! I'd sing you *The Cowpuncher's
Lament*, sweet and low, with tears in my voice. As it is, I'll
be getting the local colour a bit smudged, maybe: but I
guess— I guess,' said Caffyn—and his gaze seemed to turn
inward and become far withdrawn—'I guess—'O Hardy,
kiss me ere I die!'— No, that's wrong: it isn't the cockpit of
the *Victory*. It's the after-saloon of the Calais-Dover packet—
shortest route—and I see you two there at table, eating cold
roast beef, underdone, with plain boiled potatoes. With
plain boiled potatoes—yes, and mixed pickles.' He passed
a hand over his eyes. 'Excuse me, gentlemen; the vision is
blurred just here— if someone would kindly shoot that lady
on the stage and stop her—it's not much to ask, when she's

exposing so much of her personality—How the devil can I tell the difference between mixed pickles and piccalilli while she's committing murder on the high C? *Passez outre*.... I see you eating like men who haven't seen Christian food for years; yet you are swallowing it in a hurry that almost defeats the blessed taste; because one of you has just shouted up, with his mouth full, a command to be informed as soon as ever the white shore of Albion can be spied from deck. It is a race with Time—Shakespeare's Cliff against a pickled onion.... Oh, have done! have done!'

"'Thank you, Caffyn,' said I. 'You may come out of your trance. You have done admirably.'

"'Wonderful,' breathed Farrell; and he breathed it heavily. 'I won't say I'd actually arrived at a plain-boiled potato—'

"'But it was floating in your brain,' I chimed him down. 'Such is the province of imaginative art, of poetry, as defined by that great Englishman, Samuel Johnson. It reproduces our common thoughts with a great increase of sensibility.'

"'Mr. Caffyn has put it rightways, anyhow,' Farrell insisted. 'Look here, Doctor'—he calls me by that title and none other— 'What's the programme for to-morrow.'

"'Versailles,' said I.

"'Then we'll make it so. But, the day after, I'm for England. ... I don't mind telling you, Mr. Caffyn, that the Doctor and me hit it off first-class.'

"'I've noted it,' said Caffyn quietly.

"'And it's the rummier,' Farrell pursued, 'because him and me— or, as I should say, he and I—started this tour upon what you might call a mutual—what's the word? misunderstanding?—no, I have it—antipathy. Is that correct, Doctor?'

"'Perfectly,' I agreed.

"'T'tell the truth,' confessed Farrell, 'I've always been up against schoolmasters; yes, all my life. They've such a—such a—well, as this ain't Wimbledon, one may speak it out—

such a bloody superior way of giving you information. Now if there's one thing in th' world I 'bominate, it's information.' Farrell threw a fierce glance around the dining tables as if defiantly making sure of his ground. 'But I'll say this for the Doctor; he never gives you any. That is, you have to pump for it.... But we've had, we two, a daisy of a time. The great thing about travel, Mr. Caffyn, is that it enlarges the mind. Yes, sir, and in Doctor Foe's company you positively can't help it.'

"'I'm sorry, Farrell,' said I.

"'Sorry?' he exclaimed. 'Why should you be sorry? I *like* having a—a wider outlook on things, provided it ain't banged in a man's eye. In fact, I don't mind confessing to you, Mr. Caffyn, here in the Doctor's presence, that this has been a great experience for me. I've had a good time, as I believe, sir, they say in your country. But I look around me'—here Farrell looked again and almost theatrically around the feast of Comus—'and I say that, be it never so homely, give me Wimbledon to wind up. You and me, Doctor—or, as I might say, you and I, are for home, after all—and the old cooking. Our ways henceforth may lie separate; but we've a bond in common and any time you care to look me up at Wimbledon I shall be most happy. We'll crack a bottle to our travels.'

"'Right,' I agreed. 'Caffyn, will you make a note of at too?'

"'And Mr. Caffyn—at any time—Goes without saying,' pursued Farrell.

"'Right,' agreed Caffyn."

"That was yesterday, Roddy. This morning, as ever is, Farrell and I started, according to programme, for Versailles. I could see that his mind had been running on Caffyn's words; that he was dying to get back to Wimbledon; yes, and almost dying to be quit of me.

"I had been waiting for this. I had known that the moment would come, and wondered a score of times that it took so long in coming. As unmarried men, Roddy, you and I are out of our depth here. But surely—I hark back to it—it *must* happen to one or other of every married couple to look across the table and realise the words *Till death us do part.* When it happens to both simultaneously I suppose murder follows; or, at least, divorce.

"Talking about murder, I've to confess that at Versailles I felt the impulse again. You know that infernal Galerie des Glaces? Well, of a sudden the multiplication of Farrell's face and the bald spot at the back of his head came near to overpowering me. We had escaped, too, from the wandering sightseers, and stood isolated at the end of the vast hall.... High sniffing dilettanti may say what they like, but Versailles is what Jimmy would call a 'knock-out.' The very first view of the Grand Avenue had knocked Farrell out, at all events, and he had stared at the great fountains, and followed me through courts and galleries in mere bedazement, speechless, with eyes like a fish's, round and bulging and glassy.... He looked so funny, standing there... so small... and yet actually, I suppose, taller than the late King Louis Quatorze by three inches. ... Somewhere outside on a terrace a band was playing things from the *Mariage de Figaro*— Figaro, at Versailles of all places!... In short the world had gone pretty mad for a moment, and for that moment I felt that, in this *bizarrerie* of contrast it might dignify our quarrel if Farrell died amid such magnificent surroundings.... But I conquered the impulse all right: and this, the third time, was the easiest."

"I got him away to the Little Trianon: and there in its gardens— as you would lay in the shade a patient suffering from sunstroke—I conducted him to a seat under the spring boughs beside the little lake that reflects the Hameau. He stared on the green turf at our feet, and across at the grouped rustic buildings, all as pretty as paint, and came out of his stupor with a long sigh.

"'A-ah!' he murmured. 'That's better! That does me good.'

"Then I knew that it was coming: that I must break his fate to him. I even gave him the prompt-word.

"'Homelike,' I suggested.

"'You've hit it,' he said, and paused. 'No place like Home! I'm glad enough to have seen all that show yonder.' He waved a hand. 'But I wouldn't be one of these kings, not if you paid me.… Look here, we'll cross to-morrow, eh? Of course, if you prefer to stay behind—'

"'I'm not going to stay behind,' said I, throwing away my cigarette.

"'Capital! We'll wind up with a dinner at the Savoy—'

"'Cold roast beef and mixed pickles,' I put in.

"He chuckled. 'Clever fellow, that Caffyn—made my mouth water, he did. We'll wind up at the Savoy, and talk over another trip that we'll take together, one of these days. For I shall miss your company, Doctor.'

"'No, you won't,' said I, lighting a fresh cigarette.

"He stared at me for a moment as if slightly hurt in his feelings. Then: 'Don't contradict,' he said sharply, and laughed as I stared in my turn. 'Expression of yours,' he said. 'Sounds rude; but all depends *how* you say it. I reckon I've caught up the accent—eh?—by the quick way you looked up.… I hadn't much school and never went to College: but I've studied you, Doctor, and I'll improve.'

"'Well, then,' said I, nettled and less inclined to spare him,' I'm sorry to contradict you, Mr. Farrell, but you are never going to miss my company—*never, until your life's end.*'

"'What d'ye mean?' he blurted: and I suppose there was something in my look that made him edge off an inch or two on the rustic seat.

"'Simply this,' I answered. 'Ten or a dozen weeks ago you made yourself the instrument to destroy something twenty times more valuable than yourself. I am not speaking of what you killed in me, nor of the years of application, the records, measurements, analyses which you hoofed into nothing with no more thought than a splay coon's for an ant-heap. Nor will I trouble you with any tale of the personal hopes I had built on them, for you to murder. The gods suffer men of your calibre to exist, and they must know why. But I tell you this, though you may find it even harder to understand. Science has her altars, and her priests. I was one, serving an altar which you defiled. And by God, Peter Farrell, upholsterer, the priest will pursue!'

"He drew back to the end of the seat and fairly wilted. His terror had no more dignity than a sheep's. He cast an eye about for help. There was none. 'You're mad!' he quavered. 'If we were in England now—What is it you're threatening?'

"'Nothing that you could take hold of, to swear information against me,' I answered, 'even if you were in England now—now that April's here. Or is it May? I shall probably end by killing you; but I have tested my forbearance, and now know that it will happen at my own time, place, and convenient opportunity. That's a threat, eh? Well, there's no hurry about it, and you couldn't do anything with it, even at home in merry England. You couldn't put up a case that you go in bodily fear of me—as you're beginning to do—when I can call Caffyn ('Clever fellow, Caffyn!') to witness that only last night you desired no end to our acquaintance. Besides, my acquaintance is all I propose to inflict on you, just yet.'

"He jumped up, and faced me. He was thoroughly scared, and no less thoroughly puzzled. To do him justice, he had pluck enough, too, to be pretty angry.

"'I don't know what you mean!' he broke out. 'I don't know what you're driving at, mad or not.... The moment we crossed one another I hated you—Yes, damn you, first impressions are truest after all! Later, I was weak enough, thinking I'd injured you, to—to—' He broke down feebly. 'What sort of devil are you?' he demanded, mopping his forehead. 'You can't hurt me, I say. What is it you threaten?'

"'Only this,' said I. 'You have been a married man for a number of years, and therefore can probably appreciate better than I what it means. But you know my feeling for you, as I know yours towards me.... Well, I propose to be your companion in this world and until death do us part.... You may dodge, but I shall be faithful; you may slip, run, elude, but I shall quest. But your shadow I am going to be, Mr. Farrell; and ever, when you have hit a place in the sun, it shall be to start and find me—a faithful hound at your side. I have put the fear on you, I see. Waking or sleeping you shall never put that fear off. … And now,' said I, rising and tapping another cigarette on my case, 'let me steer you back to the railway-station. You will prefer to dine alone to-night and think out your plans. I shall be thinking out mine at the *Ambassadeurs.'"*

"So that's how it happened, Roddy. You might post me £100 to the Grand Hotel, Biarritz: for I'm running short. The hunt is up, and he's breaking for South."

"J. F."

NIGHT THE ELEVENTH
SCIENCE OF THE CHASE

I'm an imperfect Christian: but I read Jack's long letter three times over, and at each reading I liked it the less. Before posting an answer I handed the thing to Jimmy; who spent a morning over it, helping himself—a sure sign of a troubled spirit—to tobacco indifferently from his own jar and mine. When nothing troubled him— that is to say, as a rule—he invariably used mine. I left him ruminating; went out, did some business, and met him again at our usual luncheon-table at the Bath Club.

"I believe," said Jimmy reflectively at luncheon, "that my way with Farrell was the better, after all.... You'll admit that it did the trick, and without causing any offence to anybody. Well, if you ask me how to deal with the Professor, I'll be equally practical. Starve him off."

"No good," said I. "If I cut off supply, he'll only come back, demand his money and be off on the trail again. Indeed, he may turn up in these rooms to-morrow: for it's ten to one, on my reckoning, that Farrell will pretty soon break back for home."

"All the easier, then," said Jimmy. "Save you the trouble of writing a letter. When he comes for his money, tell him you're freezing on to it."

"But, man alive! it's Jack's money. You wouldn't have me thieve, would you?... As for the letter, I've written it; in fact you may say that I've written two, or, rather, assisted at their composition. Here is one of them, in copy. It explains the other, which is a half-sheet of instructions now in my lawyer's possession. I shall have to write a third presently, explaining to Jack—"

"I don't like letter-writing," interrupted Jimmy, "and I shun solicitors. Which is anticipatory vengeance: as soon as I'm called, and in practice, they'll be active enough in shunning me. Otty, you need a nurse. What the devil do you want with consulting solicitors, when you can have my advice, legal or illegal, gratis?"

"Listen to this," said I:—

"Thistleton Chambers,"

"29a Essex Street, Strand, W.C.,"

"May 12th, 1907."

"Dear Sir,—Our client, Sir Roderick Otway, Bart., has to-day transferred to our account the sum of £6,500(six thousand, five hundred pounds), representing a sum received by him from you, to be administered on conditions which, after reconsidering them, he finds himself unable to accept.

"Sir Roderick instructs us that you will draw on us at your convenience for any sum or sums under this cover. This, of course, pending notification of your wish that we should transfer the account elsewhere.

"Acting on our client's further instructions, we hereby enclose in registered envelope circular notes value £100. Kindly acknowledge receipt and oblige."

"Yours faithfully,
"B. NORGATE,
"for Wiseman and Norgate,
"Solicitors.

"To
"J. Foe, Esq., D.Sc.,
"Grand Hotel,
"Biarritz."

Jimmy looked me straight, and asked, "Is that letter posted?"

"It is," I answered. "I told Norgate that, as a matter of honour, Jack's letter ought to be answered promptly. That's why I lost no time this morning. Not being quite certain of the earliest post to France, he made sure by sending off the office-boy straight to St. Martin's-le-Grand."

"Then no taxi will avail us," groaned Jimmy, "and I must call for a liqueur brandy instead.... Oh, Otty—you must forgive the old feud: but why *did* your parents send you to Cambridge? Mine sent me to a place where I had at least to sweat up forty pages or so of a fellow called Plato. Not being able to translate him, I got him more or less by heart. Here's the argument, then.... Supposing a friend makes a deposit with you, that's a debt, eh? Of course it is. But suppose it's a deposit of arms, or of money to buy arms, and he comes to you and asks for it when he's not in his right senses, and you know he's not, and he'll—like as not—play the devil with that deposit, if you restore it. What then?"

"If I thought that Farrell was in danger," I mused; "that's to say, in any immediate danger—"

"Rats!" said Jimmy contemptuously. "Farrell's a third party. Why drag in a third party? The Professor's *your* friend; and he's made a deposit with you: and you don't need to think of anyone but him. For he's *mad*.... Now, come along to the smoking-room, where I've ordered them to take the coffee, and where I'll give you ten minutes to pull up your socks and do a bit of thinking."

"Maybe you're right, Jimmy," said I as we lit our cigarettes. "And if so, it's pretty ghastly.... He's had enough to put him off his hinge. But somehow I can't bring myself—No, hang it! I've always looked on Jack as the sanest man I've ever known. If he has a failing it's for working everything out by cold reason."

"Just what he's doing at this moment," answered Jimmy dryly. "If you don't like the word 'mad' I'll take it back and substitute 'balmy,' or anything you like. Madness is a relative term; and I should have thought that what you call working-everything-out-by-cold-reason was a form of it. I know jolly well that if I felt myself taken that way I should go to a doctor about it. And if *you're* going to practise it on the subject just now before the committee, I shall leave the chair and this meeting breaks up in disorder."

"The point is," said I, "that the letter has gone."

"What address?" he asked pouring out the coffee.

"Biarritz, Grand Hotel—Why surely you read it?"—I stared at him, but he was looking down on the cups. Then of a sudden I understood. "Jimmy," I said humbly, "I've been an ass."

"Ah," said he, "I'm glad you see it in that light.... The afternoon mail has gone: but there's the night boat. You can't telegraph, unfortunately. In his state of mind you mustn't warn him. You must catch him sitting."

"Look here," I proposed. "It will be a nuisance for you, Jimmy—it will probably bore you stiff. But if you'll only come along with me..."

"The implied compliment is noted and accepted," said Jimmy gravely. "The invitation must be declined, with thanks, though. Your mind is working better already. A few hours holiday off the L.C.C., and you'll find yourself the man you were. But the gear wants oiling. ... Do you remember your betting me ten to one this morning, in a lucid interval, that Farrell would break for home? Well, I didn't take you up. I don't mind owning that, after you'd left, and after some thought, I told Jephson to pack *both* suit-cases. But that lawyer, with his infernal notion of dispatch in business, will have put money in the Professor's pocket some hours before you reach Biarritz. Money's his means of pursuit: and it's well on the cards that you'll find both your birds flown. You are going to Biarritz, Otty, for your sins— like Napoleon III. and other eminent persons before you: and you'll have, unlike the historical character just named, to go alone for your sins. For on your ten-to-one odds that Farrell breaks for home it's obvious that I remain and keep goal. Now what you have to do is to make for the bank and get out some money, while I take a swim in the tank here. After that," added Jimmy, relapsing into frivolity, "I'll look up the Trades Directory for a respectable firm dealing in strait-waistcoats."

Well, there is no need to tell of my chase to Biarritz; for I arrived there only to be baulked. The porter who entered my name in elegant script, with many flourishes, in the Hotel Visitors' Book, informed me that the English Doctor had departed—it was four hours ago—to catch the night express for Paris. Here was the entry— "Dr. J. Foe, Chelsea, London." He had left no other address. "Had he a companion?" No, none. He had passed his time in solitary rambles: but on this, the last day, he had spent some time in writing furiously, up to the moment of departure.

The porter moved away to clear the letter-box, which stood pretty near the end of the table. I examined the register. Farrell's name was not among the entries.

They had assigned me my room, and I was about to take the lift and inspect, when I heard the porter say to himself, "*Tiens, c'est drole, maintenant.*" He had the bundle of cleared letters in his hand and held out one. It was addressed to me in Jack's handwriting.

I pounced for it. "*C'est a moi—Ceci s'expliquera, sans doute.*" The porter hesitated. "*Une lettre timbree—c'est contre les regies, sinon contre la loi... mais puisque c'est pour monsieur, apparement—*"

A ten-franc piece did the rest. I took the letter up to my chamber where I opened it and read—

[FOE to OTWAY]

"Grand Hotel, Biarritz.

"Dear Roddy,—I am obliged to you by receipt of your silly lawyer's letter enclosing £100; though what kind of salve it can spread on your conscience to commission a fellow called Norgate to do what you won't do at first hand I fail to perceive.

However, have it your own way. I have an enemy who, with a little training, won't give me time to worry about my friends.

"Farrell is improving. It was difficult at first to get a move on a man of his stupidity, and I could only work on his one sensitive nerve, which is cowardice. He has imagination enough to be terrified of that which hides and doesn't declare itself whether for good or evil.

"My own early experiments have, I admit, been amateurish. But I shall acquire skill, and the appetite shall learn refinements, to keep it in health. I don't think it was bad sport, on the whole, to open with low comedy. It tickled me, anyhow, to watch Farrell emerge from a sort of bathing-machine upon the *plage*, moderately nude and quite unsuspicious—having given me that artful slip in Paris—and, approaching the machine from the rear, to insert his shirt-collar, with my card, into his left-hand shoe.

"That was the first card I left on him. He was putting up at the *Albion*—I had no need to search; for the local paper, of course, prints a Visitors' List which it collects from the hotels, and there my gentleman was, under his own name. (Oh, we're in the simple stages of the process, thus far, and he hasn't yet had recourse to so much as an *alias*.) But I didn't call on him at the *Albion*.

"I have since learnt from him that the discovery of my card in the bathing-machine shook him up—well, pretty much as the footprint on the sand shook up Robinson Crusoe. But there's a difference, as he'll learn, between being shaken and being scared into fits. At all events, he didn't bolt: for I kept out of sight and molested him no more that day. Next morning he took courage and started off for the golf-links, which lie out to the north, beyond the lighthouse. He was enjoying his liberty, you understand: for I had made him carry his clubs about and up and down the Riviera, but never allowed him to play. That was a part of our understanding. Also he may have had some hazy notion that, golf being to me as holy water to the Devil, he'd be safe out there, within a charmed circle.

"There's something in it, too, Roddy. And I've half a mind,

if he doesn't wake up and improve, to offer him a handicap. He shall be safe, all the world over, when he can find a golf-course for sanctuary, and shall play his little game while I wait for him and:"

Sit on a stile
And continue to smile.

"I wonder what sort of a hell it would be, going round and round on endless rounds of golf—with a real Colonel Bogey sitting on the stile and watching.... But I make no promises, no offers, just now.

"He tells me that at the Club House he found a Golf Major of sorts—or, as he puts it, 'a compatriot, a military gentleman, retired, with a remarkable knowledge of India'—and seduced him into playing a round. I should gather that Farrell plays an indifferent game. At all events, the Golf Major was averse from a second round, and retiring to a table in the Club veranda allowed Farrell to call for—catch hold of your French, Roddy— '*Deux bieres, complet.*' The waiter understood it to mean liquid refreshment and not a double funeral.... Over the drink the Golf Major, who had known Biarritz for twenty years, explained the difference between its old and its new golf-course, and informed Farrell that in the old one there had used to be the most sporting hole anywhere—for a beginner. You drove slap across a chasm of the sea: if you didn't land your ball neatly you were in the devil of a hole, and if you foozled you saw your ball dropping down, down, to the beach and the Atlantic. 'Too expensive for duffers altogether, especially when the price of balls rose. Only the caddies thrived on it, at the risk of their necks.... After this tiffin we'll stroll over and have a look at it.'

"So thither they strolled, and by and by started to amuse themselves with pot-shot drives from the old tee. The Major whacked his ball across to a neat lie time after time. Farrell muffed and foozled, wasting his substance in riotous slogging. The height of the cliff, maybe, dizzied his head.

"In this way I suppose he expended all his ammunition. At any rate there came a pause, and a small Basque boy in a blue *beret* began to descend the slope very cautiously, searching for lost balls in the scree. At the foot of the gully, where it funnelled to a sheer drop, I stepped from under my shelter and met the youngster, holding out a golf-ball. 'Here is one more,' said I—'Where are the two gentlemen gone?' He told me that they had gone back to the Club House. 'Then here is a franc for you,' said I, 'and here is a card which you will take with the ball and my compliments to the gentleman who cannot play golf so well as the other gentleman.'

"The lad grinned. We climbed the cliff together, and I saw him speed off to the Club House."

"I had thus left two cards on Farrell, and it was now his turn to call: which he duly did, and next day; not, however, at the Grand Hotel, but at a far more romantic place of entertainment.

"If you don't know this place—and I do not commend it to you for entertainment towards the close of the English season—let me tell you that, walking south from the town by paths that lead around the curves of the foreshore, you quickly lose Biarritz and find yourself in a deserted and melancholy country,—a sort of blasted heath that belongs to a fairy-tale. The great military road for Spain runs hidden, pretty wide on your left, among the lower foothills of the Pyrenees: and from it these foothills undulate down and drop over little cliffs to form a moorland with patches of salt marish. In spring, they tell me, the ground is all gay with scarlet anemones in sheets; but, when I took the path, their glory was over and but a few late flowers lingered. I happen, however, to like flowers for their scent more than for their colour: and the whole of this moor was a spilth of scent from bushes of the purple Daphne—its full flowering time over, but its scent lingering ghostlily on the salt wind from the sea. And the sea was forlorn as it always is in this inner bight of the Bay of Biscay, where no ships have any business and your whole traffic is a fishing-boat or two, or a thread of smoke out on the horizon. You are alone between sea and mountains; and all along the strip that separates them, while the sky is spring, the land and the sense of it are autumn.

"Now I don't know the history of it, but can only guess that once on a time some enterprising speculator, fired by the sudden Third-Empire blaze of Biarritz, conceived the project of starting a rival watering place, here to the South, and that they were to make its beginning with a colossal Hotel. At any rate, here, rounding a desolate point of the foreshore, I came upon a long desolate beach, and a long desolate building, magnificent of facade, new and yet ruinated, fronting the Bay with a hundred empty eye-sockets.

"It broke on the view with a shock. It made me glance over my shoulder to make sure of the real Biarritz not far behind. But three or four spits of land shut off that human, if vulgar, resort. Between me and the Pyrenees this immense ghastly sarcophagus of misdirected enterprise possessed the landscape, and I approached it. Yes, Roddy:"

Dauntless the slughorn to my lips I set,
And blew. *Childe Roland to the Dark Tower came.*

"The horrible place turned out to be a mask—as I hope the Dark Tower did, after all, for Childe Roland. But it was a horrible mask. It had been started on foundations of good stone, with true French lordliness: but it parodied— or, rather, it satirised—the ambitious French tendency to impose architecture upon nature. Behind the facade, through which the wind whistled, all was an unroofed mass of rusted girders and joists; a skeleton framework about which I climbed—the first and last guest—conning and guessing where suites of rooms had been planned, to be adorned with Louis Seize furniture, for a host of fellow-guests that had never come and now would never arrive to make merry. I clambered along a girder, off which my heels scaled the rust in long flakes, and thrust my head through one of the great empty windows to take in the view.

"—Which was indeed magnificent. But my eye switched from it to a mean little human figure, moving along the foreshore with a gait which, even at a goodish distance, I recognised for Farrell's. It looked like a beetle creeping, nearing, across the flats and hummocks. But it was Farrell.

"He halted at some distance, as I had halted; arrested, as I had been arrested, at sight of the incongruous great structure, planted here. He drew close, cast a sort of questioning glance seaward, very deliberately drew a pair of field-glasses from a case slung over his shoulder, and focused them on the building, lifting them slowly.

"I had drawn back behind my window-jamb, yet so as to watch him. As he tilted the glasses upward, I leaned out.

"He stood for a moment, or two motionless. Then his hands sank, with the glasses clutched in them. He walked slowly away. When he judged himself hidden by a spit of the shore—but my window overlooked it—he broke into a run.

"I note that he is already beginning to reduce his figure.

"I returned the call that same evening. I dropped in on him as he took his seat to dine *solus* at the *Albion*. The dining-room, I should tell you, was fairly full. Usual ruck of people: sort of too-English; English you see at *tables-d'hote* and nowhere else in the world, with an end-of-season preponderance of females who stay to look after the British chaplain a little longer than he needs, or to gratify some obscure puritan pride in seeing everybody out, or because there's a bargain to be squeezed with the management to the last ounce, or peradventure because they've planned a series of cheap visits at home for our beautiful summer and one or two of the Idle Rich have remembered to be less idle than they were last year, and more restive.

"To do him credit—and it makes me hopeful for him— Farrell has a certain instinct of self-preservation. Let us never forget that he is a widower. Amid these Amazons he had fenced a bachelor table. I walked up to it straight and said, with a glance around, 'Farrell, you're lonely.'

"He passed a hand over his forehead and murmured, 'Oh, for God's sake—don't drive me like this!...'

"'Nonsense,' said I. 'Forget it, man. Look around you and say if there's one of these spinsters you'd rather have for companion. Don't raise your voice. You started in admirable key.... Let's keep to it and understand one another. I'm dining with you. If you like, we'll toss up later for who pays: but I'm dining with you. I promise not to hurt you to-night, if that helps conviviality.'

"'It does,' said he in a queer way. 'Let's talk.'

"'Well then,' said I confidentially. 'You're a solid man. You've made your way in the world, and I suppose the sort of success you've won implies some grit.... What makes you afraid of me, Farrell?'

"He drank some wine and stared down on the table-cloth, knitting his brows. 'Well,' he answered, 'I might tell you it's because you're mad.'

"'That's nonsense,' I assured him.

"'Oh, is it?' said he. 'I'd like to be sure it is.'

"'My pulse, as yours, doth temperately keep time," I quoted. 'Feel it, Farrell.'

"I stretched out my wrist. He started back as though it had been a snake.

"'On the whole you're right,' said I, drawing back my hand slowly, watching his eyes. 'If they saw you feeling my pulse the ladies around us would at once solve the doubt they have discussed in the drawing-room. All *table-d'hote* ladies speculate concerning their fellow-guests in the hotel.... . Thirty pairs of eyes were on the point of detecting you for a fashionable physician, and by this time to-morrow thirty ladies travelling in search of health would have found means to make your acquaintance and pump you for medical advice on the cheap.... Yes, Farrell, you have a lively instinct of self-preservation. I will note it.... Now tell me.—When I walked in just now, that same instinct prompted you to get up and run; to run as you did along the foreshore this afternoon. What restrained you?'

"'Why, hang it all,' he blurted with a look around; 'a fellow couldn't very well show up like that before all these ladies!'

"He meant it too, Roddy. It came out with a flush, plump and honest.

"It makes the chase more interesting. But I am annoyed with myself over the miscalculation.... I could have sworn he was a coward in grain. I marked all the *stigmata*.... And behold he can show fight!—at any rate in presence of the other sex.... Can something have happened to him, think you, since our talk at Versailles? Is it possible that I am *educating* the man?

"On top of this complicating discovery I made a simplifying one.

"You know that I have a knack with animals, in the way of handling their passions. I've never tried it on humans: for I've never laid down any basis of knowledge, and I've always detested empiricism. That study, as you remember, was to come.

"Well, I'll write further about it some day.... But I believe I have *something like* this power over Farrell.... I put out a feeler or two—to change metaphors, I waved a hand gently over the lyre, scarcely touching the strings; and it certainly struck me that they responded. You will understand that a *table-d'hote* was no place for pushing the experiment. And there were one or two men in the smoking-room when we sought it.

"Farrell found himself; talked, after a while, quite well and easily. In the smoking-room he told me a good deal about his early life: all *bourgeois* stuff, of course, but recounted in the manner that belongs to it, and quite worth listening to.

"He never wilted once, until I got up to go and drank what remained of my whisky-and-seltzer 'to our next merry meeting.' He followed me out to the hotel doorway to say Good night. We did not shake hands.

"There are indications that he will travel back north to-night. He has left for Pau, to play golf. At Dax this evening—mark my words—a solitary traveller may be observed furtively stealing on board the night express for Paris. He will be observed: but he won't be a solitary traveller.

"Your lawyer's letter—as I started by remarking—has arrived opportunely. If Farrell, as I suspect, intends to go through to London, I may reach you almost as soon as this letter, and shall add a piece of my mind for a postscript.—Yours,"

"J. F."

I slept the night at Biarritz and started back early next morning for London.

I found Jimmy recumbent in what he called his Young Oxford Student's Reading Chair, alone with the racing news in the evening papers.

"Hallo!" he greeted me. "I rather expected you just now. Let's go and dine somewhere."

"Has Jack turned up here?" I asked.

"'Course he has: Farrell too—Farrell first by a short head. Rather a good idea, my stopping at home to keep goal. Hard lines on you, though; all that journey for nothing.... If it's any consolation, the Professor was much affected when I told him of all the trouble you were taking, out of pure friendship, to fit him with a strait-waistcoat. 'Good old Roddy!' he said."

"No, he didn't," I interrupted. "And if he did, we'll cut that out. Tell me what happened."

"He said he had posted a letter to you from Biarritz: that it ought to have arrived by this time. I told him it hadn't, and it hasn't. If it had, I warn you I should have opened it."

"That's all right," I said. "I extracted it from the post-box at Biarritz, and have it here. You shall read it by and by. Go on."

"Well, in my opinion, the Professor's pulling your leg—or he and Farrell between 'em. If either's mad, it's Farrell; or else—which I'm inclined to suspect—Farrell's a born actor."

"Now see here," I threatened, "I've travelled some thousands of miles: I've spent two nights in the train and one in a French bedstead haunted by mosquitoes: I've had the beast of a crossing, and I'm in the worst possible temper. Will you, please tell me exactly what has happened?"

"You shall have the details over dinner," he promised affably. "For you've omitted the one observation that's relevant—your stomach is crying aloud for a meal. The Cafe Royal is prescribed."

"Not until I've had a tub and dressed myself. The dust of coal-brick—"

"That's all right, again.... I admonished Jephson. You'll find the bath spread and your clothes laid out in your bedder, and in five minutes or so Jephson will bring hot water in a lordly can. I, too, will dress.... But meantime, here are the outlines:

"Farrell knocked in early this morning. He was agitated and he perspired. He wished to see you at once. I pointed out that it was impossible and, as they say in examinations, gave reasons for my answer. Hearing it, he showed a disposition to shake at the knees and cling to the furniture. When he went on to discover that I might do in your place, and the furniture's place, and started clinging to me—well, I struck. I pointed out that he was apparently sound in wind and limb, inquired if he owed money, and having his assurance to the contrary, suggested that he should pull himself together and copy the Village Blacksmith.

"While we were arguing it, the Professor butted in. I'll do him the justice to say he wasn't perspiring. But he, too, was in the devil of a hurry to interview you. So I had to play band as before.

"The position was really rather funny. There, by the door, was the Professor, asking questions hard, and seemingly unaware that Farrell was anywhere in the room. Here was I, playing faithful Gelert life-size, but pretty warily, covering Farrell—who, for aught I knew, had gone to earth under the sofa. I couldn't hear him breathing—and he's pretty stertorous, as a rule.

"I kept a pretty straight eye on the Professor, somehow, and told him the facts—that you had sent the money ('Yes, I know,' said he: 'I got it before leaving Biarritz'): that you had actually gone to that health-resort in search of him. ('Good God!' said he. 'That's like old Roddy'—or some words to that effect. You wouldn't let me repeat 'em, just now.) Then he started telling me about this letter he'd posted at Biarritz, and that it should have arrived, by rights. 'Well, it hasn't,' said I, feeling pretty inhospitable for not asking him to sit down and have a drink.... But, you see, I wasn't certain he wouldn't sit down somewhere on top of Farrell.... 'Think he'll be home tonight?' asked the Professor. 'That's what I'm allowing, in the circumstances,' said I. '—But you owe him some apology, you know, because you've led him the devil of a dance.' 'Don't I realise *that!*' says he, like a man worried and much affected. 'We'll call around to-night, on the chance of his turning up to forgive us. Come along, Farrell!' says he.

"I whipped about; and there was Farrell, seated in that chair of yours, bolt upright, smirking as foolish as a wet-nurse at a christening! I couldn't have believed my eyes.... But there it was—and after what I'd been listening to, five minutes before!

"As I'm describing it, it staggered me—and the more when the Professor, looking past me, said, 'If you're ready, Farrell?' and Farrell stood up, smiling and ready, and moved to join him. But I kept what face I could.

"'You're going to look in again, you two?' I asked. The Professor said 'Yes, on the chance that Roddy may turn up'; and he looked at Farrell; and Farrell blinked and said, 'Yes, we owe him an explanation, of course.'

"'Well,' said I,' you'll be lucky if he don't throw you both downstairs for a pair of knockabout artists astray. I've a sense of humour that can stretch some distance, and with the permission of our kind friends in front this matinee performance will be repeated to-night, when Otty's sense of humour will gape for it, no doubt, after being stretched to the Pyrenees and back.'

"The Professor motioned Farrell out to the staircase. Then he came forward to me and said, pretty low and serious, 'You're a good boy, Jimmy. You're so good a boy that I want you to keep out of this. If Roddy turns up to-night, tell him that my man's for Wimbledon, safe and sound. On second thoughts, we won't bother a tired man, to-night, with any excuses or apologies. By to-morrow he will probably have had my letter, and will understand. He may or may not decide to show it to you. I hope he won't. I hope you'll let us see him alone to-morrow. Good-bye.'

"—Now what do you make of that?" demanded Jimmy helplessly.

"I make it out to be no jest, but pretty serious," said I. "But luckily Farrell's located at Wimbledon. Where's Jack?" I asked.

"Don't know," answered Jimmy.

"I'm tired enough for this night, anyhow," said I. "And here's Jephson.—'Evening, Jephson."

Jephson came in with a can in one hand and in the other a tray with a telegram upon it.

"Good evening, Sir Roderick! Glad to see you safe home, sir," said Jephson. "Telegram just delivered at the Lodge for Mr. Collingwood."

"For me?" said Jimmy. "I've backed nothing to-day. Been too busy."

He tore upon the envelope, read the message, and after a pause handed it to me, whistling softly. It had been handed in at the Docks Station, Liverpool, and it ran—

"Tell O. that F. and I sail to-night New York S.S. *Emania*.

"Foe."

NIGHT THE TWELFTH
THE "EMANIA"

I am going to spin the next stretch of this yarn—and maybe the next after it—in my own way. You will wonder how I happened by certain scraps of information: but you will understand before we come to the end.

It comes mainly from later report, but partly from documents which I have been too busy, of late, to sift. Here they are, all mixed: and I choose one only out of the heap—and that a passage which doesn't help the actual story much, though it may help the understanding of it. It occurs in a letter of Foe's written at sea and posted from New York—

"She had been reading a magazine, borrowed from the ship's library, and when she left me, she left it lying beside her deck-chair. The wind ruffled its pages and threatened to tear them: so I picked the thing up, and was about to close it, and to stow it behind her cushion, when a story-title caught my eye and agreeably whetted my curiosity. It was 'The Head Hunter.'

"I don't care greatly for short stories. Fiction as a rule bores me in inverse proportion to its length—which seems a paradox and liable to be reduced to the absurd by any moderately expert logician. Yet you will find it experimentally true of five readers out of six.... Moreover the yarn had little or nothing to do with real head-hunting—except in its preamble. I soon glanced at the end, and had no further use for the story.

"But I turned my attention back to the preamble and reread it twice. The fellow, an American, has a queer cocky irregular style: but he can write when he chooses: and in one shot he so fairly hit me between wind and water that I had to steal the book, carry it down to my cabin and copy out the passage for your benefit.... Yes, for yours: because it conveys something I've been wanting you to understand about this chase of mine, something I couldn't have put into words though I'd tried for a month. I enclose it herewith....

"When I had finished my copying, I took the thing back, meaning to slip it under Miss Denistoun's cushion. But she had returned to her chair, and so I was caught red-handed. 'So it was you?' said she. 'What have you been doing with my magazine?' 'Skimming it,' said I—which was true enough, literally, but I didn't manage it very well. 'Did you find anything to interest you specially?' she asked. 'Well, yes,' I admitted;' I picked it up and lit on something that promised well: but the story came to nothing.' She gave me a glance and I felt sure she had spotted my awkwardness and was going to pursue the catechism. But she didn't. To my relief she harked back to our previous talk. At tea-time, however, she remembered to take the magazine away with her.... It has not yet been returned to store...."

(ENCLOSURE)

"'Particularly during my stay in Mindanao had I been fascinated and attracted by that delightfully original tribe of heathen known as the head-hunters. Those grim, flinty, relentless little men, never seen, but chilling the warmest noonday by the subtle terror of their concealed presence, paralleling the trail of their prey through unmapped forests, across perilous mountain-tops, adown bottomless chasms, into uninhabitable jungles, always near, with the inevitable hand of death uplifted, betraying their pursuits only by such signs as a beast or a bird or a gliding serpent might make—a twig crackling in the awful sweat-soaked night, a drench of dew showering from the screening foliage of a giant tree, a whisper at even from the rushes of a water-level—a hint of death for every mile and every hour—they amused me greatly, those little fellows of one idea.'"

You observe that a lady has come into the story at last, as she was bound to do. (You will hear of another and a very different one by and by.) It is not my fault that she enters it so late—I tell of things as they occurred—though a clever writer would have dragged her in long before this. I wish to God I hadn't to bring her into it at all. I slipped out her surname just now....

It was through being a friend of mine that she comes into it. Constantia Denistoun and I had ridden ponies, tickled for trout, bird-nested, tumbled off trees, out of duck-punts, through forbidden ice, and into every form of juvenile disgrace, together as boy and girl. Her father and mine had been college friends, and (I believe) had both fallen in love with my mother, at a College ball, and my father won—but all on an understanding of honourable combat. Denistoun set out to travel, quite in the traditional way of the Rejected One. He was a Yorkshire squire with plenty of money, and could afford the prescribed cure. He travelled as far as to Virginia, U.S.A., where he halted, and wooed and won the heiress of a wide estate of cotton and tobacco and a great Palladian house, all devastated and ruined by the War, in which her father had fallen, one of Lee's pet leaders of cavalry.... Yes, I know it sounds like a tale out of Ouida: but such things happen, and this thing happened.... Denistoun scaled the twenty steps of the Ionic portico, cleft his way through the cobwebs and briers that were living and dying for

Dixie, kicked over the grand piano that Dinah's duster still reverentially spared, and carried off the enchanted Princess across the seas to Yorkshire: where in due course she bore him a daughter, Constantia, and, some years later, a son who eventually came into the property but doesn't come into the story.

In the meantime it had happened that *I* saw the light.... My mother died, a year later: and after seven years of widowhood my father married again. My sister Sally—the recipient of those long letters you see me inditing o' nights—is my step-sister, and an adored one at that.

There you have the family history, or enough of it. The old friendship between my father and Squire Denistoun had never been broken; and now that death had taken away the last excuse for a rivalry which had been felt but to be renounced, Constantia and I— unconscious brats—shared holidays, as it chanced at my home or hers, in nefarious poaching beside Avon or in gallops between her northern moors and the sea.

That is all, or almost all. I have to add that, having fallen into most scrapes with her, I ended by proposing one in which she gently but decisively declined to share the risk.... I am inclined to think that, having been so frank with her, and so frequent, in confidences about others to whom my heart was lost, she may have missed the bloom on the recital.... But there it was; and that's that, as they say.

I accused her at the time of a priggish, unnatural craving for things of the intellect. All my excuse was that at a certain time of her life she took a sudden turn for reading and setting queer new values on things. But she was always a sportswoman, a woman of the open air, and—here's the point—always knowledgeable with animals and always beloved by them, but always (as it seemed to me) inclined to be severe and disciplinary. To a lean pack she was Diana; they fawned behind her for no pay but hope of her word to let slip. But she would beat them off the piled platter, and from a fed lap-dog she could scarcely restrain her hands. If you think this hasn't to do with the story, I can only assure you that it has.

One thing more—She had met Foe; for the first time at a luncheon-party in my rooms at Cambridge, in May Week; a second time, it may be, at a May Week ball—but that wouldn't count, for she danced divinely and Foe couldn't compete for nuts. She may have met him once or twice afterwards, in London. It's not likely.

Anyhow (as she has told me since) she recognised him at once when he turned up on the *Emania*.

She and her mother were bound out to visit some friends at Washington, thence to fare South and stay a while with a cousin who held the old homestead in which her mother retained some sort of dower share.

Thus she recognised Foe as soon as he appeared on deck.

But he did not appear on deck until the *Emania* was well out from Queenstown; having made sure that Farrell didn't bolt there. The two—need I tell it?—had not taken passage in collusion. Farrell was escaping, Foe on his trail. But Foe had no idea of any dramatic surprise on board. Having made sure of his man, he just took a remnant first-class berth at the last moment, turned in, and went to sleep.

In all their commerce (you will have begun to remark) Foe and Farrell were apt to yield, at intervals, to an abandonment of weariness, but so that they alternated, the exhaustion of one seeming ever to double the other's fever. Foe sought his bunk and lay there like a log. Farrell, after the first shock of reading his pursuer's name in the Passengers' Book—where it sprang to his eyes fair and square—fell to haunting the passage-way, low down in the vessel, on which one dreadful door refused to open. His terror of it so preoccupied him that he forgot to feel sea-sick. But the steward of those nether regions marked him, by the electric lamps, as a lurking passenger to be watched; and wondered who, at that depth in the ship, could be carrying valuables to tempt a middle-aged gentleman who (if looks were any guide) ought to be up and losing money to the regular card-sharpers.

It was not until the second day out, and pretty late in the afternoon, that Foe emerged from his cabin, neatly dressed and hale. (Unlike some Professors I have known, Jack kept his clothes brushed and his hair cut.) As he opened his door his ear caught a slight shuffling sound; whereupon he smiled and stepped quickly down the passage to the turn of the companion way.

"No hurry, Farrell!" he called; and Farrell, arrested, turned slowly about on the stair. "Man, you're like the swain in Thackeray:"

> Although I enter not,
> Yet round about the spot
> Oft-times I hover—

"Solicitous, were you?—thought I might be sea-sick?"

"I was wondering," Farrell stammered. "Seeing that you didn't turn up at meals—"

(Here I must read you a queer remark from the letter in which Jack reported this encounter. Here's the extract:—)

"Do you know, Roddy, that silly simple answer gave me half a fright for a moment, or a fright for half a moment—I forget which.... What I had to remember then was my discovery that I had my second keyboard in reserve and could pull certain stops out of him at will.... But seriously, I wouldn't, without that power, back myself in this experiment against a man who obstinately persisted in forgiving. It came on me with a flash—and I offer this tribute to the Christian religion."

Foe's answer was, "Very kind of you. As a fact, I have been subsisting on hard biscuit and weak whisky-and-water: though I'm an excellent sailor, as they say.... It's a diet that suits me when I'm working hard."

"Working?" exclaimed Farrell. "What? Head-work, d'you mean?... Doctor, this is the best news you could have told me. If only I could know that you were picking up your interests—getting back to yourself—"

Foe took him by the arm. "It's no good, unfortunately," he answered. "Come up on deck, and I'll tell you."

On deck he repeated, "It's no good. I've been hard at it, working on my memory, trying to sketch out a kind of monograph—summary of conclusions—salvage from the wreck. But it won't do. It was an edifice to be built up on data, bit by bit, like an atoll.... Ever seen a coral reef, by the way? We'll inspect one—many perhaps—on our travels.... I'd burn in the pit rather than smatter out popular guess-work. Yes, all personal pride apart, I couldn't do it. But however badly I set down conclusions, they've all rested on data, they've all grown up on data, and I haven't the data.... I wrote out half a dozen pages and then asked myself, 'What would *you* say if a man came along professing to have made this discovery? You'd demand his evidence, and you'd be right. Of course you'd be right. And if he didn't produce it, you'd call him a quack. Right again.'... From this personal point of view, to be sure, I might take this sorry way out—print my conclusions, and anticipate the demand for evidence by throwing myself overboard.... In the dim and distant future some fellow might strike the lost path, take the pains that I've taken, work out the theory, yes, and (it's even possible) be generous enough to add that, by some freak of guessing, in the year 1907, a certain Dr. John Foe, of whom nothing further is known, did, in unscientific fashion, hit on the truth, or a part of the truth. Oh, damn! *Why* should I burn in the pit, or throw myself overboard, or go down to the shades for a quack, because a thing like you has crawled out of the Tottenham Court Road.... Eh? Well, I won't, anyhow: and so you see how it is, and how it's going to be."

Farrell leaned against the rail, and held to a boat's davit, while his gaze wandered vaguely out over the Atlantic as if it would capture some wireless message. ("I knew how it would be," adds Foe in his letter reporting this talk. "He was going to try the forgive-and-forget with me: but by this time I was sure of myself.")

"Listen to me, Doctor," Farrell began. "Listen to me, for God's pity! I didn't get off at Queenstown, though I knew you were on board—"

"No use if you had," put in Foe. "You don't think I had overlooked that possibility, do you?"

"Well, I didn't, anyway," was the answer. "And I'll tell you why. Honest I will.… We're both here and bound for America, ain't we? And, from what I've heard, there's no such expensive, bright, up-to-date laboratories—if that's the way to pronounce it—as you'll find in the States, in every walk of Science. Now, I never meant you an injury, Doctor; but I did you one—that I freely own.… What I say is, if money can make any amends, and if there's an outfit for science to be found in the States to your mind, why, I'll improve on it, sir. And I'm not saying it, as you might suppose, under any threat, but because I've been thinking it out and I mean it. I'm a childless man—"

Foe cut him short here. "My only trouble with you, Farrell," said he, "is that you may reach your grave without understanding. If I thought that wasn't preventible somehow, it would save me trouble to wring your neck here and now and throw you overboard. As it is—"

But, as it was, along the deck just then came Constantia Denistoun, with her mother leaning on her arm and a maid following. She recognised Foe and halted.

"Why, good Heavens!… and I'd no idea that you were on the *Emania*," said she. "Mother, this is Mr. Foe—Roddy's friend, you know.… Or ought I to call you Doctor, or Professor, or what?… You weren't anything of that sort anyhow, when we met— how many years ago? at Cambridge."

—That, or to that effect.… Constantia told me afterwards that she didn't remember throwing more than a glance at Farrell, whom she took, very pardonably, to be a chance acquaintance from the smoking-room, picked up as such acquaintances are picked up on ship-board. And Farrell stood back a couple of paces. To do him justice, he was in no wise a thruster.

"It's odd," she went on, "that we haven't run across one another until this moment. What's your business, over yonder? if that's not a rude question."

"It's a natural one, anyhow," Foe answered. "My business? Well, it has been suggested to me that a trip in the States, to see what they're doing in the way of scientific outfit and, maybe, get hints for a new laboratory, might not be waste of time."

"Yes, I know; I've heard," she said softly. "It's splendid to find you taking it like this... picking up the pieces, eh?... I wonder if"—she hesitated—"if I might ask you some questions? ... Just as much as you choose to tell: but something to put into a letter to our Roddy, you know. Any news of you will be honey to him.... You'll be writing from New York, of course. But one man doesn't tell another that he's looking brave and well; and yet that's often what the other may be most wanting to know."

Foe was touched (so he's told me). He said some ordinary thing that tried to show he was grateful, and Constantia and her mother passed on. He had not introduced Farrell.

Constantia told me most of the rest, some months later, pouring tea for me in her flat. There is not much in it. She said that she had taken very little account of Jack's companion; had just reckoned him up for a chance idler in his company—"a sort of super-commercial traveller"; so she described him; "not at all bad-looking though."

She went on to tell that she had been mildly surprised to see them at dinner, seated together; further surprised and even intrigued, to see them at breakfast together, next morning.

"Later," said she, "I asked him, 'Who's your friend that you didn't introduce yesterday?' 'Well,' said Dr. Foe, 'I didn't introduce him because I thought you mightn't like it. He's rather an outsider. His name's Farrell.' 'Farrell,' I said—'But isn't that—wasn't he—?' 'Yes, he is, and he was,' Dr. Foe told me very gravely. 'That's just it.' I couldn't help asking how, after what had happened, they came to be travelling in company. 'That's the funny part of it,' was the answer; 'he's trying to make some kind of—well, of a reparation.' I thought better of Dr. Foe, Roddy.... It seems so *mean*, somehow, that after what you've told me, Dr. Foe should be-what shall I say?—accepting this reparation from a man who happens to be rich!"

Constantia repeated this, in effect, some two or three nights later. We had danced through a waltz together and agreed to sit out another. We sat it out, under a palm. It was somewhere in the immediate neighbourhood of Queen's Gate, and a fashionable band, tired of modernist tunes, was throbbing out the old *Wiener Blatter*.... If Constantia remembered that sacred tune, she gave no sign of it.

"I thought better—somehow—of your friend," said Constantia.

I gave her a sort of guessing look. "You may take it from me, Con," I said, "that the trouble's not there. I'm worried about Jack. I haven't heard from him for months. But he's not of that make, whatever he is."

"Are you sure?" she asked. "I feel that I'd like to know. If you are right, why were he and this Mr. Farrell such close friends?"

"Farrell's pretty impossible, I agree," said I.

Constantia opened her fan and snapped it. "Impossible?" said she. "Well, I don't know…. Dr. Foe introduced him, later on… and what do you think Mamma said? She said that she had supposed them at first sight to be relatives. There was a trick about the eyes and the corner of the brow…. You are quite sure," she added irrelevantly, "that Dr.—that your friend—would be above—?"

"I swear to you, Con," I assured her. "I know Jack Foe inside and out."

She had opened her fan again very deliberately; and as deliberately she closed it.

"No man ever knew that of a man," she said; "nor no woman either. … You're a rotter, Roddy—but you're rather a dear."

NIGHT THE THIRTEENTH
ESCAPE

Somewhere in the bustle of landing and scrimmage past the Customs, Miss Denistoun lost sight of the two travellers; and with that, for a time, she goes out of the story.

You may almost put it that for a time they do the same. At all events for the next few weeks the record keeps a very slight hold on them and their doings. Jack knew, you see, that—though not a disapproving sort, as a rule, and in those days (though you children will hardly believe it) inclined to like my friends the better for doing what they jolly well pleased—I barred this vendetta-game of his, and would have called him off if I could. Folk were a bit more squeamish, if you remember, in those dear old pre-War days.

But please note *this*, for it is a part of his story. Jack wrote seldom, having a sense that I didn't want to hear. When he did write, however, he was liable at any time to break away from the light, half-jesting, half-defiant tone which he had purposely chosen to cover our disagreement, and to give me a sentence or two, or even a page, of cold-blooded confession. It may have been that his purpose, at that point, suddenly absorbed him, sucked him under. It may have been that his fixed idea had begun to spread like a disease over his other sensibilities, hardening and deadening the tissue, so that he did this kind of thing unconsciously. It may have been both. You shall judge before we have finished.

I will give you just one specimen. It occurs in the very first letter addressed from America. He and Farrell had spent five days in New York:

"I am going to ease the chain—to run it out several lengths, in fact. I shall still keep pretty close in attendance on the patient, but my professional visits will be rarer. A new and more strenuous course of treatment requires these holidays, if his nerves are not to break down under it.

"The suggestion, after all, came from him, and I am merely improving on it.... This continent has started a small heat-wave—the first of the summer. Now Farrell, who perspires freely, tells me that he doesn't mind any amount of heat, so that it isn't accompanied by noise: but noise and heat combined drive him crazy. I had myself noted that while the tall buildings here excited no curiosity in him, he acted as the veriest rubberneck under the clang and roar of the overhead trains; and the din of Broadway, he confessed, gave him vertigo after the soft tide of traffic that moves broad and full— 'strong without rage, without o'erflowing full'—down Tottenham Court Road, embanked with antique furniture or colourable imitations.

"He made this confession to me in the *entr'acte* of a silly vaudeville, to witness which we had been carried by an elevator some sixteen storeys and landed on a roof crowded with palms and funny people behaving like millionaires. In the *entr'acte* the band sank its blare suddenly to a sort of 'Home, Sweet Home' adagio, and after a minute of it Farrell put up a hand, covering his eyes, and I saw the tears welling—yes, positively—between his fingers. He's sentimental, of course.

"I asked what was the matter? He turned me a face like poor Susan's when at the thrush's song she beheld:"

> Bright volumes of vapour through Lothbury glide
> And a river flow on through the vale of Cheapside.

He said pitiably that he wanted—that he wanted very much—to go home; and gave as his reason that New York was too noisy for him.... A sudden notion took me at this. 'If that's the trouble,' I answered, 'one voice in this city shall cease its small contribution to the din.... We will try,' I said, 'the sedative of silence.'

"For three days now I have been applying this treatment. At breakfast, luncheon, dinner; in the street, at the theatre; I sit or walk with him, saying never a word, silent as a shadow. He desires nothing so little, I need not tell you. In the infernal din of this town he looks at me and would sell his soul for the sound of an English voice—even his worst enemy's. It is torture, and he will break down if I don't give him a holiday. The curious part of it is that, under this twist of the screw, he has apparently found some resource of pluck. He doesn't entreat, though it is killing him with quite curious rapidity. I must give him a holiday to-morrow."

I piece it out from later letters that from New York they harked out and harked back, to and from various excursions—quite ordinary ones. I might, if it were worth while, construct the itinerary; but it would take a lot of useless labour and yield nothing of importance. If Farrell, under this careful slackness of pursuit, had made a bolt for Texas or Alaska, the chronicle just here might be worth reciting. But he didn't, and it isn't. Buffalo—Long Island—Newport—and, in one of Jack's letters, Chicago for farthest West— occur in a miz-maze fashion. It is obvious to me that during these months

Farrell, kept on the run, ran like a hare (and a pretty tame one); that twice or thrice he headed back for New York, and was headed off.

I passed over each letter, as it came, to Jimmy, It was over some later letter, pretty much like the one I've just read to you, that Jimmy, frowning thoughtfully, put the sudden question, "I say, Otty, are we fond enough of him to start on another wild-goose chase?—to America this time, and together?"

"Jack's my best friend, of course," I answered after a moment. "You don't tell me—" and here I broke off, for he was eyeing me queerly.

"The Professor is, or was, a pretty good friend of mine," said he. "But you hesitated a moment. Why?... Oh, you needn't answer: I'll tell you. When I asked, 'Are you so fond of him?' for a moment—just for a flash— you hadn't Jack Foe in your mind, but Farrell."

"Well, that's true," I owned. "I'm pretty angry with Jack: he's playing it outside the touch-line, in my opinion. Except that I detest cruelty, Farrell's nothing to me, of course."

"I wonder," Jimmy mused. "Sometimes, when I'm thinking over this affair—but let us confine ourselves to the Professor. He's in some danger, if you think *that* worth the journey. They shoot pretty quick in the States, and they don't value human life a bit as we value it in England: or so I've always heard. If it's true—and it would be rather interesting to run across and find this out for oneself—one of these days Farrell will be pushed outside *his* touch-line—outside the British conventions in which he lives and moves and has his poor being—and a second later the Professor will get six pellets of lead pumped into him."

"Oh, as for that," said I, "Jack must look after himself, as he's well able to. When a man takes to head-hunting, it's no job for his friends to save him risks."

"Glad you look at it so," said Jimmy. "Then, so far as the Professor's concerned, it's from himself we're not protecting him, just now?"

"Or from the self which is not himself," I suggested.

"That's better," Jimmy agreed, and again fell a-musing. "Sometimes I think we might get closer to it yet". . . But he did not supply the definition. After half-a-minute's brooding he woke up, as it were, with a start. "Could you sail this next week?" he asked.

Well, we sailed, five days later; and there is no need to say more of this trip than that it panned out a fiasco worse than my first. At New York we beat up the police; and, later on, worried Mulberry Street and the great detective service for which the city is famous. Police and detectives availed us nothing. I knew that by the same mail which brought his latest letter to me, Foe had drawn £600 on Norgate; and Norgate had dispatched the money without delay, five days ahead of us. The address was a hotel at the then fashionable end of Third Avenue. There we found their names on the register. Plain sailing enough. Farrell had left, as we calculated (the detectives helping us), on the day the money presumably arrived, and at about six in the evening; Foe some fifteen or sixteen hours later. And, with that, we were up against a wall. Not a trace could be discovered of either from the moment he had walked out of the hotel. Farrell, having paid his bill, had walked out, carrying a small handbag (or 'grip,' as the porter termed it), leaving a portmanteau behind, with word that he would return next day and fetch it. We were allowed to examine the portmanteau. It contained some shirts and collars and two suits of clothes, but no clue whatever—not a scrap of paper in any of the pockets. Foe had departed leisurably next morning, with his slight baggage.

Our detective (to do him justice) did his best to earn his money. He carefully traced out and documented the movements of the two travellers from one to another of the various addresses I was able to supply: and he handed in a report, which attested not only his calligraphy but a high degree of professional zeal. It corresponded with everything I knew already and decorated it with details which could only have been accumulated by conscientious research. They tallied with—they corroborated—they substantiated—they touched up—the bald facts we already knew. But they did not advance us one foot beyond the portals of the Flaxman Building Hotel, out of which Farrell and Foe had walked, at fifteen hours' interval, and walked straight into vacancy.

In short, Jimmy and I sailed for home, a fortnight later, utterly beaten.

Now I'm telling the story in my own way. A novelist, who knew how to work it, would (I'm pretty sure) keep up the mystery just about here. But I'm going to put in what happened, though I didn't hear about it until two years later.

What happened was that, one evening, Jack drove Farrell too far, and over a trifle. Without knowing it, too, he had been teaching Farrell to learn cunning. They were back in New York and (it seems almost too silly to repeat) seated in a restaurant, ordering dinner. Jack held the *carte du jour*: the waiter was at his elbow; Farrell sat opposite, waiting. For some twenty-four hours—that is, since their return to New York City—Jack had chosen to be talkative. Farrell was even encouraged to hope that he had broken the spell of his hatred, and that the next boat for England might carry them home in company and forgiving. Just then the devil put it into Jack to resume his torture. He laid down the card and sat silent, the waiter still at his elbow. "Well, what shall it be?" asked Farrell, a trifle faintly. Jack, like the Tar-Baby, kept on saying nothing. The waiter looked about him, and fetched back his attention politely. "What shall it be?" Farrell repeated. Then, as Jack stared quietly at the table, not answering, "Go and attend to the next table," said he to the man. "You can come back in three minutes." The waiter went. "Now," said Farrell, laying down the napkin he had unfolded, "are you going to speak?"

Foe picked up the card again and studied it.

"Yes or no, damn you?" demanded Farrell. "Here and now I'll have an end to this monkeying—Yes, or no?" he cried explosively.

Foe pointed a finger at the chair from which Farrell had sprung up.

"I won't!" protested Farrell, and wrenched himself away. "Here's the end of it, and I'm shut of you!"

He dragged himself to the door. Foe, still studying the card through his glasses, did not even trouble to throw a glance after him. Once in the street, Farrell felt his chain broken: he hailed a cab, and was driven off to his hotel. There he packed, paid his bill, and vanished with his grip into the night, leaving his portmanteau behind with a word that he would return for it.

Foe had taught him cunning.

He bethought him of Renton, an old foreman of his; a highly intelligent fellow, who had come out to New York, some years before, to better himself, and had so far succeeded that he now controlled and practically owned a mammoth furnishing emporium—The Home Circle Store— in Twenty-Third Street. Farrell was pretty sure of the address; because Renton, who had long since taken out his papers of naturalisation, regularly remembered his old employer on Thanksgiving Day and sent him a report of his prosperity, mixed up with no little sentiment. To this Farrell had for some years responded with a note of his good wishes, cordial, but brief and businesslike. Of late, however, this acknowledgment, though still punctual, had tended to express itself in the form of a Christmas-card.

Farrell confirmed his recollection of the address by checking it in the Telephone Book, and paid a call on the Home Circle Store next afternoon, while Foe was enjoying a siesta in that state of lassitude which (as I've told you) almost always in one or other of the men followed their crises of animosity.

Renton was unaffectedly glad to see Farrell. "Well, Mr. Farrell," he said, as they shook hands, "well, *sir!* If this isn't a sight for sore eyes! And—when I've been meaning, every fall, to step across home and see your luck—to think that it should be you first dropping in upon me!" He rushed Farrell up and down elevators, over floor after floor of his great establishment, perspiring (for the afternoon was hot), swelling with hospitality and pardonable pride. "And when we've done, sir, I must take you to my little place up town and make you acquainted with Mrs. Renton. She's not by any means the least part of my luck, sir. She'll be all over it when I present you, having so often heard tell—You've aged, Mr. Farrell! And yet, in a way, you haven't.... You were putting on waist when I saw you last, and now you're what-one-might-call in good condition—almost thin. Yes, sir, I heard about your poor lady… I wrote about it, if you remember. Sudden, as I understand?… But if you look at it in one way, that's often for the best: and in the midst of life— You'll be taking dinner with us. That's understood."

"Look here, Ned," Farrell interrupted. "It's done me good to shake you by the hand and see you so flourishing. But I've looked you up because— well, because I'm in a tight place, and I wonder if you could anyways help."

"Eh?" Renton pulled up and looked at him shrewdly. "What's wrong? Nothing to do with the old firm, now, surely?… I get the London *Times* sent over, and your last Shareholders' Meeting was a perfect Hallelujah Chorus. Why, you're quoted—"

Now you'll know Farrell, by this time, for a man of his class—and a pretty good class it is, in England, when all's said and done; for a man of the sort that resents a suspicion on his business about as quickly as he'd resent one on his private and domestic honour— perhaps even a trifle more smartly. His business, in short, *is* the first home and hearth of his honour. So Farrell cut in, very quick and hot,—

"If my business were only twice as solid as yours, Ned Renton, I might be worrying you about it.... There, don't take me amiss! … I've come to trouble you about myself. Fact is, I'm in a hole. There's a man after me; and I want you to get me out of this place pretty quick and without drawing any attention more than you can avoid."

"O-oh!" said Renton, rubbing his chin, and looking serious. "And what about the lady?"

"There's no woman in this," Farrell assured him. "No, Ned; nor the trace of one."

"That's curious," said Renton, still reflective. "You being a widower, I thought, maybe... But as between friends, you'll understand, I'm not asking."

"I'll tell you the gist of it later," said Farrell. "It started over politics."

"So?... We've a way with that trouble over here," said Renton. "Now you mention it, I'd read in the London *Times* that you were running for municipal government, and then somehow you seemed to fade out.... I wondered why.... Is that part of the story?"

Farrell answered that it was. They were seated in Renton's private office, and Renton picked up a small square block of wood from his desk. It looked like a paper-weight.

"I've a certain amount of—well, we'll call it influence—hereabouts, if any man happens to be troubling you," he suggested musingly, and glanced at Farrell. "But you're not taking it that way, I see."

Farrell nodded.

"You just want to be cleared out.... That's all right. You shall tell me all about it later, boss—any time that suits you." He handed the paperweight across to Farrell. "Ever come across that kind of wood?" he asked.

Farrell examined it. "Never," he answered. "It looks like mahogany—if 'tweren't for the colour. Dyed, is it?"

"Not a bit. I could show you with a chisel in two minutes.... But you're right. Mahogany it is, and cuts like mahogany.... I keep a high-class warehouse of stuff lower down-town, and there I'll show you a log of it, seven-by-four. It's from Costa Rica. Would you care to prospect?... I don't mind sharing secrets with the old firm, as you always dealt with me honourably and we're both growing old enough to remember old kindness."

"I'd make a holiday of it," said Farrell heartily, fingering the wood. "Comes from Costa Rica, eh?"

"There's not much of it going, even there," said Renton. "Not enough, I'm afraid, to start a fashionable craze. It was brought to me, as a sample, by an enterprising skipper from Puerto Limon, and I was going to send back a man with him, to prospect. ... But it's not detracting from his character to say that he can't tell mahogany from walnut with his finger-tips in the dark—as *you* could, boss. If it's a holiday you want, with a trifle of high cabinet-science thrown in, what about taking his place?"

"It's the loveliest stuff," said Farrell, rapt, fingering the wood delicately.

"Well, now, that makes me feel good, having my old master's word for it, that taught me all I know. Look at it sideways and catch the tints under the light. 'Opaline mahogany' we'll call it. Come down-town with me, and I'll show you the baulk of it. It don't grow big.... What about cash?"

"I've a plenty for the present," Farrell assured him. "Clearing's my only difficulty."

"You trust to me, and I'll oblige," said his old employee.

Farrell went back to his hotel that evening, paid his bill and walked out with his grip. At Renton's warehouse in the lower town he changed his dress for a workman's; was conveyed to the Quay by Renton, who shipped him aboard the lime-tramp. She carried him down to Puerto Limon; where the skipper took a holiday, and the pair struck farther down the coast on mule-back for a hundred miles or so, and then inland for the Mosquito village hard by which they were to find the grove of this mysterious purple hardwood. They found it—as Farrell had agreed with Renton in expecting—to be no forest, scarcely even a grove, but a mere patch, and the timber a "sport" though an exceedingly beautiful one. On their return to Limon Farrell wrote out a careful report. The wood was priceless. It deserved a new genius to design a new style of inlay for it. Given that, with the very pink of artists among cabinet-makers and a knowledgeable man to put the furniture on the market, a reasonable fortune was to be made. With skill it could be propagated: but for two generations and longer it must depend on its rarity. He added some suggestions for propagating it and wound up, "Turn these over, for what they are worth, to someone who understands this climate and is botanist as well as nurseryman. It won't profit you or me, Ned; and we've no children. Mr. Weekes has, though"—Weekes was the skipper—"and his grandchildren ought to have something to inherit. I'd hate to die and think that such stuff was being lost to the trade. But for the standing timber, anyway, there's only one word. *Buy*. Yours gratefully, P. Farrell."

When his report was written and signed, he handed it to Weekes. "We can mail this, if you approve," he said.

Weekes read it over and approved the document. "But I don't approve mailing it," he assured Farrell. "No, sirree: your boss has a name for playing straight, but we won't give him all that time and temptation. We'll go back and hand him this together—for you come into it, I guess, on some floor or other."

"No," said Farrell. "The report's as good as it promises; but I'm out of this job. The only favour you can do me is to help me shift down this coast—as far as Colon, for instance. And I owe it to Renton, of course, to mail this letter. With your knowledge of the boats and trains, you can get to New York along with it or even ahead of it."

"That's all very well, so far as it goes," said Weekes, thoughtfully; "and I see your point. But again, what about *you*?"

"Ah, to be sure," answered Farrell, pondering in his turn. "There's the risk of leaving me behind to chip in on you both. Well… You don't run any whalers from this port, do you?"

"Whalers?" Captain Weekes opened his eyes.

"I understand," Farrell explained, "that they keep out at sea for a considerable time…. No, and it wouldn't help your confidence if I told you that there's a man in New York—an Englishman like myself—hunting me for my life…. But see here. Of your knowledge find me a southward bound vessel that, once out, certainly won't make port for a fortnight. We'll mail this report from the Quay, and you can put me on board at the last moment, watch me waving farewells from the offing, and then hurry north as soon as you please."

Well, this, or something like it, was agreed upon; and here Farrell sails out of the story for ten months, a passenger on the schooner *Garcia*, bound for Colon.

BOOK III
THE RETRIEVE

NIGHT THE FOURTEENTH
SAN RAMON

I have never set eyes on the village of San Ramon, but I have heard it described by two men—by one of them in great detail—and their descriptions tally.

It is a village or townlet of two hundred houses or so. It lies about a third of the way down the coast of Peru, close over the sea. It has no harbour: a population of half-breeds—mestizos? Is that the word?—sprinkled with whitish cosmopolitans, and here and there a real white man. But these last, though they wear shoes and keep up among themselves a pretence to be the aristocracy of the place, have really resigned life for this anticipatory Paradise where they grow grey on remittance money, eating the lotus, drinking smoked Scotch in the hotel veranda, swapping stories, and—since they know one another all too well in this drowsy decline of their day—feebly and falsely pretending to one another what gallant knowing fellows they had been in its morning. As for their shoes, token of their caste, they usually wear them unlaced by day and not infrequently sleep in them at night. With the exception of Engelbaum, who keeps the hotel, the white citizens are unmarried. With the exception of Frau Engelbaum— aged sixty and stout at that—there are no white ladies in San Ramon.

And yet San Ramon is a Paradise. A tall mountain backs it. The Pacific kisses its feet. A spring bursting from the mountain, about four thousand feet up, has cut a gorge down which it tumbles in cascades to the beach and the salt water. Where the source leaps from the rock the vegetation begins, as you would expect. It widens and grows more luxuriant all the way down. The stream comes to a forty-foot waterfall between sheer rock curtained with creepers; whence it hurries down through plantations of banana, past San Ramon, which perches where it can, house by house, on shelves hidden in greenery. There it takes another great leap into a basin it has hollowed for itself in the steep-to beach.

We have come down by nature's route. Now we'll climb back by man's. A sort of stairway, broad-stepped, made of pebbles and pounded earth, mounts in fairly well engineered zigzags to the plateau above the lower fall, and in a straighter flight beside the gorge to the hotel which is the topmost building of San Ramon. Above that it becomes a gully curved by torrential rains; above that, zigzags again as a mule-track up to a pass in the mountains—and thereafter God knows whither. Connecting the lower zigzags (I need scarcely say) are short-cuts or slides made by the brown-footed children, who plunge down almost as steeply and quickly as the stream itself when the fortnightly fruit-steamer blows her siren beyond the point.

There is no harbour, you understand. The small steamer—by name the *P.M. Diaz*—drops anchor a short mile out in a half-protected roadstead, and discharges what she has to discharge, or lades what she has to lade, by boats. Her ladings during the banana-harvest are feverish, tumultuous, vociferous. Her ladings during the sleepy remainder of the year comprise canned meats, Scotch whisky, illustrated magazines, and plantation inspectors.

It was almost twelve months to a day—I am trying to tell the story to-night as a novelist would tell it, but without going beyond the material supplied to me—It was almost twelve months from the day Foe left the portico of the Flaxman Building Hotel, New York, that he stepped ashore on the beach below San Ramon and resigned his light suitcase to a herd of bare-legged boys who offered to carry it up to the hotel, but seemed likelier to dismember it on the way and share up the shreds. They took him, as a matter of course, for a plantation inspector, arrived in the off-season. He was the only passenger landed from the *P.M. Diaz*, which had dropped anchor comfortably, in perfect weather, but would sail in the morning. A light land-breeze blew off the mountains: but it passed over a mile of water before rippling the sea, which, inshore, lay as glass. The sunset from the Pacific lit up San Ramon above him, all terraced and embowered.

Halted there, gazing up and taking stock of this Paradise before scaling it, Foe could not be aware, though he might have guessed, that half a hundred embrasures in the climbing foliage hid field-glasses and telescopes of which he was the one and common focus. Up at the hotel, one idler said to another, "Will it be Morgansen this time, d'you think?" The other passed on the question to Engelbaum, who was so far the master of his guests that he had lazily commandeered the large telescope on the *galeria*, and without gainsay. "If it's old Morgansen," the second man added, "we might trot some way down the hill to wish him well. The day's cooling in."

"It's not Morgansen," announced Engelbaum. "A new man—thinnish—Oh, yes, but an inspector. You can tell these scientific men by their cut."

"Hope they haven't sacked old Morgansen," said the first idler. "He's been a bit of a scandal, these three years. But he knows about bananas more'n a banana would own to, even with a blush."

Half-way over the hill, on a packing-case in a bare veranda, sat a man who for three months had avoided the hotel and these loungers, and been given up by all of them (by some enviously) as a lost friend. A woman reclined—good old novelists' word—in a sort of deck-chair three paces away. The windows of the house stood wide, and showed rooms within carpetless, matless, swept if not garnished, with other packing-cases stacked about and labelled. There was even a label on the chair in which the woman reclined: but her skirt hid it.

When the whistle of the fruit-steamer had first sounded, out beyond the Point, and almost before the alert young population of San Ramon could tear down the pathway beside the bungalow's discreet garden, she had risen with a catch of the breath, taken up a pair of field-glasses and scanned the offing.

"It is she beyond a doubt," she had announced.

"What other could it be?" the man had answered, pretty lazily. "And that being so—"

Said the woman—I am trying to tell this in correct fashion—"Why are you so dull?—who, when the boat used to call, would snatch up the glasses and be no company for anyone until you had counted everything she discharged."

Farrell—oh! by the way it's about time I told you that the man was Farrell—Farrell looked at the woman. Farrell said:

No, the devil! I can't tell it the professional way, after all. There's the woman. Well, the woman was young, and fair to see, dark, well-bred, with a tinge of lemon, and descended pretty straight from the Incas—"instead of which" she preferred to call herself Mrs. M'Kay or M'Kie, having been caught and married in an unguarded moment by someone who had arrived in San Ramon to push a new brand of whisky and stayed to push it the wrong way. Since M'Kie's death—or M'Kay's—whichever it was—newcomers had to choose between Engelbaum's, on the summit, and the lady, an heiress in a small way, who played the guitar, half-way down the hill, but frowned on the drinking-habit.

Farrell, you will perceive, had chosen the better way, and had become a voluntary exile from Engelbaum's in consequence. That, or the exercise of running, had done him a power of good. Just now he was bronzed, spare, even inclining to gauntness. Twelve months before, he had shortened his whiskers, as a first step to disguise. Since then, and to please this woman, he had grown a beard which he kept short and trimmed to a point, naval fashion. It was straw-coloured, went well with his bronzed complexion and improved his appearance very considerably. It may be that this growth had encouraged the hair on his scalp or stimulated it by rivalry to renewed effort: more likely the play of sunshine and sea-breeze had done the trick between them; but anyhow Farrell now possessed a light mat of silky yellowish hair on the top of his head—as the nigger song has it, in the place where the wool ought to grow. Shoes, blue dungaree trousers and a striped shirt were his clothing—the shirt opened at the throat and to the second button, disclosing a V of naked chest as healthily tanned as his face. His face had thinned too. His eyes no longer bulged. They had receded well under the pent of his brow and, in receding, taken colour from its shadow.

"I am not dull, Santa," said Farrell. "I am only content and—well, a little bit regretful, and—well yes, again, the least bit lazy. But what does it matter? Ylario has gone down to the beach. He will send off word to the skipper that all this truck will be ready on the foreshore by five-thirty to-morrow. In good weather he never weighs before seven, and the weather is settled."

The woman, at one word of his, had turned and set down her glasses.

"Regretful?" She echoed it as a question, and followed it up with a question. "At what are you staring so hard?"

He lifted his eyes and met hers very steadily, earnestly. "At your shape, Santa," was his answer. "When your back is turned, I am always looking at you so."

"Regretfully?" she asked, mocking.

"As for the regret, you know what it is and must be. How can a man feel it different, when we leave this place to-morrow? Don't women feel that way towards places where they have been happy?"

She picked up the glasses again and set them with her gaze seaward before answering. Thus the shadow of her hands screened any emotion—if emotion there were—on her face.

"I have not been happy here, all the time," she answered softly, readjusting the glass, or pretending to. "Not by any means. San Ramon to me is a hole.... Yes," she went on deliberately, "I know well what you are going to say. I have *you*: but I want something more—something I have always wanted and, it seems to me, every woman always wants—something beyond the sky-line. In Sydney, now—"

"You'll find there's a sky-line waiting for you at Sydney," said Farrell; "as like to this one as two peas—and just as impossible to get beyond"—which mayn't seem very good grammar, but is how he said it. "Now to me a sky-line's a sky-line—just something to have you standing against."

"You shall have a kiss for that, *caballero*—in a moment," she purred, and slanted the binoculars down to bear on the beach. "Only one passenger," she announced.

"Usual inspector, no doubt," said Farrell, rolling a cigarette.

"Ye-es—by the look of him.... Oh, there's Ylario, all right, talking to the boatman!... He must be a stranger, I think—by the way he's staring up at the town."

"Ylario was bred and born here; of uncertain parents, to be sure—"

She laughed. "Foolish!... I meant the inspector, of course."

"What's he like?" asked Farrell. "Report."

She lowered the glass, twisted the screw of it idly, and returned to her hammock-chair, beside which she set it down on the veranda floor.

"Now I'll make a confession to you," she said, picking up her guitar and throwing her body back in the chair. "I love you," she said. "When you are close, and alone with me, my heart feels as if it could melt into yours.... No, don't get up: you shall have your kiss, in good time. But when you—what shall I say?—when you *all-white* men are all far off, or when many of you are together, I cannot well distinguish.... Ah, pardon me, beloved! Haven't you had that trouble with people of other races than your own—among a crowd of Japanese, say? And the shepherds on the mountains behind here—have you not wondered how they can know every sheep in a flock of many hundred?"

Farrell was on his feet by this time, and in something of a passion. "Am I, then," he stammered out; "—am I, then, so like any of the others, up at Engelbaum's?"

"Calm yourself, O beloved," said Santa, brushing her finger-nails, gipsy-wise and soft as butterflies, over, the strings of her guitar. "Calm yourself, and hearken. You are all the world to me, and you know it. Yet there is something—something I could explain to you better, maybe, if I knew English better… and yet I am not sure. … Let me try, however.… It always seems to me with you English, you Americans, you white-skinned men—with all the ones I have known—that the fault is not all mine when I find you alike just at first; that every one of you ought to be a man quite different from all other men; that you, of your race—yes, every one—were meant for something you have missed—were meant to be—Oh, what is the word?"

"'Distinguished?'" suggested Farrell, standing up. "I never was that, Santa—though, back in England, at one time, I had a notion to make some sort of a mark."

Santa let the neck of the guitar fall back against her breast and clasped her hands suddenly. "Yes, that is it;—to make your mark! Every woman who loves a man wants him to make his mark somehow, somewhere.… I cannot tell you why: but it is so."

Farrell took a turn on the veranda. "My dear," he said tenderly, coming back and halting before her, "do you realise that I am fifty years old?" She pressed her palms over her eyes. "You keep telling me that, and it hurts! Besides, you grow younger every day… and—and I cannot bear to hear you say it!" She lowered her hands and smiled up, but through tears.

"The men who find their way to San Ramon from my country or from the States," he went on, picking up the binoculars absently while his eyes sought the sky-line, "do not come in any hope of making their mark—not even plantation-inspectors." Farrell fumbled with the screw, adjusting the focus. "If that is why we are going to Sydney—"

"Whatever happens," declared Santa, "I will love you better anywhere than in San Ramon: and I have loved you well enough here! The men who come to San Ramon—pah! this for them!" She thrummed an air— *La Camisa de la Lola*—on the guitar and broke off with another small sound of scorn from her throat. "*That's* what suits them, and what all of them are worth!"

She brushed the strings again: and if Farrell made any sound at all, the buzz of them covered it. He had brought the glasses to bear on the beach.

Santa started to thrum on the lower strings. Farrell swung about suddenly, set the glasses down, and walked back into the dismantled house.

Now so far I have evidence for all I'm telling you. From this point for thirty seconds or so, I am going to guess what happened. Santa went on thrumming. She heard his footsteps on the bare floor as he went through the echoing, dismantled room behind her. She heard them on the brick of the broad passage which separated the living-rooms of the bungalow from its bed-chambers. She heard him lift the latch of the outer door. She heard the outer door shut behind him. Then she waited for his footsteps to sound again on the sunken pathway which ran downhill beside her patch of garden, hidden by the cactus fence—or rather, deep below it. "He is standing on the doorstep," she said to herself, "lighting a cigarette"; and then, "but he is a long while about it. This is strange." Still as her ear caught no sound of him, Santa sprang up and slipped, guitar in hand, to the outer door—the fence being too tall for her to over-pry, and moreover prickly. She opened the door and peeped out. There was no one down the pathway. There was no one up the pathway, which here, for some fifty or sixty yards, climbed straight, full in view. "And what on earth has become of him?" wondered Santa. "He did not go down—I should have heard him. But why should he go up? He has broken with those drinkers at Engelbaum's.... Besides, it is unbelievable that, in this short time, he should have vanished. ..."

So much for guesswork. Now I come back to the story as it was afterwards related to me.

Santa, standing there in the porch, guitar in hand and leaning forward over the rail which guarded a long flight of stone steps, heard a footfall on the road below—an ascending footfall. For a moment she mistook it for Farrell's: she believed she could distinguish Farrell's from any other man's: and so for a moment she stood mystified.

Then a man hove in view around the corner... not Farrell, but the newly-landed stranger she had spied through her binoculars—the presumed Inspector. His eyes were lifted as he calculated the new gradient ahead of him, and thus on the instant he caught sight of Santa aloft in the porch-way. Something held Santa's feet.

"Many pardons, *senora*," said the Stranger, halting a little before he came abreast of the stairway and lifting his hat. "But can you tell me if this path leads to the Hotel?"

Now Santa was confused and a little abashed—it may have been because in her haste she had forgotten to drape her head in her mantilla—a rite proper to be observed by Peruvian ladies before showing themselves out-of-doors. But she could not help smiling: the question being so absurd.

"Seeing, *sentor*, that there can be no other," she answered, with a small wave of the hand out and towards the gorge down which the river cascaded always so loudly that they both had unconsciously raised the pitch of their voices.

From the pathway above came the sound of stray stones dislodged under a heavy plunging tread; and there was Farrell striding down, with his hands in his trousers' pockets.

In the right pocket he carried a revolver, which he had picked up on his way through the house. His forefinger felt about its trigger.

He had recognised Foe through the glass. He had pelted up the path in the old sweating terror, making for the mountain as if driven, to call on it to cover him.

Close by Engelbaum's gate he overtook three small boys contending around a suit-case: the point being that all three could not demand reward for carrying so light a burden. If the owner were a fool, or generously inclined (which amounted to the same thing), two of the three might put in a colourable claim for services rendered.

In white countries one boy fights with another. In San Ramon as many as fifteen can fight indiscriminately, and the vanquished are weeded out by gradual process. Farrell shook the urchins apart, driving them for a moment from the suit-case as one would drive three wasps off a honey-pot.… It lay at his feet. Yes, he'd have recognised it anywhere, even without help of the half-effaced "J. F." painted on its canvas cover. It was a far-travelled piece of luggage, and much-enduring—What are those adjectives by which Homer is always calling Ulysses?… It bore many labels. One, with "Southampton" upon it, was apparently pretty recent… and another with "Waterloo."

He turned the case over while the boys eyed him, keeping their distance. His brain worked more and more clearly. . . Foe had returned to England, then, to pick up the trail. But how had he struck it?… There was only one way.… He had, of course, been obliged to send letters home from time to time—letters to his firm, to his bankers for money—instructions to pay his housekeeper— possibly a score of letters in all. Foe must have obtained possession of one and spotted the postmark on the Peruvian stamp. …

Of a sudden he realised his cowardice; and flushed, with shame and manhood together, there in the pathway.… This thing was no longer a duel. Three were in it now, and the third was Santa.… The old scare had caught him, surprised him, and he had run from recollected habit.… It had been base.… Why, of course, Santa made all the difference! He must go back to protect Santa.

At the thought of her he felt a second flush of shame sweep up in him, quite different from the first and quite horrible. The tide of it scorched his face as if flaying it. And so—if you'll understand—in the very moment of knowing himself twice vulnerable— no, ten times as vulnerable—this

Farrell, loving this woman, became a man: and three small ragamuffins stood about him and witnessed the outward process.

The outward process ended in his fishing out three *dineros* from his trouser pocket and bestowing one on each of them—twopence-halfpenny or thereabouts is a godsend to a juvenile in San Ramon. "There, little fools!" he said. "Take the stranger's bag along and don't quarrel any more. There is nothing in this world so silly as quarrelling."

With that he went back down the hill, and so came on Foe and on Santa, talking down to Foe from the balcony porch.

"Hallo, old man!" said Farrell, looking Foe straight in the eyes: and "Hallo!" answered Foe, looking Farrell straight in the eyes. Santa, gazing down from the rail, thought it strange that they did not shake hands, as Britons and Americans do when they met.

"I found three rascals," said Farrell easily, "scrapping for the honour of delivering a suit-case at Engelbaum's hotel—a suit-case that I recognised. I rescued it, and it is now safe in the porch. … Oh, by the way, though you seem to have made acquaintance, let me do the formal and introduce you to my wife. Santa, this is Doctor Foe, an old fellow-traveller."

Foe gave him one glance, shrewd and steady, before looking aloft and again raising his hat. The thrust did not penetrate Farrell's defence.

"It's awkward," said Farrell, "that we can't even offer you a bed. We're all packed up, ready to sail by the steamer to-morrow. Mrs. Farrell and I in fact are shifting quarters.… Staying?"

"No," said Foe imperturbably. "I shall be sailing to-morrow, too. … I just heard of this place, and thought I'd like to have a look at it before going on.… Shouldn't think of troubling you."

"Curious, how small the world is," went on Farrell in a level voice. "You won't mind my talking a bit in the old manner?… It sort of puts us back at the old ease, eh?… Well then, we can't offer to put you up. But if you don't mind a packing-case for a chair and another for a table—eh, Santa?"

"We shall be charmed," said Santa.

"You understand that it will be a picnic," added Farrell.

"My good sir!" protested Foe.

"Yes?… It will be better than Engelbaum's, any way. I don't mind promising," said Farrell. "We will talk over old times, and Santa shall play her guitar to us."

That is how the two men met.

The *P.M. Diaz* plied no farther than Callao. From Callao the Farrells, with their furniture, and Foe in company, worked down by coasters to Valparaiso.

Does any one of you remember the mystery of the *Eurotas*? which regularly for about four months occupied from an inch-and-a-half to four inches space in the newspapers. In 1909… pretty late in the year. She happened to be the first ship of a new line started between Valparaiso and Sydney, and her owners had so well boomed the adventure in the Press that, when she began to be reported as overdue, the public woke up and she became as interesting as a lost dog. She was of 12,000 tons, new, Clyde-built, well-found, and carried a mixed cargo, with about twenty passengers. Two vessels reported having passed her, about three hundred miles out. After that she had become as a ship that had never been.

In his casual way—for I must remind you that he and I had lost all trace of Foe and Farrell in New York—Jimmy lit on the next item of news.

Long before the *Eurotas* was posted as "missing," the newspapers published a list of her passengers. Jimmy, seizing on this, ran his eye down it, and let out the sort of cry with which he greets all news, good, bad, or indifferent.

"I say, Otty!—here it is, and what do you make of it?

—'The s.s. *Eurotas*…. List of Passengers.
"Mr. and Mrs. P. Farrell, San Ramon, Peru.
Professor J. Foe, of London….'"

And after that there was silence for four years. The bell at Lloyd's never rang to announce the arrival of the *Eurotas*. By Christmas her underwriters were paying up, and the newspapers had lost interest in her fate.

NIGHT THE FIFTEENTH
REDIVIVUS

About seven weeks later Norgate called on me with evidence that settled the last doubt: a letter from Foe, written from Valparaiso. It was brief enough. It merely announced that he was on the eve of sailing for Sydney and wished to have credit for £600 opened with the Bank of New South Wales. "I have booked a berth on the *Eurotas*," it concluded, "and go aboard to-night. She's a new ship, owned by a new line, of which you may or may not have heard—the 'Southern Cross Line.' We hear enough about it in this town, the Company having contrived to fall foul of the dock labour here. I don't know the rights or wrongs of it, but some sort of boycott is threatened. However, this sort of dispute usually gets itself settled at the last moment; and anyhow I shall get to Sydney by some means or other. So you may safely mail there. No need to cable. I have plenty of money for immediate purposes."

"What had I best do?" asked Norgate. "Lloyd's are about giving the *Eurotas* up."

"Cable out and make sure," said I. "If he calls at the Bank, he calls; and if he doesn't, there are no bones broken. *Something* has gone wrong with the ship; and in the mix-up he may easily have lost his ready cash and be landed at Sydney without a cent."

I should have told you that, about a fortnight before this, Jimmy had solved, or partially solved, the puzzle of that entry "Mr. and Mrs. P. Farrell" on the passenger-list. Jimmy had found a good girl, and as pretty almost as she was good, and yet imprudent enough to consent to marry him. This had the effect of rendering him at once and surprisingly prudent. As the poet puts it, "he had found out a flat for his fair," and as he himself put it, "We have heard the chimes at midnight, Master Shallow: but be-shrew me, we never thought of making my bank-manager one of the party, to break him in to our ways; the consequence being that Elinor's maid will have to stick a bedroom-suite priced five-pounds-ten, while the other domestics, unless dividends improve, sleep (poor souls, insecurely) upon bedsteads liable to be spirited from under them at any moment by a Hire System that knows no bowels.... By George!" sighed Jimmy. "If we hadn't let Farrell slip through our fingers! Do you know, Otty, I've an idea," he announced. "Why shouldn't I take the Tottenham Court Road to-morrow, visit Farrell's old place of business, and kill two birds with one stone?"

"It sounds a sporting proposition," I agreed, "though sketchily presented."

"Adumbrated," suggested Jimmy. "That's a good word. I found it in yesterday's *Observer*."

"Adumbrated, then," said I. "The Tottenham Court Road—"

"—*And* two birds with one stone. No moors for me this year: I'm back on the simple life and the catapult.... You just wait."

There really is no resisting Jimmy, nor ever will be. He went up the Tottenham Court Road next day, walked into Farrell's late place of business and demanded to see the General Manager; and—if you'll believe it— that dignitary was fetched amid a hush of awe. "I dropped in," explained Jimmy, "to see one of those cheap bedroom suites you advertise, in pickled walnut—or is it *marron glace?*— suitable for a house-parlourmaid. The fact is, I'm going to get married—well, you've guessed that—otherwise, of course, I shouldn't be here.... My intended wife—she's a Devonshire lady, by the way—from near Honiton. Anything wrong about Honiton?... No? I beg your pardon—I thought you smiled.... Well, as I was about to explain, my intended wife, coming as she does from near Honiton— that's where they make the lace—likes her servants to be comfortable: at least, so she says. Your late Managing Director, had he lived—" Here Jimmy made a pause.

"You knew our Mr. Farrell, sir?" asked the present Managing Director, sympathetically.

"He honoured me with his acquaintance. If he had lived," said Jimmy ... "But there!... By the way... that second marriage of his—wasn't it rather sudden? I understood him to be a confirmed widower."

"We know nothing about it, sir: nothing beyond what he conveyed in a letter to our Vice-Chairman. In fact, sir, during the last year or so of his life, when Mr. Farrell took his strange fancy for foreign parts, it seemed to us— well, it seemed to us that, in his strange condition of mind, anything might happen. To this day, sir, we haven't what you might call any certitude of his demise. It is not, up to this moment, legally proven—as they say. Our last letter from him was dated from far up the coast—from a place called San Ramon, which I understand to be in Peru. In it he announced that he was married again, and to a lady (as we gathered) of Peruvian descent. He added that he had never, previously to the time of writing or thereabouts, known complete happiness."

Jimmy brought back this information, having, on top of it, acquired a bedroom suite of painted deal. "And there," said he, "the matter must rest. Foe's gone, and Farrell's gone. Both decent, in their way; and both, but for foolish temper, alive now and hearty."

So it seemed to be, and the book to be closed. I mourned for Jack, yet not as I should have mourned for him a year or two before. Jimmy married and left me, and soon after I moved from our old quarters in the Temple to my present rooms in Jermyn Street.

Four years passed: and then, one fine morning, my door opened, and John Foe called me by name.

"Hallo, Roddy! How goes it?"

I jumped up, in a pretty bad scare. It was the voice that did it: for, my door making an angle with the window, and the day being sunny, he stood there against a strong light—sort of silhouette effect, as you might put it. And there was a something about him, thus gloomed—but we'll talk of that by and by. The voice was Jack Foe's, and none other.

"It's all right," he went on easily. "Pull yourself together. … It *is* the Ancient Mariner come home, but you needn't imitate the Pilot and fall down in a fit.… Where's the Pilot's Boy, by the way—young Jimmy Collingwood? You still keep Jephson, I see. … I happened on Jephson at your street-door, just returned from posting a letter. Jephson performed the holy Hermit very creditably: he raised his eyes and almost sat down on the doorstep and prayed where he did sit. 'Doctor Foe!' said Jephson. 'Good Lord, send may I never—!'—which amounts to a prayer, eh?… He let me in with his latchkey, and I told him I'd run up unannounced.… Well?"

He came forward. In the old days Jack and I never shook hands; nor did we now. He set down hat, gloves, and umbrella carelessly on my knee-hole table and dropped into a chair with a long-drawn sigh. "Reminds one— eh?—of the famous stage-direction in *The Rovers*— *Several soldiers cross the stage wearily, as if returning from the Thirty Years' War*.… Well? What are you still staring at? … Oh, I perceive! It's my clothes.… Yes; I should inform you that they are expensive, and the nearest compromise a Valparaiso tailor and I could reach in realising our several ideas of a Harley Street doctor. I am going to open a practice in that neighbourhood, and thought I would lose no time. The hat and umbrella over there are all right, if you'll give yourself the trouble to examine them. I bought them on the way along."

He was right, in a way, about his clothes. (I believe I have already mentioned that Jack had always dressed himself carefully and in good form.) His frock-coat had a fullness of skirt, and his trousers a bluish aggressive tint, that I couldn't pass for metropolitan. His boots were worse—of some wrong sort of patent leather. But they ought not to have altered the man as I felt that he was altered. ... Yes, cheapened and coarsened, in some indefinable way. His hair had thinned and showed a bald patch: not a large patch: still, there it was. His shape had been rather noticeably slim. I won't say that it had grown pursy, but it had run to seed somehow. Least of all I liked the change in his eyes, which bulged somewhat, showing an unhealthy white glitter. I set down this glitter as due to long weeks at sea: but the explanation couldn't quite satisfy me. When a lost friend returns as it were from the grave—from shipwreck, at any rate, and uncharted travel—you look to find him gaunt, brown, leathery, hollow of cheek and eye, eh? Foe's appearance didn't answer to this conception... not one little bit.

"Then you didn't sail in the *Eurotas*, after all?" said I, finding speech. "We saw your name on the list."

"Oh, yes, I did," he interrupted. "And, by the way, we shall have to talk about her—or, rather, about what I ought to do.... Yes, I know what you'll be advising. 'Go straight to Lloyd's,' no doubt."

"Man alive," said I, "why not? If you were aboard of her—and if, as you tell me, you fetched somehow to Sydney—why in God's name hasn't Lloyd's heard of it months ago? There are such things as cables. ... Unless, to be sure, you have a reason?"

"I have and I haven't," said Jack. "My turning-up doesn't hurt anyone, does it? The *Eurotas* went down, sure enough: and *I* didn't scuttle her, if that's what you suspect."

"Please don't be an ass, Jack," I pleaded.

"Well, I don't see," he continued, ruminating, "—I don't see any way but to go to Lloyd's and tell them about it. Yet equally I don't see what good it can do. The underwriters have paid up, eh?"

"More than three years ago," I told him.

"Well, then... I was perfectly well prepared to answer any questions at Valparaiso. I landed in my own name. I went back to the same hotel. And 'Foe' is not the most common of names, especially when you write 'Doctor' before it.... No, I'm wrong. Farrell had entered our names on the register, and had entered mine as 'Professor.' On my return I wrote it 'John Foe, M.D.' But anyway, not a soul in the hotel recognised me.... I think my looks must have altered, somehow.... So I let it go. I dare say you won't understand, not knowing the kind of experiences I've been through, nor the number of 'em. But you may understand that after a goodish while as a castaway I was tired beyond the point of answering more questions than I should happen to be asked.... So I gave Valparaiso a silent blessing, and came home by the first ship, to consult you and Collingwood. What—let me repeat—have you done with Collingwood?"

"Jimmy?" said I. "He's married, a year since, and is already the father of a bouncing boy. I acted as his best man, by request. He has a delightful and tiny wife who keeps him in order, which he passes on to the County of Warwickshire as Justice of the Peace and Coram.... But about the *Eurotas?*" I persisted. "I don't think you quite realise. There were passengers on board: and for months—"

"Of course there were passengers," Foe agreed. "It won't help their relatives (will it?) to know for certain what they pretty well know already. As I hinted to Norgate in my last letter, there was a labour crisis on when we sailed. Some aggrieved blackguard on the dock, acting on his own or under command of his 'Union,' shovelled half a dozen bombs in with the coal. Simple process. Between seven hundred and a thousand miles out, this particular batch of coal was reached and shovelled into the forward furnaces. I counted four explosions. Two of them blew her bows to pieces, and she sank by the head and was gone in twenty minutes.

"Must I tell it, when I am home and dying to ask questions?—Oh, very well, then.... I shall be perfectly truthful so far as the history goes; but I warn you that at a certain point you won't like it, and you'll go on to like it less. You and I have been friends, Roddy, and you naturally suppose that I've come straight to you, as my first friend, to be welcomed and to ask for counsel. But you suppose wrong. I am come asking neither for advice, nor for a sympathy— which I know I shan't get."

"My dear Jack—" I began to protest.

"Oh, be quiet," said he, "and let *me* do the talking! I've had no one to talk to, these five months around the Horn, but a Norwegian skipper, a first mate of the same country, a fellow-passenger shipped off as a dipsomaniac for a cure (we lost him somewhere in the worst of it—I've an idea he let himself be swept overboard), and a mixed crew that I helped to cure of *beri-beri* at St. Helena. So I want to do the talking, with your leave.

"—And I want to say this first, foremost, once and for all. I am come *simply to tell you.* I understand the devil of a lot about hatred by this time— more than you will ever begin to guess. But you taught me, anyhow, this much about friendship, that I couldn't bear to go along with you without your knowing every atom of the truth. That means, we're going to be clean cuts, when I've done…. You'll loathe the tale. But, damn it, you shall respect me for this, that I cut clean, for old sake's sake, and wiped up the account, before we parted as strangers and I started life afresh."

"All this is pretty mysterious, Jack," said I. "You know that, for all the hurt he'd done you, I shied out of helping your pursuit of Farrell…. Tell me, what happened to Farrell? Went down in the *Eurotas*, I guess, and so squared accounts. That's what you mean— eh?—by your clean cut and starting life afresh?… If so, for your sake I'm glad of it."

"He didn't go down in the *Eurotas*," Foe answered gravely: "As a matter of fact I dragged him on board one of the boats with my own hands."

"What?" said I. "Farrell another survivor?"

"Upon my word," he answered, lighting a cigarette, "I can't swear to Farrell's being alive or dead. Probably he's dead; but anyway I've no further use for him, and that's where the clean cut comes in. I had to quit hold of him because a woman beat me…. Now sit quiet and listen."

FOE'S NARRATIVE

"Did you know that Farrell had married?… Yes, at San Ramon, a little portless place some way down the coast of Peru. The woman was a Peruvian and owned a banana-strip there, left to her by her first husband, a drunkard, in part-compensation for having ill-used and beaten her.

"When I ran Farrell to earth there, after he'd given me the slip for twelve months and more, this woman had married him and almost made a new man of him. In another month or so I don't doubt she'd have converted him into man enough to tell her all the truth, and let her deliver him.

"As it was, he passed me off for his friend—the ass!… I shipped with them, and we worked down the coast, by fruit-ship and sloop, to Valparaiso, intending for Sydney…. Now at this point I might easily make myself out a calculating villain. Farrell was enamoured to feebleness, and to make love to his Santa was an opportunity cast into my lap by the gods…. But actually, before I could even meditate this simple villainy, I had fallen in love with her because I couldn't help it.

"Now I had never been in love before, and I took the disease pretty severely. And I should say that I took it rather curiously: but you shall judge, for I'll set out the credit side of the account just as plainly as the other.

"I hated the man, as you know: I loved the woman, as I've told you. But—here's the puzzle—strange to say, at that time, and for a long while, these two passions did not conflict or even contend at all, as neither did they help. I couldn't hate Farrell any worse than I did already. If I'd hated him just a little less, I might have killed him, to get him out of the way. But I give you my word, I never thought of shortening the chase in that way. Farrell, you may say, had become necessary to me: by this time I couldn't think of living without him.... Now I know what's crossing your mind. I might have piled up the torture on Farrell, and at the same time have played on that other passion, by setting myself to debauch Santa. No, I'm not complaining. You shall have as bad to condemn before I've done, so you needn't apologise. But, as it happens, I wasn't that sort of blackguard. Moreover, it wouldn't have worked, anyhow. Santa was as good as her name—

"No, damn it! I will clear myself of *that*!... You'll understand that I loved the woman, and—well, in the old days, as you'll do me the justice to remember, I hated men who played loose among women. As for 'making love' to Santa—oh, I can't explain to you, who never saw her, how utterly that was beyond question on either side.... Almost white she was, with the blood of the Incas in her—blood of Castile, too, belike—and yet all of a woman, with funny rustic ways that turned at any moment to royal.... And she loved Farrell—my God!

"I wonder now if she guessed—guessed at the time, I mean. They say that women always guess; which in these matters is as good as knowing.... But I'm holding up my story."

"The *Eurotas* went down in something like 36, south latitude, longitude 105 and a half west. That's as near as I make it: that is to say, some three or four hundred miles from any known land save Easter Island, which lay well away north and to windward, for we were down where the main winds set between W. and N. That's as close as I can give it to you. In seafaring matters I leave seamen to their own job, and don't worry about reckonings and day's runs. It's their business to take me, mine to trust their skill. You will own, Roddy, that if fools had only kept their noses out of *my* job in life, I shouldn't be having to tell you this story.

"Anyhow, Macnaughten—that was the skipper's name—took all the ship's instruments with him on board his own boat, which was the last to quit.

"He was a good man, and I couldn't but admire his behaviour, first and last. The *Eurotas* went down within half an hour of the first explosion; which had surprised us passengers on deck as we were chatting and watching the sunset. The sea was calm as a pond, with a bank of cloud to northward, all edged with gold on its western fringes.

"I think this calm, resting over sea and sky, may have helped us through the catastrophe. The only irritation I felt was at the slowness of it all, between the moment we knew we were lost and the moment when the vessel went down. Yet every moment between was used to a nicety, almost as if Captain Macnaughten had been preparing for the test. He commanded us, crew and passengers alike. Four stokers had been killed below: another and the engineer officer badly hurt. These two were fetched up while some of us lowered the accommodation-ladder and others swung out the boats on the davits. These two sick men were carried down to the first of the three boats launched. Four women passengers followed; three married, one a spinster. The three husbands were ordered down after them.

"The *Eurotas*, as I've told you, was a new ship, well found to the last life-buoy. The directors of the Company had lunched on board before she sailed and drunk to her health, having seen that everything answered to advertisement. The boats were staunch, newly painted and smart: the crew as well-picked a lot as the Board could find. So far as I can recall those hurrying minutes, I remember them as being almost intolerably slow. I cannot say how many of them it took before we realised for a certainty that the ship was going down. But I know that as, by order, I went down the ladder to the second boat, I had a sense of irritation at the long time it was taking and the methodical way the skipper was getting out stores and water-breakers and having them hefted down.

"Another thing I must tell you. As I went down the ladder—the ship's bows already beginning to dip steeply—I had a sense of being in no *time* at all, but in eternity. There around us, spread and placid, stretched the emptiest waste of the Pacific, with God's sun deserting the sky above it, sinking almost as fast as the ship was sinking.

"Santa had wrapped her mantilla over her head. She went down the ladder before me, following Farrell. Our boat was white-painted on thwarts and stern-sheets.... I was keeping my foothold with difficulty, loaded with a water-breaker.... A man took it from me, all in silence. I gripped Farrell's hand and hoiked him on board. There was a great silence hanging, as it seemed, about those last moments.

"We pushed off a little way. The third and last boat was lowered down, and we saw the last half-dozen, with the captain at their heels, tumbling down in a stampede.

"The *Eurotas* took her plunge just as we heard them unhook from the davit-blocks."

NIGHT THE SIXTEENTH
CAPTAIN MACNAUGHTEN

(Foe's Narrative Continued)

"I once read a novel called *One Traveller Returns*. That's all I remember of it—the title.

"Well, I am that traveller: and if ever I write down the story of the *Eurotas*, and in particular of what was suffered on board her boat No. 2, I have no doubt that nine readers out of ten will forget the details just as soon and just as completely. There is a horrible sameness about these narratives, Roddy; and the truer they are (as I've proved) the nearer they resemble one another. Monotonous they are—these drawn-out agonies—as the sea itself upon which they are enacted. From time to time you sit up half-awake out of your stupor, and then you know that something is going to happen, and also that it is something you've read about somewhere, something that you've *lived* through (or so it seems) in dreams, or in a previous existence. You hardly know which; and you don't care, much. It's going to be horrible, you know: it's going to be all the more horrible, in its way, for being conventional. You want to get it over and pass on to the next stereotyped nightmare. That's the feeling.

"So I'm going to confine my tale pretty closely to myself and what pulled me through.... But before I get to this I must tell you of two shocks that fell on me before I came to it, and seemed to promise that the books were all wrong and not half vivid enough. I dare say that quite a number of survivors have tried to paint the sense of loneliness that swooped on them in the first few seconds after their ship had slid down. But I'll swear I had read nothing to prepare me for it.... It's not a ship—it's a continent—that vanishes. The little hole it has made in the water calls to the whole ocean to cover it, and the ocean widens out its horizon by ten times all around, at once pouring in and spreading itself to isolate you ten times farther from help.... Nobody who hasn't been through this and felt it for himself can understand how promptly and easily— without help of quenching their thirst in salt water—men go mad, in open boats, at sea.

"But I believe the shock of loneliness at sunrise was even more hideous. One is prepared for it, in a way; otherwise it would, I am sure, be far more hideous. Santa confessed to me, on the second day, that she had felt—and, she believed, could feel—nothing more dreadful. As she put it, 'You see, my friend, when the sky lightens at length, you have assurance of God, and that God is help. Then, when He sends up no help, but a great staring sun to watch your misery, hour by hour, God turns to devil and you only long for night—when, at least, the dew falls.'

"Between sunset and sunrise, however, I was kept fairly busy. For the *Eurotas* had scarcely been twenty minutes under water, and night had barely fallen, before the captain's boat ranged up to us. She carried a lantern in her bows, and I had found one and was lighting it after his example.

"'Names on board!' he demanded. We gave them through Grimalson, the second mate, who was in charge. He said no more for about half a minute, during which time no doubt he was running through the list in his head. Then, 'That's all right,' he announced cheerily. 'You'll set watches, Mr. Grimalson, and keep her in easy hail. The weather will certainly hold fine for a bit, and early to-morrow I'll be alongside again with instructions. Plumb south our course lies, for the present. I'll tell you why, later. You have a sail?"

"'Ay, sir,' answered Grimalson.

"'Right. But don't hoist it unless I signal.... Yes, yes, not a draught at present. But if a breeze should get up, don't hoist sail without instructions. We keep together—that's the main point. Just pull along easy—I'll set the pace—and keep in my wake, course due south. Those that aren't pulling will act wise to trust in God and get some sleep.... Is that Doctor Foe there forra'd, with the lantern?'

"'Ay, sir,' I answered up.

"'Then as soon as you've fixed it, sir, I'll ask you to jump aboard and along with us for to-night. I've poor Jock Abercrombie here— fetched him and Swainson out of No. 1 boat'—These were the two injured men: Abercrombie, our Chief Engineer, by far the worst burnt—'I doubt if he'll last till morning: but we've been friends from boys, Jock and me, and if you can do aught, sir, to make his passing easier—'

"I asked him to wait while I fetched my medicine-chest, and was transhipped with it into the captain's boat. They had laid Abercrombie in the stern-sheets, with the stoker Swainson beside him. Abercrombie's plight was hopeless; flesh of chest and arms all red-raw from the scorching, and the man palpably dying from shock.

"'I had him into my boat, sir,' Macnaughten explained gravely, 'because we'd shipped the ladies—all but Mrs. Farrell—in No. 1, and I don't want 'em to be distressed more than necessary.... A man can't think of everything all in five minutes, but I got him out of it, soon as I could. There's no hope, think you?'

"'Between you and me, none,' said I, sinking my voice.

"'That's what I reckoned,' said the skipper, with just a nod of his head. He had taken the tiller and sent all the crew, saving four men rowing, forward whilst I examined the patients. 'Jock wouldn't be one to let out a groan if he knew there were women by to be scared by it.... Also, Doctor, if he's dying, I'd like to be handy by, if you understand. I got him this berth. We were friends, always.'

"I found some cotton-wool and a tin of vaseline, and coated the poor man's hurts as well as I could. Then, as he still groaned, though more feebly, I got out my phial of morphia and a needle. As I held the bottle against a sort of binnacle-light by which Macnaughten sat steering, I caught his eyes staring down on me, quiet and solemn. I tell you, that man was a man, Roddy.

"'Yes, I know, Doctor,' he said quietly. 'You're calculating how much there is of it, and how you may have to use it before we're through.... What about Swainson?'

"'He'll pull around,' said I. 'The vaseline will ease three-fourths of his trouble within ten minutes.'

"'Keep your voice low,' said the skipper, 'as I'm keeping mine.' He bent forward, pretending to consult the compass. 'I've sent all these fellows forward, though they put her down by the head so that it's like steering a monkey by the tail.... Now I reckon that you'll be wishful to go back to-morrow, or as soon as may be, and join your party. That's so?'

"'That's so,' said I, as I finished the injection and turned to deal with the stoker.

"'Well, I'd like to have you here aboard,' said the skipper. 'But so's best. We want some brains in No. 2 boat; and, between ourselves, Grimalson hasn't the brains of a hare. He's a second-cousin-twice-removed of one of our directors. He's no seaman at all; and his navigation's all a pretence.... I suppose, now, *you* can't navigate?'

"'Good Lord, no, sir!' said I. 'I just understand the principles of it—that's all.'

"'It's a damned sight more than Grimalson understands, I'll bet,' responded Captain Macnaughten, studying the binnacle and speaking as though we were discussing the weather and the crops. 'You may push your finger into that man anywhere, he's that soft and boggy—no better'n slush—*and* pink.... Don't you despise a pink-coloured man? Still, I want you to understand, Doctor, that he's the superior officer on No. 2, for the time being.'

"'I understand,' said I, looking up from my business of unguenting the stoker, who was not badly burnt.

"'But if Grimalson should turn rotten.... Well, now, I've had an eye on you, sir, and I judge I can share off on you a bit of trouble I wouldn't share off on most.... *You* must know as well as I do that the chance is pretty thin for us all, even if this weather holds. I reckon there's no nearer land than Easter Island, four hundred good miles norr'ard, and a beat in light winds.... I've heard too much about long beats in open boats—heard enough to make the flesh creep. Anyways, I'm responsible. I've turned it over in my head: and I'm giving orders—you take me? We're not steering for any land at all. We're steering the shortest way, due south—what wind there is drawing behind us—on the chance to hit in with the way of traffic—Sydney ships making round the Horn.... You'll not argue that, I hope?" he demanded.

"'On the contrary, sir,' I agreed, 'I just know enough to be sure that you are doing the wisest thing.'

"'Nobody but God can be sure,' said he, and sat musing. 'Well, I take the responsibility God has seen fit to lay on me of a sudden. You won't hear me speak of this again: but you're an educated man, and you've nerve as well as brains—I marked ye by the head of the ladder, when the first boat was getting out. I reckoned you for one that doesn't speak out of his turn; and it came over me, just now, that I'd like one such man, and him a gentleman, to bear in mind that if I set my face pretty hard in the time that's ahead of us, it won't mean that I ain't feeling things at the back of it.'

"'Thank you, Captain Macnaughten,' said I, pretty earnestly. 'The best I can answer is the simplest—that you're doing me much honour.'

"'That's all right,' he said lightly: 'all right and understood. One man often helps another in funny little ways in this funny old world.' After a pause he went on yet more lightly and cheerfully, 'Well—and I've noticed you've a trick of beginning your sentences on that word 'well': it's a habit of mine too, they tell me—as the ladies say ashore, we're going to be worse before we are better, so we'll call those fellows aft a bit and ease the steering.... Stay a minute, though, before I call to them.... A clever man like you ought to be able to pick up a bit of navigation in a few lessons. While our boats keep together (as, please God, they will to the end) it wouldn't be a bad notion if you dropped alongside just before midday for a morning call, and I'll learn you how to handle a sextant and prick down a reckoning.... It'll be sociable, too.... Yes, I'll signal the time to you: but, to be ready for it, you might set your watch by my chronometer here.... I wonder, now,' he inquired oddly, 'if you've forgot to wind yours up to-night?'

"Well, Roddy, it's the truth that I had forgotten. I looked at him, pretty foolish, and with that we both laughed—yes, there and then, a sort of laugh, low and quiet, like well-water bubbling.

"'Now I'll tell *you*,' said the skipper, 'I caught myself winding up mine the moment after the ship went down... that's funny, eh? Five minutes to nine was the hour.... I'd hooked the old timepiece out of my fob, and there I was, winding, for all the world as if ashore and going to bed.... See here— three turns of the winch and she's chock-a-block again, if you ever!... And, come to think, I may as well correct *her* by the chronometer, too.'

"So we solemnly set our watches together, there by the binnacle light. A queer fancy took me that the act was a sort of ritual, not devised by either of us—a setting and sealing of friendship.... Ought a fellow, Roddy, shipwrecked in the South Pacific, to complain while he has these three stand-by's—a woman to love, a man to admire, and a man to hate?"

"The engineer died just before dawn. Indeed, the day broke of a sudden as I finished straightening his body and wrapping it for burial; and I looked up in the new light, and around me, to take in that second gush of loneliness of which I told you.... It was appalling. It swept in on me from the whole enormous circumference of empty waters, and I fairly cowered from it over the corpse I had been tending.

"I never had that sensation again, or in anything like that degree, during the whole voyage; and I shall presently tell you why. But it was Macnaughten who taught me my first deliverance.... I knelt there, huddled, not daring to turn my face up for a second look and expose my cowardice. I seemed to be drowning in the deep of deeps, and fragments of the first chapter of Genesis swirled past me like straws—*And the earth was without form and void.... And the Spirit of God moved upon the face of the waters. And God saw the light, that it was good*—but here it was, and it was not good. *And God said, Let there be a firmament in the midst of the waters*— but there was no firmament. *And God divided the waters... and the gathering together of the waters called he Seas: and God saw that it was good*—oh, my God! *And God said, Let the waters under the heaven be gathered together unto one place, and let dry land appear: and it was so*—But it wasn't!

"Captain Macnaughten's voice spoke through this misery of mine quite matter-of-factly and simply, dispersing it like so much morning mist.

"'Signal the other boats to pull close,' he commanded. 'Someone tell me where the Bible and Prayer-Book were stowed. I saw them handed down, with my own eyes.' Then to me: 'These things—packed as we are... the sooner over, the better, and the less they'll prey on anyone's mind.' He looked down. 'Jock would have liked it so, I reckon.'

"The other two boats were called close. The summons was explained, and the burial service decently read. 'It don't seem altogether a lively beginning,' said he to me at the close—and the water was scarce dry on his cheek that had run down suddenly as he read out *I heard a voice from heaven, saying*—'But,' he added, 'it'll sober 'em down to what they'll have to face.... And now we'll sober 'em up with some cheerfuller business no less practical.'

"The boats having gathered close for this ceremony, he commanded them to stay so while the crews cooked breakfast. 'I saw the coffee handed down into No. 1,' he announced. 'Fetch it out, you!... And, after breakfast, I'll overhaul all three boats and see that each has her share fairly apportioned.'

"I tell you, Roddy, that this Macnaughten, who aboard the *Eurotas* had been an ordinary skipper conning his ship, and nowise hearty or communicative, of a sudden proved himself as great as any man I've read of in history.... You may smile if you will. But here was a man abandoned by Heaven in the waste of the South Pacific, with all his prospects blasted and all the hopes built on the *Eurotas* line (in which, I learned, he had piled his money); with a wife at home, moreover, and a daughter. Yet for the seven days we kept company he stood up to duty, fathered us all, never showed sick or sorry. He had a fairish baritone voice, and it was he that started us singing to fill up the endless time. How does it go?—"

> Thus sang they in an English boat,
> A holy and a cheerful note—

God! I can hear his voice now, trolling *Nancy Lee* back across the waters, defying them, until the night quenched it.

"Through these seven days, regularly and towards noon, he signalled and I went aboard No. 3 for a lesson in navigation. It was the third day that, returning, I found Grimalson didn't stomach these visits. Grimalson was a mean man, and incompetent; the sort that knows he's not trusted, knows there's good reason for it, and resents it all the time. I thought him just a sulky brute, and noted that on some excuse or other it was always inconvenient to be close up with No. 3 boat as it drew towards midday and my time (as he put it, growling) for 'taking the Old Man's temperature.' He was misguided enough, on the fourth day, to let off a part of this rather feeble joke upon the captain himself, and found his bearings pretty smartly. He had so managed things that at ten minutes to noon it became pretty clear I must miss my appointment. All three boats carried sail now: the weather being perfect, with a nor'-westerly breeze, light but steady: and the three were running before it pretty well abreast like three tiny butterflies on the waste of water—for I should tell you that all three were twenty-four footers, built to one whale-boat model on the same moulds, and carried small Bermuda, or leg-of-mutton sails, cut to one pattern—when Grimalson took it into his head that our down-haul should be tautened in, cursed the man who was doing his best to execute a silly order, ran forward, and so messed matters that the sail had to be three-parts lowered and re-set. It was quite deliberately done, as even a landsman could see; and it lost us a couple of hundred yards off the captain's boat, sailing to starboard of us.

"Things were scarcely right with us before Macnaughten had brought his boat about close to wind and came ranging alongside. He had his watch in his hand.

"'Mr. Grimalson,' he demanded, 'why were you fooling with that sail, just now?'

"'She wasn't setting proper,' explained Grimalson; 'and I told Jarvis to take a swig on the downhaul. He got messed up in the slack somehow, and—'

"'Before you go any further,'—the captain cut him short—' I may just tell you that your sail was setting perfectly, and that I saw the whole business through my glass.… Hasn't Doctor Foe told you that I require him, while this weather holds, to be on board this boat regularly at ten minutes to noon, to take observations?'

"'Observations?' grumbled the second mate. 'I thought observations to be a seaman's job. I reckoned that what doctors and suchlike took was temperatures, and five minutes up or down wouldn't put anyone out.'

"'I'm sorry,' answered Macnaughten, very quiet, after a moment's thought,—'I am very sorry to tell you before your crew and passengers what, with a ship under me, I should have called you aft and below to hear in private. But if you ever use that tone with me again, Mr. Grimalson, I shall take *your* temperature with my revolver. And if you dare to disobey my smallest order, as you deliberately did just now, I shall transfer you to this boat and clap you in irons. For it seems to me I have to explain to you what the others,—crew and passengers alike—know by the light of common sense: that until God's mercy delivers us my least word is the Ten Commandments rolled into one, we being where a hand's turn is either a hair's-breadth or broad as the Pacific.... Now cast off, and set your behaviour by No. 1 boat, where Mr. Ingpen has come up to wind and is waiting for us.... A cable's length on the port, and level with us—that's the order, and you'll watch it until I give the next. You have lost us twenty minutes. Happen *that* might turn out the hair's breadth I was speaking of—the difference between life and death—and the whole Pacific ain't wider.'

"We were down in latitudes where the current sets southeasterly, and this was helping us all the time. But on the sixth and seventh days, although the wind held fair and light and steady, a considerable swell had been following us, warning of trouble somewhere to northward; and on the eighth night it overtook us.

"It was—not to speak irreverently—in itself ten times more trouble than ten thousand Grimalsons could have raised; a tearing gale of wind which, all of a sudden, converted the oily summits of the swell into bursting white waves. I don't suppose the height from trough to summit actually increased as it did to view, but in twenty minutes, and with night shutting down the lid on us, each successive wave astern seemed to grow taller by feet. The rain appeared to have no effect in flattening their caps, though it came down with a weight that knocked half the breath out of our bodies, and with a roar above which it was hard to hear an order shouted. We could spy the other boats' lanterns but at long intervals, partly because of this down-pouring curtain and partly, I suppose, because when we topped up over a crest they would nine times out of ten be hidden in a trough, dipping or rising.

"We carried, by Captain Macnaughten's orders, a hurricane lamp on our fore-stay. Someone had lit a second amidships, where we huddled in oilskins and under tarpaulins like a congregation of eels.... Jarvis, our best seaman, had the tiller. He sat, all hunched, crouching forward over a third small lamp—the binnacle lamp with which our boat, like the others, was providentially fitted. The rain, however, beat on its glass in such sheets that he could not possibly have read the compass card floating by the wick. Nor—I am sure—was he trying to read it. He just sat and steered by the feel of the seas as they lurched ahead and sank abaft. The lamplight glowed up on his cheek-bones, but was lost under the pent of his sou'wester, which had a sort of crease or channel in its fore-flap, that shed down the rain in a flood. Though we lay, we passengers, on the bottom boards we could see nothing of his face, so far forward he bent.

"Then Grimalson lost his head. He was seated at Jarvis's shoulder in the stern-sheets, with a hefty seaman (Prout by name) on his other hand tending the sheet—the both of 'em starboard of Jarvis. Of a sudden he started up, reached forward, snatched the midships light, and held it aloft against the wall of a tremendous sea arching astern. At sight of it the fool lost all his remaining nerve, and yelled to the two seamen forward to lash a couple of oars to the painter and cast overboard. 'If we ran another hundred yards, we were lost: there was no hope but to fetch around head-to-sea and ride to it.'

"—Which, after some seven or eight sickening minutes, we did. He was master, and Jarvis put down the helm and obeyed. Twice we were heaved, tilted and slid sideways down, like folks perched on the window-sills of a falling house. Then she came fair about and rode to it, every crest flinging more or less of spray over us, hour after hour....

"But I must tell you one thing. From time to time we were roused up in the darkness, to bale. Our work performed, we three passengers— Santa and Farrell and I—would creep under the tarpauling anew, out of the drumming rain, and coil there to sleep.... Ay, and once in the pitch blackness under, she, mistaking, reached two arms around my neck and with a long sigh, dead-beat, sank asleep. That was all. ... Farrell lay as he had tumbled, like a log across my ankles. ... I held her, crooked by my elbow against my side, her head drowsed on my shoulder, her body pulsing against mine. I am telling you all, and I tell you that I did not dare to kiss her. Lying awake, with Farrell across my feet, I held her to me, feeling her breathe.

"At hint of dawn Jarvis, who had been watching the seas the night through, barked us out of cover. The rain had ceased, the gale had swept southward as fast as it had come. The sea heaved almost as steeply as ever, but the toppling waves no longer flung any spray over us, or any to mention."

"Day broke, and the after-swell still tumbled us heavily: but nowhere within the great ring of horizon did it heave one of the other boats into sight. The sea smoothed itself down with a quite wonderful rapidity, and still its great surface was a blank."

"I cannot somehow believe that so able a handler of his boat as I knew Captain Macnaughten to be allowed himself to be swamped in that gale. His orders had been to carry on and only heave-to upon signal. Jarvis—who (as I have said) could sail our boat running by the feel of her, maintained that we had never been in the worst of danger, that the skipper could sail a boat for ten to his own one, that he had just held on, in his straight way, upon the orders he had given, and left us at the back of the horizon while we fenced seas under Grimalson's orders.

"Since nothing apparently has been heard since of those other boats, I shall go on hoping that Jarvis was wrong, and that Captain Macnaughten's boat and Mr. Ingpen's, in one way or another, met with a short sharp end in that gale.

"But if they did last it out and over the horizon to drag it out and die and never be reported to Lloyd's, then I, who know the sort of things they must have suffered, assure you, who have read them accurately reported in books, that whenever or wherever Captain James Macnaughten perished, the Recording Angel has him entered up for a seaman and a gentleman."

NIGHT THE SEVENTEENTH
NO. 2 BOAT

(Foe's Narrative Continued)

"One must use ugly words for ugly things.

"Grimalson, staring—as we all stared—over the blank sea, vomited the natural man within him in some fourteen or fifteen words for which he was never forgiven by any of us.

"'Gone, by Gosh! And that bloody old fool was teaching *me* to handle a boat!'

"All heard it. Not a soul spoke. I glanced at Jarvis in time to catch the twitch of his mouth—one of those twitches I used to study in angry dogs, and snapshot and measure: but he continued to gaze across the waters. After half a minute or so he glanced at me, looked seaward again, and observed quietly, 'It don't seem probable they would run mast-down in the time. And yet I don't know: 'twas blowing powerful fresh just after midnight. Hull-down, a boat might easily be; and supposing sail lowered, what's a boat's mast better to pick up than a needle in a bottle o' hay?—let be they might be dismasted. There was weather enough. And No. 1 carried a bamboo—which is never to be trusted, if you ask *me*.'

"'Who the devil's asking you?' demanded Grimalson.

"'Nobody, sir,' the seaman answered, respectfully, but without turning his head. 'Words spoken in a l'il boat like this be for anybody's hearin'; and anybody's heard or no, accordin' as they choose.'

"'Well then,' Grimalson retorted, 'I happen to be boss here aboard, and I don't choose. So drop you that, prompt, and start baling her.'

"'One moment, Mr. Grimalson—' I began. But he took me up quicker than he had taken Jarvis.

"'Dear me, now!' he snarled in a foolish sarcastic way. 'And who may this be that I have the honour of addressing?—Captain Macnaughten's ghost? or his next-of-kin, belike? Or may be his deputy understudy?—with your *One moment, please*?... You sit down on that thwart there, and don't you dare open your face again until I give you leave…. That was the old fool's way with *me*—hey? And now you recognise it.'

"'I do,' said I, pulling out my revolver. 'You may quit fumbling in your pocket, for it's wringing wet and these cartridges are dry, as I have assured myself…. *You* sit down on *that* thwart, and don't you dare open your face until I give you leave to get up and wash it. That's *your* trick of speech, and maybe you recognise it."

"As I covered him, Jarvis touched my elbow. 'I beg your pardon, sir, but you're a gentleman and a passenger, and Mr. Grimalson's our senior officer, when all's said, *and* in command…. I'm not talkin' about the rights of it nor the wrongs of it,' Jarvis went on, as I still held the revolver levelled:' but 'tis flat mutiny you're committing; and me and my mates'll have to range up on the side of order. Whereby you'll be no match for us…. Oh, sir,' he pleaded, 'let up with quarrelling, and let's all die decent, if we must, when the time comes—and with a lady in the boat!'

"'Thank you, Jarvis,' said I; and lowering my revolver drew out the cartridges pretty deliberately. 'I beg your pardon, Mr. Grimalson. I shall not, on any provocation, interfere with you again. But before you start baling the boat, I'll ask you to note that the third water-breaker is stove, and it was the only full one. Saltish this water may be, but nine-tenths of it is honest rain from heaven.'

"'My God, sir, and it's truth!' verified one of the seamen who had scrambled forward. The full breaker had jerked loose from its lashings and lay awash under the bowman's thwart: worse—it had loosed the other two, and these, floating light, had washed away overboard and gone out of ken.

"Grimalson stood up, slightly dazed. In the rock of the boat he seemed to be shifting his weight deliberately from foot to foot.

"'Why didn't one of you report?' he shouted, in a fury at which I smiled; it being so senseless and at the same time so cunning, as a ruse to let him arise with dignity from the thwart. 'Why didn't somebody report?' he repeated in an absurd official manner, quite as though he had been a station-master interrogating a group of porters on the whereabouts of a missing parcel.

"'Well, sir,' I answered as politely as possible; 'it was I that first found the casks were loose, and by the accident that the rim of the full one struck me pretty sharply, in the night, between the shoulder-blades. I got it trigged up, as you see, before it ran amuck to do further damage. In securing it I found that it had lost its bung and was almost empty: but that hardly seemed worth mentioning, with such a flood of rainwater washing around. There was nothing to be done at the moment; the breaker in a way was refilling itself, as soon as I had it jammed, by the water washing over it; and, after a bit, judging it full or nearly full, I ripped off a corner of my oily and made a sort of bung, as you see."

"All this had, in fact, cost me some labour, and I related it, no doubt, a bit too complacently. Worse, I rounded it up by saying, 'The captain, sir, was more anxious about the water than anything, as he told me yesterday.'

"At this his temper boiled over—yet not (as I could see) until he had flung a glance at Jarvis and the crew, to make sure they were submissive still to the old habit of discipline. 'Macnaughten was always full of wisdom,' he sneered; '—so full that he's dead of it! ... And so you didn't think it worth mentioning?'

"Do you know, Roddy, I didn't think the fool worth any further attention.... One can't really hate two men at one time... at any rate, *I* can't. It's too fatiguing. There sat Farrell, three feet away, looking dazed, as he'd looked ever since the *Eurotas* went under. As for this Grimalson, I didn't reckon him worth powder and shot. I knew that he would bluster before the men, to save his face, and then climb down. To secure the water on board was such an obvious measure that, bluster as he might, he couldn't miss coming to it finally.... I heard Jarvis explaining that an empty pork-tub, with a tarpauling inside of it, would hold quite a deal of the rainwater washing above the bottom-boards. I took no more trouble than to turn my back on Grimalson, who was arguing that all this water was mucking the dry provisions.

"'They're pretty well mucked already, sir, by the looks of 'em,' answered Jarvis: 'all but the canned meats, and few enough they are. Five cans, as I counted the last stowage.'

"'Oh, very well, then,' came the order which I had known to be inevitable. 'Run a tarpauling inside of that cask—and bale, you, Prout and Martinez!'

"And so, behind my back and almost as I shrugged my shoulders—so, within twenty minutes of the sunrise that told us we were eight human beings isolated from all help but that which we could afford to one another—in a casual, unpremeditated stroke the curse fell on us.

"The seaman Martinez, kneeling in water, was asking, rather helplessly, for someone to pass him a baler or invent one—our regulation dipper having gone overboard in the gale. It was a silly, useless question: but Grimalson, already rattled, swung round upon a man he knew to be weak. 'Damn me!' cried he in a gust of rage, 'if I can't teach it to doctors, I'll teach *seamen* who gives orders here!' and snatching out a marling-spike from a sheath in his belt, hurled it full at the seaman's head.

"The act was brutal enough in itself; for the iron, though a light one, was full heavy enough, flung with that force, to lay a man out. It did worse: for Martinez, instead of ducking his head, made a spring to his feet, putting out his hands much as if fielding a cricket-ball. The marling-spike, miss-aimed, struck the thwart in front of him, turned point up with the ricochet, and plunged into his thigh. As I splashed forward to his help, blood came creeping, staining the water around my ankles. The steel point had pierced slantwise through his femoral artery.

"Well, I was quick: and Santa was quick, too—tearing in strips the damp pillow-case on which her head rested of nights when it wasn't resting against Farrell's shoulder. (But not *this* night, I thought as I worked—not this blessed night just passed!) With the pillow-case and the very spike that had done the mischief I made a good firm tourniquet and saved Martinez's life for the time.

"But he had lost a lot of blood. All the drinking water awash in the boat was foul with it, and this bloodied flood was running, as the boat rocked, in and out among our small bags of pork and ship-bread. My job ended, I looked aft. Farrell was leaning over the gunwale in uncontrollable nausea. The face of Prout at the tiller, was dogged but inexpressive. Grimalson stood like a man dazed.

"'Will he live?' he asked, his eyes meeting mine. 'Of course I never intended—'

"'It wasn't a very pretty thing to do, was it?' I answered quietly.

"'Well, this settles it,' said he, staring down at the water. 'We must clean out this filthy mess and overhaul the stores.'

"'And *then*?' I asked.

"'Oh, it'll rain,' said he, affecting confidence. 'It rained for a hundred last night, didn't it? We've run south of the dry latitudes and soon we'll be getting more rain than we've any use for. There's the small keg of rum, too.... Great thing as we're situated,' the fool continued, 'is to keep everyone in heart. And anyway I don't stomach water with blood in it—specially Dago blood.... Jarvis and Webster, fall to baling: and you, Prout, hand us over the tiller and dig out something for breakfast.'

"I had found a plug of tobacco in my pocket and seated myself to slice it: and as I cut it upon my palm, my eyes fell on Farrell's yet-heaving shoulders.... Of a sudden then it came upon me that, even with the luck we'd carried, men can't go through seven days and eight nights in an open boat and emerge quite sane. Macnaughten had put up a gallant, a magnificent pretence. 'The Old Man's Penny Readings,' as Grimalson had dubbed those evenings when the boats had closed up and the crews sang Moody and Sankey or *My Mary*—'The Old Man's Penny Readings, or Pea-nuts on the Pacific'—had been just as grandly simple as anything in the Gospel. No: that's wrong—they had come straight out of the Gospel, a last chapter of it the skipper had found floating and recovered, and would carry up, a proud passport to his God.

"But Macnaughten was gone, and with him the whole lovely illusion. He had kept us in a nursery, separated from hell by a half-inch plank; and here we were all beasts, consigned to ravening and to die of unsatisfied bestial wants—yes, and commanded by a monkey-man who chattered of keeping everyone in heart! *He!*"

"So there it was. I told you, Roddy, that it all happened like a nightmare—or, if you prefer it, a composite photograph—of any dozen stories you can recall. Here are the facts; and I will try to give them succinctly, as in a police-report.

"We were eight in the boat:"

Grimalson.	In command.
Davis.	A.B. Seaman.
Prout.	A.B. Seaman.
Webster.	Ordinary Seaman.
Martinez.	Ordinary Seaman.
Farrell.	Passenger.
Santa.	Passenger.
and I.	Passenger.

"Our victuals were:—4 lb. of pork (about) and 7 lb. of ship-bread, all messed with blood: 3 cans of potted meat, 2 of preserved fruit, one tin of sardines: for liquid, half a gallon of rum and, in the breaker, about 3 pints of water.

"We were, as we calculated, four hundred miles at least from any known land, and we had no chart on board: we might be within a hundred miles of the fringe of traffic.

"The sea was calm: the wind came in intermittent light draughts from the north. The sky was a great burning-glass, holding no hint of rain."

"Now from the very beginning—from the moment we left the ship—I knew that, if we were to perish of hunger or thirst before sighting help, I should be the last survivor. No; you needn't stare: it's perfectly simple.... I doubt if I ever told you that in the old days, when experimenting with the animals, I found that my will—or brain-power, if you prefer the term—worked torpidly for a while after meals, although, as you know, I was never what they call a hearty feeder. So I took to cutting down my rations. Then of course I discovered that this was all right enough up to a point, beyond which the stomach's craving made the brain irritable and impatient. So for a long time I let it go at that, and ate pretty frugally at fairly long stretches... until one day, in some book about Indian fakirs, I picked up a hint that if this interval of exhaustion were passed—if I stuck it out—my will might pick up its second wind, so to speak, and work more strongly than ever. I was curious enough, anyway, to give it a trial or two. The results didn't amount to much: but I *did* discover that I had a rather exceptional capacity for fasting, and promised myself to practise it further, from time to time, as an experiment on my own vile body.

"But now we'll come to something more important. In the matter of thirst I had persevered: being, as you may remember, hot-foot upon rabies just then and the salivary glands.... Well, in the matter of thirst, I trained myself to do my three days easy without swallowing a drop. That last night you invited yourself to dinner— the night I first met Farrell, by the way—you unknowingly ended a four days' experiment. I told Jimmy Collingwood about it, the morning he breakfasted with me...."

["I remember Jimmy's telling me something about it, in the taxi," I put in. "He said you were either the saviour or the curse of society—he wasn't clear which: wouldn't commit himself until he'd read your forthcoming treatise on *Thirst, Its Cause and Cure*. He added that you were mistaken if you thought the topic non-controversial."]

"He needn't be afraid... Farrell smashed me up for good as a benefactor of my species.... I shall put up a brass plate in Harley Street and end my days as a pottering empiricist—Remember Jimmy's trouble with that word?—alleviating particular complaints for cash. If it hadn't been for Farrell—well, just you remember *that* when I stand up for judgment!...

"Anyhow, that infernal boat gave me all the personal experiment I wanted.... I promised not to tell you all about it.... Martinez went first, of course, being weak as water. He died muttering for water. Grimalson came next... two days later.

"But I shall go on telling you about myself. Physically I suffered very little, mentally a good deal at sight of the others' torments— but only from time to time. By the fourth day (the eleventh after the *Eurotas* went down) we were all more or less mad, I reckon. But my lunacy took the form of light-headedness with a strange, almost persistent, sense of exaltation. I kept my strength so much better than they that almost unconsciously they left most of the trimming and steering in my hands. And I sat and steered as a god, in a world blank of all but miserable happenings. I looked on Santa, and she was the woman I loved but should never enjoy. I looked on Farrell: and he was *here*, brought here by *me*. What worse woe could possibly lie in store for him than this agony over which I presided it was impossible to tell and hard indeed to imagine. But I did not want him to die. On the contrary, it was for *him* that I searched the horizon, that a ship might rescue us and he might live. I would see to the rest!

"They say that living with an enemy in a confinement such as ours, makes you hate him worse and worse.... It wasn't so with me. My hate, by this time, was set and annealed, so to speak; quite cold, and almost judicial. I had no more jealousy than Jove. The air that, to the others, quivered so damnably, so insufferably around the boat under a sky without shade, swam around me like incense.... As for Farrell, his eyes watched mine like a dog's.

"Oh, yes, we went through it all! I'll have to tell you about Grimalson (as shortly as possible, though), because Farrell gets mixed up in it, hereabouts. Even in their suffering, the three seamen—Jarvis, Prout, and Webster—had nursed poor Martinez almost tenderly; and I suppose, amid their mutterings forward, they had hatched out their form of protest. And it was fit for comic opera— ghastly comic opera—if you can imagine Lucifer sitting in the stalls.

"Noon of the third day it was—I count from the time of our losing the other two boats. We had lowered Martinez overboard about an hour before, and the seamen should have been preparing our diminutive ration. (Salt pork boiled in sea-water, if you can imagine it, Roddy!) I was steering: Santa sat a foot away, staring over the waters, sometimes bringing her attention back to a line which Grimalson had cast overboard, trying for a fish. Grimalson lounged on the after-thwart—facing me, as you might say, and with his back to the men, but lolling sideways over the gunwale. He felt the line with his left hand. Close by his right lay a useless gaff. He had exhausted our third and last tin of sardines for bait, without effect, and— what was worse—had drained the oil down his throat impudently, without an offer to share it. Also he had been drinking salt water—and I had not troubled to restrain him. Farrell I could hate, but this man was naught. Farrell lay on the bottom-boards at my feet, breathing stertorously, with his head in what shade Santa's gown and the side-sheets together afforded. But this fool seemed intent on baiting the Pacific with a plummet, a hook, and a lump of salt pork.

"As if this wasn't enough of grisly opera, of a sudden, in my light-headedness I saw the three men stand up, join hands solemnly in a sort of cat's cradle fashion, and advance aft, for all the world like a comic trio, with the after thwart for footlights. They came to a halt, close behind Grimalson, and—even as though I had ordered a burlesque—Jarvis cleared his parched throat painfully, very formally, and spoke across to me. You must picture the three, if you will, still holding hands while he spoke.

"'Doctor Foe, sir,' said Jarvis oratorically, 'me and my mates, not knowing the law, but being wishful to behave conformable as British seamen, have cast it up together. And we allow 'tis no mutiny, being situated as we are, to say as this Martinez was a shipmate, when all's said and done, though a Dago, and Mr. Grimalson, meaning no disrespect, done him to death by bloody murder. Which, consequently, attaching no blame, we three, as loyal British seamen, two A.B. and one ordinary, and giving our opinion for what it is worth, hold that Mr. Grimalson was probably off his chump when he done it, and hasn't behaved subsequently in a way to inspire confidence in a crew left as we are. Whereby, Doctor Foe, not having pen and ink handy to make a round robin of it, we hereby respectfully depose Mr. Grimalson, and request of you to take over command of this craft, trusting you to be a gentleman and being well aware of the consequences and ready to face 'em. The others having said *Amen*, we'll consider the matter finished.'

"There's farce somewhere in every tragedy, Roddy. Here, against the glare on the Pacific, it challenged all doom, broad and unashamed. I need hardly tell you that Grimalson, at the opening of this harangue, had dropped his fishing-line, clutched his gaff, and whirled about furiously. But he faced three determined men, and Webster's loose hand played with a revolver. Twice or thrice Grimalson essayed to interrupt; but Jarvis was a man with a prepared speech: and, backed by Webster's free hand, he delivered it straight out at me to the last word over Grimalson's shoulder.

"Then, as he concluded, there ensued the beastliest scene of all. Grimalson, from facing these three slow, determined men, took a swift turn right about and struck at me with the gaff. They clutched at him and he faced about again, dropping the gaff, springing to the thwart and hitting right and left. Webster sprang also to the thwart and landed him a stunner on the point of the jaw which sent him overboard from the rocking boat.

"Now Webster was, in ordinary life, a religious man, and a Methodist. At sight of what he had done he ran to the boat's side, making ineffectual grabs to recover the body, which floated for a moment or two, with the senseless hands afloat or spread on the waters, as if in ghastly benediction. And then, as I put up helm, as if hauled down on a line, the trunk and head disappeared from view and a bloody smear came up, oozing and spreading. Jarvis called out that he had seen a shark's fin.

"I did not see it, being occupied in rounding up the boat to recover the body: doing this, too, with my left hand, in no small pain. For Grimalson's stroke with the gaff had lacerated my right fore-arm, tearing away a strip of my rolled-up shirt-sleeve.

"And then.... My God, Roddy!—Farrell, who had roused himself up at the scrimmage, had his mouth fastened on my arm, mad with thirst, sucking the blood! Oh, you have to go through these things to understand!... And I said I wouldn't tell.... I beat at him; but it was Santa who pushed him off.

"Webster had sunk, sobbing, with his face on his hands that gripped the gunwale. We were all mad. I held out my bleeding fore-arm to Santa, who was tearing a bandage for it.

"'Your husband has drunk,' I said.

"'Ah, pity!' said she, softly, taking the first deft turn of the bandage. 'Must you, too, be a beast?'

"Jarvis, meanwhile, like a man dulled to all tragedy had gone to the boat's side and was hauling in Grimalson's futile line. He brought up the sinker.

"'God help us all!—there's hope yet!' he barked through his parched throat, and held up the sinker all clothed about and clogged with greenish-brown shore-weed."

NIGHT THE EIGHTEENTH
"AND SO THEY CAME TO THE ISLAND..."

(Foe's Narrative Continued)

"That night, as I was steering, I heard a sound as of a bucket dipped over the bows. Needless to say, we had hoisted no lantern on the forestay since the night the other boats had driven away from us or gone down. To help a vessel to pick us up on that expanse of water it would have been about as useful as the tail of a glow-worm—and moreover the crew *had drunk all the oil.*

"I had the sheet well out and was running under a light, lazy night-waft of breeze. A thin moon was setting somewhere behind my right shoulder, and the glimmer of it played on the canvas.... I had supposed all the others to be sunk in merciful sleep, when Webster stood up and, staggering forward, ducked under the foot of the sail, which at once hid him from me.... When I heard the *plunk* of a bucket—as I supposed—it suggested at the worst that here was another fool dosing himself mad on sea-water; and, as values counted by this time, it was not worth while to awake four other souls to consciousness and misery for the sake of preventing him. ... And then the man's face went swimming past me, upturned to the moonlight, momentarily sinking as I grabbed at his beard which floated up like seaweed.... I grabbed, and missed. God knows what I should have done had my fingers tangled themselves in that beard, to get a clutch on it.

"He had slipped himself overboard, to drown quietly.... And we were now five, and Prout was plainly a dying man. (I'd have you note, Roddy, the order in which the men on board went; for it rather curiously backs up my theory that there's ever so much more vitality in what we call brains than in what we call physique.) Martinez was a weakling, of poor breed: Grimalson, big as bull's beef, had a brain rotten as a pear: Webster, a docile fellow, was strong as Hercules and surprisingly stupid. These were gone, in their order. The two A.B.'s, Jarvis and Prout—canny men, resourceful, full of seamanship—survived, and we three passengers. What kept Farrell going, and saved his reason, was a great capacity for sleep. He slept all the night and most of the day; and though by consequence he helped us little or nothing, seemed (as he declared himself to be) constantly dog-tired. His momentary ferocity, when he fastened on my bleeding forearm, had been a gust only, and after it he sank deeper and deeper into drowsiness. As for Santa—frankly, I don't know. They tell us that women sleep more lightly than men, and can endure suffering far more patiently—which some explain by saying that their nerves are less sensitive to pain, and (I suppose therefore) to pleasure. But I don't know: I have never studied the subject. She sat very quiet, sometimes for hours together, without stirring; but she took very little actual sleep.

"The end of Jarvis and Prout was one of those inhuman, ghastly farces which, as I've said, break the spell of a sudden and are worse than the tragedy itself. They had struck up a quaint, almost canine friendship—Yes, that's the word, though I can't stop to explain what I mean by it more than by saying that they would sit together by the hour, like two dogs before a fire. The odd thing about it was that they had twice been shipwrecked before on the coast; and had come through the double experience respecting one another as capable seamen but forming no attachment until—But it's ludicrous past guessing. On the second day in the boat it was discovered by a chance word that they had a common acquaintance in 'Frisco: and he wasn't much of a friend either. I never heard his name right and full, and I doubt if they knew it. They called him Uncle Tibe, and I gathered from their earlier conversations that he was a Jewish dealer in marine stores and a money-lender; of mature years; and afflicted with a chronic and most Christian thirst, which he alleviated by methods derived from the earliest patriarchs of his race. Of these his favourite was to attach himself to some young seaman with money in his pocket and, having insinuated concurrently the undoubted truths that he possessed great wealth but was averse to spending it (even on Scotch 'smokes'), to insinuate further that the victim had to an extraordinary degree crept into the affections of a childless old man,—yea, might hope indeed, by attentions which in practice worked out to ordering whisky and adding 'Make it two,' to inherit his real and personal estate.

"Silly as you like!—But the discovery that each had been hoaxed by Uncle Tibe, and the comparison of their foolish experiences, with reported tales of the dupes yet more heavily befooled and bled, caught and bound these men in fellowship. They had both met with some queer ones in their travels, and they compared notes: but they always came back to this superlative old fraud. After long wise and disconnected talk about the set of the wind, or the rates of pay on various lines, or stowage, or freights, or rigs, or currents, or the characters of various skippers and mates, or the liveliness or sulkiness or homeliness or fickleness of this or that kind of cargo, they would revert extra-professionally to Uncle Tibe: of whom the old stories would be repeated over and over, with long pauses, chuckles, slow appreciations—'Ay, Tibe!... He was a none-such, if you like!'

"Will you believe me that, in the end, these two honest fellows murdered each other over this more-than-half-mythical Tibe? No, you can't guess what it's like, towards the finish. They sat side by side on the mid-thwart, fishing over either gunwale—or leaning over, pretending. They were almost too weak to haul in a fish over four pounds had they caught one, and for two days their throats had been parched so that speech came with difficulty. Of a sudden Jarvis let out 'Tibe!' with a sort of ghostly cackle, and Prout cackled 'Tibe!' in an echo even thinner.... And, with that Jarvis stood up and started raving of what he would do when the money came to him, as he allowed it would, after all. Mighty queer ways of spending wealth he mentioned, too, before Prout was up and, yelling at him for a thief and supplanter, drove at his throat with a knife. He missed: but the next instant, these two fond friends, whose friendship had fenced us others off almost as strangers, were wallowing and knifing one another on the bottom-boards,—all over the visionary legacy of a Jew, thousands of miles away, whose picking of their pockets had been their common reminiscence and their standing joke through days of horror! And political economists used to tell us that money is a medium and symbol of exchange!"

"Well, after that we were three in the boat, and I was the only one strong enough to heft the bodies overboard. If they could only have held on to their wits for another twenty-four hours, or even for twelve!

"When I had done this work, and redded up the boat, I looked rather anxiously at Santa, who had been watching me: for I feared the effect this scene of shambles might have upon her. She sat, with Farrell's head resting against her knee, and still gazed unmoved.... Then I knew why. She had passed beyond these vain phenomena. Her eyes saw them and saw them not.... She was dying.

"Yet she sat erect. She even smiled, very faintly, and made a feeble motion of the hand towards her guitar-case, which I had lifted out of the reach of the blood and set on the seat at a little distance from her. Then I understood that she *had* seen, after all.... For I must tell you that, in the early days, Santa's playing and singing had brought great cheer to the crews, and our boat was envied for carrying this music. But there had come a day when Jarvis and Prout sent aft very respectfully to beg that there might be no more of it, for it dragged across their raw nerves: and from that hour the guitar had lain in its case. It could be set free now.

"I took it out, and she half held out her arms for it, as a mother might for her newly-born child.... But she would never play on it again. The strings were all loose but one, and that one broken. She had no strength, and I no skill, to re-tune the thing.

"But she thanked me in a sort of throaty whisper, and sat for a while letting the neck of the guitar lie against her shoulder, while her left hand went up to clasp it and finger it in the old way. And her right hand lifted itself once or twice towards the sounding-hole, but dropped back to her lap.

"'You are very good to me,' she said, after some seconds, still in the same whisper. 'Why is it that you hate Pete so?' Then, as I did not answer, she went on, 'I am dying, I think. It would be quite safe to tell me, now.'

"'When two men love one woman—' I began. But she shook her head, and her eyes accused me. Santa had very beautiful eyes, and in this agony they were perhaps deeper in colour and more beautiful than ever. But they had changed, somehow.... I cannot explain it but they recalled another pair of eyes... another woman's.... Whose?... I don't know! My mother's, maybe. She died, you know, when I was quite a small boy.... Anyway, these eyes quite suddenly looked at me out of the past—out of my memory, as it were. They were Santa's and yet they were not Santa's....

"'Ah,' said she, 'do not lie to me, now! It hurts so!'

"'Well, then,' I told her, 'your husband once, back in the past, did me a very great wrong. It—well, it wrecked the work of my life, and I have never forgiven it. Now let us talk no more about it.'

"A look of relief, almost a happy look, dawned on her face. 'I *knew* it was not about me! For I saw your two faces when you met on the hill, under my porchway.... Do you know that, at moments, you are very much alike?... Oh, in general, of course, there is no likeness at all.... But at certain moments.... And it was so when you met, there on the hill: I had to look from one to the other. It was plain in that instant that you hated one another—yes, and it might have been for a long time... ages and ages. But it could not have been about me, for you had not set eyes on me but within the minute.... I am glad, anyway, that it is not for my sake that you hate.'

"Her words came in faint, hurrying wafts, much as for days the wind had been ruffling after us. The sunset struck slantwise across her cheek and hung entangled in the brown tress that drooped low by her right temple. I tell you, Roddy, that if the old gods and goddesses in our school-books ever turned out to be mortal after all, she was one, and thus looked, and spoke as she died....

"'I understand well enough,' she went on, 'the small things over which women quarrel.... Though they all seem very far away just now, I was a woman and could be jealous over *any of them*. But I never understood why *men* quarrelled, except for me, of course. ... Was it over your work, do you tell me?'

"'Surely,' said I, 'a man's work—'

"'Yes. I know that it is so,' she answered me with a small sigh. 'Do you know that, far back, I come down from the Incas? and I dare say they thought less of work than of other things.... It is all thanks to your working that we three are alive, now.... I understand a little why men so much value their work.... But yet I do not understand why they drop their work to quarrel as they do. I understand it no better than the fighting of dogs.' She paused on that last word, and then, as though it had put new life into her, she sat erect and opened her eyes wider upon the horizon as she put the amazing question, 'Was it over a dog that you two hated?'

"It staggered me: but I caught at the first explanation. 'Oh, I see,' said I. 'Your husband has been telling you?'

"She didn't answer this at once.... At length, and as though my voice had taken long in reaching her, far out on the ocean where her gaze rested— 'No,' said she, 'Pete has told me nothing. ... I never asked.... But if it is true, *ay de mi!* then that which I behold is not true.'

"'Of what are you speaking?' I asked.

"'I saw an island,' she answered, as one in a dream: 'and again I see it. It has two sharp peaks and one that would seem to be cut short. Lawns of green climb up to the peaks between forests. There is a ring of surf all about the shore... but the boat has found a passage through... and you and Pete are landing... and— strangest!—there is a dog leaping about on the shore to welcome you.'

"I was silent, not caring to break in upon her happy delirium. 'But I am not there,' she whispered, almost in a moan. 'Why should a dog be there and not I?' Still getting no word from me, she turned her eyes full on mine and repeated the question imperatively, almost indignantly. 'Why should it be a dog?—and not *I*, over whom you never hated?'

"'Santa,' said I, 'if there were such an island as you see—'

"'But there *is*,' she interrupted quick as thought. 'There *is*, and it is near, though I shall not see it, except from the boat.'

"'Say, then, that there is such an island—' said I. It was just possible: for during the last two days we had sighted many sea-birds.

"'And near—quite near,' she insisted. 'It has groves of coco-trees, and streams tumbling down the rocks—on which no boat can row with men cursing in her and fighting with knives.'

"'Then you shall land on that island, O beloved!' said I, 'and we will live on it, and love—'

"'Ah, I know what you mean! You mean as they love in heaven? Yes.' And she added quite simply. 'I have had great trouble with men.'

"'Not exactly as in heaven,' said I, and took out from a breast-pocket under my jumper a small flask of yellow Chartreuse, which I had snatched up among other small belongings from my state-room locker ten minutes before the *Eurotas* went down. I had nursed it with a very jealous purpose.... Farrell should not slip through my fingers by dying, while I could yet force a stimulant down his throat, to linger him out.... It was a tiny 'sample' flask, and had been pressed on my acceptance, as a small flourish of trade, by a German wine-dealer in Valparaiso.... And here at the crisis, with Farrell dying at my feet, on an instant I renounced my purpose.

"'Drink this,' I commanded Santa, 'and you shall live some hours yet. And then, if there *be* an island—'

"She caught at it with a delighted cry, her hands suddenly vitalised. The guitar slid down from her lap. She drew out the glass stopper, holding the flask up a moment to the setting sun and letting it blaze through the liquid. Then swiftly, as I made sure she would carry it to her lips, she bent over Farrell and whispered some soft word of the night that pierced his stupor so that he stirred and lolled his head around.... Yes, and for a farewell kiss— which I watched without jealousy....

"But as their mouths drew apart, and before his swollen lips could close again, she had slipped the mouth of the flask between them and the cordial was pouring down his throat....

"She had defeated me.... I watched her without uttering a word. Farrell let out a guttural sort of *ah-h!* and sat up somewhat higher against her knee, opening his chest and breathing in new life as the Chartreuse coursed through his veins. Santa turned the flask upside-down, and handed it to me.

"'I have won!' she said softly. 'Men at the last are—what is the word?— magnanimous, mostly: and that is why a woman can usually win in the end.'

"'You have thrown away,' said I, 'so much of life as I gave you, renouncing much. You have sacrificed yourself.'

"'That was *my* share of the price, my friend. Now continue to be great, as for these many days you have been good. There is a bad pain about my heart. With that other small bottle of yours, and with that needle I have seen you use... You will? Ah, how much better it is to be friends than enemies, when the world—even this little shrinking world—is so wide yet—so wide—'

"So I took her wrist and, she scarcely wincing, injected the last drop of my morphia: yes, Roddy, and kissed the spot like any poor fool, she not resisting!... Her last words were that I should lay the guitar back again on her lap.... Oh, damn it, man! it was everything your damned sneerer would choose to call it.... But I tell you I held my ear close to her breast for hours; and in my light-headedness I heard the muted music lulling her: and in and out of her breathing, when she was long past speech—and above the stertorous snoring of my enemy laid at her feet—I heard distant waves breaking in a low chime to some words of a verse I had once quoted to her on a night when her song had made the crews sorrowful for a while before lifting their hearts again to make them merry—music to ripple, ripple:"

'—Ripple in my hearing
Like waves upon a lonely beach, where no craft anchoreth;
That I may steep my soul therein, and craving naught, nor
fearing, Drift on through slumber to a dream, and through
a dream to death.'

"My ear was close to her breast, listening, as the last breath went out with a flutter... and Santa was dead, having conquered me— conquered me far beyond my guessing; but up to the moment having subdued me so effectively that my sole kiss of her had been taken, kneeling, upon the wrist, as one kisses faith to a sovereign, and had never been returned. Through the night I held her wrist until it was cold."

"Towards dawn, and just at that moment when a watcher's spirits are at their lowest, Farrell stirred, stretched out his legs, drew them up again, and asked how things were?... For his part (he added, sitting up weakly), he felt a different man.

"'It behoves you to be,' said I with some sternness. 'Take the tiller and— yes, you may hold on to it with some firmness. Your wife is dead.'

"'Santa!' he gasped. 'Oh, my God!' and cast himself upon her body, seemly bestowed as I could serve it.

"'Get off of it,' I shouted, 'before I brain you!' I held the very gaff with which Grimalson had torn my arm. He had plucked the tiller from the rudder-head, and with these two weapons in our right hands we faced one another, each with his left feeling for the revolver he carried.

"Then Farrell, who stood facing the bows, shot out his right as if jabbing at me with the stick, a foot short of my shoulder. The action was, as a stroke, so idiotic that, although it might so easily have meant death to me, I turned half-about to where the stick pointed, as the helmless boat yawed.

"And there, above the low-lying wisps of morning fog, stood three peaks: two sharp and the third blunted: and, below the fog, ran a thin white ribbon of breaking water!

"We had run down upon it so close in those hours of darkness that the beat of the surf had, as I now recognised, confused itself into Santa's last breathings: so close that, as the sun took swift mastery of the mist and dissolved it, disclosing, below the peaks, the variegated greenery of lawn and forest pouring down to the seamed cliffs and pouring over them to the very beaches in tapestries of vines and creepers, we were almost in the ring of the surf: and it came as a shock to me that the lazy swell on which we had so long lifted and dropped, heeding it least among many threats, could beat on this islet so terrifically.

"The sight so vanquished Farrell that he yielded the stick over to me, obedient as a child. I thrust it back in its socket, hauled sheet and fetched her up close to the wind outside the surges.... Without a word said, he turned to pointing out this and that inlet between the reefs where there seemed a chance to slip through.

"For two miles at least we fended off in this way, until we came to the base of the hill which, from seaward, had appeared so curiously truncated. As we opened its steep-to sides, they rounded gradually into a high curve at the skyline, and, at the base, into a foreshore of tumbled rock through which ran a cleft with still water protected by sheer rocks—a narrow slit, but worth risking with the wind to drive us straight through. So I upped helm on the heave of a comber, and drove her for it, the walls of rock so close on either hand that twice the end of our short boom brushed them before Farrell, who held the sheet, could avoid touching.... And then, rushed by a heave of the swell through this gorge, we were shot into a round lake of the bluest water I ever set eyes on; a lakelet, rather; calm as a pond except by the entrance, where the waves, broken and spent, spread themselves in long ripples that melted and were gone.

"You know Lulworth Cove? Well, imagine Lulworth, with a narrower entrance, its water blue as a sapphire shot with amethystine violet, its cliffs taller, steeper, hung with matted creeper and, high aloft, holding the heaven in a three-part circle almost as regular as you could draw with a pair of compasses. We were floating in the cup of a dead volcano, broken on the seaward side; and broken many hundreds of years ago—for on our starboard hand, by the edge of the rent, swept down a slope of turf, cropped by the gales, green as an English park; with a thread of a stream dropping to a small wilderness of ferns, and, through this, to plash upon a miniature beach of pink sand, on the edge of which the sea scarcely lapped. Sea-birds of many kinds circled and squawked overhead. Yet it was not our boat that had frightened them.

"They had risen in alarm at the sound of barking, high up the slope. A dog came leaping down it, tore through the fern, and, as our boat drew to shore, raced to and fro by the water's edge, barking wildly in an ecstasy of welcome. A yellow dog, Roddy—a largish yellow dog—and, as I live by food, the living image of my murdered Billy!"

NIGHT THE NINETEENTH
THE CASTAWAYS

(Foe's Narrative Continued)

"A miracle? Well, I had always supposed poor Billy to be a mongrel of such infinite variety of descent that the world might never hope to behold his like. But, after all, the strains even of dogs are limited in number; and what Nature has produced she can reproduce.

"But the apparition, just there, and at that moment, was a miracle to me. I sat staring at it even when the boat's stem took the beach gently, and it was Farrell who first crawled over her side to land. His knees shook, and the dog, leaping against him, nearly bowled him over. Then the sight of water seemed to galvanise his legs, and he tottered frantically up the small foreshore to the cascade, beside which he fell and drank, letting the spray drench his head, neck, and shoulders. The animal had gone with him, gambolling and barking, and now ran to and fro and leapt over his body three or four times, still barking. All his welcome was for Farrell. To me, as I followed, staggering, the animal paid no heed at all, until he saw me drawing close, when he suddenly turned about, showed his teeth and started to growl. His tail stiffened, the hairs on his chine bristled up, and I believe in another moment he would have flown at me.

"Partly of knowledge, however, and partly of weakness, I checked this. My feet had no sooner felt firm ground than I found myself weak as a year-old child. The strength of will that had held me up through that awful voyage—and it was awful, Roddy—went draining out of me, and the last of my bodily strength with it, like grain through a hole in a sack. As the dog bristled up, I fell forward on hands and knees, laughing hysterically, and the dog winced back as if before a whip, and cringed.... You know, I dare say, that no dog will ever attack a man who falls forward like that, or crouches as if to sit, *and laughs*?... So I dropped from this posture right prone by the edge of the basin hollowed by the little waterfall, and drank my fill.

"What next do you guess we did?... We rolled over on the sand under the shade of the cliff, and slept....

"We slept for three mortal hours. I've no doubt we should have slept oblivious for another three, had not the making tide aroused me with its cool wash around my ankles. The sun, too, was stealing our resting-place from us, or the comfort of it, cutting away the cliff's shadow as it neared the meridian.... The boat, utterly neglected by us, had floated up, broadside on, with the quiet tide, almost to our feet. The dog sat on his haunches, waiting and watching for one or other of us to give sign of life.

"I roused up Farrell.... My first thought was for Santa's body, laid within the boat on the bottom-boards. 'Are we man enough, between us, to lift her out?' I asked. 'Or shall we moor the boat and climb for help?... There are certainly people on this island, since this dog must have a master somewhere.'

"'She is a light weight,' said Farrell simply. 'Let us try.... Her soul forgive me for leaving her, even so long as I have, in that horrible boat!'

"So, weak as we were, we managed to lift Santa's body ashore and carry it up the few yards of sand beyond what we judged to be a faint tide-mark, close under the ferns.... After this we fetched ashore the tool-chest and some loose articles that we judged to be necessary—such as the cooking-pot, binoculars, and a spare coil or two of rope and a ship's mallet; and Farrell searched the undercliff for sea-birds' eggs, whilst I gave the boat a cleansing with baler and sponge, redded her up after a fashion, and finally moored her off with a shore-line, some twenty yards out on the placid water. While thus occupied, my mind was wondering what kind of people inhabited this island, and why they kept such poor watch.... We had run in openly in daylight, and yet it would seem that only this dog had spied us.

"If they were savages, why, then, I had only my revolver with a fair number of cartridges.... Some of my stock I had blazed away during the last two days in vain attempts upon the life of the sea-birds that ever wheeled out of fair range. The tool-chest, indeed, contained a shot-gun, or the parts of one: but I had never pieced them together, for the simple reason that all the cartridges belonging to it had, through Grimalson's careless stowage, been soaked and spoilt during the night of the gale.... Somehow, I could not mentally connect savages with the ownership of this dog. But the day wore on, and still no one hailed us from the cliffs or the green slope.

"Now I must tell you that the boat's locker yet held a chunk or two— less than a pound—of brined pork, hard as wood and salt as the Dead Sea, that none of the crew at the last had a thought to boil in the sea water, which only made it more intolerable. None of us, indeed, after a trial, had been able to get a morsel past our swollen tonsils. But I had a boxful of matches in my trouser pocket, half-emptied: and, as it turned out, Farrell had preserved another. So in this most vital necessary we were well supplied. Therefore, when Farrell, with the dog at his heels, came back along the shore, holding up two cray-fish that he had taken in a rock-pool at the turn of the tide, I tossed the gobbets of pork overboard to desecrate the clear depth. Indeed, apart from fish and fowl, I had seen as we neared the island that we had no fear of starving: for an abundance of cocos and palms grew all around the ridge of the crater and had but to be climbed for as soon as we found strength. The tool-chest contained a saw and a hatchet.

"It also contained an engineering-tool, part pick, part digger. I handed it to Farrell, and he understood. 'But first,' said I, 'let's make a fire and fill the pot. There's a plenty of small dead wood everywhere, and we're too weak just yet to heave this gear any distance up the slope before sunset. We'd best light a fire here; and when we have it started, I'll mount the slope some little way where I see a plenty of limes growing. I may go some way farther, to prospect. The smoke of the fire ought to attract the attention of these very careless islanders; and if they turn out to be unfriendly, well, I have my revolver and you'll have ample warning to clear off to the boat.'

"'Savages?' muttered Farrell. 'I never thought of that…. Go you up, if you will, and take the dog for company. You can leave me to light the fire, and—'tisn't a request I've dared to make to you since God knows when—but if you've any pity anywhere in your bowels, just now I'd like to be alone.'

"'I haven't,' said I: 'but I have some sense in my head, and I'm going to prospect. I'll leave you at anchor here for an hour or so.'

"I whistled to the dog, and the dog, after long hesitation and having been thrice shoo'd in my wake by Farrell, followed. But he hung some twenty yards behind, and showed no sign of desire to lead me to the people to whom he belonged. By and by he came to a dead halt and, for all my whistling and calling, broke back for the beach again and disappeared at a gallop….

"I held my ascent, still beside the downward-pouring stream, and on my way noted fruit-bearing trees in plenty. I reached a point where the volcanic hill ran down landward in rounded ridges, and crossed two or three of these: but no sign of human habitation could I discern.

"When I descended again to the beach, with the lap of my jumper full of limes and wild grapes, it was to find the dog stretched beside a sizable fire and Farrell busy nailing together some lengths of long timber. I had heard the sound of his hammer from half-way down the slope.

"'Good Lord, man!' said I, staring. For he had pulled in the boat and sawn almost the whole of the port-side out of her. 'You have cut us off now, whatever happens!'

"'You don't imagine,' said he, 'that I'd ever set foot in that blasted boat again?'

"What is more, he had cut a couple of cloths out of the sail, for a winding-sheet.... But the pot was near to boiling; and after we had supped on the crayfish and the fruit, he fell to work again, nailing together a rough coffin. He explained that he had served his time in quite a humble way before embarking in business, on borrowed capital, as a tradesman. Then, under the risen moon, by the scarcely audible plash of the beach, he told me quite a lot about himself and his early days, as he fashioned a coffin for the woman into whose arms I had driven him, as I had driven him with her corpse to this lost isle.

"In the midst of it I said, 'You know, I suppose, that she saved your life?'

"He checked his hammer midway in a stroke, and stared at me, the moonlight white on his face.

"'You know,' I repeated, 'that she gave her life to save yours?' and I told him how. At the end of the tale, if ever hatred shone in a man's eyes, it shone in Farrell's; and yet there was incredulity in them too.

"'What!' he gasped. 'And you let her do it, there in front of you, when with a turn of the hand—O my God!' he broke off. 'I've thought at times you must be the Devil himself, you Foe: but I never reckoned you for as bad as all that! The wonder to me is I don't kill you where you sit.' He clenched the hammer, and twice again he called on his God. The dog growled.

"'Steady!' said I, showing him the revolver. 'Steady, and sit down. You can't kill me, my good man, unless you do it in my sleep—against which I'll take precautions. So you may quit wondering on that score.... And I can't kill you; for you're too precious—doubly precious now, *having been bought with that price*.... Sit down, I tell you, and order that infernal dog to be quiet: else I'll pump some lead into him and, dog against dog, you may count it quits.'

"'Quits?' he echoed.

"'In the matter of two yellow dogs only: and I have given up keeping pets, having *you*.... Now listen: Did you ever guess that I loved your wife?'

"It took him like a blow between the eyes. 'No, I didn't,' he answered slowly, and then with a sudden rush of malignity, 'I wonder it didn't occur to you, then—I wonder you didn't try to—to—tamper with her.'

"'You would,' said I. 'It's the sort of man you are, you Farrell. The next thing, you'll be capable of wondering if I didn't…. Pah! and *you* call *me* Satan!' I spat. 'Now, take hold on your fool head and think. For *her* sake I grant you ease of that suspicion, though in dealing with you it would be priceless to me. Think what a peck of torture I'm letting run to waste, as that waterfall yonder runs to waste in its basin. But it wouldn't be true. Your wife was an angel. Drink that comfort—drink it into every cranny of your soul…. And now hold your head again. I loved Santa, I tell you.'

"'You let her die,' he muttered sullenly.

"'Think, you fool—think!' I commanded. 'If she had lived, you would have died, and she would be sitting where you are sitting at this moment, and I here, and the moon swimming above us two—Would you have had it so?'

"'My God!' he blurted, wiping the back of a hand across his eyes. 'This is too much for me….'

"I stood and picked up the engineering tool. 'For me, too,' said I, 'it is enough…. Now come and choose the spot, and I will fall to my part of the work.'

"But to this he demurred, saying vaguely that he was upset; that the spot for the grave must be chosen with care and by daylight; that he must first finish the coffin, and then take some rest. There would be time enough after we had breakfasted.

"I believed that I understood…. He wished to wash and wind the body. So at dawn—by which time the coffin was ready—I told him that he should be alone for a couple of hours, and went up the hill again in the first light, to prospect. Again I tried to whistle the dog after me: but this time he refused even to budge.

"I climbed no farther than before; that is, a little beyond the ridge. For it gave upon a wide undulating valley to the slopes of the second crater, which again partly overlapped the cone of the third or highest. To descend and cross this first vale would cost from two to three hours' hard walking, and my design was merely to con the prospect for sign of those inhabitants to whom the dog must belong. For he was little more than a puppy in age. Also, though lean, he was not at all emaciated: but the traces of rabbit-dung on the slopes told that a deserted dog might manage to sustain life here. Also it promised that the island was inhabited, and by white men, for rabbits are not indigenous anywhere in the South Pacific. They must be brought.

"I studied the hollow and searched it with my binoculars for some while: but without picking up any trace of mankind. Far below me a sizable stream here showed itself through the tropical vegetation as it hurried down to a hidden cove. The wide ocean spread southward to my right. Of how far the island might stretch beyond the taller and more distant cone I could make no guess.

"A desire for sleep came upon me, and I stretched myself in the shade of a bush under the lee of the ridge. After an hour's nap I rose and descended again to the beach.

"Farrell sat by the fire, cooking breakfast, the dog watching him. There was no coffin, nor any sign of a grave, and the tide was making. He had made haste to bury Santa during my absence.... He said not a word about it, and I did not question him. But he had played me this trick. Henceforth I felt no further pity."

"You may remember my saying, Roddy, when I first started to tell you about Santa, that it was impossible for me to hate Farrell worse than I did. Well, I thought so at the time. But now on the island I was to find myself mistaken, and this trick of his set me off hating him in a new and quite different way.

"I believe now, looking back, that this was the real beginning of Santa's revenge; or the first evident sign of its working; unless you count the behaviour of the dog—of which I will say more presently. At any rate I had no longer that cool godlike sense of mastery over the man which had sustained me in the boat. It may sound incredible: but whereas, cooped in that narrow shell of boards, I had found his presence gratifying, here on an island of wide prospects, where we could have parcelled out a kingdom apiece and lived by the year without sight of one another, I found it irritating and at times even intolerably so. He had found power, through her dead body, to give me a grievance against him, when I had supposed him too low and myself too high for anything to affect me that he could do.... It is always a mistake, Roddy, to falter once in an experiment. It is disloyalty in a man of science to renounce one at any point. Now, I had renounced, in handing Santa the flask; and again I had faltered, in a moment of generosity when I left him beside her corpse.... And of that act of generosity—and of delicacy, too, by the way—this thief had taken advantage.

"Oh, yes—I know what you will be wanting to say—that the man was her husband, hang it all!... I answer that he *had been* her husband and my darling's flesh I had resigned to him, as was meet and right.... But if you'll understand—if you've ever read what the Gospel quite truly says about marriage, to take it in—the man had no tyrant's monopoly beyond the grave. She was mine now—his, too, if he would—but mine also by right of my great love for her.

"You see, I am shaking, even as I speak of it. I had this grievance, and it festered and raised the whole temperature of my hate.… And this wasn't the worst, either. The worst was a sense that, lying somewhere with closed eyes under the ebb and flow of the tide, my beloved was working against me, watchfully, by unguessable ways, and weakening me. There was this dog, for example.… Yes, *that* had been the first token. How had it passed from me—this power over animals that had used to be exerted so easily?"

"But I had not lost my power over Farrell, although there were times when I mistrusted it. His eyes had given me the first warning, when I returned that morning and found myself tricked. They were half-timorous but also half-defiant, and wholly sly. It disconcerted him that I made no comment on his silence and asked no questions.

"On the fifth morning—by which time we had picked up enough strength to attempt a day's exploration of the west side of the island, and within an hour of the time fixed for our start, he found me fitting and nailing a short cross-plank to the boat's mast.

"'Hallo!' said he. 'What job are you spoiling there? I'm the carpenter of this party, or believed I was.'

"'And I'm the captain,' said I; 'and duly appointed—though I have no witness but you to the fact—if you choose to lie about it.… I'm doing a job which you have neglected: fixing a Cross for Santa. It will be a comfort, as we fare inland, to know she has a Christian mark over her grave.… You have the bearings accurate no doubt,' said I, lifting the heavy cross and, as I stooped to shoulder it, picking up the ship's mallet, which lay at my feet. 'Will it be here—or here?' I asked, choosing the spot and prodding the sharpened foot of the cross into the sand.… His face blanched. 'You accursed fool!' said I, 'do you suppose I haven't, these four days, been watching you and the dog?'—and, as I said it, the point of the mast struck upon timber. 'Come and help me to drive it deep,' I commanded. 'If we can work it down within reach of mallet, three taps will drive it so that it will stand firm above such tides as reach this anchorage of hers.'

"He came down the beach heavily and we heaved our strength together, driving the cross down by the coffin's head. 'The mallet is handy by you,' said I. 'Pick it up and use it while I hold steady.'

"This work done, without another word between us, we returned, picked up axe, saw, and a wallet to collect any specimens of fruit we might find on our way, and, still without a word, breasted the hill side by side, the dog running ahead of us.

"We got no farther that day than to the stream which ran between our hill and the second volcano, the edge of which—like that of our own broken and truncated one, ran down steeply to the western shore. The wood beside the stream grew so thick, interlaced with tendrils of tropical plants, that we were forced to turn aside and make for the coast in hope to find a crossing.

"We descended into the sound of the beating surf before we found one: and there an impish fancy took me. I had been losing grip on Farrell, and despite my small triumph of that morning, I felt a sudden desire to test him. Pretending that my purpose was only to cross and report, I waded the stream and dodged upward through the undergrowth; recrossed it, about a hundred yards above, crawled another yard and again recrossed, all to baffle the hound's scent, since from Farrell I could have hidden by this time securely enough. In a very few minutes I heard his voice hallooing to me, and then the dog's yelp began to chime in with it. By and by the beast, well baffled, was baying hard through the undergrowth between me and the surf.

"After a while of this play I crept out and strolled easily back to my first ford, my hands in my pockets.

"'What the devil's up with your beast?' I asked, wading across to the bank on which Farrell stood.

"His face was white. 'My God!' he said. 'I thought, for a while, we had lost you!'

"Then I knew that he dared not be alone, and that I had him, whatever happened."

NIGHT THE TWENTIETH
ONE MAN ESCAPES

Before continuing Foe's story, I should warn you not to be surprised that hereabouts it takes on a somewhat different tone. I am trying to give you the tale as he told it: and so much of it as related to Santa, he told bravely and frankly, here and there with a thrill somewhere deep beneath his voice, and exaltation on his face. He was, in short, the Jack Foe of old days, opening out his heart to me; and all the more the same because he was different. By this I mean that never in life had I heard him speak in just that way, simply because never in life had he brought me this kind of emotion, to confess it; but, granted the woman and the love, here (I felt) was the old Jack opening his heart to me. It rejuvenated his whole figure, too, and, in a way, ennobled it. I forgot—or rather, I no longer saw—the change in him which had given me that secondary shock when he walked into the room.

I cannot tell you the precise point at which his tone altered, and grew hard, defiant, careless and—now and then at its worst—even flippant. But it was here or hereabouts, and you will guess the reason towards the end.

Another thing I must mention. You have already guessed that the tale was not told at one sitting. Between the start and the point where I broke off last night, we had lunched, taken a stroll Piccadilly-wards, done some shopping, and chatted on the way about various friends and what had happened to them in this while—Jack questioning, of course, while I did almost all the talking. It was in the emptying Park, as we sat and watched the carriages go by, that he told me of Santa's burial and what followed it, so far as you have heard. I broke off last time at the point where he broke off, stood up, and said he would tell me the end of it all over dinner at the Cafe Royal, where we had called, on the way, to reserve our old table.

I saw afterwards why he had arranged it so: as you will see. But for the present it only needs remembering that what follows was told in a brilliant, rather noisy room—at an isolated table, but with a throng of diners all around us.

I had ordered wild duck as part of the dinner: and when it came to be served he looked hard at his plate, and, without lifting his eyes, slid from casual talk into his narrative again:

[Foe's Narrative Concluded]

"Wild duck—? good! Yes, we used to have wild duck on the island. … There were lagoons on the east side, fairly teeming with them, and we fixed up a decoy. I don't pretend that we fixed up an orange salad like this, with curacao: but in the beginning we practised with limes, and later on I invented one of sliced bananas, with a sort of spirit I brewed from the fruit. Also we found bait in the pools, not so much unlike the whitebait we've been eating—I used to frizzle it in palm oil. And once I achieved turtle soup.… He was the only fellow that, in two years, we ever managed to collar and lay on his back; and the soup, after all was no great success. But turtle's eggs.… I can tell you all about turtle's eggs. That dog had a nose for them like a pig's for truffles.

"Don't be afraid, Roddy. In this sophisticated den of high living and moderate thinking I'm not going to give you the Swiss Family Robinson; though I could double no trumps and risk it on the author of that yarn—whoever he may have been—if he had only dealt from a single pack, which he didn't. Farrell and I didn't build a house in a tree, because we didn't need to; and we didn't ride on emus, because we didn't want to, and moreover there weren't any. But we did pretty well there for two years, Roddy: and could say as Gonzalo—was it Gonzalo?—said of another island, that here was everything advantageous to life. And we found the means to live, too.

"I may say that I took the role of Mrs. Beeton: hunted for fruits, fished, told Farrell (of my small botanical knowledge) what to eat, drink, and avoid, and attended to the high cuisine. Farrell, reverting to his old journeyman skill, sawed planks and knocked up a hut. When one hut became intolerable for the pair of us—for in all that time we never ceased hating—he knocked up a second and better one for my habitation. He was my hewer of wood and drawer of water. Also it was he who—since I professed no eagerness to get away—did the conventional thing that castaways do: erected a flag-staff, and hauled piles of brushwood up to the topmost lip of our volcano, for a bonfire to be lit if any ship should be sighted, lest it might pass in the night. I had resigned the binoculars to him, but he never brought report of a sail.

"On two points—which served us again and again for furious quarrels—the fool was quite obstinate. He would not budge from our first encampment—that is to say, out of sight of Santa's grave; and he flatly refused to fit new planks to the ruinated boat which now lay, a thing of ribs, high and dry as we had hauled her close underneath the fern-brake beside the cascade. Again and again I pointed out to him that, patched up, she would serve me for fishing. To this he answered, truly enough, that we had

Foe-Farrell | 203

a plenty of fish in the rock-pools and a plenty of oysters on the shore. Then I urged that, if we sighted a ship—though it didn't matter to me—we might need a boat to get out to her. He retorted that, though it mattered to him, he would never set foot again in that cursed craft or help me to set foot in her. Finally, one day when I was absent on an expedition after food, he broke her remains to shreds.

"Upon this we had an insane quarrel—the more insane because it all turned on my dwelling on the detriment to his chances of escape and his reminding me of my indifference. We argued like two babies. But I had now another grievance: though it was the devil to me to be falling back on grievances.

"I still held the whip-hand over him in this—I could always thong him by a threat to part company and live by myself on the east side of the island. He mortally feared to be left, even with the dog for company.

"The dog remained a mystery. Although, as time went on, we explored the island pretty thoroughly, we never found his owner, nor any sign of human habitation. The conies which bred and multiplied on the hills were our only assurance that man had ever landed here before us—that is, until we discovered the strange boat: and it was through the dog that we discovered it."

"During the first three months we made no lengthy excursions, being occupied in cutting and sawing timber for the two living-huts and a store-hut; in making a small net (this was my task), and in sun-drying the fish I caught in it—for, knowing little about these latitudes, I feared that at any moment the heavenly weather might break, and we be held prisoners by torrential rains, traces of which I read in some of the seaward-running gullies. Also Farrell refused to budge until he had built his bonfire. When this was done we had another pretty fierce quarrel because, tired of waiting, I took a humour to punish him by making him wait in his turn while I did some tailoring.... No: we didn't dress in goatskins. There were no goats. But I had visions of piecing up a rabbit-skin coat and, in the meantime, of cutting up the boat's sail into drawers and jumpers, our clothes by this time being worse than a disgrace. But I believe that I held out chiefly to annoy him; and, having annoyed him sufficiently, I gave way to his final argument—that our boots were wearing out fast and, if we didn't make the expedition at once, likely enough we never should.

"So we started on what proved to be a two days' tramp, and thereby came pretty near to wrecking ourselves.

"The third cone, which—in that clear atmosphere—seemed to stand close behind the second, turned out to be separated from it by a good five miles as the crow flies. But on the north-western shore the sea had breached the reefs and swept in to form a salt lagoon in the great hollow, so that we had to fetch a circuit of at least seven miles to the southward, avoiding a tangle of forest in which the lagoon ended, and clambering along a volcanic ridge with the sea often sheer on our right. It was in this lagoon, by the way, that we afterwards learned to take our wild duck, scores of which paddled about quite tamely on its surface, their tameness promising poorly for human hospitality on the farther side of the hill.

"We gained the side of the great cone at length and, rounding it, beheld all the northern part of the island spread at our feet—in form a narrow strip of land curving around a delicious bay and ending in a small pinnacle of high tumbled cliff and wood. Quite obviously this bay was the one anchorage in the island for any ship of burden; and no ship could have asked for a better: for it made almost three parts of a circle, and, while not completely land-locked, held recesses in which any gale might be ridden out.

"Here, if anywhere, as I told Farrell, we should come upon human life or the traces of it: here, if anywhere, if vessel ever made this island, to water, she would drop hook. 'Fools we have been, to waste months pitching camp on the other side, when this is the place of places, and this hill gives the citadel prospect of all!'

"Farrell sat down on a rock and broke into curses. 'Damn you,' he moaned, 'for bringing me so far! I wish I had never seen it. Wasn't it comfortable enough where we were?... And now I can't go back!'

"I had taken the binoculars and, engaged with the view, for a moment paid no heed. I was accustomed to his explosions of fury, as he to mine. But, turning about for a while, I saw that he had unlaced his left boot and was holding it out.... The sole had broken loose in our scramble over the tufa rocks, and hung parted from its upper.

"'That's bad,' said I. 'Well, I stuck a ship's needle in the tool-bag here before we started—*you* never think of anything! When we get down to the shore we'll see what can be done: that is, if we don't find a cobbler.'

"'Cobbler? you funny ass!—' he began.

"'Look here,'—I stopped him. 'If you won't attend to me, attend to Rover. What's up with that dog of yours?'—for the dog which had been following all day pretty obediently, except for a wild dash down to the lagoon to scatter the wild duck, had of a sudden picked up bearings and was running forward, halting, returning, wagging his tail, running forward again, turning, asking dumbly to be understood, in the way all dogs have who invite you to follow a trail.

"'Here's business,' said I, and hurried after him, leaving Farrell to limp down the hill-side in our wake. For once the dog recognised me as more intelligent or, at any rate, prompter than his master, and gave his whole attention to me.... I tumbled down the hill after him in a haste that fairly set my temples throbbing. Once sure of me, he played no more at backwards-and-forwards, but bounded down the slope towards the innermost southern corner of the bay, where a grove of coco-trees almost overhung the beach. A curtain of creepers bunched over the low cliff at their feet and into this he plunged and disappeared.

"But his barking still led me on; and presently, as I avoided the undergrowth and creepers to follow the foreshore, sounded back to me across a low spit of rock. I climbed this and came all unexpectedly upon a diminutive creek.

"It was really but a fissure between the rocks, with deep water between them and an abrupt, dolls'-house-beach of sand and shells above it, terminating in a flat, overhanging ledge. And on this ledge rested a white-painted boat, high and dry! From the stern-sheets the dog barked at me joyously, wagging his tail, with his fore-feet on the edge of the stern-board.

"I ran to it. Within the stern-board, in cut letters from which the cheap paint had scaled, was a name plain to read—*Two Brothers*. Two paddles lay in her, neatly disposed: a short mast and sail tightly wrapped and traced up in its cordage; her rudder, with tiller-stick, two rusty rowlocks of galvanised iron, and a tin baler, all trimly bestowed under the stern-sheets—and that was her inventory, save a pig of iron ballast, much rusted. How long she had rested there, clean and tidied, half protected from the sun's rays, there was no guessing. But her seams gaped so that I could push my little finger some way between her strakes. She had no anchor; and her painter had been cut short at the ring, sharply. Only the knot remained.

"I was examining this when Farrell overtook me. He came over the rocks, limping; halted; and let out a cry at sight of the boat. Then, as by chance, he peered into the cleft at his feet, into the fathom-deep water past which I had run; and, with that, let out a sharper cry, commanding me to him.

"Down in the transparent water, inert but seeming to move as the ripple ran over it, lay the body of a man, face down, with a trail of weed awash over its shoulders. Peering down through the weed, I saw that a cord knotted about its right ankle ended in another pig of ballast, three-parts covered by the prismatic sand.

"'My God!' said Farrell, and shivered.

"'Well, he's no use to us, even if we do fish him up,' said I, pretty grimly. 'Here's the dog's owner, and that's as far as we get. Since a dog—even so intelligent a pup as Rover here—can't very well attach a weight to his master's ankle and cast him overboard—let alone pulling his boat above high water and stowing sail—we'll conclude that this fellow deliberately made away with himself. As I make it out, the dog, thus marooned, struck pretty frantically for the high ground. Lost dogs—and lost children, for that matter— always make up hill, dark or daylight. I suppose it's the primitive instinct to search for a view.... But anyway, here's a boat. She's unseaworthy, as she lies: but her timbers look sound enough if we can staunch her, and the first thing is to get her down to the water and see how fast she fills. We've a baler, to cope with the leak... and when we have her more or less staunch, here's the way around to our camp. Hurry up your wits!' I added sharply.

"'If we launch her here,' he twittered, 'she'll settle down on *that!*'

"'Then run,' said I, 'and, with all the knowledge you ever picked up in Tottenham Court Road, fetch every grass and fibre you can collect, to stuff her seams. I'll do the sailing while the wind's fair offshore, as it is at present. When it heads us, I'll do the pulling. Man alive! think of your burst boot! For my part, I'm willing enough to stay here as anywhere: or you can stay, and I'll start back for camp, and we'll share this island like two kings, you keeping this imperial anchorage.'

"But of course this had him beaten. He helped me launch the boat and ran to collect stuffing for her seams, while I sat in her and baled, baled, baled.... It was pretty eerie to sit there alone—for the dog had gone with Farrell—fighting the water, and feel her settling, if for five minutes I gave up the struggle, down nearer and nearer upon the shoulders of that drowned corpse with the hidden face. By sunset Farrell returned with an armful of sun-dried fibre. We hauled the boat high again and he began caulking her lower seams, that already had started to close.

"'She'll keep afloat now for a few hundred yards,' he announced after a while. 'Let's launch her again and run her round the point and beach her. I left a bundle of bark there that, early to-morrow, we'll cut in strips and tack over the seams, and she'll do fine to carry us home.'

"'Home?' echoed I grimly.

"'You know what I mean, you blighter!' he snarled. 'Oh, for God's sake, no—we mustn't start bickering alongside of *that!*' He forced his eyes to look down again at the corpse, and shuddered. 'The tide's going down, too.'

"'It won't go down far enough to uncover *him*: and that you ought to have sense to know," said I.

"'But the farther it goes down the nearer he'll come up, or seem to,' he argued.

"'Well, night's coming on, and you won't see him,' I suggested, playing on his nerves.

"'D'you think I'll sit here in the dark, alongside of—oh, hurry, you devil! Hurry!'

"I chuckled at this. It came into my mind to refuse, and declare I would sit out the night here by the boat. I knew that the shore beyond, though it curved for two good miles, would not be wide enough to contain his agony through the night hours.... But I had pushed him far enough for the time. So we launched the boat again and paddled her around and beached her on shelving sand: and soon after, night fell.

"Farrell slept poorly. Three or four times I heard him start up, to pace to and fro under the starlight: and each time the dog awoke and trotted with him....

"But he was up, brisk and early, with dawn; and he made quite a good job of tacking bark over the boat's seams, while I sat and cobbled up his boot with sailmaker's needle and twine. He made, indeed, and though swift with the work, so good a job that, inspecting the boat when he had done, I judged she would stand the strain of sailing— whereas I had looked forward to a grilling pull in a craft that leaked like a basket.

"At a quarter to ten, by my watch, we pushed off, stepped mast and hoisted sail—a small balance-lug. We carried a brisk offshore wind—a soldier's wind—which southerned as the day wore on, and again flew and broke off-shore as we neared home. I steered: Farrell, for the most part, dozed after his labours. He had not, I may say, one single faculty of a seaman in his whole make-up. He could mend a boat or make an imitation Sheraton wardrobe; but, when the both were made, he'd have sailed the one about as well as the other.

"He dozed uneasily, with many twitchings. Once he woke up and said, 'I thank God he lay so as we couldn't see his face. Would it have been swollen much, think you?... Bleached, I make no doubt....'

"'What about worse?' I answered. 'I noticed a crab or two.' "He put up his hands to his face. 'How the devil can you talk so!' he stammered.

"'It was you who started questions,' said I.

"'Suicide, you think?' he asked, after half an hour's silence, during which his mind had plainly been tugging away from the horrible subject only to find it irresistible.

"'All pointed to it,' I answered. 'As for the motive, we can only guess.'

"'Where's the guesswork?' he demanded fiercely. 'Cast here, in this awful loneliness—' I saw him look around on sea and cliff with a shiver.

"'He had the dog,' said I. 'You find Rover here a companion, don't you? I had a notion, Farrell, that you were fond of dogs.... I used to be.'

"We downed sail hereabouts, and pulled in for the cleft and the anchorage we called home. The sea under the smoothing land-wind ran through the passage as calmly as through a miller's leat: and I will own it was happier to be by that shore where my cross still stood over Santa than by the other, where that other body lay, face-down, with the weight whipped to its ankle. "'Wonder who he was?' said Farrell late that evening, as we parted to go to our quarters. 'A missionary, I shouldn't be surprised.'

"'If so,' said I, 'he tumbled on a sinecure. Since your mind runs on him and you want to sleep, make it out that he was a bishop, and home-sickened for the Athenaeum.'"

"I'm coming to the end, Roddy; and you shall have it sharp and quick, as it happened.... As I've said, we stuck it out on that island for two years, and a little over, hating one another as two lonely men will come to hate, on island or lighthouse, even when they don't start on a sworn enmity. Oh, you must have been through it to understand!... We even quarrelled—and came almost to blows—over the day of the month; though God knows what it helped either to be right or wrong, and, as it happened, we were both wrong by a fortnight or so."

"And then Farrell took ill.

"It was a kind of fever he caught while duck-snaring in the lagoon. He'd start off there for a long day with his dog, the two practising cleverness at the sport. I always felt somehow that, when his grief came, it would come through the dog.... Well, he took a fever which I couldn't well diagnose, to say whether it was rheumatic or malarial. It ran to sweats and it ran to dry skin with shivering-fits, the deuce of a temperature, and wild delirium.

"I nursed him, of course, and doctored him, keeping the fever at bay as well as I could with decoctions of bark—quassia for the most part— and fresh juice of limes. But it was the vigour of his frame that pulled him through—as I believe all the skill in London could not have availed to do in the days of his prosperity when he was fat and fleshy. Hard life on the island had thinned him down and tautened and toughened him so that I wondered sometimes, washing his body, if this was indeed the man with whom I had vowed my quarrel.

"His ravings in delirium, however, left no doubt on that score! I tell you I had to listen to some fairly obscene descriptions of myself and his feelings for me—all in the best Houndsditch.… Yet here again was a queer thing—again and again this gutter-flow would check itself, drop its Cockney as if down a sink, and, bubbling up again, start flowing to the language of an educated man.… The first time this happened it gave me a shock, less the abruptness of the break than by its sudden assault upon my memory. All insensibly, and unmarked by me, Farrell's accent and way of speech had been nearing those of decent folk. They were by no means perfect, but they had amazingly improved.… Now, when his delirium plunged him back to Houndsditch, though it gave me a jerk, I could account for it as reversion to an old habit that had been put off before ever we met. What beat me was, that his second style, accent and choice of words—though still fluent in cursing—far surpassed in purity any speech I had heard from him in health.

"And there was something else about it.… While the gutter ran Houndsditch, the man was a cur, cowering and yelping out terror under strokes of a whip-lash. When it shifted accent, he lost all this and started to *threaten*. Something like this it would run: 'Gawd! Oh, Gawd, he's after me again.… See his rosy eyes follerin' like rosy naphthas.… Oh, Gawd, hide me from this blighter.… Look here, damn you! I'll trouble you to know who's master here. You will halt where you are, you Foe, and not wag a tail until I give you leave. That's better! Now, if you will kindly state your business at that distance I'll state mine.… Is that all? Quite so: and now you'll listen to me, and maybe reconsider yourself …' That, or something like that, is the way it would go.

"I had a sense all the while, Roddy, that he was almost slipping through my fingers, and I fairly dug in my nails to hold him to life. On that point my conscience is clear, anyhow. No man ever had a doctor to battle harder for him, or a more devoted nurse.

"Well, I pulled him through, and nursed him to convalescence. I thought I knew something of the peevishness of convalescents: but Farrell beat anything I had ever seen, or heard, or read of. By this time I was worn weak as a rat with night-watching and day-watching: but of this he made no account whatever. He started by using his greater weakness for strength, and he went on to dissemble his growing strength, hiding it, increasing it, still trading it as weakness upon my exhaustion. He came back to life with a permanent sneering smile, and a trick of wearing it for hours at a stretch as he leaned back on the cushions I had painfully made for him of plaited flax and stuffed with aromatic leaves, daily renewed.... Yes, Roddy, as a doctor I played full professional service on him, and piled it up with every extra kindness one castaway man could render another.... And the devil, as he recovered, lay watching me, under half-closed eyes, with never a sign of gratitude, but, for all my reward, this shifty sneer.

"There came a day when his new insolence broke out with his old hate. 'You Foe,' said he, 'I reckon you're priding yourself on your bedside manner, eh?... I can't keep much account of time, lying here. But, when I get about again, I'll have things in this camp a bit more shipshape, I promise you.... I've been thinking it out, lying here: and my conclusion is, you're too much of the boss without doing your job.... How long is it since you've strolled up to the look-out?'

"'About a fortnight,' said I.

"'And that's a pretty sort of watch, eh?' he continued irritably: '—when you know that I never missed a day.... I tell you, Foe, that, after this, we'll have to come to a reckoning. One or other has to be master on this island, and it isn't going to be *you*!

"I went up the hill obediently with the binoculars. I went up thoughtfully...."

"I came back some fifty minutes later, and said, 'You're too weak to walk; too weak even to crawl.'

"'What's the use to tell me that?' he asked, still keeping his air of insolence. 'Drop your bedside manner, and present your report.'

"'I will,' said I. 'One of us two has to be master on this island? So you said, and you shall be he; sole master, Farrell, with your damned dog.... There's a schooner at this moment making an offing from the anchorage where, as I've always told you, we'd been wiser to pitch our camp. I guess she put in to water, and I've missed her whilst I was busy curing your body.... Well, better late than never! She's hauling to north'ard, well wide: so you'll understand I'm in something of a hurry.... You're on the way to recovery, Farrell, and this makes twice that I've saved your life: but as yet you can neither walk nor crawl, and I give you joy of your bonfire, up yonder. In five minutes I push off, alone.'

"He raised himself slowly, staring, and fell forward grovelling, attempting vainly to catch me by the ankles.

"'You won't—you can't! Oh, for God's pity say you don't mean it! Say it's a joke, and I'll forgive you, though it's a cruel one.' Then, as I broke away from the door—'Have mercy on me, Foe—have mercy and don't leave me! *I can't do without you!*'"

"These were his last words that I heard as I plunged down the sand and pulled in the boat's shoreline handover-fist. I had just time to jump in and thrust off before the dog came bounding after me, barking furiously. The brute was puzzled, but knew something to be wrong. He even swam a few strokes, but turned back as I hit at him with a paddle. He made around the curve of the shore, still barking. But I had sculled through the narrows of the passage before he could reach it. I had a sight, over my shoulder, of Farrell, who had crawled to the doorway: and with that I was through the strait and sculling for open water, while the baffled dog raced to and fro on the spits and ledges astern, pausing only to bark after me as though he would cough his heart out.

"In the open water I hoisted sail, with the wind dead aft, and soon, beyond the point, caught sight of the schooner. After running out almost three miles, she had hauled close to the wind and was now heading almost due north…. She could not miss me, and yet I had made almost two miles before she got her head-sheets to windward and stood by for me.

"As I drew close, a thin-faced man with a pointed beard hailed me from her after-deck.

"'Ahoy, there! And who might *you* be, mistaking the Pacific for Broadway, New York?'

"'I'm from the island,' I answered.

"'What ship's boat is that you've gotten hold of?' he bawled.

"The *Two Brothers*.'

"'Lordy! I *thought* I reckernised her…. Then you're old Buck Vliet's missionary, that he marooned.'… Shall I go on, Roddy?"

I dropped my cigar into the ash-tray. "You may stop at that," I answered, unable (that's the queer part of it) to lift my eyes and look him in the face, although I knew very well that he was leaning back in his chair, eyeing me steadily, challenging the verdict. "Yes," said I, slowly turning the cigar-stump around in its ash, "I'm sorry, Jack… but I don't want to hear any more."

"I knew you would take it so," said Jack quietly, with a sort of sigh.

"Well," said I, "how else? Of course I know you'd had a damnable provocation, to start with. And I'm no man to judge you, not having been through the like or the beginnings of it…. You were rescued, for here you are. That's enough. But—damn it all!—you left the man!"

"—And the dog. While we are about it, don't let us forget the dog," said Jack wearily. "Shall we toss who pays the bill? Here—waiter!"

We parted under the porch-cover, in the traffic of Regent Street. I have told you that, in our best of days, Jack and I never shook hands, meeting or parting. It saved awkwardness now.

BOOK IV
THE COUNTERCHASE

NIGHT THE TWENTY-FIRST
THE YELLOW DOG

About two months later—to be accurate, it was seven weeks and two days—my flat in Jermyn Street was honoured with a totally unexpected call by Constantia Denistoun. Constantia has a way of committing improprieties with all the *aplomb* of innocence. She just walked upstairs and walked into the room where Jephson and I were packing gun-cases.

"Hallo!" said she. "You seem to be in a mess here."

"Please sit down," said I, removing a sporting rifle and bundle of cotton-waste from the best arm-chair.

"What is the matter?" she asked, arching her brows as she surveyed the general disorder.

"We're packing," said I.

"It may surprise you to hear it," said she, taking the seat, "but so I had guessed. What is it? Preparing for the pheasants, or for Quarter Day?"

"Neither," I answered. "I'm going to South America, that's all. … That will do for the present, Jephson. You may get Miss Denistoun a cup of tea."

"Sudden?" she asked, when Jephson had withdrawn.

"Well," I admitted, "I booked my passage only two days ago, but I've had the notion in my mind for some time."

"Alligators, is it? or climbing, this time? Or just general exploring?"

"You may call it exploring, though I may have a shy at the Andes on the way. These fits come upon me at intervals, Constantia, as you know, ever since you determined to be unkind."

"Don't be absurd, Roddy," she commanded, tracing out a pattern of the carpet with the point of her sunshade. The tracing took some time. At length she desisted, and looked up, resting her arms on her knees. "Roddy, I'm engaged to be married."

A bowl stood on the table, full of late tea-roses sent up from Warwickshire.... As the blow fell I turned about, and slowly selected the best bloom.

"I hope," said I, "the fortunate man, whoever he is, doesn't object to your calling around on us poor bachelors and breaking the news. However, Jimmy Collingwood is up, with his wife, and will be coming around from his hotel in a few minutes. He'll do for a chaperon. Meanwhile"—I held out the rose—"I wish you all happiness from the bottom of my heart.... When is it to be?—and shall I be in time with an alligator for a wedding present?"

"Now that's rather prettily offered," said Constantia, half-extending her hand to take the flower, her eyes shining with just the trace of tears. "But you and I are a pair of humbugs, Roddy. To begin with *you*—I don't believe there are any such things as alligators on that island."

"What island?" I stammered, and my fingers gave a small, involuntary jerk at the rose's stem as hers closed upon it.

"The island about which you wrote that queer short note to—to Dr. Foe—two days ago, asking if he could supply you as nearly as possible with its bearings."

"Are you telling me—?" I began.

She nodded, searching my face. "Yes, your old friend is the man; and that's where *I* come in as a humbug. The reason of this call is that I want to know why you two, who used to be devoted, are no longer friends."

"Good Lord!" I exclaimed, not loudly, but more or less to myself. "You must forgive my lighting a cigar, Constantia.... My mind works slowly." While lighting it I made a miserable attempt to fob her off and gain time. "When an old friend cuts in and carries off—"

"That's nonsense," she interrupted sharply; "and you know it; and you ought to know that I know it."

"Well, then," I protested rather feebly, hating to hurt her, "you must allow that his behaviour to that man Farrell was a bit beyond the limit. Of course, if you can forgive it—well, I don't know. It's odious to me to be talking like this about the man to whom you're attached—the man I used to worship. And for me, who still would lose a hand, cheerfully, now as ever, to spare you pain! ... My dear girl, let's talk of something else."

"No, we will not," said Constantia firmly. "I came to talk about this, and I will.... Of course I know it was wrong of Jack to pursue Mr. Farrell as he did. You remember my telling you I was worried, that day we talked about him after my return from the States? At that time I imagined he was allowing himself for a bribe to be friends again with this man, and it distressed me; because— well, women have their code, you know, as well as men, and—and I may confess to you now that, even at that time, I had begun to take an interest—"

"I see," said I dully, resting my arm along the chimney-piece and staring down into the grate, where Jephson had lit a small fire: for the day, though bright, was chilly.

"You assured me, you remember, that Jack was above any such meanness; and so far you relieved me, for I saw you were telling the truth. But," she continued, "I saw also that it wasn't the whole truth: that you were hiding something. So I went away puzzled. Afterwards, I got the truth out of Jimmy Collingwood."

"Well?" I prompted her, as she paused.

"Well, it was shocking of Jack, I admit. But, after all, this Mr. Farrell had ruined his life, and—of course I don't quite understand men and their code— but isn't it a trifle uncharitable of you, Roddy, not to allow that the shock may have unhinged his mind for a time?… No, I'm playing the humbug in *my* turn, and I'll own up. It was wicked, if you will: but it was great in its way, and determined… and women, you know, always fall slaves to that sort of thing. It was straightforward, too: Jimmy said Jack had given his man fair warning. Jimmy—but you know that boy's way—gave me the impression that he didn't condemn Jack's craze as unsportsmanlike: merely for being, as he put it, a thought bloodthirstier than any line of sport he himself felt any inclination to follow. 'But I'm no judge, Con,' he added—I remember his words—'for the simple reason that I never had a career to be ruined.'… Well, for the rest, Jack says he came straight to you as soon as he set foot back in England, and told you the whole story.—That's so, I guess?" Constantia, in her agitation, relapsed into her mother's idiom.

I nodded, bending my head still lower over the high chimney-shelf, still staring down into the fire.

"Then you *know*," she said; "and I *do* call it rather dull of you, Roddy— not to say insensate—and unlike you, anyway.… When, at the end, he turned and behaved so finely, nursing this man through his last illness.…"

I tell you, it was lucky that I still kept my face turned sideways, still staring down on the fire.… It took me like a mental nausea, and all my thought for the moment was to hold steady under it. I felt my fingers gripping hard on the ledge and holding to it, as the waves went over my poor brain.

Through the surge of them confusedly I heard her voice pleading: and yet her voice was calm, well under control. It must have been the waves in my own head that broke her speech into short sentences.

"You were his friend... his best friend... mine, too, Roddy. You took it so well, just now... I *do* want—"

What in the world could I say? How lift and turn my face to her? How answer?... And yet within a second or two I must lift my face and make some answer. Her voice was already trailing off plaintively. I heard her catch her breath—

And then—thank God—I heard a brisk, happy footstep in the outer passage, and Jimmy burst into the room with his accustomed whoop.

"Ahoy, within! How goes it with Gulliver?" He broke off, staring, and let out another joyous whoop, upon which chimed the merry rattle of tea-things, as Jephson followed close on his heels with a tray. "Eh? No—but it is! In the words of the Bard, What ho, Constantia!" He threw his bright top-hat across the room, hooked his umbrella over his left arm, and ran forward with both hands held out. "Oh, Con! this is good! Give me a kiss, with Otty's leave—a real good nursery kiss!"

"There!" agreed Constantia. "And now sit down and be a good boy. Where's Lettice?"

"Shopping in Knightsbridge: and the nurse walking the infant up and down, more or less parallel, just inside the Park, that he may watch the wheels go round.... I broke away. Shouldn't be surprised if Lettice taxi'd around here presently. I hinted at tea, and she knows where to find me.... Oh, by George, yes! Lettice always knows where I am, somehow. Meanwhile, here's your good staid chaperon." He dropped into a chair. "Otty, you're looking serious. What were you talking about, you two?"

"Well, it's like this," said I, after a glance at her; "Constantia's going to be married—to Jack Foe."

He had started up at my first words, to congratulate her. As I dropped out the last three, with admirable presence of mind—"When in doubt, apply cake," said he hoarsely, cramming a large piece into his mouth to stifle his emotion.

"I am not in doubt," said Constantia serenely; "and I suppose that is why you help yourself as first aid, before offering me some bread and butter, while Roddy lets me pour the tea. Thank you," she added, as he whipped about with an apology. "Don't speak with your mouth full: it's rude.... And now listen to me. Roddy, here, is off for South America, he tells me. Two days ago he wrote to Jack, asking for the latitude and longitude, as near as might be, of a certain island. Jack showed me the letter.... You know about this?" she asked Jimmy, shooting out the question of a sudden.

I interrupted it. "Jimmy knows about it," said I. "No one else."

She looked at us calmly, taking stock of us. "Very well," she said; "and Jack has told me the whole story too, of course. I didn't know till this moment that Jimmy knew: but I'm so glad he does, for it makes us all four-square. Now, when first Jack got your letter, Roddy, He was for sending the information in six words on a post card, as being all that was due to an old friend that had so misjudged him. But I persuaded him, and—"

The outer door slammed upon the word, and a brisk footstep sounded in the passage. I recognised it at once. So did Constantia.

"—And here he is!" exclaimed Constantia, without rising, "—come, as it happens, to have it out with the pair of you.... Hallo, Jack!"

I am bound to say that my first look at Jack Foe gave me a start, as he too started at sight of Jimmy, whose presence, of course, he had not expected. He was pale in comparison with the tan of two months back: but at every other point he was wonderfully set up and improved. It was Constantia's doing, belike: but he had become again in appearance the Jack Foe of old times—a trifle more seamed in the face but with a straightness and uprightness of carriage that rejuvenated him. His clothes, too, were of the old cut, modestly distinguished.

"Collingwood too?" said he, nodding easily. "That's better than I looked for.... You have told them?" he asked Constantia with a frank look of understanding. Then his eyes wandered, naturally, over the disorder in the room.

"Roddy is packing," said Constantia.

"For South America," said I.

"And after that? Yes, you needn't tell," he went on with an ease which I could only admire. "It's the island, of course—I had your note and was going to answer it, but Miss Denistoun—Constantia— insisted that I should call round and tell you. The latitude is—"

"One moment," interrupted Jimmy. "You let the door slam behind you, Professor: and your dog is protesting."

"My dog?" Foe turned about, as Jimmy stepped to the passage. "What are you talking about, Collingwood? I don't own such a thing."

"I'll be damned if there isn't one snuffling at that outer door," said Jimmy, and went quickly out into the passage. I heard the lock click back and, upon the noise, a scuffle and gallop of a four-footed beast: and, with that, a great yellow dog burst in at the doorway of the room, took a leap forward, crouched, and slowly stiffened itself up with its legs, its back hunched and bristling. There it stood, letting out its voice in a growl that sounded almost like a groan of satisfied desire.

"Great Scott!" exclaimed Jimmy, following. "If this isn't your Billy, Professor, come to life!"

And I, too, cast a quick glance over my shoulder at Foe—against whom the hound evidently stiffened, as a pointer at its game. Foe, white as a sheet, was leaning back, his shoulders propped against the edge of the mantelshelf.

"He is not my dog," he gasped out. "Take him away: he's dangerous!"

"Looks so, anyway," said Jimmy calmly. "Well, if he's not your dog, here's his owner to claim him."—And into the room, staring around on us, walked Farrell.

For the moment I stared at him as at a total stranger. It was only when, almost ignoring the rest of us, he took a step forward, pointing a finger at one man—it was only when I turned about and saw Foe's face—that the truth broke on me—and then, at first, as a wild surmise, and no more. Even when I wheeled about again and stared at the man, full belief came slowly: for this Farrell was thin, wiry, gaunt; sun-tanned, with sunken eyes and a slight stoop; wearing the clothes of a gentleman and, when at length he spoke, using the accent of a gentleman.... But this came later.

For some seconds he said nothing: he stood and pointed. I glanced at Constantia, preparing to spring between her and I knew not what.

Constantia, leaning forward a little in her chair, with lips slightly parted, had, after the first glance, no eyes for the intruder, whom (I feel sure) she had not yet recognised. Her eyes were fixed on Jack, at whom the finger pointed: and her hand slid along the arm of her chair and gripped it, helping her to rise and spring to his side. Jimmy's face I did not see. He had come to a halt in the doorway.

"*You hound!*"

"Roddy! Catch him—oh, help!"

It was Constantia's call ringing through the room. I sprang about just in time to give support as Jack fell into our interlacing arms, and to take the most of his weight as we lowered him flat on the hearth-rug in a dead faint.

"Call off your damned dog, sir, whoever you are!" shouted Jimmy, running forward to help us. "We'll talk to you in a moment."

I heard Farrell call "Rover! Rover!" and the dog must have come to heel instantly. For as I knelt, occupied in loosing Jack's collar, of a sudden a complete hush fell on the room. Jimmy had run for the water-bottle. "Don't ring—don't fetch Jephson!" I had commanded. "Get water from my bedroom." When I looked up to take the bottle, Farrell still stood implacable before the doorway.

Constantia also looked up. "Who is this gentleman?" she demanded.

"My name is Farrell," answered the figure by the doorway. "Miss Denistoun may remember a fellow-passenger of some years ago, on the *Emania*."

I heard the catch of her breath as she knelt by me, staring at him. I heard Jimmy's muttered "My God!" My arm was reaching to catch Constantia if she should drop backward.

But she pulled herself together with a long sob—I felt it shuddering through her, so close she knelt by me. Again silence fell on the room. Jimmy had fetched my bath-sponge along with the bottle. I poured water upon it and bathed Jack's temples, watching his eyelids. After a while they fluttered a little. I felt over his heart. "He is coming round," I announced: "but we'll let him lie here for a little, before lifting him on to the couch."

"One question first," commanded Constantia. "Answer me, you two. … Is this—is this thing true, Roddy? *Did he leave-this man—on the island?*"

For the moment I could put up no better delay—as neither could Jimmy—than to call "hush!" and pretend to listen to Jack's faintly recovering heart-beat. But Farrell heard, and answered,—

"It's true, Miss Denistoun.… I had no notion to find him here; still less to find you and distress you. I came to Sir Roderick. But the dog here was wiser. *He* knew the scent on the stairs, and raced in ahead.… I am sorry to say it, Miss Denistoun: but that blackguard yonder took ship and left me solitary,—to die, for aught he knew. Let him come-to, and then we'll talk."

Constantia rose. Slowly she picked up her gloves and sunshade. "No, we will not talk," she said, after a pause. "That talk is for you four men. I—I have no wish to see him recover."

As she said it, she very slowly detached from her breast-knot the rose which had carried my felicitation, and laid it on the table: and, with that, she walked out, Farrell drawing aside to make way for her.

NIGHT THE TWENTY-SECOND
THE SECOND MAN ESCAPES

Now that exit of Constantia's, I must tell you, had an instant and very remarkable effect upon Farrell, though she swept by him without perceiving it.

A moment before he had stood barring the doorway, his legs planted wide, his eyes fierce, his chest panting as he waited for his enemy to come back to life, his mouth working and twisting with impatience to let forth its flood of denunciation.

As Constantia walked to the door he not only drew back a foot to let her pass. He drew his whole body back, bowed for all the world like any shop-walker letting out a customer, even thrust out a hand, as by remembered instinct and as if to pull open an imaginary swing-door for a departing customer of rank. In short, for a moment the man reverted to his past—to Farrell of the Tottenham Court Road…. Nor was this all. As she went by him he slewed about to follow her with his eyes, kicking aside the dog that hampered him, crouching against his legs: and still his gaze followed her, to the outer door.

Not until she had closed the outer door behind her did he face about on the room again; and still it was as if all the wind had been shaken, of a sudden, out of his sails. His next words, moreover— strange as they were— would have stablished his identity with Farrell even had any doubt lingered in us.

"Funny thing," said he, addressing us vaguely, "how like blood tells, even down to a look in the eyes. I was husband to a woman once, thousands of miles from here and foreign of race: but she came of kings, though far away back, and Miss Denistoun, Sir Roderick, she reminded me, just then—"

"Look here, Mr. Farrell," I broke in; "with your leave we won't discuss Miss Denistoun, here or anywhere—as, with your leave, we'll cut all further conversation until Dr. Foe is fit for it, which at this moment he pretty obviously is not. It may help your silence if I tell you that the lady who has just left is, or was, engaged to marry him."

"*Christl!… And she knows?*" He stared, less at us than at the four walls about him.

"She does not," said I: "or did not, until a few minutes ago."

"But *you* knew!"—Wrath again filled Farrell's sails. "*You* knew— and you allowed it.… And you call yourselves gentlemen, I suppose!"

"If you take that tone with either of us for an instant longer," I answered, after a pause, "you shall be thrown out of that door, and your dog shall follow through the window. If you prefer to stand quite still and hold your tongue—will you?—why, then, you are welcome to the information that I only heard of this engagement less than an hour ago, and Mr. Collingwood less than ten minutes before you entered."

"But you knew *that other thing*," Farrell insisted.

"Yes, I knew," said I: "and for the simple reason that Dr. Foe told it all to me. And Mr. Collingwood knows, for I told it to him. We two have kept the secret."

"And," sneered Farrell, "you still keep being his friends!"

"No," I answered; "as a matter of fact, we do not. But you have taken that tone again with me in spite of my warning, and I shall now throw you downstairs.… You are an ill-used man, I believe, though not by me: and for that reason, if you come back—say at ten to-morrow morning—and apologise, you will find me sympathetic. But just now I am going to throw you out."

"You may if you can," retorted Farrell, eyeing my advance warily. "I've spoilt this marrying, I guess: and that's the first long chalk crossed off a long tally."

I was about to grip with him when Jimmy called sharply that there were to be no blows—Foe wanted to speak.

Foe had recovered under the brandy and lay over on his side, facing us, panting a little from the dose—of which Jimmy had been liberal.

"Have it out, Roddy," he gasped, "here and now. I'm strong enough to get it over, and—and he can't tell you any worse than you both know, of my free telling—and I don't want to trouble either of you again. Let him have it out," implored Foe, between his sharp intakes of breath.

"I am glad you excepted *me*," burst out Farrell. "You'll trouble *me* again fast enough: or, rather, I'll trouble *you*—to the end of your dirty life. Are you shamming sick, there, you Foe?"

"You know that he is not," said Jimmy, holding back my arm. "Tell your story, and clear."

"My story?" echoed Farrell in a bewildered way. "What's my story more than what you know, it seems? What's my story more than that, after sharing hell for days in an open boat, and solitude on that awful island, this man left me—choosing when I was sick and sorry: left me to hell and solitude together—left me to it, cold-blooded, when I was too weak to crawl—left me, in his cursed grudge, when he could have saved two as easy as one? Has he told you that, gentlemen?"

"He told me quite faithfully," said I. "We—Mr. Collingwood and I— both know it."

"Ay," Farrell retorted, "but neither you nor your Mr. Collingwood, when you say that, understands a bit what it means…" He broke off, searching for some words to convey the remembered agony to our brains that had no capacity (he felt) even to imagine it.

"No," came a dull voice from the couch—startling us, dull though it was. "Only you and I, Farrell, understand what it means. Tell them just the facts, as I told the facts, and no more. Tell them, and me, how you escaped."

"By the same ship as you did, if you wish to know—the *I'll Away* schooner, Captain Jefferson Hales. And I'll tell you something even more surprising.—Your ill-luck started the very hour you left me and Rover to die like two dogs together. When you stepped aboard the *I'll Away*, you stepped aboard as a lost missionary. You had your own bad reasons for not wanting to tell too much: and Hales had his own very good reasons for not putting too many questions. To start with, he didn't like missionaries as a class, *or* their conversation: and I gather that his crew likewise didn't take much truck in them; neither in the species nor in you as a specimen: least of all in you as a specimen. I'm sorry for it, too, in a way: because, at first, I pictured them asking you to put up a prayer, and pictured your face and feelings as you knelt down to oblige. Well, that was one of the pretty fancies that ought to come true but don't manage to, in this world. As for the next, there's no saying. You passed yourself for a missionary, and if Satan has humour enough to accept you on that ticket, a pretty figure you'll make, putting up false prayers in hell…. Anyhow, you didn't make friends on board that schooner—eh?"

"I did not," Foe answered listlessly.

"You weren't over comfortable with that crowd when you changed me for it?"

"I was not, if that's any comfort to you."

Farrell grinned. "Of course it's a comfort to me. They sent you to Coventry more or less; and I'll tell you the reason, if you don't know it. There was a whisper going round the ship forward.... One of the hands—it being a clear day—had heard a dog barking from the shore. Another fancied that he had. Then a third called to mind having heard somewhere—he couldn't remember the public, or even the port—that when old Buck Vliet marooned his missionary he'd left a dog with him in compassion.... I should tell you two gentlemen that the yarn about Vliet and how he caught a missionary by mistake, and how he'd short-circuited him somewhere in a holy terror, was a kind of legend all along the coast and around the Eastern islands. I dare say it crossed to the Atlantic in time: for again it was the kind of story that starts by being funny and gets funnier as each man chooses to improve on it.... All I can say is, that if the body you and I, Foe, looked down upon, that afternoon, belonged to Vliet's missionary, I don't want to hear any more fun about it.... So you see, gentlemen, this God-forsaken lot, down in the *I'll Away's* fo'c'sle, patched it up amongst them that this man, in his hurry, had deserted his dog. Now, as I shall tell you, if they had reasoned, they'd have known that the dog wouldn't starve, anyway. But they didn't reason. They were a God-forsaken lot—mostly broken men, pliers about the islands—and it just went against their instinct that anyone should forsake so much as a dog. If they'd known you had forsaken a man, you Foe, they'd have tarred and burnt you.

"—Captain Hales, as it happened, hadn't caught the barking or any faint echo of it: the reason being that he was hard of hearing, although in the rest of his senses sharper than all his crew rolled together, and in wits or at a bargain a match for any trader between Chile and Palmerston. Also I have heard it rumoured that he had run a bit wild in his youth, found himself within the law or outside of it (I forget which), and come down to the South Pacific for the good of his health. But that was many years ago. He was now a middle-aged man, and had learnt enough about these waters to call you a fool if you suggested by way of flattery that what he didn't know about them wasn't worth knowing.

"—Something, at any rate, in his past had turned him into a silent, brooding man, seldom coming out of his thoughts until it came to a bargain, when he woke up like a giant from sleep. His deafness helped to fasten this silent habit deeper upon him. Also he was touchy about his deafness: didn't like at any time to be reminded of it; and was apt to fly into a sudden rage if anyone brought up a reminder, even by a chance hint. And that, belike, was the main reason why he alone on board—barring yourself, Foe—never heard tell of this barking which he had missed to hear with his own ears.

"—And now for one thing more, Foe—and it'll make you squirm by and by! Like most deaf men he was a bit suspicious: and looking at you sideways as you came on board—what with one thing and another, not liking missionaries as a line in trade, and, in particular, mistrusting the cut of *your* jib, he thought things over a bit and altered his helm.

"—I'll explain. You see, you not only came aboard looking what you are, but you came aboard fairly slimed over, in addition, with all that had ever been told or guessed against Buck Vliet's missionary. The stories didn't agree about his sect: but they agreed that Vliet, though a ruffian, hadn't marooned the man just for fun—that he must have been a hard case somehow. The stories might vary concerning Vliet's reasons: but they agreed that the man hadn't come to it by sheer over-prayerfulness: and the conclusion was— reasonable or unreasonable—that you, Foe, must have been a bad potato somehow, or at best a severe trial, if so hardened a stomach as Vliet's hadn't been able to keep you down. Worse; he guessed you for a spy.

"—Here, Sir Roderick and Mr. Collingwood, I must tell you that Vliet and Hales, as masters in this knock-about off-island trade, had grown to be rival kings in their way, and Hales in his brooding fashion as jealous as fire. From all I've heard, Vliet hadn't the ambition to be properly jealous: all *he* objected to was his business being cut.

"—Vliet was an old man—a regular hoary sinner, who kept his trade secrets by a very simple method. He stocked his crews entirely with lads of his own begetting. White, black, he didn't care how many wives he carried to sea, or how much of a family wash he carried in the shrouds on a fine day. He ran his trade on secrecy and close family limitations. He had no range. His joy was to have a corner unknown to a soul else in the world. Fat, lazy, wicked, and sly— that was Vliet. He belonged to the old school.

"—Now, for years, Hales—of the new school, and challenger—had been chasing after a rumour that chased after Vliet from port to port—a rumour that Vliet drew on an uncharted island, in those latitudes, known only to himself and to so much of his progeny as the old Solomon didn't mistrust enough to lose overboard.... Well, the belief at Valparaiso is that old Buck Vliet, with his schooner—on which he grudged a penny for repairs—had found an ocean grave at last, somewhere. The guess is that he overdid the *Two Brothers* in the end, being careless of warnings, with a top-hamper of wives. There is also a legend—likely invented to account for the name of his schooner—that he left all his money to a twin brother in business in Salt Lake City, and that the brother and his brother's wives had fitted out a new schooner to hunt for the island's whereabouts.

"—Listen, you Foe! While I was lying sick, and you neglecting the look-out, Hales made our island, and anchored in the bay. While I was lying sick, and you neglecting the look-out, Hales made our island, that had been his dream for years; landed there, or on the far side, took its bearings to a hair, of course, and went ashore with a party to prospect. What do you say to that?"

"I say," answered Foe, still languidly, shifting his head a little on the cushion, "that I always told you we were on the wrong side of the island, and that you would never listen."

"They landed, anyway," pursued Farrell; "and for a whole day, after watering, they explored. They never got over the crest that looked down on our camp."

"And if they had they would never have seen us," said Foe, responding like a man in a dream. "You had chosen the site too cleverly; the fern-brake would have hidden us, anyway. Let that pass."

"But there was the bonfire and the look-out, both unattended."

"Oh, if we're to start re-arguing arguments that kept us tired for about three years," answered Foe, "you built the bonfire on the wrong slope, as I always told you. And I'd cut down your flagstaff."

"We won't quarrel about *that*, since here we are," Farrell retorted with a savage grin. "So I'll drop it and get on with the story. And the next thing to be mentioned in the story, Foe, is that for a clever man, you're about the biggest fool alive. You have no end of knowledge in you, which I admired on the island. The way you found all kinds of plants and things and turned them to account, and explained to me how traders and practical chemists could make fortunes out of them—why, it was wonderful. But it wasn't so wonderful to me as that, with all this knowledge, you'd never turned it to account, so to speak, when, with a third of it, at your age, I'd have been a millionaire. And the ways and manners of a gentleman you had, too; which I could easier set about copying—as I did. It won't bring you much comfort to know that, half the time, I was sucking education out of you, grinning inwardly and thinking, 'Now, my fine hater, the more you're taking the superior line with me the more I'm your pupil all the time; the more you're giving me what I'll find priceless, one of these days, if ever we get back upon London pavements.' In the blindness of your hatred you never guessed that Peter Farrell, all through life, might have had a long way with him—a way of looking ahead—and all to better himself. You never guessed *that*, all the time, I was letting you teach me.

"—But in practical matters—in all that counts first with a business man—I saw pretty early that you were little better than a fool. Yet I couldn't have believed you or any man such a fool as you showed yourself on the *I'll Away*: and even you couldn't have missed sensing it but for one thing—*you couldn't dare return to the island.*

"—A place so rich as that, unknown, uncharted!—reeking with copra, not to mention other wealth—fairly asking to be sold and turned over to a government, to a syndicate, to develop it! Man! you and Hales had a million safe between you when you boarded the schooner; and I can see Hales's mind at work when he spotted your boat and sized up the share he was losing by your turning up. The marvel to me is, he didn't turn you a blind eye. But Hales is a humane man. He did time in his youth, but he's not the sort that you are, Foe—the sort that could leave a man to die solitary and forsaken. Belike, too, the prize was so great in his grasp that he didn't care how much, in reason, might run through his fingers.

"—Listen! When you sighted him, he had made a careful offing of the southern reefs, and had hauled up close to his wind. Where do you suppose he was bound? He was fetching up to beat back to Valparaiso. Being Yankee born and not a stocking-banker like old Buck Vliet, he was all for Valparaiso with an island to sell to the Chilian Government, and a concession and a syndicate fair in view. This cargo of beads, cheap guns, sham jewellery, canned meats, and rum, that he had aboard for the islands, would keep: the rum would even be improved by a little Christian delay. But, if he sank it all, all was nothing to the secret he carried.

"—And then you hove on his view, for partner: and he took you in. … I hope you'll remember him gratefully after this, Foe. He chose to sight you—and he hadn't heard the dog. If he had, it wasn't in him to guess that you had left any better than a dog behind.

"—Then you fairly flummoxed him. Missionary though you were, he'd accepted you as prospective shareholder. It wasn't for him to guess that you dared not go back.

"—He's told me that, accepting you, for a day and a half he held on his course, close-hauled. Is that so? But he was suspicious, as deaf men are. He took a notion that you—you, keeping mum as a cat, having to pass for somebody else and avoid questions—were just lying low, meaning to slip cable at Valparaiso and hurry in with a prior claim. I am sorry to say it, Foe: but altogether you did not create good impression on board the *I'll Away*. To the crew you were an object of dark suspicion. To the skipper you were either a close knave, meaning to trick him, or an incredible idiot. After a while, and almost against hope, he determined to try you for an idiot. He ordered his helm up, and watched you. You did not protest. He put his helm farther and farther up, and headed for the Marquesas. Still you offered no objection. So he landed you—on Nukuheva, if I remember. And from Nukuheva, somehow, I guess, you got a slant out of your missionary labours to Sydney or else 'twas back to Valparaiso—I haven't tracked it: but from one or other you picked up some sort of a passage home. Anyway, lost men as the *I'll Away's* crew might be, they were glad enough, having traded you for nothing, to up-sail and lose you out of their sight.... And this man I find you two gentlemen treating as your friend, whom the scum of the earth (as you would call them) abhorred! And you *know*, whilst those poor men only guessed!"

"Stay a moment, Farrell," interposed Jimmy. "Sorry to interrupt ... but will you kindly take a look around this room. Not entirely a neat apartment, eh? A few odd cases and cabin trunks lying around?... You and Sir Roderick were almost at blows just now. But if you're curious to know the reason of all this mess, it is that, when you paid us this timely call, he was packing to search for you."

"So?" Farrell drew back, regarding me, and the upper lids of his eyes went up till they were almost hidden by his brows. "So?" he said slowly. "But why?"

"Put it at a whim," I said sharply, "and get on with your tale. ... If you interrupt again, Jimmy, I'll strangle you, or attempt to. You may have observed that I'm ready to fight anybody, this afternoon."

Farrell looked at me earnestly. "I see what you would be driving at, sir," said he, becoming the humble tradesman again. "And I admire. But, by God, sir!" he broke out, "it won't do! It shan't do! No man is going to shoulder that man's sin, to rob me of him!"

"Get down from that horse," said I. "You can mount him again, if you choose, later on; but, first, finish the story."

"All very well," said Farrell, "to put it in that dictatorial way, when you've taken the heart out of a man.... Well, Hales headed back for Valparaiso, scarce believing his luck. There he interviewed the ministry, got a provisional concession, and started out for the island again, to make good—and found another inhabitant alive and kicking.

"—He behaved just as well as before, and better—for I was frank with him and knowledgeable. He couldn't understand missionaries, real or sham: but he understood a square deal, and didn't charge interest on bowels of mercy. His only grumble was, 'I'll put you on your honour. Tell me, please, there's no more of you hereabouts. It's a long passage to and fro: and if you're a man, you'll see that I'm almost as crowded as you are lonesome. Don't start me beating *all* this brush for skunks!'

"—He sailed me back to Valparaiso, after we had spent three days prospecting the property together. At Lima I left him to fight out details with the Minister of the Interior—who, for some mysterious reason, turned out to be the person charged with trafficking for an islet three hundred miles from any interior—while I trained north and, crossing the Isthmus, sailed north for New York. The only man I knew in the whole Western Hemisphere was a friend of mine there, Renton by name, and I made for Renton, to raise capital.

"—I found that he could walk into Wall Street, and, arm-in-arm with me, raise the money easily. Moreover I found that he had stored some twelve thousand dollars for me as my share of an investment I'd helped him to in Costa Rica. Some day, gentlemen, I'll tell you of this little episode, if you care to hear about it. It was a deal in a queer sort of mahogany he had asked me to inspect.

"—But to return to the island, and wind up. Hales found me there, alive and hearty, Foe. For why? Because I had found a purpose in me—to wait and, when time came, to hunt you to the ends of the earth. It's *my* turn now. You've taught me, and I'll improve on your teaching. You've bought a practice, I've learnt; and now I learn that you've fixed up to marry this Miss Denistoun.

"—Don't I know why?… Didn't I see that look in her eyes as she walked past me, just now?

"—Yes.… Santa's look.… No secrets between you and me. But, by God, you shan't! I'll save her from *that*. Sooner than she shall be wife of yours, I'll marry her myself!"

"Mr. Farrell," said I, "you have learnt much and learnt it sorely: but you haven't learnt enough. Pick up your hat, take your dog with you, and walk out."

"That's right enough," said he; "and I'm going. I'm only half a gentleman yet, and my feelings get the better of me in the wrong way. But you'll never rob me of that fellow, and so I promise you two, and him.… Come along, Rover!"

NIGHT THE TWENTY-THIRD
COUNTERCHASE

I went to the South Pacific, after all.

Farrell called on me, next day, and before I could countermand my passage. He came, as he said, to offer me his deep apologies. "I grant you, Sir Roderick, that I behaved ill to you and Mr. Collingwood, and specially to Miss Denistoun. I had no business to drag her into the talk.... But I'm only a learner in the ways gentlemen behave. It doesn't come to me by nature, as it comes to luckier ones, whose parents and grandparents have bred it into the bone. You may put it that I've hair on my hoof and have to shave it carefully. What taking trouble can do I can make it do, and don't count the time wasted. But it's the unexpected that catches out a man like me.... You see, I came up thinking to find you alone: and I was so keen to see you, I paid no attention to the dog, queerly as he was behaving. I thought, maybe, he'd smelt a cat. There weren't any cats on the island, or aboard the *I'll Away*, or the cars, or the *Oceanic*.... And then I burst in after the hound, as soon as I realised that he meant mischief of some sort; and, of a sudden, there was Foe face to face with me, and you others treating him friendly as friendly. Was it any wonder that, coming on him like that and after hunting him more than half the world across, I let myself go?"

"Well, first of all," I answered coldly, "you may disabuse your mind of any notion that Mr. Collingwood and I were chatting with Doctor Foe in the way you suspect. As a matter of fact, after you left, we told him what we were trying to avoid telling him in Miss Denistoun's presence at the moment when you broke in—that, through his treatment of you, he had forfeited our friendship."

"Had he come to hear that?" asked Farrell,—"if it's a fair question."

"It's a perfectly fair question," said I, "and the answer is that he had not. He had come to give me in person some information for which I had written to him.... Can you guess? It was the precise latitude and longitude of your island.... And now, question for question. You hadn't tracked him here, for you have just said that your finding him in this room took you fairly by surprise."

"Almost knocked me over," Farrell agreed.

"Then what had been your purpose in calling on me?" I asked, "—if that, too, is a fair question."

"Well, I'll admit I was calling, in part, to get his address or discover his whereabouts. But that wasn't my only reason. My real reason and foremost—But before I tell it, Sir Roderick, will you answer me yet another question? Was it true, what Mr. Collingwood said?—that you were actually packing to search for me?"

"Mr. Collingwood," I answered, somewhat embarrassed, "certainly would not have said it if it hadn't been true."

"Well, it fairly beat me," said Farrell, staring. "And it beats me again, now you confirm it. Searching for *me*?—Why? You couldn't have guessed there was money in it."

"It may sound strange to you, sir," said I pretty icily; "but I took that fancy into my head neither for your *beaux yeux* nor for profit. Moreover, if you don't understand without my help, I'll be shot if I can provide you with an explanation that won't strike you as wildly foolish.... However, if you must know, the thought of a fellow-creature marooned on that island, and of the bare chance that he might yet be alive to be rescued, had been preying on my mind ever since I heard Foe's tale, and parted with his friendship on account of it. Also it may appear extravagant, but through that old friendship I felt a sort of personal responsibility, as if Jack had left his trespass in my keeping.... But why discuss all this? You're back, safe and sound, and the trip is off. When Jephson has finished unpacking, he'll step over to Cockspur Street and pay forfeit for the two berths."

"*Two* berths?"

"Jephson was going with me. I fancy he looked forward to the adventure, and is a trifle disappointed this morning."

Farrell nodded to show that he understood. Yet he seemed to be considering something else, and kept his eyes fixed on me in a queer way.

"Sir Roderick," he said, after a pause, "your arrangements are all made for this voyage?"

"Oh, yes," said I. "Your turning up like this is quite a small nuisance in its way. I'd arranged with my lawyers, arranged with my bankers, let my flat here furnished from the first of next month (*that's* the worst), taken out letters and passport, made my will, stored my few bits of spare plate. Last week I spent down in Warwickshire, clewing up the loose tackle, holding heart-to-heart conversations with Collingwood and my steward.

Collingwood's my neighbour down there, you know, and will help to look after things."

Farrell considered all this, slowly. "Excuse me, Sir Roderick," said he, "but is there no chance of your going back to your intention and re-packing?"

"Why on earth should I?" was my very natural question.

"Why, it's like this, sir," said Farrell, "—and now I'll come to the real reason that brought me yesterday. My real reason was a matter of business.... You may remember my telling you that, in New York, I'd consulted Renton, an old friend of mine, about raising the capital to take over and develop Santa Santissima, as we've agreed to call the island; and that Renton had no difficulty to raise the money. What I didn't tell you—not thinking it wise before company— was that from the first I'd stipulated—with Hales as well as with Renton—that half the shares should be held in Great Britain. Hales didn't care, as he put it, where in thunder the money came from, so long as it was good. Renton—as being British-born, though naturalised—made no objection and only one condition, that the syndicate should be a small one. If I could get half the capital raised quietly in England by one or two persons, why, so much the better. He could raise the other half without calling on Wall Street or starting so much as an echo.... Now, I don't mind telling you, Sir Roderick, that I had you in mind all the while. That island is a gold mine: the copra alone there represents whole fortunes running to waste: and even if old Buck Vliet still sails the waters—which I doubt, for the *Two Brothers* hasn't been spoken or sighted within these four years, and he wasn't provisioned for whaling—still, the concession papers are made out in Hales's name and mine, and the duplicate documents stored.... All I can say is, that I'm ready to put my own little pile upon it, to the last guinea. And I thought of you from the first; you having done me a good turn more than once, or tried to. Yes, sir: but the best of all would be your going out and making sure for yourself. You, that was preparing to go that distance to find a lost man—I say, sir, it would be heavenly, if you went and found a fortune instead. I've arranged a cable to Hales, and the *I'll Away* will be waiting for you at Valparaiso. But in case he should miss—which he won't—here are papers for you: bearings of the island, sketch-map, copy of bond of agreement with him, copy of agreement with Renton. All these I was bringing to put into your hand yesterday. But, my God! Sir Roderick, now that I've heard what I've heard—that you were preparing to search the South Pacific for me, and for no worse reason than that a poor devil was cast away there, I'd ask you on my knees to sleep in the berth you've booked and travel to better purpose."

It has occurred to me since—and more than once or twice—that although the man and his offer were honest, he had a secondary purpose all this while: to get me out of the way lest I should embarrass his pursuit of Foe and his other scheme of which I am to tell.

But, on the whole reckoning, I incline to think the man was perfectly sincere, and even eager to do me this kindness; which—as things turned out—was really an extravagant one, on the monetary calculation.

At any rate, after studying his face for a while, I called Jephson out from my bedroom and told him that I had changed my mind: we would sail, after all, and he might start re-packing at once. Jephson fairly beamed.

"But there's one thing I'd like to say," put in Farrell, while it was obvious that this order overwhelmed him with joy. "I want to have it clear between us that, joyful as I am at your acceptance, and grateful as I am for your seeing things in this light, it doesn't in any way compromise my dealing with Foe."

"If you take my advice," said I, "you'll drop Foe, and all this silly business of hatred. He has tried it on you, and up to a certain point it answered. You played him—I'll grant you, unknowingly—a perfectly damnable trick. Don't smear your soul with any flattering unction, Mr. Farrell. You wrecked his life; and, in return, he set himself to wreck yours. Up to that point I can understand, though it all seems to me infernally silly. But in his monomania he went just that step too far, and has exchanged thereby the upper hand. You have the cards now: yet I warn you against playing them. For, as sure as I sit here, I warn you that in the act of destroying him you will destroy yourself. I look back on his miserable pursuit, and I prophesy the end of yours."

"Well, it has taken me through fires of hell," said he; "but I wouldn't have missed it. I'm the man now, and he's the coward."

"Quite so," said I. "Then be thankful and drop it. Do you want to retrieve his soul as he has found yours?"

Farrell mused over this for a while. "I can't explain it to you," he said. "I can't explain it to myself. But that man and I simply can't give one another up. As I woke it in him, so he wakes in me something that I can't be without, having once known it. It seems to be a necessary part of myself."

"There are a great many 'Can'ts' in that confession—for a strong man," was my comment; "and a trifle too much 'myself' for a man who has found himself. But you remember that meeting at the Baths, when you and Jack Foe first made acquaintance? Of course you do. Well, there was a little man seated in the hall, fronting you, and he read the explanation and gave it to me later, as he helped me on with my coat. I made no account of it at the time: but he said that he'd seen another man looking out of your eyes, for a moment, and it gave him a scunner."

Again Farrell pondered. "I dare say he was right, too," he said thoughtfully. "When two men are made for one another, I guess their souls—if that's not too good a word—must exchange flesh and clothing now and then, so that for the moment there's a puzzle to separate t'other from which.... Has Foe told you about *her*— about Santa?"

"He has," said I.

"Yet he can't have told you all: for he doesn't know it all—about Renton, for instance, and how I did that bolt from him to Costa Rica, and from Costa Rica to San Ramon. You must hear all about that, if you will: because, when you've inspected the island for yourself, your next business will be with Renton, and I want you to understand the man you will be dealing with."

Thereupon he told me: and that is how I was able, the other night, to relate what happened in Costa Rica and at San Ramon.

One of these days, when you're fairly rested, you shall have a full, dull, true, and particular account of the voyage upon which I started, next day, with Jephson, as per schedule: with a detailed description of Santa Island, or Santa Santissima (to give it its full name). But this story isn't about me: it concerns Foe and Farrell: and therefore it's enough to say here, that I reached Valparaiso and found Captain Jeff Hales waiting for me with his schooner fresh from dock, and fleet: that he and I took to one another in the inside of ten minutes; that our voyage, first and last, went like a yachting cruise; that we made the island and spent something more than two months on it, prospecting, mapping, choosing the sites for our factories that were to be, even planning a light tramway to cart their produce down to the grand north-eastern bay which (as Foe had warned me) proved to be the only anchorage. But Santa's cross was there, standing yet on the small beach where the castaways had landed, and no doubt it stands yet. No storm ever seriously troubles the water within that lovely protected hollow.

Returning to Valparaiso, I travelled north by steamer, by rail, by steamer and rail again, to New York, hunted up Renton, and found that my luck held; that I was dealing with a man as honest as Hales and keen as either of us. With half a dozen cable messages, to and from Farrell in London, we had everything fixed, and our company as good as a going concern, when the Chilian Government interposed a long, vexatious delay which, at one point, appeared to hint at an intention to repudiate the bargain.

Back I travelled; this time with Renton in company, and Renton mad as fire. It all turned out to be a bungle by some clerk that had taken to drink and forgetfulness; but it cost us a month or two before the Government of Senor Orrego, having no case, decided to do us justice without troubling the Courts. Renton and I returned in triumph through the grilling heats of July, and reached New York to find the papers announcing this war for a certainty: whereupon, without unpacking, I pelted for home.

From Southampton I made for London, and had two short interviews with Farrell amid the rush of rejoining the H.A.C., collecting kit, and the rest of it. Our talk was entirely about business, and was conducted at the National Liberal Club—the hostelry to which I had addressed all my letters and cables. I gathered that he used it almost as a permanent residence, having sold or given up his house at Wimbledon. He said nothing of Foe, and I forbore to ask questions.

From the H.A.C., in the general catch-as-catch-can of those early weeks of the war, I found myself on one and the same day pushed into a temporary Commission in the R.F.A., commanded down to Warwickshire to recruit for it; and met at my lodge-gate with a telegram ordering me off to Preston to collect a draft there and report its delivery at Aldershot. Funny sort of home-coming for a man returning after two years' absence! But there it was. I had just time by smart driving to catch the next down train at our local station: so, without even a glimpse of the ancestral roof, I put the dog-cart about and posted back.

For the next week or so, as Jimmy put it of his own very similar experience (he had joined up in the Special Reserve as a gunner three years before the war), I didn't spend a night out of my train. Then came a morning—I had rolled up with my latest draft, from Berwick at 4.30 a.m.—when the Colonel sent for me to come to the orderly-room some ten minutes before he opened business, and then and there asked me if it was to my liking to come out to France with the division then moving, on the ammunition column of his brigade.

I walked back to the R.F.A. mess, picked up a newspaper in the ante-room, and dropped into a chair. My heart was beating like a girl's at her first ball. "France" — "France" — the very "r" in that glorious word kept beating in my ears with the roll of a side-drum. I gripped the *Times*, steadied myself down to master the short little paragraph on which my eyes had been fixed, unseeing, for a couple of minutes, and found myself staring at this announcement:

> "A marriage has been arranged, and will shortly take place, between Peter Farrell, Esq., of 15a The Albany, and Constantia, only daughter of the late George Wellesley Denistoun, Esq., J.P., D.L., of Framnel in the West Riding of Yorkshire, and of Mrs. Denistoun of 105 Upper Brook Street, W."

NIGHT THE TWENTY-FOURTH
CONSTANTIA

The drumming in my ears died suddenly out to silence, and then started afresh more violently than ever, and more sharply, for the long pinging of an electric bell shrilled through it. The pinging ceased sharply: the drumming continued; and I looked up to see the mess sergeant standing over me, at attention.

"Telephone call for you, sir."

I went to the instrument like a man in a dream. Something suddenly gone wrong with Sally's healthy first-born? Jimmy starting for France and ringing me up for farewell? Farrell—damn Farrell!—to talk business? Jephson, with word that he had achieved the urgent desire of his heart and been passed as a gunner, to join me, *quo fas et gloria ducunt*? These four only, to my knowledge, had my probable address.

"Hallo?" I called.

"Hallo!" came the answer sharp and prompt, in a woman's voice which I recognised at once for Constantia's. "Is that you, Roddy?"

"Yes—Roddy, all right," I spoke back, mastering my voice.

"Have you seen—?" Her voice trailed off.

"D'you mean the announcement? Yes, two minutes ago. Is it congratulations you're ringing up in this hurry?"

"Roddy, dear, don't be a beast!" the voice implored. "I'm in a horrible hole, and I think only you can help me. Is it possible for you to get leave, and come? Mamma asks me to say that there's a room here, and—and we want you!"

"As it happens," returned I, "there'll be no trouble about getting leave. We're to start—report says—at the end of the week, and I must be sent up to collect a few service odds-and-ends. As for sleeping, I'll ring up Jephson, and if he's already conscripted, I can doss at the Club. All that is easy. But tell me, what is the matter?"

"Oh! I can't here." Constantia's voice thrilled on the wire. "It's pretty awful. I never gave him leave—*never*!"

"You're getting pretty incoherent," said I. "We'll have it out when we meet. Dinner?… No, I shall pick up a meal on the train. … Mustn't expect me before 8.30; I have to put a draft through and see them off. Odd jobs, besides.… These are strenuous times."

"Roddy, you're an angel!"

"Not a bit," said I; "and I warn you not to expect me in that capacity. You'll observe that I haven't congratulated you yet." I put this in rather savagely.

"You're also rather a brute," answered the voice. "But you'll come?"

"Please God," said I.

"Thank God!" answered she; and I hung up the receiver.

Well, in my jubilation I had forgotten to ask for leave to run up and get kit. But leave was no sooner asked for than given. From Victoria that evening I taxi'd straight to Jermyn Street, where I found Jephson, warned by telegram, elate at the prospect of soldiering. I was able, after a talk with my Colonel, to inform him that he had also a prospect of coming along as my servant, and this lifted him to the seventh heaven. Then I went out, picked up a dinner at Arthur's, and walked on to Upper Brook Street.

In those days London had not started to shroud its lamps. One stood a few paces short of the porch of Number 105; and as I turned into Brook Street I saw a man come hastily down the steps, and enter a taxi anchored there. The butler followed and closed the door upon him. The night had begun to drizzle, and there was a sough of sou'westerly wind in the air. I turned up the collar of my service overcoat and, as the taxi passed, walked pretty briskly forward and intercepted Mrs. Denistoun's butler, who, after a stare at the retreating vehicle, had reascended the steps and was about to close the door. Recognising me by the light of the porch lamp, he opened the door wide, and full upon the figure of Constantia, standing in the hallway. She gave a little gasp and came to me, holding out her hand.

"You were always as good as your word, Roddy. Come into the library. Where are you sleeping, by the way?"

"In my flat," said I. "Jephson will not be called up for a day or two. He has a fire lit, and will sit up for me."

"He may have to sit up late," replied Constantia. "Mamma will be down presently.… There has been something of a scene, and she is upset.

You saw Mr. Farrell go away, just now? You must have passed him, almost at the door."

"I did," said I, "though I don't know if he recognised me. Child, what is the matter?"

"Child?" echoed Constantia. "It does me good to be called that, for that's exactly how I am feeling.... He had no right—no right—" and there she broke off.

"Do you mean," said I, "that he put that announcement in the *Times* having no *right* to do it?"

"I dare say," moaned Constantia, waving her arms feebly, pathetically, "he understood more than I meant him to."

"Let us be practical, please," said I, becoming extremely stern. "Have you, or have you not, engaged yourself to marry Farrell?"

"Certainly I have not," she answered with vivacity. "He asked me, and I—well, I played for time."

I couldn't repress a small groan at this: or, rather, it was half a groan and half a sigh of relief. "Has he spoken to your mother?"

"No."

"Does your mother know about it?"

"Yes. I told her."

"Does she approve of this announcement in the papers? Has she sanctioned it?"

"Of course she does not—of course she has not.... Roddy, sit down and don't ask so many questions all of a heap. Sit down and light your pipe, and pass me a cigarette. Furnilove will bring in some whisky for you by and by."

"Thank you, Constantia; but I don't feel like staying. I've always maintained—oh, damnation!" I broke off.

"What have you always maintained, Roddy? Sit down and tell it. Are you not here because I sent for you? And didn't I send for you because I am in trouble? We are in a tangle, I tell you, and I'm asking you, on my knees, to untwist it. So light your pipe and, before we begin, tell me—What is it you have always maintained?"

"I have always maintained," I answered slowly, even more stern than before, "that no woman can be safely trusted to know a cad from a gentleman. If the cad can flourish a trifle of worldly success in front of her, or if he's a mere adventurer and flashes himself on her boldly enough, *or*, if she has persuaded herself to pity him, she's just fascinated, and you can't trust her judgment ten yards. There!... I've burnt my boats."

Constantia sat for some while pondering this, breathing out the smoke of her cigarette, gazing into the fire under the shade of a handscreen.

"I'll tell you another thing, Roddy," she said at length; "and it's as true and truer. No woman thinks worse of a man for burning his boats.... But it isn't quite worldly success to be wrecked and left desolate on an island three hundred miles from anywhere. It all started (as you hinted) with my pitying him and admiring his strength of will after the awful experience he had tholed."

"He left you just now? I saw him drive away, and his infernal dog with him."

"Yes: there had been a pretty bad scene. I was furious, and Mamma was so much upset that I doubt if she'll be fit to talk to-night. But it's a blessed relief to her, now that she knows you are anchored here for a while, to protect us, and that, at the worst, we can ring up Jermyn Street."

"Why," I exclaimed, "what the devil is there to protect you from?"

"Jack—Mr. Foe, that is—has been watching this house for days. He haunts the pavement opposite, all the hours he is off duty. Mamma is sure that he means evil, and I wish I was sure that he didn't. He has gone under, Roddy. It is awful to look out, as Furnilove draws the blinds, and see that figure there stationed, reproaching us—yet for what harm that we have done him? He is even ragged.... I should not be surprised to hear he was starving. Yet what can we do?"

"Tell me his address," said I.

She hesitated. "Why should you suppose that I know his address?" she asked, shading her face.

But I took her up bluntly. "I am sorry," I said, "to be discharging apophthegms upon you to-night: but you must hear just one other. Every woman follows and traces a man who has once laid his heart on her altar. I am sorry, Con, to call up an instance from so far back in the past: but you knew where to 'phone even for me, this morning. ... So own up, child, and tell me, where is Foe?"

"I believe," she answered after a while, the handscreen hiding her face, "he has found work in one of these emergency hospitals they are putting up.... It's at a place called Casterville Gardens, down by Gravesend. When first he started watching this house, he was in rags; but for the last fortnight he has worn khaki, and it improves his appearance wonderfully.... Besides, when a man is in the army, you have the comfort to know that, at least, he isn't starving."

"Was it so bad as that?" I asked. "Well, and now about Farrell?"

"Ah!" said she, "when you saw him get into that taxi, I had dismissed him. He was going—or said he was going—straight to Printing House Square to get that abominable paragraph contradicted. I told him that he was to return to-night and bring me his assurance that it was contradicted— either that, or never to enter this house again.… And now, Roddy, as he may be late—as I would only be content with his seeing the Editor in person— and as editors, I understand, come down late to their work—suppose you mix yourself a whisky-and-soda: for here is Furnilove with the glasses.… Furnilove! keep the latch up for an hour or so, and the door on the chain. Mr. Farrell may be calling late with a particular message. Do not admit him beyond the hall, but come and report to me here. Sir Roderick will receive him in the hall and take the message."

"Yes, miss," said the obedient Furnilove.

"That is all." Constantia pondered.—"Except that you may tell the housemaid not to worry about the room for Sir Roderick. He will not sleep here, after all. And you may send Henriette up with word to Mamma that all is right and Sir Roderick stays only to receive Mr. Farrell's message. He will probably be going at once on receipt of it, and then you can lock up. The others can go to bed when they choose."

"Very good, miss," said Furnilove, and withdrew.

"And now," said Constantia, "since he is late, keep me amused. Tell me all about the island."

So I told her this and that of my voyaging; and the time drew on until the clock on the mantelpiece chimed a half-hour. It was one-thirty.

"The dickens!" said I, pulling out my own watch and consulting it. "Farrell is a long time at Printing House Square. In my belief, Con, he won't be returning."

Just at that moment the front door bell pealed loudly.

We stood up together. We heard Furnilove padding towards the door, and we both moved out into the passage as he slid up the latch and unhooked the chain. Constantia, in her eagerness, had pressed a little ahead of me.

A man rushed in, disregarding Furnilove, shouldering him aside—a man in a furred overcoat. Expecting Farrell, for the moment I mistook him for Farrell. Even when above the fur collar I caught the sight of common khaki, for another moment I took him for Farrell. But he ran for Constantia, stretching out his arms as if to embrace her; and as he stretched them, under the hall light, I saw that one of his hands was bleeding.

I had enough presence of mind to spring in front of her and ward him off. It was Foe.

"It's all right," he gasped, staring at me. "No need to make a fuss. ... I have killed him." And with that, still staring at me horribly, he sank slowly and collapsed in a huddle at my feet, raving out incoherent words.

Furnilove behaved admirably. Having assured himself that Miss Constantia was safe, and that I had the intruder under control, he went smartly to the telephone.... Amid Foe's ravings I heard him ringing up the exchange and, after a pause, summoning the doctor.

"We had better have the spare room prepared again, after all," said Constantia. "We can't turn him out, in this state.... And there's a dressing-room, Roddy, next door, if you can put up with it.... But what has happened, God knows."

"God knows," said I. "But he's a lunatic, unless I'm mistaken. We'll hear what the doctor says.... But he shan't sleep here, to trouble you.... Furnilove, whistle up and have a taxi ready...."

"Oh, what is he saying?" moaned Constantia as the body on the floor still twisted as if burrowing to hide itself, now muttering and again shouting in a voice that reverberated along the passage, "Kill him! Damn that dog!—kill him!"

I knelt on the body and held it still. It was the body of my best friend, and I knelt on it, almost throttling him.

"One can't ring up a lunatic asylum, at this hour of the morning," I found myself gasping. "He's for my flat, to-night, if your doctor will take charge of him with me." And with that I looked up and caught sight of Constantia's mother at the head of the staircase.

"It's all right, Mrs. Denistoun," said I, glancing up. "It's my friend, Jack Foe—my friend that was. With the doctor's leave I'll get him back presently to Jermyn Street, where Jephson and I will look after him for the night.... Jephson used to worship him, and will wait on him as a slave."

And with that—as it seemed amid the blasts of Furnilove's whistle in the porchway and the *toot-toot* of a taxi, answering it—a quiet man stood above my shoulder. It was the doctor: and Furnilove had been so explicit on the 'phone that the doctor—whose name I learnt afterwards to be Tredgold—almost by magic whipped out a small bottle from his pocket.

"Water," said he, after a look at the patient, "and a tumbler, quick!"

Furnilove dashed into the library and returned with both.

"Bromide," said Dr. Tredgold. "Let him take it down and then hold his head steady for a few minutes…. Right!… Now the question is, where to bestow him? I can't answer for him when the dose wears off: but it's no case to leave with two ladies."

"There's a taxi, doctor," said I, "if we can get him into it. I have a flat in Jermyn Street, and a trustworthy manservant. I suggest that he'll do there for the night."

"Right," said Dr. Tredgold again; "and the sooner the better. I'll come with you, when I've bound up this wound on his hand. It's a nasty one…. It looks to me—Yes, and it is, too!"

"What is it?" I asked.

"A dog-bite."

"So *that* was what he killed!" thought I, and aloud I said, "Thank God!"

"Eh?" said the doctor. "A dog-bite's a queer thing to thank God for."

"It might have been worse," I answered.

"H'm: well it's bad enough," Dr. Tredgold replied, busy with his bandaging.

NIGHT THE TWENTY-FIFTH
THE PAYING OF THE SCORE

Next evening, my leave being up, I returned to Aldershot. Dr. Tredgold had called around early, and after overhauling his patient and dressing the hand, had assured me there was no cause for anxiety. The fever had gone down, and this allowed us to tackle the main mischief, which was malnutrition. In short, Jack was starving.

"Your man makes an excellent nurse," said the doctor. "I'll tell him to go slow at first, with beef-tea and milk, and to-morrow he can start the works up with a dose of champagne. But I'll drop in to-morrow, to make sure. The wound?—Oh, it's a dog-bite, safe enough, and a rather badly lacerated one. But we cauterised it in time last night, and it shows no 'anger,' as the saying is. Has he told you how he came by it?"

"No," said I. "He has been lying in this lethargy ever since you left him. He wakes up and takes his medicine from Jephson, and then drops back into a doze. I thought it best not to worry him."

"Quite right, too.… And I'll not ask questions, either, beyond putting it that he's a friend of yours, gone under, and you're playing the Samaritan.… Well, you can go back to duty, and Jephson and I will see this through. It's queer, too.… I seem to have seen his face somewhere.… But what's queerer is that he isn't dead. He must have had some practice at fasting, poor fellow. I should say that his stomach hadn't known food for a week."

I duly 'phoned the doctor's report to Constantia. To Jephson my last words were, "Write daily. When Dr. Foe can sit out, dress him in any old suit, shirt, and underwear. I don't see myself out of this khaki for a long time ahead. He will be fit again long before Monday week, when you're to join up: and when he is able to walk, there's an envelope for him in the top right-hand drawer of my writing-table."

Jephson wrote twice to report that Dr. Foe was "going on favourably," and on the third day, that he had even dressed himself and taken a walk. He had been away four hours and more—"which caused me much anxiety," added Jephson.

But on the fourth day, on the eve of our starting for Rouen, I got the following letter, in Jack's own handwriting:

"My dear Roddy,—I shall use the old name, since it is the last time I shall address you; and you, starting for France, will have no time to reach me and say that it is forbidden.

"I have killed Farrell. It was a stupid and a sorry ending. At the last it was even quite brutal—bestially different from anything I had imagined—and I had imagined many ways—while I had control of the show.

"I have gone through madness. That again was part of the bestiality I had not reckoned with.… And unless I take steps I shall soon be back in worse bestiality, worse madness. But I am taking steps.… And in the meantime, when you read this you are to be sure that it is written by a man perfectly sane.

"It is nothing that I have killed Farrell. I could have killed him, as he could have killed me, at any time. I still think that, while the pursuit lay with me, my methods were the more delicate, and that I should never have goaded him to strike as he goaded me.

"But I will grant that his methods were effective enough: and along one line I should have allowed them to be original, if I didn't know that he had picked up the hint of it on the *I'll Away*. It was *rumour* that had cursed me there, and he started to work upon rumour. I had put up a plate in Harley Street, as you know, upon the dregs of my capital. This meant a certain bluff upon credit. If my reputation lasted me out six months, all would be well. He divined this and struck at it. To do him justice, I suppose that if he had walked up brutally to the Medical Association and given them his story, I should have been struck off the Register. He worked more subtly than that. Indefinable reports started up, spread and followed me. Out of the skies a net of suspicion descended between me and my quite reputable past. For no reason given, my fellow-practitioners began to shun me.

"I had a bad case, and no money to carry it through. I have heard, Roddy, that he let you into the secret of the island and that you are like to prosper on it: and I wish you well. But I, who brought him to it, lingering him to land—I, but for whose treasured flask he would never have lived to see

Santa Island— could set up no claim on any of that wealth.

"I had deserved this. It was all quite right, and I make no complaint. But I had to throw up Harley Street, and for two years I steadily sank. In the end I came to know worse hunger than I was prepared for. Though you won't have me at any price, I think you would pity if I told you of some of the holes to which I have crept to sleep.

"I suppose—and now I think of it, I might have borrowed some comfort from the thought—I suppose that all the while, being rich, Farrell had hired eyes to watch me. It is certain that he ran across me—always at night, and always in evening dress. Once, on the Embankment, as I was coiling on a bench, he came down from the Savoy and along, bringing his dog for a walk. The dog scented me and growled; but I lay out stiff, pretending to sleep.

"Even when it came to a Salvation Army shelter, we were disturbed by a company of the benevolent; Farrell one of them, in a furred coat with an astrachan collar. He saw me stretched there with closed eyes, and said that one half of the world never knows how the other half lives.

"It was going like that with me when the War broke out. Then—broken, beaten, and in rags—I put all pride in my pocket, walked across the bridge to Silversmiths' College, rang in on Travers, and demanded a job.

"Travers was shocked.... I could see also that he was suspicious. Rumour had been at him, too. Finding him less than frank, I turned more than proud: and, his back being up and his conscience uneasy, he did what I could have pardoned in a weaker man; lost his temper, to excuse himself in his own eyes for treating me unjustly. He had scarcely spoken six words before I detected the slime of Farrell's trail. The man had managed to sow rumours, somehow, within the gates of Silversmiths' College, of all places!—rumours that had nothing to do with the island, but suggested that, after all (there being no smoke without fire), there *had* been dubious and uncleanly experiments in the laboratory during my professorship. I believe that this, when I came to think it over, started my recovery: yes, my recovery. For it showed me that Farrell was deteriorating, and, renewing a little of my old contempt for the man, raised me by so much above the abject fear of him into which I had sunk. From that moment hope was renewed in me, and I nursed it. So long as he worked on the truth he had me at his mercy: playing with falsehood in this fashion, he was vulnerable, might come to be mortally vulnerable if I watched and waited, and then I should regain the lost mastery, dearer to me than life.

"For the moment, however, Travers claimed all the scorn I carried inside me for use. He hinted that the College had suffered by the scandal of the riot: which no doubt was true to some extent, but not true enough to hide a lie or to cover a meditated betrayal. He said that he had always looked a little askance on my researches, and particularly upon my demonstrations; that they were doubtless astonishing, but had lain, to his taste, a little too near the border-line of quackery,—Yes, Roddy, he said the word, and it did not choke him. On the whole and speaking as a friend (yes, he used that word, too), he must express a hope that I would not press to renew my connection with the Silversmiths' College. It would pain him inexpressibly, remembering old times, to be forced to give me a direct refusal.... But was there anything else he could do for me?

"That, Roddy, was the valley of the shadow of my death, and I had no rod or staff to comfort me.

"I did not answer him in words. I gave him a look, and walked out.

"My purpose had been to apply for temporary work, to relieve some younger teacher who wished to enlist for medical work at the front. Had you been in London, Roddy, I'd have pocketed shame and come to you, and borrowed the price of a suit of clothes; inside of which— and may be with your support—I might have walked up boldly for a commission in the R.A.M.C.—for there was nothing definite against me: only I was ruined, and my old credentials, set against my present squalor, were so comparatively splendid as to raise instant suspicion of drink and disgrace. But it was part of my just punishment that, when I most needed help, you should be far abroad searching for the very island on which I had shipwrecked all.

"Finally I found work as a dresser in one of those temporary hospitals which sprang up everywhere in such hurry as the streams of wounded began to pour back from France. Ours was pitched in a derelict pleasure-ground on the right bank of Thames some way below Greenwich.… I don't suppose you ever visited Casterville Gardens: as neither had I until I entered them to do stretcher-drill, tend moaning men, and carry bloody slops in the overgrown alleys that wound among its tawdry, abandoned glories. It had a half-rotted pier of its own, upon which, in Victorian days, the penny steam-boats had discharged many thousands of crowds of pleasure-seekers. The gardens occupied the semicircle of an old quarry, on which the decorative landscape gardener had fallen to work with gusto, planting it with conifers and stucco statues in winding walks that landed you straight from the sightless wisdom of Socrates and Milton, or the equally sightless allurement of Venus, shielding her breasts, upon a skittle-alley, a bandstand, a dancing-saloon, or a bar at which stood, for contrast, another Venus, not eyeless, dispensing beer. The conifers, flourishing there, have grown to magnificent height. The effect of rain upon the statues has not been so happy, and I have set my pail down to pick a snail off the saddle-nose of Socrates and meditate and wonder what he would have thought of it all.

"The dancing-saloon—still advertising itself as 'Baronial Hall'—had been converted into a main ward, holding forty beds. It was there that Farrell found me at work, that night. He had interviewed the Adjutant—as we called the harassed secretary who, brayed daily between the upper and nether millstones of official instructions and 'voluntary effort,' never left his desk nor dared to wander abroad for fresh air—the gardens having been specially laid out to trick the absent-minded and induce them to lose their way. Farrell had simply told the Adjutant that he wished to see me on urgent personal business. The Adjutant could not hesitate before a presence that might, in its dress-clothes and sable-lined overcoat, have stood among the statues outside for personified Opulence.

"'Very good,' said he. 'Oh, yes, certainly. I will send for the man.... Your business is private, you say?... I am very sorry: we are all at sixes and sevens here, with every office crowded. But there's an empty saloon—one of those absurdities with which the management in old days sought to tickle the public taste. They are going to turn it into a ward in a couple of days, and that's why we have left it unoccupied. If that will do, and you'll come with me, we'll see if the electric light functions. I believe the fitters were at work there this afternoon.'"

"That, as Farrell told me ten minutes later, was how it happened. For me, when answering the message that a stranger had called to see me on urgent business, I walked as directed, across the matted moonlit lawn to this building which I had never visited before—and when, pushing the door wide, I saw Farrell standing under the electric lamps, with his dog beside him—I fell back a pace and half-turned to run for it.

"For he was alone, yet not alone: a hundred Farrells stood there. No, a battalion, and all of them Farrells! And a battalion of dogs!

"I stepped back from the ledge of the threshold. Above the doorway an inscription in faded gilt letters shone out against the moon—'VERSAILLES GALLERY OF MIRRORS. ADMISSION 3D.'

"Then I understood. This absurd and ghastly apartment was lined, all around its walls, with mirrors, in panels separated only by thin gilt edgings. Dust lay thick on the floor; cobwebs hung from the ceiling in festoons; there was not a stick of furniture in the place. But a battalion of Farrells stood in it, and there entered to it, and stood, under the new electric fittings, a battalion of Foes.

"Farrell's aspect was grave. His eyebrows went up at the choke of half-insane laughter with which I greeted him. 'Foe, my man,' said he, eyeing my khaki. 'So you have come to this, have you?'

"He said it pompously, with a fine air of patronage, and I stifled a second laugh, hugging it inside my ribs: for now I felt that the time would not be long—that, at long last, he would pass me over the cards. 'We both seem to have come to this, don't we?' I answered with a shrug and a glance around.

"'I have run down here,' he went on, still betrayed back to his old Tottenham Court Road manner, 'because I have an announcement to make to you.... Have you read your *Times* to-day?'

"He was priceless. Oh, he was falling to me—falling to me like a ripe peach! He held out a scrap of paper.

"'Do I look like a man that takes in the *Times*?' I purred '—at twopence a day, and the price likely to go up, they tell me.... But I can guess your news, for I've watched the house. ... You've come all this way to tell me that you're going to marry Constantia Denistoun.... Well?'

"'You have been watching the house?' asked he, staring, as it took him aback.

"'Of course I have.... And she didn't tell you?... Gad! If she didn't tell you, she isn't yours yet, and I've a doubt if she's ever like to be. Did she give you leave to put in that announcement?'

"Farrell cleared his throat. Before he could answer I had chipped in—'No, you liar! I hate men who clear their throats before speaking. It was an old trick of yours, of which I believed myself to have cured you at some pains.... So you have played over ardent, and there has been a row, and you have come down here to take it out of *me*.... Man, you thought you would: but I have you beaten at last; for I see you—as she will see you—dissolving back into the cad you always were.'

"'I am going to marry her,' Farrell persisted. 'Let that eat into your soul.'

"'It has eaten,' said I, 'these weeks ago, just as far as ever it will get; and that's as far as a rat can gnaw into a marlinespike.... Come out of this into fresh air,' said I with another look round on our images repeated in the mirrors. 'There are too many Farrells and Foes here. When I ran the game, at Versailles that afternoon, it had a certain dignity. … But, you!… Your primal curse, Farrell, reasserts itself at length. I have done my best with you, but you reproduce it in tawdriness. Out of the Tottenham Court Road you came: and back to your vomit you go.'

"'I am going to marry Miss Denistoun,' he repeated dully. 'I felt sure it would interest you to know.' He was losing grip.

"'Oh, yes,' said I. 'Whistle your dog, and let's get out of this for a walk by the river.… There's too many of us in this room, and we're all too cheap.… Damn it! I believe I could forgive you for anything but for lowering our hate to *this*!'"

"We went out past the sentry, and walked down by the sullen river's edge, the dog padding behind us.

"'You have been provocative,' said Farrell, after a while, checking himself by an afterthought in the act of clearing his throat. 'Considering our relative positions, I am rather surprised at your daring to take this line.… But you used a word just now. It was 'forgive.' I came not only to say that I am going to marry Miss Denistoun, but to propose that henceforth the account is closed between us. You must tell yourself that I have won; and, having won, I bear no further malice. I would even make some reparation on the shrine of my affection for Miss Denistoun. She would esteem it, I feel sure, as a tribute. … Dear me, how fast we are walking!… You'll excuse me if I stop and take off this coat.… In the old days, as a working-man, more than half my time I walked without a coat, and an overcoat to this day always sets up a perspiration.… Well now, shall we shake hands at the end of it all and cry quits?… Say the word, and I'll go one better. They've formed the syndicate for that island of ours. What do you say to a thousand shares, and to coming in on the Board?'

"He was on the river side of me, quite close to the brink. I had been playing for some minutes with the knife in my pocket; and as I leapt on him and drove it in over the breast, he fell straight backwards. All the end of Farrell was a gasp, a sharp cry, and a splash.

"And both cry and splash were drowned instantly by the raging yelp of the dog as he sprang for me. I fisted him off by his throat and he fastened his teeth in my right hand, tearing the flesh down as I slipped the knife into my left hand. Then with my left I jabbed sideways under his ribs, and his bite relaxed, and he dropped.

"The embankment was steep. I ran down a little way and came to a disused landing-stage—four or five planks on rotting piles. Kneeling there, I lowered my bleeding hand, to bathe it. … As I knelt the body of Farrell came floating down-stream and was borne in towards me by the eddy. It lodged against the piles, chest uppermost, its white, wide-open eyes turned up to the moon.

"—And I stared on it, Roddy, crouching there. *And I swear to God it was not Farrell's face but my own that I stared into.*

"Yes… for I stared and stared at it—there, plain, looking up far beyond me, sightless—until a swirl of the tide washed it clear; and, as it passed out into darkness, it seemed to be sinking slowly, slowly.

"I dragged myself away and ran back to the dead dog. Farrell's overcoat lay close beside it, and his hat—which had fallen short of the edge of the embankment as he pitched backwards.

"I picked up the coat, put it on, and felt in its pockets. They were empty, but for a railway ticket. I picked up the hat, and smiled to find that it fitted me. Lastly I stopped, lifted the dog's corpse and flung it over to follow its master. All accounts thus closed, I stepped out for the station and caught the last train for Charing Cross.

"You know the rest.

"I borrowed your clothes, yesterday, and went down to the inquest. They admitted me to see the body, on my pretence that I had missed a relative and might be able to identify it. Farrell had gone back to his old features; death had made up its mind to hide the secret after all…. I am afraid that, having overtaxed my strength, I broke down on the revulsion, and may have given myself away.

"But it doesn't matter. That dog has done for me. Your Dr. Tredgold is a good fellow and has nursed me very prettily back from starvation. But I happen, as you know, to have studied canine virus with some attention, and I have an objection to rivalling some effects of it that I have witnessed. Before you receive this, I shall be dead. I shall not trouble your hospitable roof, and I am sorry to trouble Jephson. But the searchers may find my body in Bushey Park.

"So long!—and, on the whole, so best.... I find, having lost Farrell, that *I cannot do without him.*

"You have been endlessly good to me. Remember me as I was once on a time, and so I shall always be—Yours,"

"Jack."

That is the end of the tale [concluded Otway], except for this—

Twelve months later, being on leave and wanting to clear up the mystery of the newspaper report, I took a train down to C—, past Gravesend, made inquiries of the police, and finally hunted up the juryman who had shown so much emotion at the inquest. I found a little whiskered grocer, weighing out margarine in a shed that was half shop, half canteen. All I extracted from him was this—

"Yes, to be sure, sir, I remember it perfectly. I only wish I didn't: for I dream of it at night: and, being a widower, I can't confide the trouble. The fact is, I must suffer from nerves and— what do they call 'em, sir?— hallucinations—yes, that's the word. But I was fresh from inspecting the body, and when that person broke in, wearing a face like the corpse's twin-brother, well, it knocked me clean out. Of course, it must have been a hallucination; none of the others saw the least resemblance—as they've told me since. But at the moment, I'd have wagered my life...."

EPILOGUE

"Yes, that is the story," said Otway, sorting back the documents into his dispatch-case.

"Is it quite all the story, sir?" asked Polkinghorne, breaking the silence that followed its close.

Otway frowned, re-sorted the last three or four papers, laid them in the case and closed it with a couple of snaps.

"That's all," he answered, "that exists for publication. That is, unless you want a moral. I can give you *that*, all right: and if you have any use for it you may apply it to this blasted War. As I see it, the more you beat Fritz by becoming like him, the more he has won. You may ride through his gates under an Arch of Triumph; but if he or his ghost sits on your saddle-bow, what's the use? You have demeaned yourself to him; you cannot shake him off, for his claws hook in you, and through the farther gate of Judgment you ride on, inseparables condemned.

"—And, oh, by the by! I am taking my leave next Wednesday. Sammy has been nosing suspiciously, these five days, around a wine-case which on the 22nd he shall have the honour of opening. It contains, if our friend the Transport Officer hasn't been beforehand with you, some Pommery 1900; with which you are to do your best. For it turns out that, with luck, I am to be married on that day. No flowers, by special request."

Otway re-opened the dispatch-case and again made sure of his last two exhibits, which he had not exhibited. The first was a note, folded three-corner-wise, which ran:

> "Dear Roddy—Your last word to me was that you had no patience with people so clever that they lacked sense to come out of the rain. Well, I am willing to learn that silly skill, if you remain willing to teach me.—Yours,"
>
> "CONSTANTIA."

The second of these exhibits, not exhibited, was a creased envelope containing the shredded petals of a rose.